THE
GLITTER
SCENE

A NOVEL

MONIKA FAGERHOLM

Translated from the Swedish
by Katarina E. Tucker

OTHER PRESS
NEW YORK

The translation of this work was supported by a grant from FILI

Production Editor: *Yvonne E. Cárdenas*
Book design: *Simon M. Sullivan*
This book was set in 12 pt Bodoni BE Light
by Alpha Design & Composition of Pittsfield, NH.

10 9 8 7 6 5 4 3 2 1

LIBRARY OF CONGRESS CATALOGING-IN-PUBLICATION DATA

Fagerholm, Monika, 1961-
[Glitterscenen. English]
The glitter scene : a novel / Monika Fagerholm ; translated by
Katarina E. Tucker.
p. cm.
Originally published in Swedish as Glitterscenen by Albert Bonniers
Forlag, Stockholm, c2009. Simultaneously published in Finland.
ISBN 978-1-59051-305-7 (trade pbk.) — ISBN 978-1-59051-420-7
(e-book) 1. Teenage girls—Fiction. 2. Family secrets—Fiction. 3.
Identity (Psychology)—Fiction. 4. Cities and towns—Finland—Fiction.
5. Psychological fiction. I. Tucker, Katarina Emilie. II. Title.
PT9876.16.A4514G5513 2010
839.73'74—dc22
2011013072

THE GLITTER SCENE

Also by Monika Fagerholm

The American Girl

Wonderful Women by the Sea

There is goodness in blue skies and flowers, but another force—a wild pain and decay—also accompanies everything.

DAVID LYNCH: *Lynch on Lynch*

Orpheus was going to fetch his Eurydice from the underworld. He loved her so much that the gods who had taken her there took pity on him. Go down to her and she will follow you, but do not look back, do not turn around until you have come up again. Hold her hand, she will follow you.

JOHANNA'S PROJECT EARTH

CONTENTS

I

THE AMERICAN GIRL IN A SNOW GLOBE
(Johanna and the Winter Garden, 2004–2006)

II

THE MASK, THE ROSE, THE SILVER SHOES
(An entirely different story, or maybe not?)

THE ANIMAL CHILD AND THE LAW
(THE GIRL FROM BORNEO)
(Maj-Gun Maalamaa, November 1989–January 1990)

THE GLITTER SCENE

*THE OLD SONGS (From The Return of the Marsh
Queen, Chapter 1, Where did the music start?):
The Summer of Love, a bench in the park.
The Marsh Queen: I don't know about music,
if what I mean with music, is music.*

*1967, the Summer of Love, a new hour of creation, we are
the Woodstock Nation.* And so it was Jimi Hendrix who
was playing "The Star-Spangled Banner." He played it
like a scream, just the guitar, no words. Without wrath,
without the slightest hint of being bothered or as if he
wanted to beg for some kind of sympathy. He played the
national anthem like it had never been played before, so
that there was room for *all* meanings, nuances.

And DeeDee on a bench in the park, 1967, 1969? It
was the summer of hate in any case, the summer of hate,
and for me it wasn't just about going and watching Jef-
ferson Airplane in Central Park and enjoying LSD. It was
about sitting on a bench in the park, drinking wine and
doing double hits of heroin.

And I wondered if there was some systematic plan
somewhere with the purpose of fucking up people in this
country, deliberately letting all of the drugs in the country fuck up idiots like me whom they saw as a burden.
Everyone knew that the CIA was on the opium smug-
glers' side so that the countries they ruled over wouldn't
be sold to Communist China and become red. And because it was so profitable, drugs are money, and where
did all of those orange methadone crackers come from?
Was it just part of the deal?

1

IN ANY CASE IT IS DAMNED DISCOURAGING
BEING SIXTEEN YEARS OLD SITTING ON A PARK
BENCH KNOWING THAT NOTHING NOTHING
NOTHING NOTHING IS GOING TO CHANGE.

I

THE AMERICAN GIRL IN A SNOW GLOBE

(Johanna and the Winter Garden, 2004–2006)

The Winter Garden exists, does not exist.
On the Second Cape, a place.
At the same time. A dream, a utopia.
An island that grows inside your head.

THE ROOM, THE HOUSE

THE CHILD, FLUORESCENT. Johanna. In the room of dreams, time, history. Pins *The Child, fluorescent* on the wall. The woman on the meadow with the child in her arms, a black-and-white photo, in a thunderstorm, lightning. The child of light/in the light.

An explosion, transcendence.

She is the Child, fluorescent.

Johanna in the room, looks out the window.

The meadow, which reveals itself on the other side of the windowpane in the light of the Winter Garden, dusk is now falling. A corner of the woods farther away, Tobias's greenhouse on the side of the road, like a quivering yellow spot in the rain.

Lille. Breathes on the windowpane, an island of mist spreads over the glass, erasing the view. Breathes over and over again, so that the island becomes very large and then writes LILLE in the mist in large, clear letters with her index finger.

Several times over, faster and faster, until the name is obliterated and the window is clear and transparent again.

The road, on the side, the Piss Factory.

From The Return of the Marsh Queen, Chapter 1. Where did the music start?

Patti and the factory, the Piss Factory. Somewhere, where there really was not anything, not the friendly middle-class family you grew up in. But poverty, the factory, ugly, fat ladies in the factory. During your lunch break you snuck out to the bookstore to buy your Rimbaud, and then you sat by the conveyor belt and tried to concentrate, your Rimbaud in your head: Rimbaud who was supposed to save your life but you could not know that yet. You thought you were stuck there, forever, in the factory.

The road is about thirty feet from the house where Johanna lives: one direction leading toward the Second Cape, the Winter Garden, and the main country road and the town center and the school in the other. The road: a shiny, dark line cutting through the deserted landscape.

See the road as a line—

She is Johanna, the child in the light/the child of light. She is the Child, fluorescent.

•

The house where they live, she and her aunt Solveig. At the foot of the hill on the First Cape, just the two of them. Earlier, quite often, there was also a small cousin, Robin, who had a mother, Allison, who worked on boats and was gone a lot. Robin liked being with Solveig and Johanna—especially Johanna, in Johanna's room. They built the world's largest race car track, yellow plastic rails joined together across the entire room, a thousand loops. Released small cars on the track, they traveled quickly, too quickly, flying out. But then Allison and Robin moved to another city and Robin stopped coming altogether. Stopped working on the boats, making *beauty trips,* as people said about her in Torpesonish. "And how are the storks in Portugal doing?" she would ask Johanna, happily ruffling her hair. Then Solveig would get so angry at her there would almost be a fight.

Allison was Torpe's sister, the Torpe Solveig once was married to—back then they were living on the Torpesonish homestead at the Outer Marsh. Torpe is in Germany now, remarried, works on different construction sites there. Solveig had a cleaning business once, but now and for a long time already she has been working in real estate. Here, in the District. Has almost always been here. And in this place, not in this house, but in another one. It was called the cousin's house, it burned down, the outbuildings and the barn were torn down and Solveig built this instead.

But otherwise, *been there done that,* you do not talk to Solveig about the past. She has closed that chapter, a lot of troubles. Almost the only thing Solveig wants to remember from her childhood and that she talks about sometimes is how when she was little and went to the swimming school at the Second Cape, she saved another little girl, a classmate in the swimming school named Susette Packlén, from drowning. She, Solveig, Sister Blue, the teacher's assistant in Tobias's swimming school; together with her twin sister Rita who was Sister Red. They were called that because of the color of their swimsuits, otherwise it was almost impossible to tell them apart, they looked so much alike. Solveig's twin sister, Rita. Solveig has closed that chapter too. And the Winter Garden, *Rita's Winter Garden. Ritsch.* Solveig has closed the curtains in the kitchen. To Solveig the Winter Garden does not exist.

But Tobias exists. As said, he once was the teacher at the swimming school. Yes, the same Tobias who has the greenhouse on the side of the road a little ways away from the house. Johanna likes Tobias, likes going to the greenhouse and spending time with him there.

There used to be another cousin in the house, Irene, Solveig's girl, Much older, already grown up. The fall before the Winter Garden opened on the Second Cape, New Year's Eve 1999, Irene moved away from home to start studying in another town to be a nurse. Later she went to Norway, works at an EMT station high up in the mountains. Beautiful cards, which Solveig hangs on the refrigerator, come from there, from Norway. Beautiful landscapes, restful. Reminiscent of how Irene is, or was, when she was still living in the house.

Someone who played the recorder and went to choir practice, a calm and low-voiced type. But—it was impossible not to like her. And to be allowed into Irene's room across from the kitchen on the other side of the hall, in the evenings, in the rain, the black darkness on the other side of the window. Irene perched on her bed, on a light blue bedspread, knitting long scarves in subdued colors, or playing the recorder, the sheet music on a music stand next to the bed. Or, with a book: one of the four boy or girl books she had in her possession, the kind that when it is raining it just says, "The rain beat against the window."

But to be allowed to come into this neatness, just ordinary things there: hairbrush, music stand, boy book, girl book, knitting, Johanna loved it regardless. Remembers how she used to stand in the doorway and stare at Irene, who was playing, stare and stare until Irene noticed her and put down her flute and looked up: "Hi, Lille, what, cat got your tongue?" And laughing, stretched out her arms toward Johanna. "Come here, you small silly changeling!" And at full speed Johanna had rushed right into her arms.

•

When Irene moved away from home, Johanna got her room. For a while, in the beginning, she tried to live like Irene, maintain the order and the neatness. But it did not go very well: little by little everything was, is, one big mess anyway. Things—paper, books, pictures, this and that—all over the place, everywhere.

But still, with Irene, as if there was a fundamental difference between the two of them. Despite everything having been so different in the District when Irene was growing up; there was no Winter Garden or high school or school for artistic expression and theatrical performance where she would have had the opportunity to develop her recorder music to a *professional level*, like there would be later—the school Johanna attends, and Ulla Bäckström from Rosengården 2. So like a fish in water you might think that the school had been designed just for her; *the theater, the dance, and the music*, the singing about Ulla Bäckström in the corridors at school.

But still, Irene on the one hand, Johanna on the other: in Irene there was nothing that ran wild, that could take its own wild paths, become too much of too much—

•

So for the time being, this is Johanna's room. *Everything that brings you to the music.* The Story of the Marsh Queen, the Return of the Marsh Queen, Chapter 1: a never-ending first chapter that washes over the room and buried the yellow plastic cars a long time ago.

The Marsh Queen who rose from the mire. The material that will be made into a story is constantly growing. Quotations, clippings, informations. All over the place, everywhere.

"Write her into the story. There aren't many women in the history of music. At least make her a footnote. In *The History of Punk Music*."

It is Råttis J. Järvinen, a music teacher, who said that to Johanna at school. In school there they are doing Project Earth; it is supposed to be a story, inspired by the myth of Orpheus and Eurydice. This is what Råttis J. Järvinen says, and it is beautiful: "To be young is to lose an innocence but find a treasure—like Orpheus who loved his Eurydice so much he was prepared to follow her to the underworld."

Project Earth. A project that is supposed to be about something that touches you, *someone else's story about you*. The person you are, the one you could be and want to be, to the music. "Make the music yours, in your own language."

Everything that brings you to the music. The Marsh Queen who says: "Being on stage is so terrible, they tear you to bits with their admiring looks, admiring hands, you could just die."

The Marsh Queen who says: "The Glitter Scene is my life."

Patti, Debbie, Ametiste, and the Marsh Queen, who once grew up here in the District in the house in the darker part of the woods: her name was Sandra Wärn.

So when it is at its best in the room, the room with broad views, big vision. The Marsh Queen. Johanna. "Take the world by storm." Wembley Arena 2012. "The Glitter Scene is my life."

But first it is a matter of: from here. The window. See the road like a line. The field. Tobias's greenhouse stands like a dirty yellow spot on the side of the road, in the cool abstract glow of the Winter Garden. The Winter Garden that is shining, shining.

"See the road like a line." Patti and the women, in the Piss Factory. Patti at the assembly line, *away from here*, reading *her Rimbaud* during her lunch break.

The Piss Factory.

Johanna and the Child, fluorescent on the wall.

•

Johanna turns off the lights, crawls under the covers in her bed across from the window, does not close the curtains. Wants to have the light, a dull glow from the Winter Garden. The room, the dreams, the Marsh Queen, time, history, vision: you can float in it, like a boat.

But calmly, all of the lights in the house in the background. Solveig's and Tobias's voices from the kitchen: Tobias has a habit of stopping by in the evenings after he has been at his greenhouse before he bikes back to the residential housing for seniors where he lives up in the town center. He is stubborn about that bike, despite the fact that it is more than six miles and he is old, his legs are getting worse and worse. But if the road conditions are bad Solveig convinces him to let her drive him—not so easy, Tobias is woven of a stubborn cloth. But still: voices in the yard, car doors slamming, she will be back soon.

Or, other evenings, Solveig who is watching television in the living room, the volume turned down very low, a quiet hum in the background. Sometimes Johanna gets up and goes to her, lies down on the sofa in the living room, her head resting in Solveig's arms. *Steep stairs, white houses* on television: women, men who are running up and down stairs, meeting in hallways, talking,

talking and having relationships with each other. Johanna does not follow along, Solveig's fingers in her hair, she is not thinking about the Marsh Queen then either, not thinking about anything in particular, or about the houses. The houses that Solveig sells, supplies through her business. Blueprints, photographs, sometimes Johanna is allowed to be at a showing. To walk through the empty apartments, through the houses, *imagine*, all sorts of things. Brochures about Rosengården 5 and 6 and 8, residential areas, all of them alike. Old brochures about the Winter Garden before it was finished, a special language in them. *Kapu kai.* The forbidden seas. *The hacienda must be built.*

Not the Winter Garden that would exist later, for real. But the Winter Garden when it was still just an idea on paper, presented in brochures: the one planned by the *Rita Strange Corporation*—with all the history, stories from the District. The American girl. *It happened at Bule Marsh.*

In reality, the Winter Garden became something else. But still, what it was supposed to be does not disappear from your mind just because of that. The Winter Garden, an island that grows inside your head, that connects to you personally. To what is most personal. Because there is so much in the Winter Garden that affects you. You know it, you just cannot put your finger on exactly how. Or maybe you just do not want to.

So the Winter Garden that exists in your head cannot be shared with anyone, not with Solveig, for example. *Ritsch,* Solveig has closed the curtains in the kitchen. To Solveig the Winter Garden does not exist.

And yet, there are things Johanna would like to ask Solveig, which Johanna knows belong there, to *the Winter Garden.*

On TV *Steep stairs, white houses.* "I love you." People in pastel-colored clothes who really do not say anything to each other. "Are you really my daughter?" "Yes, yes, I love you." "My daughter! I love you, too."

"Solveig," one might want to ask, "who is my mother?"

•

But thoughts. Sometimes, quite often, Johanna grows tired of all the thoughts, is just sleepy. Solveig's warm fingers, the smell of the woods and leaves in her nose, coming from her own skin.

"Aren't you going to clean your room?" Solveig might whisper. Nah nah. Sleeping now. *ZZZZZZZZZ* to *Steep stairs, white houses.*

Of course it happens that Johanna grows tired of the mess in her room, of everything. During the day, puts on her clothes, goes out. To the Boundary Woods, alone, where it is quiet; that is Johanna's world.

THE BOUNDARY WOODS/SCREAMING TOYS, 2004–2006

2004, THE BOUNDARY WOODS. What is left of the large woods that were once large and uninterrupted, with the Outer Marsh farthest to the north. Now it is a small belt running between the Winter Garden and the mainland: stretching across all of the First Cape and then inland.

Great, desolate woodlands that over the years have been leveled by logging, construction work: new residential areas that have sprung up, called things like Rosengården 2, 3, and 5 and of these Rosengården 2 is the farthest to the south, toward the sea, the very nicest and oldest. It was built already during the 1980s, long before all of the other Rosengårdar and many years before a place like the Winter Garden on the Second Cape had even been imagined. But despite the new houses, Rosengården 2 remains as an unattainable ideal: the place that all other Rosengårdar try to imitate. These family homes, several thousand square feet in size, with gardens surrounded by wall-like fences that allow no one to see in but from where the sound of barking dogs can be heard; Spanish wolfhounds, no terriers exactly.

But still, it does not help. Rosengården 2 remains what it is: the most special and luxurious. And: the only gated residential area in the District. In order to get in you need a key card with a code, which is inserted into a machine at the entrance gate.

Private Property: the ones who live in Rosengården stay put. They do not come out—not to the Boundary Woods, anyway: in their eyes and in the eyes of many there is nothing there.

No lit walking path to work out on and cell phones with poor reception because the Boundary Woods are under radio silence compared to the Winter Garden.

And of course: here and there some fairly nasty places too. Bule Marsh, *the abode of suicide*, where unhappy people come to take their own lives. Maybe they are drawn to the marsh by a certain atmosphere of seclusion, timelessness: tree branches that hang over the dark, still water. Or egged on by an old story of something tragic that happened there once. The American girl who was pushed into the water from a cliff in the summer of 1969 by her jealous boyfriend, was sucked into the whirlpool and disappeared, and when her boyfriend understood what he had done he became so beside himself he went off and hanged himself. It is a story that can also be found in the Winter Garden.

The place, the Winter Garden on the Second Cape. Next to the wide-open sea through a grove of pine trees where the road stops, then you are there. Which is not true of course. You do not get there just like that. There is a security system. Fencing. Starts below the hill on the First Cape, which also belongs to the Winter Garden, but there is only a regular fence there, the real security measures are found farther inside. In any case: fences. Press your face against the square grooves, leaves a mark on your skin.

•

So. The Boundary Woods, others do not spend much time there.

An invisible boundary line, which applies not only to the inhabitants of Rosengården 2 but to almost everyone in the District as a whole.

Except one, of course. Ulla Bäckström who is exactly where she wants to be and everywhere in every place. *Private Property*. All of that means nothing to her.

Rosengården 2. Where she lives, with her family in an architectonic masterpiece of stone, tile, and glass in three and a half stories—she is the only child and has the entire attic at her disposal. "The Half Floor" or "the Glitter Scene" as Johanna hears her say as she sweeps past in the halls at school in the middle of a group of like-minded students, ones from the junior and senior classes. The Glitter Scene, the half story: slightly joking, of course, but still not without a grain of seriousness. Because Ulla *is* special and ingenious and very artistically gifted, really truly. *The theater, the dance, and the music*: how they sing about her there where she is walking, that is what she says she lives for . . . Ulla Bäckström, laughing in the hallways, filled with her own babble; everything she does and "creates." And it comes about up there, she explains, on the Glitter Scene, her room. Ulla Bäckström, glittering eyes, capturing her friends with her talk, her laugh, with how she is—also capturing the ones standing off to the side watching her, like Johanna, for example.

There, on the Glitter Scene, EVERYTHING is there: all the thoughts, the ideas, and all the music. All the music books, all the manuscripts. And IF Ulla Bäckström is exaggerating then it is only just a little. Because already at the age of seventeen, her age when she dies in November 2006, she has played the lead role in *Miss Julie*, *A Midsummer Night's Dream*, and *Singin' in the Rain*, a musical; she loves to sing, has a fantastic singing voice, deep and magnificent. And a few years earlier she was the American girl in a play she wrote herself, which was based on an old story about something that happened in the District.

"Places have their stories that define them, cover them like a scar, a curse . . ." Ulla Bäckström who talks like that on the stage in one of the school's many auditoriums. "*The American girl who died, and all the death that gathered around her.*"

And Ulla Bäckström has a band, or, she has had several bands, but one called *Screaming Toys*.

•

The Glitter Scene, Rosengården: and yes, it happens that when Johanna is in the Boundary Woods she finds her way to the northern edge, finds herself alone under the protection of the woods' last tree and looks up. At Bäckström's house, it is the last one. High above all the walls, enclosures, it rises up, the attic at the very top. No ordinary attic, there is a high ceiling in there, you can see that, large windows.

And yes, of course, maybe it is possible to see it as a stage. A theater stage, so shimmering and elusive, with promises. Dark fall nights, Johanna below, among the trees.

A faint light trickling out from beneath the heavy, dark red curtains pulled closed over the windows, like just before a performance is about to start.

The curtain that is pulled to the side. Ulla singing: *Don't push your love too far, Eddie.*

Or: Ulla standing at the window. Just standing. There is a door on the stage, in the middle of the window, a door made of glass. She has opened the door. She is standing there, at the edge, in white clothes, shimmering. It is windy. Just standing there, singing.

In the wind: how it is blowing around her.

Don't push your love too far, Eddie. Ulla Bäckström sings, screams out over the Boundary Woods.

But it is like this, all the more often too. That: the bird has flown the coop. Darkness in Ulla's window. Ulla is not where you think she will be. *Ulla everywhere, Ulla across all borders.*

And when you see her like that, a glimpse in the Boundary Woods, a glimpse on the field that starts outside Johanna's window in Johanna's room in the house below the hill on the First Cape where Johanna and Solveig live together, a glimpse below Tobias's greenhouse while Tobias is still alive, a glimpse on the path in the copse on her way to the Second Cape . . . then she is not surrounded by all of her thousand friends but almost always alone.

•

Ulla Bäckström, the Flower Girl, in a field, November 2004. Ulla Bäckström comes walking over the field, butterflies are falling out of her large, light, rough hair; velvet insects in different colors are shimmering softly in the light of the Winter Garden, where she is headed. Ulla Flower Girl, a basket with roses over her arm: she has begged them off of Tobias at his greenhouse, she is going to sell them at the Winter Garden.

Long white coat, long white dress, white ankle boots— dress-up clothes, because this is when she is writing her play about the American girl: Ulla, the Flower Girl, is going to gather material in the Winter Garden, the clothes are her camouflage.

The basket is filled with dark roses when she meets Johanna on the field.

"Hey, Lille." Sets her basket down on the ground, trains her beautiful brown eyes on Johanna.

"Shall I tell you about the Winter Garden? Have you heard?

"You know." Ulla Bäckström lowers her voice to a whisper, points at the frozen ground between them. "It's like a hole in the earth. You can . . . fall. Down. And swish, you're in the underworld.

"And Lille, it's magical down there. There's an inner kingdom. *Kapu kai.* Lots of rooms. *The forbidden seas.* Have you heard?

"Places almost nobody knows about. Secret rooms where only a few have been. And in the rooms, Lille, there are stories. The walls talk: *It happened at Bule Marsh.* Is it familiar? You find out the truth about everything there.

"Do you think it's true, Lille?" she says, staring at Johanna again, but Johanna, suddenly struck dumb by her own shyness, does not get a word out.

But then Ulla Bäckström takes out the snow globe. Rummages around in her basket on the ground, under the roses.

"Look here." It is round, made of plastic, fits in the palm of her hand.

"*The American girl in a snow globe,*" she whispers. "From the Winter Garden. You can buy it at the souvenir shop." Holds up the snow globe in front of Johanna and

Johanna sees: two plastic figures in a watery landscape. Boy, girl, on a cliff—the dark water of the marsh under them with white ripples that are supposed to represent the foam on the waves; the background of the snow globe a shimmering silver.

The boy in the foreground, with his back toward you, hand raised, turned toward the girl on the edge of the cliff in the moment right before she falls headfirst, is sucked up by the whirlpool and disappears. You see only her terrified face over the boy's shoulder. Mouth wide open, sharp red lips surrounding a silent and eternal scream.

Ulla on the field shakes the snow globe, snow falls inside it: soft plastic flakes that swirl around in the water, mixed white and silver. Glitters in the light from the Winter Garden, which is falling over the field in the November twilight.

"They say she died from love," Ulla Bäckström whispers. "The one who killed her loved her too much. The boy. With his back toward us. But, Lille, who is he? You can't see the boy's face.

"I mean," Ulla Bäckström continues, as if she wants to reveal a secret, "which one? There were two, after all. Who loved her. One was named Björn, the other named Bengt. *The Boy in the woods.* That's what they called him.

"But it was Björn who was her real boyfriend, they were closer in age. The Boy in the woods was only thirteen and she had just turned nineteen. And Björn, her boyfriend, he became so sad when she died that he went and hanged himself.

"But the other one. The Boy in the woods. You wonder, Lille, can you ever really know what it was actually like?

"Because he, Bengt, he loved her just as much. If not even more . . . I don't know," says Ulla Bäckström, after a brief pause, shrugging her shoulders, standing up straight. "Maybe it's a riddle, Lille. But, in any case. Hard to know. Since all of them are dead now.

"But—oh! Have to go now. Sell my roses, in the Winter Garden.

"The snow globe, isn't it pretty?"

Johanna nods attentively.

"Do you want it? You can have it."

And Ulla Bäckström gives the snow globe to Johanna.

She laughs again, and now, suddenly, it has started snowing; large, heavy flakes descend over the field. "All of them dead now . . ." Ulla Bäckström hums in the first snow, almost elated, a new melody that suddenly has floated into her head. "Dead, Lille." Opens her mouth and stretches out her tongue to catch a few snowflakes on it. "I'm obsessed with death. *Ille dille death Lille*," Ulla sings and lowers her voice. "And I'm not Ulla but Ylla, Ylla of death. Listen Lille, in this silence on the field, doesn't it sound good?"

Johanna mumbles, "Yeah, maybe," a bit gruffly because she had to say something even if she would really like to say something else, something better, something more in line with the special mood.

"But, Lille," Ulla continues, "maybe it's like this. That there's a lot of goodness . . . blue skies, flowers, beautiful music . . . and at the same time, as if another force, *a wild pain*, and mortality is working inside everything."

And then suddenly, with those words, she is gone. Has lifted up her basket with red roses and continues across the field toward the Winter Garden.

Ylla of death. Skirts flapping, so white in the light of the Winter Garden rising up in front of her.

And Johanna, alone on the field, wants to call out, Wait Ulla, wait! Take me with you! But just stands there, dumb and silent. And futilely of course. Ulla Bäckström has probably forgotten everything already and Ulla Bäckström *does not* wait.

Johanna stands where she stands, a snow globe in her hand.

She takes the snow globe to her room and puts it away among all her things, looks at it sometimes and fantasizes. The field that starts outside the window. Blows mist on the glass. *Lille,* she writes in the mist, peers out through the letters. Empty. The light of the Winter Garden. Ulla does not come.

The play about the American girl begins and then ends, new plays come, new music. Ulla who sweeps by in the corridors at school, the theater the dance the music, how they sing about her there where she is walking. Johanna tries to make eye contact. It does not work. Or, if Ulla sees, then she looks through Johanna, caught up in her own things.

And at home: Robin moves away, Tobias becomes ill and does not come to his greenhouse anymore. The greenhouse deteriorates, Tobias dies, Solveig and Johanna are alone in the house.

•

The American girl in a snow globe. The Winter Garden. An inner kingdom. Kapu kai. But it happens that Johanna finds her way to the edge of the Boundary Woods anyway. Like always, she stands at the edge and looks

up, into the darkness. Ulla's room, high up above Rosengården's fence.

"Maybe I went away because I wanted to be with people who were called Jack, Vanessa, Andy, and Catherine."
Sometimes Ulla still stands there in her room, on the
Glitter Scene. The glass doors open, the white dress flapping in the window. Singing a song, "Death's spell at a
young age," that one, another one? Or just stands, looking out at everything.

Then it is over, everything is normal. The door is
closed, Ulla leaves the window. The curtains, like a theater curtain, are pulled closed again.

And still, often, just darkness, *the bird has flown the
coop.*

But sometimes when Johanna stands alone at the edge
of the woods and looks up at the Glitter Scene she imagines that she is there. With Ulla on the Glitter Scene, the
theater, the dance, the music . . . no, not like that.

But so. "Maybe I went away because I wanted to be
with people who were called . . ." Ulla and Johanna with
the Marsh Queen, all of her songs. "And now you're
going to get to hear what it sounds like." How Johanna is
going to come to Ulla Bäckström in her room, and they
are going to listen to it up there.

Death's spell at a young age. They are going to be Orpheus who goes to the Underworld, the Winter Garden,
bring back Eurydice. Their Project Earth. The Marsh
Queen, the Winter Garden, the American girl in a snow
globe, how everything is going to coincide.

They will have Project Earth. They will have everything. The two of them.

Patti, Debbie, Ametiste, *Imagine, my* Rimbaud and the Piss Factory. Screaming Toys and Wembley Arena 2012, everything will lead there.

"Being on stage is so terrible, they tear you to bits with their admiring looks, admiring hands, you could just die . . ." To talk like that in an interview, sign autographs.

Or like that. Just like that. Listen to the Marsh Queen and her songs. The Marsh Queen's voice, mellow like Ulla's, but even darker and more mysterious. "Lie down here," Ulla Bäckström will say on the Glitter Scene while the song is playing, "and we'll dissect the Marsh Queen's inner life, all her dark corners . . . close your eyes . . ." And the insects, the butterflies, will glitter in her hair there on the Glitter Scene, among the music, the books, all the music and the dress up clothes, all the manuscripts.

But when that song has finished playing, new songs will come. And Ulla will sit up and shake the butterflies from her hair, *klirr klirr* as metal and velvet rain down on the floor around her.

The Glitter Scene is my life. New songs, other songs, their own songs.

Well. Just a story, a fantasy. It does not happen. Nothing happens, in reality. Aside from time passing, months, years. Robin who moves, Tobias who dies, the greenhouse that deteriorates on the side of the road. It becomes the fall of 2006, the months of October and November. A glimpse of a stranger in the Boundary Woods. She is called the Red One, a woman in her fifties, and she wears red clothes.

The Red One, from the Winter Garden.

The American girl in a snow globe. Sometimes Johanna thinks about it too. Lonely thoughts. Two characters in

a watery landscape. *Don't push your love too far, Eddie.*
Ulla on the Glitter Scene, Johanna down below at the
edge of the woods, alone like always, in the dark.

Ille dille death, Lille. "There is so much death." The
memory of Ulla from two years ago, 2004. *"I am Ylla
of death."* Ulla Bäckström catching snowflakes on her
tongue on a field.

•

The house in the darker part, November 2006. If you follow the longest path into the Boundary Woods, which
starts behind what was once Tobias's greenhouse next to
the road, and you continue across all of the First Cape
to where the sea meets you on the other side, you will
come to the house in the darker part. Though, it should
be mentioned: in those outskirts you do not exactly think
sea when you see the water, it is such an inland-located
overgrown muddy bay—the poles of an old jetty sticking
up out of the water.

But in any case there is a house next to that beach, the
only house in all of the Boundary Woods, an old alpine
villa in the mud. Has been standing empty for many
years, a great staircase takes up almost the entirety of
the front of the house leading up to the entrance on the
second floor. Many wide steps in gray concrete, cracked
in places; during the summer moss and weeds grow tall
from within the cracks. One large staircase in the middle of nowhere: can look like that from a distance during the fall and winter when all the leaves have fallen
from the trees and all the undergrowth has withered
away. Isolation and such loneliness around the abandoned house where a special darkness rules, even during the day. Almost timeless, without a season—or as

if it were the same season all year round. Late fall, just before the snow.

A feeling that endures after the Winter Garden comes to the Second Cape, which is located just a few miles away and illuminates all of its surroundings with its powerful lighting systems. But the light does not quite reach the house in the darker part: just streams down carefully among the tall conifers or grows stiff, into aurora borealis–like streaks across the sky during the cold, clear winter evenings.

But the house, someone lived there once. A small family, mother, father, child who came to the District straight from the international jet-setter's lifestyle which, during the winter, took place at various Central European ski resorts. But the dad, he was called the Islander, loved his wife more than anything else on earth and in secret had the house in the darker part built based on the model of a lodge that the mother had fallen in love with during a sunny winter walk high up in the Alps and he gave it to her as a surprise.

It was supposed to be their new home, here, in the District, they would plant roots and live as a family here for real in the darker part of the woods. Of course it was not very successful. Wrong place, wrong foundation for a house, and the architecture and the construction were not really to anyone's credit either so the mother could not put up with the marshiness; rather she left and remarried and the father and daughter were left alone in the strange house. Then they lived there just the two of them, father and daughter, until the daughter grew up and became the Marsh Queen and went out into the world, to *the punk music,* to become a footnote.

But in the house, large wild parties were held there once. They could last for days because the Islander loved glitz and glamour. Even after his daughter had grown up and left home and he was living somewhere else, he would come back during the hunting season and then there were parties, for days and nights. Until it gradually ebbed out on its own: one party was the last party and the Islander stopped coming altogether. It was like this: you could stand in the forest, in the darkness, and watch the parties from the sidelines. Like a ship, an island of light—which was traveling by. Then suddenly the house was evacuated and it was empty and dark all over again.

Johanna goes to the house sometimes—there is a panorama window on the ground floor at the back through which you can see the basement. She cups her hands around her face, looks in: an old earth-filled swimming pool, filled with disgusting water that seeps up from the ground through the cracks in the tiling. Trash floats on the calm surface. Paper, scraps of fabric, bottles, the like.

•

But it was here, exactly right here in the pool, that she, the Marsh Queen, had grown up. The Marsh Queen whom she later became, when she went out into the world, to the punk music. *The Marsh Queen who rose from the mire.* Lived alone in the house with her father the Islander, her name was Sandra Wärn: a little girl who collected matchboxes and silk fabric—her mother had owned a silk fabric store that had gone bankrupt and all of the unsold fabric was brought to the house in the darker part and when her mother left, everything was left behind. Bundles, packages from a closet on the upper floor were unwound in shimmering, colorful lengths and spread out over the entire house. Down in the swimming pool too, when the Marsh Queen was a child, was just a square, sloppily tiled hole in the ground, never filled with water—there was so much about that house that in some way was unfinished. The girl hung out down there in the swimming pool, it became her world. And a moment in her life, childhood, *the only world*, for a time she came to share with a friend who became everything to her, they were always there. But that friendship ended abruptly and tragically, they had a falling out, the friend went and shot herself. And then in some way, Sandra Wärn had lost everything, there was nothing left.

•

Imagine: Sandra Wärn after her friend's death. Among all the fabric, in the waterless swimming pool. Colorful, shimmering lengths she wrapped herself in, and fell asleep. Slept and slept, in sorrow, inconsolable, wrapped in fabric. But from them, like from a cocoon, the Marsh Queen was born, the one who went out into the world, to the music. Never returned, but—forgot nothing. All of it, the house, the swimming pool, her and her friend's world, all of the fabric, she took them with her to the music. Wrote songs about them, such as one called "Death's Spell at a Young Age."

She has talked about it in interviews. But smack, back to reality. At that point in the story the Marsh Queen stops herself, almost throws everything away, tears the silk fabric into pieces ... "Oh, maybe it's just a way of saying something else. Maybe I left because I wanted to be with people called Jack, Vanessa, Andy, and Cathe—"

•

"She cuts rags for rugs, Lille."

And that is just about how it is, at the basement window in the house in the darker part, that day, one afternoon in November 2006, when Johanna suddenly hears a voice behind her, turns around fast as lightning, and stands face-to-face with Ulla Bäckström.

The same Ulla yet another one, different. Certainly older than two years ago in the field, wearing completely ordinary clothes now. Jeans, dark blue quilted jacket, a red hat pulled down over her ears, out of breath, as if she had been running. And she has something in her hand. A toy mask.

"*Crehp, crehp,* Lille. Through fabric, long strips. Curls down into a bucket. While she's talking, talking, *Djiissuss*—you never get away.

"Maybe she's crazy, Lille. You must know who I'm talking about. The Red One. What's her name? Maalamaa.

"But Lille," Ulla adds, looking around, confused and at a loss, "it's as if you've put a ball in motion." She grows quiet for a moment and then Johanna understands what it is about her that is different. Ulla Bäckström is afraid. An ordinary empty rotten day in the woods, cold, the first snow is about to start falling again.

But terrorstruck, the fear stinks, screams in her for a few seconds even though she immediately does everything in her power to fend it off.

"My God, Lille," she calls. "I am so DAMNED tired of it. I'm not interested anymore, I *never* think about it."

"About what?"

"The American girl. It was just one project among many. I'm doing new roles now, new manuscripts. The world is filled with manuscripts, Lille..."

"What are you talking about?"

Ulla Bäckström comes closer, the fear is suddenly blown away, her voice is steadier. "You know, Lille, it was like this, when I played the American girl, played her on stage. Or it *becomes* like that. If you do the same thing over and over again, play the same story in the same way, beginning middle and end, the same scenes, same same, over and over again . . .

"Are on the cliff and die of love, fall fall, every time the same way . . . that, well, it becomes a bit monotonous. And then it can happen that you start thinking about other things. Or just this repetition that makes you uncertain, you start asking yourself: *was* it really like this?

"You know, with that story. The American girl. You start thinking about other possibilities.

"Björn who killed himself. Her boyfriend, after she had died. But Bengt, the other boy, the one in the woods, who loved her too. Who was he?

"*If* it was him . . . And then, when you start thinking like that you sort of became unsure about everything.

"I gathered material. Sold flowers in the Winter Garden. But I didn't get anywhere. Then you start asking around elsewhere, here and there. Putting balls in motion, Lille. Google, write some messages . . . and then, gradually, you come across someone"—Ulla pauses— "whose name is . . . Maalamaa.

"Well, there's not so much to say about that. But now, Lille. The Red One, *now* she's here. In the Winter Garden. And I've been there.

"And she talks about completely different things—

"Strange things. Like, well, that change everything.

"And suddenly, even though you don't want to hear any more, you get hooked.

"She cuts rags for rugs, Lille. Heavy scissors, *crehp crehp* through the fabric, curling down into a bucket on the floor—"

"What does she talk about?" Johanna suddenly asks, loudly and eagerly.

Ulla Bäckström stops herself, stares so intensely into Johanna's eyes that Johanna almost regrets asking.

"Well." Ulla shrugs. "Just different stuff. She knew that boy, Bengt. Well, he wasn't a boy then any longer, a grown man . . . the one who died here, burned in the house.

"But that—maybe there was another secret. About what happened. Also with the American girl. Where everything started. *Three siblings*, Lille, who were united by a secret that should have kept them together but instead it drove them apart and everyone turned against each other. Is it fam—"

"What three siblings?" Johanna interrupts her.

But then Ulla suddenly laughs and puts on the mask she has in her hand.

"*You* know, Lille," she yells, with the mask on. "And *her* name is the Angel of Death Liz Maalamaa—and *your moooootheeer HA HA HA!*

"And SO, Lille, it becomes an entirely different story. About two people and a newsstand. Maybe you know it too? HA HA, Lille! Buhuu!"

And with these words Ulla turns around and walks away, November 2006, for the last time.

"Dark boring groupie," she yells. "EVERYTHING can be stuffed into your head!"

•

But that same evening, though much later, almost night by that time, Ulla Bäckström is standing on the Glitter Scene, the glass door wide open. And she falls, flies out.

A shadow behind her, that mask. The Angel of Death. Liz Maalamaa.

To add to the Winter Garden. Ulla falling, the mask, Screaming Toys.

It howls through this experience, screams, *Screaming Toys.*

•

But Johanna, still during the day, has run home from the woods, the house in the darker part, to her room.

The American girl in a snow globe.

Bengt in the woods.

Three siblings united by a secret.

Solveig closing the curtains in the kitchen. Ritsch. *To her the Winter Garden does not exist.*

Rita's Winter Garden. The Rita Strange Corporation.

From The Return of the Marsh Queen, Chapter 1. Where did the music start?

The Marsh Queen: I don't know about music, if what I mean with music, is music.

"Wembley Arena, 2012." Everything that brings you to the music. "Maybe I left because I wanted to be with people called Jack, Vanessa, Andy, and Catherine." *A new hour of creation, we are the Woodst* . . .

But of course, fantasies only. Leftovers of a Project Earth, the Marsh Queen, in the wastepaper basket, torn to bits.

•

"You have to know your history, to know who you are."

It was Tobias who said that once. But Tobias is dead, the greenhouse is dark, at the side of the road. It obscures the field.

And Johanna is alone with a story, a very different one, one she does not know what to do with.

A gust of wind, November 2006, Child, fluorescent on the wall.

And it is blowing through this experience.

THE STORY, TOBIAS'S GREENHOUSE, 2004

TOBIAS HAS A greenhouse, he grows roses there, lots of different kinds, you can remember names, such as one called Flaming Carmen.

Tough, sharp stems are forced up from plants and he is not very good at it. A rather hopeless task too if you think about the climate, he explains to Solveig sometimes, a bit vaguely as always when he is talking to her about his greenhouse that he built on property Solveig has rented to him. He certainly has all sorts of fertilizer in there, strong chemicals and strange lamps to "stimulate" the vegetation, he says with authority, even though it does not help. Tobias does not really have the knack; all the knowledge he has acquired about plants, and mainly about roses, he has gotten from books. According to Solveig, it may all be beautiful but in reality it just is not enough.

Maybe Solveig is right, Johanna does not know. On the other hand: Johanna does not care about greenhouse gardening, the art of getting roses to grow or die; she likes Tobias, likes going to the greenhouse, being there with him. Just the two of them, Solveig has asthma and cannot handle the air, but sometimes she shows up anyway. Suddenly standing in the doorway, reminding Tobias to wear his gloves. This period, the last period, Tobias in the greenhouse before he gets sick and dies, he often had to come to Solveig in the kitchen and get Band-Aids, his hands covered in small cuts.

But for the most part it is just Johanna and Tobias in the greenhouse, on their own. Tobias moving up and down the rows, cutting and pruning. Johanna in her place, a stool made of an upside-down bucket next to the water hose and the books by the entrance. Yes, there is a bookshelf with books in Tobias's greenhouse, next to all the greenhouse equipment and a record player playing opera music: a part of Tobias's large library that he could not take with him when he moved from the apartment on the hills north of the town center to the senior housing facility by the square. For example *A Lesson in History—A Sense of Belonging to the Village, Architecture and Crime,* and *History and Progress,* which was once Tobias's favorite work of reference: a heavy, worn bundle, several pounds of it, on the top shelf, mold on the edges.

"You need to know your history in order to know who you are." Tobias was once someone who said things like that, with a pedagogic fervor that had pretty much left him even before he left the teaching profession; he had taught history at the coed school and the high school. He had also been Solveig and Rita's teacher, that is how long Solveig and Tobias have known each other. Even longer too: they became friends at the swimming school where Tobias had taken notice of the twins' swimming talent, the twins' talent in general, the twins always did well in school too.

You have to know your history, Tobias said to Johanna once and started telling her about some local history but her concentration started fading while listening to the Old Men's Choir over five generations, the like. That's not mine, Tobias, she had wanted to say, but on the other hand: her own history, in that way, what would she have to add? The Marsh Queen, the corridors at school, to the music, but Råttis J. Järvinen who also says that *then, Johanna, one might also learn how to play an instrument, practice a little*. Nah. My story. Not exactly elated at the thought.

So they have not done a lot of talking there in the greenhouse, it just turned out that way. Just been there together, the damp everywhere, Tobias's music playing on the record player. Tobias slowly moving up and down the rows between the plants, Johanna on her bucket, and the titles of the books her gaze rests on, the scissors, the knives. The dusk falling outside can be seen through a hole in the plastic wall, *see the road like a line*, the light, the Winter Garden.

"Tell me about the American girl, Tobias."

In any case Johanna is thinking about what Tobias said about needing to know your history when she goes down to Tobias in the greenhouse after meeting Ulla on the field the first time, after being given the snow globe, from the Winter Garden.

"Project Earth, Tobias. It's something we're doing at school."

Tobias stops what he is doing, surprised, but at the same time, what else is there to say about that?

"I know, Tobias," says Johanna, "that Bengt is my father and he loved the American girl and that Björn, the one who killed her, was also from here, the cousin's house—

"And now, Tobias, I want to know everything. You know just as well as I do that Solveig doesn't say anything. I want to know. Tobias. Everything."

THAT RHYTHM AND THE QUIET CHILDREN, 1969

TOBIAS TALKS ABOUT THE DISTRICT like another world, even though it is not more than thirty–forty years ago. About the capes: the Second Cape, next to the sea, where he, at the beginning of the 1960s, runs a swimming school for the District's children before the summer settlers take over the beautiful cliffs of the archipelago. A housing exhibition of the vacation homes of the future is being built on the Second Cape, the first of its kind in the country, it is finished in 1965. Modern houses in a bold, new architecture are sold as summer camps for people who can afford to buy them because they are expensive houses—mostly outsiders, from the nearby city by the sea for example. Located just forty miles away and there is a road the whole way so it makes the area especially attractive. Thus the Second Cape is transformed into a secluded place, rather inaccessible for the District's own residents. The public beach is moved to the woods behind the First Cape, Bule Marsh.

The First Cape is located right behind the Second Cape, a bit off to the side, farther inland. It has more reeds, no sandy beaches or jetties there. The tall hill on which at that time there was only an old three-story house on it with turrets can be seen from a distance, far out at sea as well, like a landmark. In the very beginning, when Tobias comes to the District as an elementary school teacher in 1959, the house is empty and there is no sign of any owner making claims to the house. In and of itself it is not striking at that time: after the war, the entire District was a military base for the occupying power and was closed to all outsiders and when it is returned and opened again, not everyone who had been evacuated returns. The devastation was immense, homes, properties destroyed, burned down—not something you particularly want to see.

And below the hill then "the cousin's property," a red cottage with outbuildings and a tumbledown baker's cottage where the twins, Rita and Solveig, will come to live and grow up together. The cousin's property: named after the old man who owns the place; he is called "the cousin's papa" and nothing else. A jovial name for a grouchy and obstinate man who, shortly after the District becomes an open area, comes out of nowhere together with his brother and his brother's wife and their three small children and has, it turns out, papers saying that he is the new owner of certain land on the First and the Second capes. He won them in a poker game from one Baron von B. who, naturally after the game had taken place in some military barrack at the end of the war, tried to do everything in his power to invalidate the transaction. But it was futile, Baron von B. had signed over portions of his property in the presence of witnesses, nothing to be done about the matter.

In other words, such a strange, small clan: maybe you think what kind of loose rabble—who, without asking anyone's permission, settles down in the house on the hill on the First Cape and do not leave voluntarily; a countryman is needed to get them to leave. A bit amusing; here today, somewhere else tomorrow, people like that, as it were. But they do not disappear, they just move down to the foot of the hill and when you realize the cousin's papa actually owns *that* place (and large sections on the Second Cape as well, which he later sells to the company with the housing exhibition) you adjust your attitude a little. All this ownership still musters an ounce of respect together with the fact that shortly thereafter a terrible thing happens, the mother and father to the three small children die in a car accident. Crash into a hill at a high speed on the way to a dance competition (that was what they were, circus performers, professional dancers). And three small orphaned children left to fend for themselves with the man in the cottage, in that mess . . . and children are children despite everything, you can see from a long way off how it is going with those children. You try and do what you can for them, get them clothes, food, even if it needs to happen in secret so that the old man, who mainly spends his time sitting in his room boozing, will not become angry.

The children stay out of the way—like shadows, timids, during the day. But they can be seen at a distance: on the hill on the First Cape, sitting in a row, backs leaning against the stone foundation of the house where they had lived for a while. Tall, big for their ages, look older than they actually are. And when you see them like that, it can happen that you feel a certain . . . maybe it is not the right word, but worry, discomfort.

As if it were still hanging in the air, the music from the house from the time the children's parents were still alive and practicing dance moves on the salsafloor on the ground floor. Rumba tones, sneaking out through the crack in the open window, behind closed curtains.

On still, hot summer days: energetic rhythms, certainly "southern," certainly "happy," but in the silence where only the music and the pounding of feet could be heard it became something else entirely. Something pulsating, threatening, hypnotically absorbing.

That rhythm and the quiet children. And so, the children at the foot of the house on the hill, *the three cursed ones.* A memory, like a sensation, that springs up again a few years later when tragedy befalls the house again in connection with the American girl's disappearance and death at Bule Marsh.

Not for Tobias, of course, but for many others. Something about those children . . .

Tobias, on the other hand, after having met the twins at the swimming school and having known them for a few years, asked them what they do up there on the hill. "Play," the girls replied. "The Winter Garden." "What kind of a game is that?" Tobias asked with friendly interest. "A sibling game," Solveig explained and Rita elbowed her and added cryptically, giggling, "A world. An own world. We're building. In our heads."

But then when Tobias was about to ask more, both girls were evasive and giggled even more and started teasing him instead in a way that would gradually become an amusing pastime and a special jargon among the three of them. "Will you ask Rita?" one of them said, or "Are you talking to Solveig?" And whether Tobias nodded or shook his head it was always wrong. "I'm Solveig," one of them said. "No, me, I'm Rita." And they carried on like that to confuse him because of their likeness—and at the time the twins still looked so much alike that it was impossible even for Tobias to always tell them apart.

And little by little, about a year before everything with the American girl happens, things become pretty good for the kids in the cousin's house. A new woman comes to live there about a year after the car accident. A simple one, fond of children, who gets the house in order and has a boy of her own with her, his name is Björn and he is a few years older than the other children who become his "cousins" in the cousin's house. *The cousin's mama*: her real name is Astrid Loman, she is countryman Loman's daughter from the next county over and she is the kind that opens her arms to all children.

And God knows in those years, during the aftereffects of the war, there are enough homeless, abandoned children to go around. A little girl like that starts hanging around the cousin's house too: Doris Flinkenberg, an abused, mistreated child from the Outer Marsh. A special child, filled with light—and who, after Björn's death, is taken in as a new cousin in the cousin's house.

But first, now, the three siblings: the twins Solveig and Rita and their older brother Bengt. The twins catch Tobias's eye at the swimming school in other words: their exceptional talent, not only when it comes to swimming but in general, their strength, courage. Makes them assistant teachers in the school and that is where one of them, Solveig, distinguishes herself early on and saves a girl named Susette Packlén from drowning and gets the Lifeguard's Medal, which she keeps under her pillow a long time afterward, many years—there is so much of the child in her too.

There at the swimming school one of them, Solveig, is called Sister Blue, and the other, Rita, is Sister Red, so that the young students will be able to tell who is who.

Tobias takes the twins under his wing, not just at the swimming school but otherwise too. He visits them in the baker's cottage where they live on their own on the other side of the field across from the cousin's house. He encourages them in school, gives good advice.

And he is the one who finds them a new place to swim at Bule Marsh when the Second Cape becomes private property. Rita and Solveig are going to become swimmers, have decided that little by little. And if you are going to become a swimmer, you have to train hard and be goal oriented, with discipline. Bule Marsh becomes their training location where they go early every summer morning—and it is there, at the quiet beaches of Bule Marsh, in the middle of the woods' isolation, where they eventually meet the baroness from the Second Cape. They teach the baroness to swim, something she maintains she does not know how to do. In return, in exchange for the swimming lessons, the baroness teaches the girls English, which is one of the many world languages she has mastered.

For a time, a few summers at the end of the 1960s, the twins and the baroness are at Bule Marsh almost every morning. And Tobias himself as well, if he happens to come by on one of his morning walks. Like a small family there on the beach; Tobias, the baroness, the twins. Though it ends forever after that morning, late summer 1969, when the American girl dies there at the marsh.

Falls from Lore Cliff and disappears, is sucked into the water's currents. And the current *is* strong, especially under the cliff, and it is very, very deep.

•

Bengt, Rita and Solveig's brother, walks in the woods on his own, or on the Second Cape—even after the summer residents settle there. Tall and gangly, eleven, twelve, thirteen years old, but looks older. And a sketch-pad under his arm more often than not: but if you ask him what he is drawing, which Tobias does once, tries to start a conversation that way, for the most part you receive no answer or perhaps just a few evasive mumbles in response.

But, "maps," "special buildings," "architecture"—on a rare occasion he finds his tongue, even becomes excited. Then for the most part, his cousin Björn is with him and Björn is the one who explains it as a way of introduction, with admiration in his voice too. But then when Bengt relaxes and starts talking on his own it does not become much more intelligible; Björn rolls his eyes and starts laughing in the middle of everything. "You aren't right in the head, Einstein," he says but with respect, so to speak, as if being crazy is a sign of honor, and Bengt thaws even more and suddenly words start gushing out of him. Then you see the age difference too, of course—despite his gruffness and seriousness, how much of a little brother Bengt is in relation to his cousin Björn with whom he shares a room on the upper floor of the cousin's house; his best friend, his only friend, before the American girl comes in any case.

Björn and Bengt, together the two of them make a rather odd couple, as it were. Bengt who is five years younger and still a head taller than Björn. And no, they do no talk very much, not always and especially not in large groups. *The collective silence* you sometimes say when you see the cousins together. But for the most part it is that ordinary teenage shyness too; in any case with Björn, none of that restless, quiet anxiety about him.

Björn is kind, someone everyone likes, nothing strange about him. A perfectly ordinary boy who tinkers with his moped on the cousin's property; he bought it with his own money, he works at the gas station up in the town center and is going to be a car mechanic when he grows up. And of course, something that becomes very clear later on when he gets together with the American girl, eventually get married and start a family and have many children with her.

It is in the middle of June 1969 when she comes walking from the Second Cape where she is living that summer, the American girl Eddie de Wire. Cuts across the cousin's property with her eyes trained on Björn who is working on his moped outside the barn, the transistor radio hanging on a hook on the wall of the barn. Teenager drawn to teenager, like a fly to flypaper—Eddie to Björn and, of course, despite the great shyness, vice versa. Eddie who sits down in the opening of the barn, lights a cigarette and smokes. Björn toying with his moped, screwing and screwing because he has no idea what to say but for everything in the world he does not want her to go away. And then he finally builds up some courage and lifts the radio down from the hook on the wall, takes it in one hand and Eddie in the other, and then they go for a walk. So Björn becomes Eddie's official boyfriend that summer. The one she "is going steady with" as it is called in the pop songs that should be playing on that radio as they walk up and down Saabvägen, backward and forward; but for the most part there are just talk shows, or the news and the weather report.

Eddie and Björn, by the barn on the cousin's property, many evenings that summer. And gradually, after a while, Bengt joins the group. As shy as a weasel at first, a quiet presence—but does not go anywhere, remains there.

•

"The architecture," "the buildings" that Bengt talks about, they are his world. Architecture, houses, dreams about houses—both in fantasy and reality. For example the houses on the Second Cape that were once part of the housing exhibition: he loves them, has them on his mind, as if they in some way *are* his. He was on site already when they were being planned and built, asking the builders and architects questions and trying in different ways to make himself useful to the construction workers. But without progress: Bengt is not, so to speak, despite his wild and strange mind, the slightest bit practically oriented.

Also after the summer guests have taken possession of the Second Cape he continues going there, moves around just as he pleases and at whatever time of day suits him. He does not pay attention to the property lines, ignores the sign PRIVATE PROPERTY that is eventually put up in the little copse of trees that naturally demarcates the summer world on the Second Cape from the remaining parts of the District. The strange boy, you notice him. There is nothing obviously charming or childishly attractive about him either; almost something a bit frightening where he is wandering among the houses and on the cliffs, sketch book under his arm, tall and gangly. Stirs, yes, a certain discomfort, thoughts that cannot really be uttered out loud, in any case not if you are an adult and a parent on the Second Cape because he is, after all, you can see that too, just a child. A child like your own children, who have their own eyes and ears to see and hear with as well of course, who can monitor what they hear in the voices of the adults, the kind of underlying things that cannot be said in public.

So maybe that is why no one on the Second Cape really intervenes when the children finally take matters with Bengt into their own hands. Attack him, chase him into the woods behind the houses, surround him, and punish him. Many times, over and over again.

Before the American girl arrives and becomes his friend and gets involved, saves him. And the time that follows, a few intense weeks in July and the beginning of August 1969, you can see them on the terrace of her boathouse. Mouths moving, especially Bengt who is talking the hind legs off a donkey—all that dark gruffness and shyness in him blown away.

·

But punishment or not, and also before the American girl: nothing can beat Bengt. Sooner or later he is back again.

On the bare cliffs by the sea, for example, looking up at the Glass House where the baroness lives. One of the most elegant houses on the Second Cape, with the entire front made of glass. Windows from floor to ceiling and a veranda in the middle which, from a certain perspective, off to the side, looks a bit like it is floating above the water.

"That boy is different." It is the baroness who says that about Bengt to Tobias when Tobias visits her in the Glass House. They sit down there on the veranda on long, light summer evenings and talk to each other. The American girl is not there yet, it is the summer before the catastrophe that changes everything. Changes the baroness too—and in those times, the baroness is not the baroness but rather just "Karin," to him.

Many times later in life Tobias will remember how she said it, "Karin," the baroness; without anything condemning, no customary District suspiciousness in her voice. But softly, with admiration. The calm, the softness . . . like an extenuating circumstance because he liked her very much once, keeping in mind everything that happens later.

Up there on the veranda in the Glass House, Tobias and "Karin," at the beginning of time. Him talking, her listening with interest when he tells her about Bengt and his two sisters—about their tragic family history, of course, but also about their talent, fantasy. And about the game they have, the Winter Garden, they are building their own world, with their own language that only they understand. *People float freely away from themselves. In the middle of the Winter Garden there is* Kapu kai, *the forbidden seas. The hacienda must be built . . .*

How he has taken it upon himself to support and help the twins, in school, in all ways, sneak them a little money now and then, "granting small scholarships." With swimming as well; they are talented, good swimmers, both of them: one of them saved a little girl named Susette Packlén from drowning at the swimming school that Tobias held for the District's children a few years ago, right here, on the Second Cape.

"The hacienda must be built." The baroness laughs on the veranda of the Glass House, and it is as if she is enlivened for real, likes what she is hearing. "You are kind, Tobias," she says as well. "It must mean a lot to them that you are here." And Tobias shrugs and says nothing but it touches him of course that she, the baroness, "Karin," which she is for him during this time, says that.

And he will also like thinking that the baroness getting to know the twins at Bule Marsh has something to do with what he is telling her about them, that it makes her interested, so to speak, so that she wants to be involved, take part in something.

She starts coming to the twins at Bule Marsh, precisely in the mornings.

They teach her to swim and she, who is widely traveled and knows a great deal about most things, talks to the girls about life and the world that is large, the many interesting places to visit, a lot of interesting things to see along the way. But the world in a metaphorical sense as well, like the world inside you: that you can be and become yourself. It being your duty as a human being to take advantage of all these possibilities. *I have placed you in the center of the world . . .* The baroness quotes Pico della Mirandola there at Bule Marsh. The world as a garden. *Welcome girls to my lovely garden—*

Pico della Mirandola, the Renaissance there at Bule Marsh, of course, you can smile a little. *I have placed you in the center of the world.* On the other hand, completely realistic.

And Tobias comes there often. Like a small family on the beach—or what should you call it; but a somewhat special kinship, a unit, a possibility. But in some way, at that time, he is already thinking—so fragile.

"I can't swim, Tobias." The baroness laughs as it were there on the veranda many times. "So it's about time I learn. But funny girls—"

But, of course, on the veranda, they also talk about other things. Their own things, interests they share. About gardens, plants, the woods, and nature. "I'm going to have my winter garden here on the veranda." The baroness laughs. "My hacienda. My own world."

•

Below the Glass House, at the edge of the beach, there is a boathouse, a small hut on poles stuck between the rocks on the beach, a terrace facing the sea. That is where she spends her time, the American girl Eddie de Wire, a short time, a few months during the summer of 1969 when she is in the District.

She has come from America, the baroness has taken her under her wing, they are distant relations. She lived with her since the winter and comes with her to the summer residence on the Second Cape. Meets Björn who becomes her boyfriend and Bengt who is six years younger but the two of them become good friends as well, gradually spending a lot of time together, just the two of them.

But otherwise, Eddie de Wire, who is she? You do not really know. It is one summer—yet, like a question mark, a mystery. It is also a bit like this with the American girl: one day she is in the District, and few months later she is gone. Just nineteen years old when she falls from Lore Cliff at the beginning of the month of August and tumbles to her death in Bule Marsh.

"Blood is thicker than water." It is the baroness who says that to Tobias on the veranda at the Glass House, where they are sitting, talking to each other that summer before all of the horrible things happen. She says it many times on various occasions, in various tones of voice. Sometimes ironically, sometimes excusing herself, sometimes as if "despite everything," officiously and decidedly.

The blood, the water, the kinship. It is about the American girl, who is such a disappointment to her. She makes no secret of it either: after Eddie de Wire's death several others in the District will be able to hear those words ringing in their ears, "such a disappointment."

So Eddie de Wire living in the boathouse and not up in the Glass House with the baroness can be seen as an expulsion. Which the baroness, "Karin," herself does not say outright, not even to Tobias but it can be gathered by the mood. Something that is suddenly so different this year: the baroness's exhaustion, hesitation, anxiety—or, pure fear? Can also be seen in the mornings with the twins at Bule Marsh. Yes, the baroness is there this summer as well, but not as often. Clearly irritated sometimes, snaps at the girls, "Don't stand there and dawdle like the cat's got your tongue." Says things like that, which make the girls confused, careful and clumsy, nervous. And then when she still tries to be like before, starts talking about all of her trips, about Italy, the world, Pico della Mirandola, the Renaissance . . . it often happens that she just stops. Does not get in the water, wraps her bathrobe more tightly around herself, remains sitting on the beach.

"Such a disappointment . . ." Not even with Tobias, when it is just the two of them on the veranda, does she explain it any further. On the other hand: Tobias does not ask, as if there were a distance between them that neither really understands. But at the same time, when they got together it was as if they were both so preoccupied with bridging the gap they were unable to focus on anything else.

Put your finger on what has changed, try and stumble your way forward to an old fellowship. "Karin," "Tobias," "Karin," "Tobias" . . . and then they sit there saying staccato lines to each other that begin with the same terms of address, "Karin," "Tobias," meaningless, like an old parlor game. Find a manner . . . it slips away.

For example, a certain afternoon in the Glass House at the end of July 1969: "Karin," "Tobias," in the Winter Garden—Tobias who suddenly says to her that he is going away.

"To Italy?" "Karin" asks then. It comes out in a hurry, sharp and almost ill-tempered. Tobias laughs. "Well. Not now anyway."

No, no, Karin: Tobias is going to an in-service training seminar in another city, will be gone almost a week, which he says with a sober severity in his voice too, as if he is reprimanding her, like the teacher he is in real life. With the purpose of underlining the difference between the two of them: *he* is never anywhere, much less abroad, does not have the possibility. It hits home, of course, "Karin" understands perfectly, laughs acidly, shrugs her shoulders, picks up a book. Once she came to him—now, all of this alienation, and he regrets it of course—at the same time, the reality in everything, when you understand that it is the last time. And at the same time: a dreadful parlor game, "Karin," "Tobias."

Like this too: in the next moment Tobias stands and walks to the window. Stands on the glassed-in veranda— of course, for real; glass against the world here—and looks out. The boathouse off to the side, where Eddie de Wire and Bengt can be found even on this late afternoon. On the terrace, just the two of them, babbling away.

Eddie and Bengt: feet dangling over the water, the sea opening up in front of them. Eddie with the guitar she is plucking at amusedly, Bengt drawing, *talking*. He who was always so quiet, as if transformed, suddenly something a bit happy about it.

And on the Second Cape otherwise, the summer life that is carrying on on its own, separate path. The children from the fancy houses, in the middle of their "sea life" with sailboats, skiffs that they devote themselves to as silly hobbies, fishing gear, motorboats.

But again, the unusual figures on the terrace of the boathouse. Brace yourself against them. In this moment, as if *they* ruled, were queen/king over everything. The boy's babbling, the girl's laughter, the only closeness.

They have a game, the Winter Garden.

The baroness, "Karin," has at this point in time, July 1969, stopped saying "odd" about Bengt. Says, when speaking of Bengt and Eddie on the terrace of the boathouse, nothing. Pretends not to see them.

Northern wind. The sea dark, foam on the waves.

Still, a beautiful image. Eddie and Bengt. Ideas flying around them. Such invincibility.

What is Bengt saying?

The hacienda must be built?

Something else?

Cannot be heard of course. On the other hand: does it matter if you know it in hindsight? Because that comes to an end as well. Just a few days later the American girl is dead, and Björn, her real boyfriend, has hanged himself in the most distant outbuilding on the cousin's property.

And Tobias then, who never goes anywhere but has now been to a training seminar in another city, comes back as if to another world.

•

And this is how the American girl's death is going to be taken down in history: like a teenage love&jealousy drama with a violent end. Björn who argues with his girlfriend Eddie de Wire when he realizes that she has deceived him and he becomes furious and chases her through the woods and they end up at Bule Marsh where he pushes her from Lore Cliff into the deep water with the strong current. It happens quickly, in just a few seconds, how she falls, is sucked into the whirlpool. And Björn, when he understands what he has done, cannot live with it: love is pure, he loved her after all.

Eddie's body disappears. Becomes stuck on the bottom, the dredging that year results in nothing—not strange in and of itself since the water at Bule Marsh is deep.

Floats up a few years later, after a long period of drought, at the end of another summer, 1975.

But you know that she fell, there are witnesses who have seen it—

•

But, as said, above all. This will become a story. *He who killed for the sake of love.* A story about young love and violent death that lives on in time, lives on in the District.

And will also, many years later, be at a place called the Winter Garden.

Where you can, for example, buy the American girl in a snow globe at the souvenir shop. Two figures in a watery landscape.

"It was a great love, Lille." Ulla Bäckström with the snow globe, on the field in 2004 . . . in the first snow, which is falling around her. Looks at Johanna, absorbs her with her beautiful eyes. "Ylla of death . . . I am obsessed with death." Ulla-Ylla who is catching real snowflakes on her tongue.

And Ulla Bäckström as the American girl. How she stands on the Glitter Scene, her room in the woods, at the highest point in the wonderful house where she lives in Rosengården 2 and Johanna below, alone among the last trees of the Boundary Woods, in the darkness. Streaming lights, like searchlights. She IS the American girl, so real you can almost see the following: how she falls, crashes down to the ground—

"Don't push your love too far, E—"

•

But Tobias, in the greenhouse, shrugs impatiently. As if he wanted to say something else now, with authority: once upon a time all of that was real.

And he—just like Solveig—is not interested in the Winter Garden. As if he also wanted to say: don't bother with all of these stories, tales, productions, which come later.

Because once upon a time, as said, all of this was FRESH and real. And the loss that followed, life changing.

•

"I didn't want it to happen that way."

The baroness on her veranda, tired, stammering, waiting for the two sisters of the dead Eddie de Wire.

"Maybe I didn't understand her." Says the same thing over and over again in different ways when Tobias comes to her at the Glass House when he is back from his trip; on her veranda, and it is the last time.

"I should have understood, Tobias," she says, "but—"
She carries on like that, ruffled and confused and beside
herself. "I was going to send her away, I thought I had
sent her away—

"And that poor boy who was wandering around with
her little bag . . . I took him under my wing. I meant well,
but—"

•

Then, almost a week after that fateful morning, the following has also taken place. Bengt has been at the baroness's. He was the one who found Björn in the outbuilding
and has gone into shock, become mute, weeks will pass
before anyone can get a sensible word out of him.

So the baroness went to the cousin's house and offered to take Bengt to the Glass House for a while, after
everything. So he will get some peace and quiet and be
able to get away from everything but also to make things
easier for the cousin's mama who has been beside herself during this time—about Björn, inconsolable. But as
luck would have it, things get better for her later, when
Doris Flinkenberg is allowed to move into the cousin's
house.

And of course, the baroness has had such a bad conscience too. She does not hide it at all.

"I should have understood, Tobias. I didn't mean
everything I said. About Eddie, I mean."

And she has gotten nice drawing materials for him.
Been into the city and bought real painting supplies: an
easel and paint, watercolors, oil paints, chalk, expensive
felt pens. And is not the least bit quiet about the potential absurdity in that *that* is what she does, goes to the
city and buys all of those things in the middle of all of

the chaos. "I was so beside myself, Tobias. Didn't know what to do."

There in the Glass House, in one of the largest rooms with a view of just the sea—in other words in the opposite direction, so he would not have to look at the boathouse all the time—she decided Bengt will have peace and quiet, to paint, in all placidity, if he wants to.

Bengt has been there. One day, maybe half, before he disappeared without the baroness even noticing it, and, still, without saying anything at all. Is just gone. And later back at the cousin's house where he furnishes a room for himself in the barn and lives there. Eventually bringing in a bed and a Russian stove, and insulating the walls.

But after that, for Bengt, when he gradually starts speaking again (but then it is later in the fall and the baroness has left), there is no talk about the Second Cape; his solitary wandering has also ended. The boy with the sketchpad. Does not exist.

·

"I didn't WANT it to turn out like this . . . But, Tobias," says the baroness, "it was when that boy left that I understood you can't push things aside. You have to . . . face. Your responsibility, your shortcomings . . . I didn't understand that girl."

The baroness hysterical, babbling, telling Tobias an incoherent story about the last evening, night. A disturbance, a fight, and how she had phoned an acquaintance who came with a car to take the American girl away. And how they had driven away from the property, the last she had seen of the American girl. And Bengt who had come to her, upset, asking to see the American girl and not believing her when she said that she had sent her away.

Bengt, stood there bewildered, with the American girl's
bag—

"They were going to go away, Tobias. Had decided to
run away. The two of them, Tobias. Or whatever she had
hammered into him, Eddie. My God, that poor boy."

And how she had seen him leave—so alone, so crest-
fallen, all of him. As if all the air had left him . . . that her
having gone looking for him again later, afterward, was
maybe her way of trying to make things right, asking for
forgiveness.

Later, early in the morning, how Rita in her swimsuit
had come running to the baroness in the Glass House
from Bule Marsh. In need of help, wanting to tell her
about something terrible at Bule Marsh—

And then she told the baroness, "Karin," but in the
middle of everything just stopped, as if she was pushing
all of it away.

"Blood is thicker than water, Tobias. Maybe I've
learned that now. But it was an expensive lesson, Tobias.
And not worth it.

"I was afraid of Eddie, Tobias. She wasn't honest. In
the end I didn't know who she was. And maybe I don't
know now either. But this: it is just terrible. I'm sorry,
Tobias, I didn't want it to turn out like this—"

And the baroness on the veranda of the Glass House,
so alone, pitiful.

And how she appealed to him about an old friendship,
fellowship, solidarity.

"Blood is thicker than water, Tobias. But it isn't
everything."

But still, Tobias left. She is no longer "Karin" to him.
Just . . . nothing.

Because she said other things as well. About the twins, not directly, but paraphrasing, which in some way was even worse.

"I don't know if it's right, Tobias. And please don't ask me to explain. But I want to stay out of this, Tobias. Completely. Everything. God knows I have enough problems of *my* own now. Of course I don't mean you, Tobias. But—I'm asking you to respect my decision."

So that is how it went when the baroness abandoned the twins, when she refused to have anything to do with them anymore.

And for Tobias, who cannot believe his ears yet in some way it is not exactly a surprise either. "Karin." What "Karin"? A silly dream.

And Tobias leaves the baroness and he never comes back again either.

And that is how it is. The baroness disappears, ceases to exist—for Tobias, and for the twins. And shortly thereafter, as said, she has other people around her, new youths. *Blood is thicker than water*: her *own* relatives, a pair of sisters to Eddie de Wire, they come from America—and Kenny, the younger sister, comes to live with the baroness permanently.

In some way she might look a little bit like her sister Eddie, but still, so completely different. Essentially different, so light, Kenny de Wire in white clothes. But a delightful person and above all nothing mystical or mysterious about her.

But in some way it is, will be, in another time, in another world.

Because already during the winter after the American girl's disappearance the baroness is diagnosed with cancer and that is what she dies of six years later after a course of illness that had been lengthy and painful. The baroness loses the ability to move, has reduced vision and hearing, treatment and medicine make her bloated.

Sometimes you can see her at a distance, from the high hill on the First Cape. The baroness next to her house on the veranda where a winter garden was going to be constructed but it never materializes because of her illness. See her, an ungainly bundle in a wheelchair, wrapped in blankets in the middle of a warm summer day, but turned facing the sea, in large, dark sunglasses.

With her then, the new girl, Kenny de Wire. A calm voice that echoes for a long time in the warm, still summer evenings. A pleasing, soft laugh—that charm, that affability.

None of the alienation that once hovered over her sister Eddie de Wire, with Bengt, on the terrace of the boathouse.

•

"But Tobias!" Johanna interrupts him impatiently in the greenhouse. "What happened? At the marsh? The baroness never said anything?"

"But she wasn't there, Johanna," Tobias says and adds, after a short pause. "No, no, Johanna. I spoke with her as I said. I have a feeling that everything she told me was true. I know, Johanna. I knew her—"

"But Rita then? Who went to the baroness? What did she say?"

Tobias shrugs—"What she saw—"

"But Tobias," Johanna starts again. "Rita and Solveig then? Did they have anything to do with that . . . at Bule Marsh? Was that what the baroness meant?"

And, for a second, Tobias looks at Johanna blankly, completely perplexed. As if: my God, no.

"It was just that she abandoned them. Because she had so much else going on. Her own relatives. And it was already so terrible, everything, for her, she thought. But the twins became very lonely, of course."

•

Yes, of course. Life goes on, everything passes gradually. But it takes time. *The one who killed for the sake of love*: Björn who caused his girlfriend's death at Bule Marsh. Also before that story—which is also a bit beautiful, the young love, so shimmering but unconditional—can come out.

The gloom rests heavily over the District, over the cousin's house. The poor cousin's mama who lost Björn, and is beside herself, inconsolable.

But something good happens to her during this time too, which at least makes the sadness a bit more manageable, she gets something new to live for. That girl, Doris Flinkenberg, the knocked-about trash kid, whom the cousin's mama who loves children, *wants all the children to come to her*, has also been attached to earlier, gets to come and live with the cousin's mama in the cousin's house. It is arranged so that Doris gets a new home in the cousin's house and Doris, who is beside herself with joy in the middle of all the grief, moves into Björn and Bengt's old room on the top floor of the cousin's house.

Small, remarkable Doris, the mistreated one from the Outer Marsh who, after all of the terrible things she has experienced in her early childhood, finally gets some peace around her. And someone like the cousin's mama loves her one hundred percent and wants what is best for her.

And how they have such a good time together, the cousin's mama and Doris Flinkenberg. In the kitchen, in the cousin's house, with crosswords, the music streaming from the radio, the family magazines, *True Crimes* . . .

Doris, despite her terrible past, is still in some way so bright. And it soon infects everyone who comes in contact with her, *Doris-light*.

But, as said: it takes time. Some weeks, months later everything is still open, raw. Maybe also because Eddie de Wire's body was not found right away makes it difficult to move on. The body floats up out of the marsh where it has been lying, wedged into the mud on the bottom, six years later, at the end of an unusually dry and hot summer in 1975. And then: what is left of the body is just a skeleton, in a red plastic raincoat—*plastic is an eternal material*. It is Doris Flinkenberg who makes the macabre discovery.

And the other shock: that something like that can happen *here*.

A period of tittle-tattle, creepiness, feeling ill at ease and a lot of thoughts, other thoughts, about what happened at Bule Marsh when the American girl drowned. Thoughts that do not really belong anywhere, but they still do not leave you alone during this strange time.

•

You think for example about the baroness—though these thoughts really start coming when the baroness and Eddie de Wire's sisters, who came from America, have traveled back to the baroness's winter home in the city by the sea.

You knew of course, everyone in the District had known, that the baroness and Eddie de Wire had not gotten along. "That girl is such a disappointment to me": how the baroness herself had gone around saying it, increasingly irritated toward the end of the summer as well. And how even then rumors were spreading that the fact the baroness and Eddie de Wire were at each other's throats was more than just the usual grudges that can arise between an adult and a teenager. But more serious things: for example that Eddie de Wire was said to have stolen things and money from the baroness, forged her signature on proxies, the like. And it had already been going on during the winter in the apartment in the city and the baroness had tried to send Eddie de Wire away during the winter in the city by the sea. But Eddie de Wire had quite simply refused, as if she was dead set on staying. "Where am I supposed to go then?" Played innocent and stupid when the baroness had driven her into a corner, tried to force her to leave.

And followed her to the summer residence as well. Where the baroness put her up, not in the house but in the boathouse. An existence that Eddie de Wire was dissatisfied with in the beginning but later found tolerable after all. And she found herself a boyfriend, of course, one boyfriend, maybe two. But you can also remind yourself about something else you heard the baroness say one time while Eddie de Wire was still alive. That after the summer the American girl would not be there anymore: the baroness had no plans whatsoever of taking Eddie de Wire with her to the winter residence.

And in that light, think about the fact that the baroness herself had also spent quite a lot of time at Bule

Marsh where Eddie de Wire had died. That she had a habit of going there almost every day for her morning swim. But that is to say—you have stopped yourself at· the thought—morning*swim*? At Bule Marsh, in the middle of the woods? The baroness from the Glass House on the First Cape that is located by the *sea*: my goodness, why didn't she swim *there*?

But you knew the answer to that too. A fact that is cast in a new light.

The twins. Rita, Solveig, from the cousin's property. They were the ones she would meet at Bule Marsh, they were the reason she was there: the twins who were always at Bule Marsh—already early in the morning when ordinary, honest people were still in bed, asleep. In order to "train"? Were going to become *swimmers*, whatever *that* was? There was so much talk about a "talent for swimming," which they were seen as having. How they had gone around bragging about it left and right as if they were saying it just to each other but loud and clear enough so everyone else would be sure to hear it too. About everything "that was required," "all the sacrifices," "training, training, training . . ."

Sure. This was added on silently in the District back then too, before everything. Who did they think they were? Ha-ha. Really, seriously, *nothing* to write home about exactly. That "cousin's property," for example, which they came from, what kind of a place was it anyway?

Now, in this context, you remind yourself of what you know about them, not much, but strange things. The terrible man, the "cousin's papa" who won the property in a card game, the parents who died, dancers, circus artists? And so, a memory that strikes down like light-ning. Dance music coming from the open window, closed curtains. *Rumba tones.* A persistent, absorbing rhythm in the still, hot summer days around the house on the First Cape. The dancer, his wife, who were training for dance competitions on the salsafloor.

The rhythm, and the quiet children. *The three cursed ones.* And later, after the accident, sitting outside the house, the three children in a row. Tall kids who seemed so much older than they were, backs against the stone foundation.

Rumba tones, absorbing, as if they could still be heard around them.

That kind of inheritance, that kind of evil blood in the genes.

A shiver ran through you. *Those* children. The boy, who was friends and maybe more than friends with the American girl, and Rita, Solveig, the twins.

Back to Bule Marsh. *Those girls* with the baroness who did not get along with her young relative Eddie de Wire who died right there, at Bule Marsh.

Nothing you walk around saying out loud, you dismiss the thought as soon as you can. But still, difficult to get it out of your head once it has gotten in. And because all of it *cannot* be said out loud, *after all they are only children*, strengthens the feeling.

And so it becomes that much of that vagueness, the fear, the discomfort, the suspicions that were hanging in the air after the American girl's death without a goal or a direction gather around the twins, unspoken. Rita, Solveig, exposed for a short while; the eyes of the District upon them, stolen looks.

•

And a circle of emptiness around them, which only Tobias does not care about at all and pushes his way through. Continues visiting the twins in their cottage, just like before. Encourages Rita and Solveig to focus on school: the world is large, is open to them, and so on. Everything that had also been said in the woods at Bule Marsh with the baroness—but that sounds different now. Pedagogically severe and square so to speak, yes, he certainly hears it. But someone has to say something, he cannot remain quiet. Do not throw away your talent: high school, college, university! Reminds them of their old nicknames, which existed before "the swimmers," before everything. "The astronaut," "the nuclear physicist." Which were of course *also* what they were going to become . . . and the twins nod and start bickering a bit loose-limbed about who was going to be what, as they had a habit of doing during the time when they enjoyed teasing Tobias because even he did not want to admit that he also had a hard time telling them apart because they looked so much alike. "I AM the nuclear physicist, not Rita." "No, me Rita." An old jargon but without any energy in it: grown out of it, not very much fun anymore.

They do not talk about swimming, at all. Never again. Naturally unthinkable to continue training at Bule Marsh as if nothing had happened. But there are swimming pools, in the city by the sea for example where you can easily get to by bus, not to mention one in the next county over. And when it becomes summer again, other public beaches in the District.

"Shall we go and swim? Rita? We can bike." Solveig will be heard nagging at Rita a few times. But Rita is determined. Does not listen at all, *all of that* is over and done with.

So, what do you mean "swimmer"? Two ill-fitting swim-suits that are hanging, forgotten, on a clothing hook in the hall of the twins' cottage under shirts, coats.

An old Lifeguard's Medal that is hidden away in a desk drawer is forgotten. A reminiscence from another life.

•

So in the very beginning, it is like this, you cannot escape: Rita and Solveig on shining late summer days and in the fall that follows August of 1969. September that becomes October and the beginning of November. High blue skies, wild white clouds, and the play of colors when the leaves fall from the trees, the ground grows hard, the first snow.

Sitting on the steps of the twins' cottage on the other side of the field, across from the cousin's house.

Rita, Solveig, just the two of them while everything continues around them.

On the cousin's property, for example, about three hundred feet in front of them on the other side of the field: the new girl in the cousin's house, Doris Flinken-berg, she is jumping rope. Concentrated, persistent, does not look around, in the middle of her own per-sonal game, as if she had personally discovered the art of jumping rope. And not just any old, rotten jump rope she is handling either, but a brand-spanking-new one, which the cousin's mama has bought for her in a real store with her own money from cleaning houses that she has saved in a tin can in the cabinet in the kitchen. In addition to the glossy photos and the stationery of a kind that not only a small child like Doris Flinkenberg could be made happy with, printed with Keep-on-going-and-smile suns at the top edge. Not to mention the radio cassette player, a real *radio cassette player*, which also suddenly appears at the house instead of the old transistor that belonged to Björn and had been broken into a thousand pieces.

Welcome-Doris-presents is what they are called. Gifts that are given to Doris Flinkenberg to make Doris happy, Doris who has had such a difficult time and has now finally gotten a real home. With the cousin's mama, in the cousin's house. *"Today I've gotten, and tomorrow I will get and get . . ."* That is how Doris's little song goes, the one she walks around humming during this time too.

·

Doris who is jumping rope a few hundred feet away. *"Stipplo."* One of the twins says it, so that only the other one hears. *"Stipplo."* But in the next moment how it actually happens: Doris on the cousin's property, a desert away from them, trips over the rope, tangles her legs in it, falls flat on her stomach. Dump on the ground, she is not particularly graceful. And Doris, there where she is lying, looking around, a brief moment of astonished hesitation—as if she really did not know how she was going to deal with this unexpected mishap, with what kind of reaction. On the one hand: naturally just a trifle, what is tangling yourself in your jump rope compared to all of the horrible things you experienced in your early childhood in the Outer Marsh that fortunately for that matter is now over? On the other hand: *objectively* speaking it is *also* damn painful falling flat on your face, not to mention skinning your knees. But such a normal evil for a normal child can be blown away by a normal mother. And as if she was thinking just that, she casts a quick glance in the direction of the cousin's house and the kitchen window where the cousin's mama can be found on the other side . . . and first then, how her face wrinkles and she starts crying at the top of her lungs.

"Maamaa!"

The cousin's mama is out of the house in no time, running to Doris Flinkenberg, taking her in her arms. And then the scrapes on Doris's knees are inspected by the cousin's mama and Doris Flinkenberg together. Whereupon, cheeks ballooning, *puust* on the owie and soon Doris stops sobbing because it is so much fun and she starts puffing as well. And the cousin's mama helps Doris to her feet and they disappear inside the house. To the kitchen, where a snack is being served and pop songs and crosswords are filled in family magazines and there is reading from *True Crimes*.

A funny little scene, of course, not even the twins on the steps on the other side of the field can resist smiling just a little.

"You said it. *Stipplo*," Solveig establishes later. "And then it happened."

"Nah, it was you," says Rita.

"I heard you, Rita. Don't even try." ′

Rita suddenly gets angry. "Yes, but just imagine if you would shut up! IMAGINE if you would stop getting involved in things. It just gets screwed up!"

Tobias, within hearing distance, closes in with quick steps. Rita sees but does not stay and wait, gets up and leaves. Solveig gets up as well, shilly-shallies a brief moment as if standing between two fires but then follows after Rita. Waves to Tobias, "Be back soon." Tobias waves, calls out something friendly, "See you," then remains standing at a loss before he slowly walks off in a different direction to return when the twins are back.

Tobias stands and watches: the twins heading up the steep path to the hill on the First Cape. To the house, the overgrown garden that will be tended by a family by the name of Backmansson who will eventually move in there. But still, a short while, a few years, a place for dreams, utopias . . . "They have a game, the Winter Garden," the silver ball in the middle of the tall grass, overgrown rosebushes, reflecting light in the middle.

Rita first on the path, Solveig a little way behind. Rita who is in a hurry, Solveig trying to keep up with her.

Because also: *those children* . . . A shadow falls over them. Which Rita tries to escape, by breaking free of her sister, separating herself. Rita, suddenly, how she turns around and bellows, "I want to be alone. Do you *have* to follow me around all the time?"

Solveig flinches, stops. Rita who continues, upward, upward.

Still Solveig, she does not want to stay in the shadows either. Or shadow and shadow, maybe the grandiose just was not for her—because one difference among many, which starts presenting itself between the twins during this time as well, is that Solveig broods less, is maybe a bit slower but more here and now. But quite simply: does not want to be left behind, alone.

"Rita, wait!" And Rita still hears, regrets it. Waits for her sister and when Solveig has caught up with her the siblings walk the last bit like two friends, arms around each other.

•

"They have a game, the Winter Garden." A game with its own language, like a separate world, a dreamworld, a utopia. With its own rules, its own language. *The hacienda must be built.*

Beautiful. But: it fades. Lacking the energy to maintain it, or force&resistance. *The cursed ones.* The eyes of others that become their eyes. Rita, Solveig frozen in time. Rumba tones, stone foundation, an unexplainable threat hanging in the air around them. Another story that is taking over all the time.

And yes, there comes Bengt. Who does not spend very much time with his siblings anymore, or at all, with anyone. Has started speaking again, but does not say very much—on the other hand, it was always like that. And soon, rather soon too, he will pretty much leave the sketch book altogether to become oneofthose teenagers for real. One with bags of beer, flower power cap on his head, to attract "women"—girls from the District and so on . . . who in some way will actually flock around him, for a while. But Bengt becomes stuck there, so to speak, the beer, et cetera . . . drifts here and there, one who comes and goes, things with him go to hell in a handbasket, he becomes nothing. And many years later, 1989, then he is around thirty-five, he is completely dried up, kaput. Comes "home," to the cousin's property and ends things. Also there, in that cursed cousin's house. Maybe a logical fate—

A sad story, a story about the unnecessary.

Tobias who stands by and watches. Remembers "Karin" too, not often but sometimes. Her desertion, and his. The baroness who soon after the catastrophe said confused, stammering: "That is what you do. First. Instead of doing what you should be doing. Go to the city with 'Astrid' "—that is the cousin's mama's real name, which only the baroness has ever used—"and buy things." As if it would make things easier. Art supplies for Bengt, a radio cassette player. Yes, it is "Astrid" who suddenly wants it but it is the baroness who pays for it. She tells Tobias about Astrid who had a tin can filled with coins in her authentic checkered milkman shopping bag, which she had insisted on taking with her on their visit to the city; she had suddenly taken the can out in the appliance store and opened the lid and poured the contents out on the counter. "Is this enough?" With tears in her eyes, and the baroness explains that it was first in that moment that she understood how, behind the cousin's mama's calm, sorrowful façade, such a daze had been hidden, that she herself had fallen silent. And in some way also understood that she should do something. Not just for Bengt, but for everyone, for everything. Those children, so defenseless. But at the same time she realized the opposite. She could not, cannot—has enough problems of her own: Eddie de Wire and the guilty conscience about her own shortcomings, everything that went wrong.

The cousin's mama who had stood in the shop like a child, chasms that had opened for the baroness. But the only thing she had been capable of doing was collecting the coins and getting out her checkbook and paying for that gadget—at the same time as she hated herself, her checks, her money, her possibilities.

Everything you should have done but did not while there was still time. "Time is the time we do something else, Tobias," the baroness had said to Tobias on the veranda and said that there was a poem that went like that which had suddenly popped into her head and Tobias never hated her like he loved her in that moment.

•

"WHERE IS EVERYONE? I WANT TO PLAAY!" Doris out in the yard again, had become a bit bored with just the cousin's mama and the crosswords in the kitchen. And the music: *I go up to the mountains with my lonely heart*—a pop song of the day as good as any other, which she hums where she is standing there on the steps, looking around with a hardtack sandwich in hand.

"WHERE?" Doris yells. Deadly silence. No one answers Doris. But then Doris catches sight of Rita and Solveig and Bengt on the hill on the First Cape.

"I'm comiiing!" And Doris heads off in the direction of the path that leads up to the hill. But no one stays there and waits for her. Bengt disappears and Rita and Solveig make their way down on the other side, leaving the garden and the house that will soon be occupied by others: *let's get out of here* as they say in the District.

Enough of that. But also, enough of the twin-unity. What happens happens there even though no one notices until it is impossible to hide it any longer. A crack that becomes a sore that is widened until it can be seen by day, red and gaping. Doris starts running up the hill.

Rita and Solveig walk down, as said. You can see them strolling down the hill, out of Doris's sight, leaving the garden and the house that will soon be inhabited by other people, *let's get out of here.*

Lose yourself. Because what you are, have been together, is not good enough.

And you have started hating what you are.

The game. The Winter Garden, on the hill. Can be

determined. Silly. Realized. The utopia. More fantasy was needed than what they possessed in order to make the game, which was really never a game but an own world, real—a possibility. Well, been there done that and no one there is interested in witnessing the development of the fall, from A to B in that way.

And: what remains. The astronaut. The nuclear physicist. A damned many years until college, university.

But at the same time—these are just movements that can be sensed under the surface.

And are never spoken about, almost no fights, reconciliations.

An old Lifeguard's Medal that Solveig still sleeps with under her pillow. A sign of luck. Talisman. *Pathetic.* But it disappears, as Rita starts saying: "You are, Solveig, a pathetic."

•

But Doris comes to the twins' cottage that same night. "Today I got, tomorrow I will get and get." Doris warbling her own little song, a few hours after she raced up the hill on the First Cape only to discover that the siblings had escaped.

Doris in the twins' cottage, jumping around there too: clumsy dance steps on the floor, tippytoe, today . . . tomorrow . . . GET! Doris everywhere, at the table where Solveig and Tobias are trying to focus on her math homework . . . but mathematics, sigh, Doris does not *want* that one, yawns theatrically, you become bored after all. So Doris continues on, to the bookshelf, takes out the Swedish Academy's word list that was Tobias's Christmas present to the twins and that Solveig used to take with her to the cousin's kitchen as an aid for the cousin's mama with all of the crosswords she was solving before all of the terrible things happened and Doris Flinkenberg came to the cousin's house. Some strange, funny word that Doris can find and take away from there; and Doris flips, flips until she realizes, which she says too, with delight, "*I* am so little, I can't read!" And moves on to picking up different things at random, whereupon she stretches out on her stomach on Solveig's bed, "get and get," but drowsy now, and then of course after a moment of motionlessness as if she were sleeping, so to speak, she sticks her hand under the pillow.

"Damn it, Doris!" Solveig's voice suddenly surprises all of them, resounds loud and wild in the cottage. "You put my medal back!" And everything stops, is frozen. Doris above all. Doris sits up, so small pitiful afraid—as if all of the terrible things she has been through bubble up inside her, gather in her eyes in an unbearable way. Opens her hand, it is empty, but says, stammering, "Sorry, sorry . . ." bottom lip quivering, like a preparation for crying.

"Now, now, girls," Tobias says but Solveig gets up and walks out, slamming the door behind her.

And later, that night, Solveig goes to the outbuilding farthest away on the cousin's property alone and she has newspaper and matches with her.

The place where Björn was found when he was dead. It is definitely burning, but just a little, nothing dangerous. The outbuilding itself will fall down under its own weight during a storm, but not until the following year, in the spring.

But suddenly Bengt is there, with the water bucket, and puts it out.

And everyone sees: Solveig standing and crying by the outbuilding. Rita coming, taking her hand, leading her home. They walk, Solveig crying, Rita putting her arm around her. Past the cousin's mama who is standing on the steps of the cousin's house, and Doris, heavy with sleep in her pajamas and big boots, just below. Rubbing her eyes, but then, shoots into the cousin's house and as fast as lightning she is back with a blanket and runs after Rita and Solveig on the field and "if you are freezing, here," and wants to put the blanket over Solveig's shoulders. And Solveig stops, turns around, says a soft but very emotional "thank you" to Doris Flinkenberg.

And it is—all of the small things that happen that evening, that night, the only release.

·

But later, gradually, everything evens out. In the District too: life goes on, everything acute and inflammatory comes to rest, the whispering as well. Is pushed aside by new happenings, bad, good, everything imaginable from day to day, big and small, which draws attention to itself. And Rita, Solveig—they are of course on the other hand completely ordinary youths in the District, students at the school, the coed school and the high school up in the town center. And that is finally what wins over everything that does not exist, that is not left: like the American girl and the baroness and the other summer residents. And the winter comes, the spring, the summer, several summers falls winters seasons.

And at the cousin's property, in the cousin's house, there is something about Doris Flinkenberg for real. Her mood, her joy, her *light*. Which infects everything and brings about a change. Something about Doris, so smart, wonderful—she gradually wins everyone's heart. With the exception of the cousin's papa's of course, but he does not count. He has withdrawn to his room next to the kitchen, closed the door. Sits there and boozes by himself, sometimes does not even come out at mealtimes.

The effect Doris has, Doris-light. Doris who, despite everything, comes and makes everything normal again. And when after that scene with Solveig in the twins' cottage Doris's own present-getter zeal becomes weaker, it becomes more fun for the twins and for Bengt to be around her. So that you notice that you WANT to give Doris a lot of things—especially when she is not there in person begging for them.

·

Doris came like the first orange after the war. The cousin's mama says many times when she becomes herself again. And Doris laughs, nods and agrees. WANTS to be an orange, but also banana and pear and large green apples of the kind that can be bought at the real store—*the whole* fruit basket.

"Look, it's me!" The fruit basket standing on the prize table at the Christmas bazaar at the fellowship hall in the middle of December: all of those wonderful fruits under the crackly cellophane and the red silk bow around the handle. First prize, of course, and Doris points at it, laughs. And Rita and Solveig and Bengt and Tobias and the cousin's mama laugh too, it is funny of course and Bengt, who has inexplicable good luck with games, buys a few lottery tickets and wins that basket too, which he then, in full view of everyone, hands over to little Doris Flinkenberg.

So heavy, so large, she barely has the strength to carry it, has to drag it behind her on the floor of the fellowship hall but she gladly does it of course, a fine show besides. But then *CRUNCH* someone is suddenly there sticking her hand in through the cellophane, swiping the largest most delicious green apple: it is the Pastor's daughter Maj-Gun Maalamaa, almost as little as Doris, who has been running around among the guests at the church bazaar with a terror-inducing old lady mask, "Here comes Liz Maalamaa, buhuu buhuu!" as if she wanted to frighten people and maybe it is a little creepy because the mask looks dreadful but no one wants to play along with those kinds of games NOW in the whirl of the general Christmas bazaar with the elves and the Christmas peace and the candles, so no one pays any attention. Just her brother who is slightly older, wearing a suit and white shirt with a tie even though he is probably only eight–nine years old, he is trying to keep an eye on his little sister, who the less attention you pay her the more high-spirited and unbearable she becomes.

But she is standing there now, the Pastor's daughter Maj-Gun Maalamaa, with the apple from Doris's basket in her hand. Takes off the mask and takes a big bite of the apple right in front of Doris, *smack*, and "ha-ha-ha" to Doris. "Give it back!" Doris yells. Give it back. But suddenly Doris, when Maj-Gun does not pay her any attention, so pitiful and suddenly almost afraid. "Stop!" she almost whispers, but Maj-Gun does not stop, only when her father the pastor shows up and pulls her ear, does she yell bloody murder, "NO!"

"Don't pay her any attention," says Solveig, who has been standing next to Doris the entire time; and it turns out all right later, because the Pastor comes and apologizes and takes Doris and Rita and Solveig to the kitchen of the fellowship hall where he has sweets that he lets his disobedient daughter Maj-Gun offer them. Especially Doris, who will get the nicest piece, a shiny red chocolate heart with a truffle inside wrapped in paper. "Maj-Gun should apologize," says the Pastor. And Maj-Gun finally says it, sorrysorry.

The fear, how it had flamed up in Doris's eyes. The Pastor had also seen it. And probably thinks it is a matter of the old lady mask so he explains to Doris Flinkenberg who has her mouth so full with delicious chocolate that she cannot speak but just makes her eyes wide—that the mask is not dangerous at all but represents the face of a famous actress, Ava Gardner, does Doris want to try it on?

But just as Doris is going to nod yes please there is a furious howl from Maj-Gun Maalamaa who snatches the mask out of papa Pastor's hand and yells that it is not a movie star but her horrible godmother Liz Maalamaa! And Doris recoils, almost frightened—but Maj-Gun has run away, with the mask, the apple, before the pastor has time to become even angrier with her.

But the fear in Doris's eyes, you think about it later. That it is still there beneath everything. Under the surface of this that and the other—jump rope jumping, cassette player, song of the day *I go up the mountain with my lonely heart* in the cousin's kitchen, crosswords, *True Crimes* with the cousin's mama . . . and the cousin's mama!—it remains. Like the scars in her skin, the burns from the grill, the cigarettes, under her clothes.

Can pass, but never leave.

A fear that exists there and can be called forth.

Like an omen as well. Because that fear, it disappears for a long time but returns when she gets older and contributes so that she, many years later, in her teens, will take her own life: goes and shoots herself at Bule Marsh.

Just sixteen years old—and incomprehensible. At the same time not. Because by that time there is also another story. Doris's own, private one. Because what also happens and very soon, already the following spring, after Doris arrives at the cousin's house, is that she starts going out on her own. On the prowl for a companion of the same age, a friend of her own. Because despite everything, things become a bit humdrum with the cousin's mama and the older cousins at the cousin's property.

And she finds her way to the house in the darker part, completely new then. And a girl the same age lives there. Her name is Sandra Wärn and she becomes like fat on bacon with Doris for many years. A friendship that becomes love for Doris and that Doris enters into hook, line, and sinker. But it ceases, a fight, some misunderstanding, as can happen between two who are close, maybe too close—and when it suddenly ends Doris is skinless.

Beaming, smart Doris, who is still so fragile under the surface. It does not disappear even though it cannot be seen.

A betrayal, a love that died: the most important in Doris's life, the only one that existed. Yes, of course, there would certainly have come more events, and experiences, a new time. But a blow, and it is decisive and fateful, there is nothing for Doris, no real time.

To be sucked into a black hole: then there is all of the old stuff, other betrayals, tattooed into the skin and an unbearable fear then, of everything, which flares up inside her. A betrayal, a love that died, the most important in Doris's life.

And so then. Doris, conquered by a time that has run away with her—to another time.

And suddenly trapped in that time.

"The folk song. A repetition in time and space. Such a different way of understanding time."

Maybe it is like that. Because that is what she does during the final months of life, Old Doris who is New Doris: sings folk songs in a band. Her boyfriend at the time Micke Friberg, *Micke's Folk Band*—they are together a few weeks that last fall—Doris sings and talks about the folk song in between the songs.

"I'm Doris, this is Micke, and we have a band, it's Micke's band, *Micke's Folk Band*. We sing old folk songs in modern arrangements, they're Micke's arrangements—"

But regardless of how hard Doris tries to devote herself to the music that Micke Friberg talks about, regardless of how she tries to be Micke Friberg's girlfriend, everyone already knows it is a lie. There was someone else, Sandra, whom she loved.

•

But that is later, not yet. And Rita and Solveig, this is what happens to them. Turn twelve, thirteen, fourteen, fifteen, and continue living together in the twins' cottage on the other side of the field across from the cousin's house. For a long time anyway, up until Rita, just after Doris's death, leaves the District for good in the fall of 1976.

But she spends a lot of time in the house on the First Cape as well; where new inhabitants come. First a group of women who rent the house for a few years, have a collective of some sort or another and Bengt and a boy from the Second Cape, Magnus von B., whom Bengt starts spending a lot of time with, running around among them, trying to curry favor, make themselves useful in every way. Yes, yes, Bengt has "a way with women," but it is still girls from the District who fall for him most of the time—not those women who make fun of him there where he is standing with his "flower power cap" on, talking about big things, about revolution and things like that.

But then the house is bought by a real family from the city by the sea: they are called Backmansson and they have a boy, Jan, the twins' age, and Rita starts going with him just about as soon as the family moves in. And intensely; gradually Rita is at Backmanssons' on the First Cape almost all the time when the family is there, more or less moves into Jan Backmansson's spacious room in the tower. They cultivate mutual interests there, for Rita, new interests—nature photography, for example.

What is it? Real teenage love. Maybe. On the other hand, Rita has other boyfriends too when the Backmanssons are not home and they are not always around because the parents are field biologists and travel quite a bit: boys from the District, ones like Järpe and Torpe Torpeson, for example.

And it is hard to know with Rita, becomes harder all the time, she is not exactly someone who explains herself, in that respect she definitely does not become a speech maker with age. Says nothing about her business, gradually not even to her sister Solveig, not to mention Tobias who continues supporting her and Solveig as best he can. Opens his wallet, "gives scholarships," just as fair with both of them.

But Rita, she slips away more and more . . . and there is something wild and unmanageable about her. More and more too, with time, as if Rita in some way is two people. One who spends time at the Backmanssons' house when they are home and otherwise another who exists in the District, in school, outside class and makes several of her classmates afraid. Rita Rat, she who provokes, allows herself to be provoked, and does not hold back, the one who hits.

But at the same time, despite everything and all of the time: Rita does well in school, has good grades in just about every subject. "The astronaut," "the nuclear physicist," it still matters, at least to her. In reality Solveig is the one who starts fading away and it does not turn around either: later when Rita leaves the District in the middle of high school, Solveig becomes pregnant shortly thereafter by one of the Torpeson boys from the Outer Marsh. Drops out of school and it is left unfinished despite the fact that she miscarries after a few months. Starts cleaning full-time for the cleaning company Four Mops and a Dustpan, which the cousin's mama leaves behind.

•

But Rita, still during that final period when she remains: drags certain youths with her from the District over to the Second Cape in the fall when the summer residents have gone home. Rita and the Rats: break into the abandoned vacation homes, make them theirs for the night, have parties, but mostly are just there, *creepy crawling*, invading. Do not destroy, vandalize to leave a mark behind: *we were here.*

Solveig is there too of course. Still, something in Rita
Rat those final weeks that also makes Solveig keep her
distance. Rita is always the one who keeps on to the bitter end, if someone goes too far it is always Rita. One of
the last nights Rita is in the District: how she breaks into
the Glass House, starts breaking the windows on the veranda, with a cane, furious. Solveig remains standing on
the hill, smooth as glass, hard, shiny, as if frozen in the
moonlight—and watches.

It is Rita's last fall in the District, the Backmansson
family has been gone quite a while, it is more than a year
now actually. The house on the First Cape has burned,
not completely but it was damaged in a forest fire that
spread at a violent speed. The Backmanssons were not
home then but the house has become inhabitable and
it needs to be repaired, and in the meantime the Backmansson family is living in their apartment in the city
by the sea again. The intention is that they will return
as said, but time is passing—the renovation never gets
started and for a long time, it will be many years, the
house just stands there on the hill with a dark, open gaping hole on the side, deteriorating even more until it is
torn down at the end of the 1980s.

But when the Backmanssons left they promised Rita
that she might be able to come and live with them in the
apartment in the city, finish high school there, in one
of the city's schools. But time is passing, as said, and
nothing happens: the house on the First Cape stands
where it stands, as if the Backmanssons have forgotten
what they said to Rita before they left. It is not mentioned when Rita visits her boyfriend Jan Backmansson
in the city by the sea and the visits have also become

fewer and farther between the final months Rita is in the District. As said, the Backmanssons travel a great deal and then Jan Backmansson has his own hobbies that Rita does not share but that his parents suddenly think he should make time for in addition to his demanding schoolwork. *Scouting* and something called "convent activities." Rita does not even know what it is, but things like that, similar things.

And she waits, waits—until she does not have the strength to wait anymore.

•

No one says out loud that Rita is the one who goes after the windows on the veranda of the Glass House, no one tells; a crime no one gets any clarity in. It is Solveig who explains to Tobias much later how it was.

And the baroness passes away that fall, never hears about it.

Besides, so many other things happen that fall— everything. Doris dies, Rita leaves.

As if everything culminated, but in an entirely separate story. That cursed October night when Doris Flinkenberg due to *her* unhappiness, her rejected, defrauded love, gets it into her head to go and shoot herself.

Doris, the amazing, who despite the darkness within her was so light on the outside: goes down to Bule Marsh, out onto Lore Cliff, has a pistol, presses the muzzle to her temple and fires.

•

And the night after Doris Flinkenberg's funeral, that is when Rita heads off. To the Backmanssons in the city by the sea, without asking permission or telling anyone about her plans ahead of time.

One Saturday night in November 1976 Rita is suddenly standing below the Backmanssons' third-floor balcony on a calm and civilized street in the chic southern areas of the city center. Dirty, slightly intoxicated, everything she owns in a shabby plastic bag.

Calls out to the people standing on the balcony, guests of Mr. and Mrs. Backmansson who are having a large party that night.

But Rita waits on the street, and is let in.

•

That is how it is told to Solveig later by a few youths from the District whom Rita bummed a ride from into the city after she wrecked Solveig's tiny rickety old car that she had driven off in from the twins' cottage while Solveig was in the shower. Certainly deliberately: out into the field, toward a tree at a low speed, then walked to the main country road with her things in a plastic bag.

Not even Solveig's own car but her boyfriend's at the time, Järpe Torpeson, who had fixed it up for Solveig so that she and her sister would be able to sputter around on the small roads and to the Outer Marsh, Torpesonia, where he lived.

Broom. How Solveig, in the bathroom, had heard the engine start. Gone out, seen the little car disappear into the darkness—the last of her twin sister Rita. Forever.

All of Solveig's attempts at getting in touch were in vain. Rita cuts all cords, does not get in touch.

•

And what is left? At the cousin's property, the cousin's house?

Doris's song, maybe. A voice on an old cassette tape.

"The folk song has many verses, the same thing happens in every one. Over and over again: Such a different way of looking at time."

Doris's voice, soft, a bit hoarse, just a few weeks before she takes her own life. Becomes the first in a long line of those who will go down to Bule Marsh and die at their own hand. Because it is, in real time and history, what Bule Marsh is gradually transformed into. A cursed place, *a sanctuary for suicidals.*

But no, it has nothing to do with any old stories anymore. Like, once upon a time, *Rumba tones, the three cursed ones.*

Just a darkness that falls over the cousin's property, over and over again. Woe followed by woe, like pearls in a necklace. With some places, some people it is like that. They are cursed, so to speak. Things happen, and continue to happen.

Affected by time, another time. The time of the folk song.

"The folk song. A repetition in time and space. Such a different way of understanding time."

But—with the folk song comes realism; it is a shame about Solveig, who is left behind, all alone.

•

Because: the one who is left behind is left behind. Being in the world, in the cousin's house, without *Doris-light.*

The cousin's mama who has no strength left for anything. She collapses completely in the spring and is taken to the District Hospital by ambulance and when she gets better she moves back to the neighboring county where she originally came from. Never returns to the cousin's property, to the cousin's papa: because *he* does not die of course, has eternal life in him.

And Solveig then, with all of this. Rita in the world, and Bengt who stopped being responsible for his actions a long time ago—a restless one, sometimes here, sometimes there. In the city by the sea, in other places, in other cities and comes and goes in the District. Wanders off, but unlike Rita nothing becomes of him, he deteriorates more and more.

•

Solveig. Nah, she did not become an astronaut or a nuclear physicist. Eventually she moves in with her boyfriend Torpe Torpeson, whom she has taken over after her sister Rita, to his home at the Outer Marsh, Torpesonia. Is expecting a child with him; that child and another end up as miscarriages before she finally has Irene in 1984.

By that time she has been living in Torpesonia for a long time; has taken over the cleaning business as said, Four Mops and a Dustpan, business is decent, makes a living off it and eventually has an employee, Susette Packlén from the District.

The cousin's papa dies of natural causes but not until the end of the 1980s; he becomes deathly old. And Bengt—it is an accident of course—falls asleep with a cigarette that sets fire to the cousin's house and when the fire department arrives, there is nothing that can be done to save him.

And Solveig, it is a turning point for her.

She sets herself free from it, turns her back to it, the old stuff no longer exists for her.

Tears down, builds new, moves in with Irene and eventually Johanna as well.

Closes the cleaning business, starts a real estate business instead.

But from the ashes of the old ruins: finds a Lifeguard's Medal, an old sign of luck, a talisman.

•

"But Tobias," Johanna has started in the greenhouse in the fall of 2004, when Tobias has finished telling the story. A sad story, in a remarkable way a beautiful story, of course, but still, inside Johanna, it has been pounding there, not grown quiet. All of the questions, suddenly millions, wanting to go back to the really old stuff that Tobias has not spoken about. The morning at the marsh, the American girl, Björn who hanged himself.

Rita and Solveig, the twins at the marsh. Were they there? What did they see?

And Doris Flinkenberg, the knocked-about marsh kid, was she not running around in the District then too? And then—*the Boy in the woods*, Bengt. What did he do?

Don't push your love too far, Eddie.

Ulla on the field. "There was not one who loved her, but two. They say she died from love. The one who killed her loved her too much."

Bengt and the American girl Eddie de Wire, on the terrace of the boathouse. Her own father, Bengt.

"But Tobias—" Johanna, with an urgency that could no longer be concealed.

Then Tobias himself suddenly looks up at her and says, "Johanna. To you this isn't about Project Earth, is it?"

And Johanna nodded, carefully, but could not get a word out anyway, suddenly mute in some way. And Tobias was just about to say something, had taken a few steps forward and then staggered. As if still, tired of his own words, tired of everything, of the age in his body too, all the energy leaves him. The plants he does not have the energy to look after, as if he saw it in that moment too: how they are becoming overgrown, have grown above his head, roses, thick full stems and thorns that tear at the skin on his hands because he has of course forgotten his gloves somewhere again.

A record on the record player, *Carmen*, it has finished playing. And the uncertainty about what to do next, fumbling, what was he going to say now? Has taken the spray bottle to fill it with water but stumbled and hit the bookshelf next to him, it rocks and damp books from the top shelves come tumbling down. *History and Progress* and several others, Tobias has to duck in order to avoid getting the books on his head and almost loses his balance so that Johanna has to grab him and help him down on the stool where she had just been sitting and then she gathers up the books on the floor.

Among them too *Architecture and Crime*, poorly bound, old glue on the sides is falling off—not just the covers, a quick stolen look, loose pages as well.

Drawings, characters in dark lead, blue watercolor. "In the woods a body of water reveals itself. It happened at Bule Marsh." And a name on the first page of the book, "This book belongs to" with straggling letters and then his name, Bengt.

The Boy in the woods, with the sketchpad. Bengt.

A blue girl on a cliff.

"*Sister Blue.*" How it sweeps through her head.

Rita. Solveig. Bengt. A crack that became a wound that was opened. A secret that drove them apart.

Solveig. Sister Blue.

Solveig who pretends the Winter Garden does not exist.

Ritsch! The kitchen curtains.

The book in Johanna's hand. At first she thinks about asking, "Can I borrow it?" but changes her mind and says straight out, "This book was my father's. Can I take it?"

"What is it Tobias? Put on your gloves, Tobias?"

And right then, before Tobias has a chance to answer, Solveig is suddenly standing in the entrance to the greenhouse.

•

Sometime later, spring 2005, Tobias becomes ill and does not come to the greenhouse anymore. Falls off his bike, it is slippery, an early morning on his way to the greenhouse, he is lying in bed with a cast on his leg. An accident, he has fallen off his bike before.

But never really recovers again. Develops other problems. His stomach, his heart, and he dies in the month of April 2006.

The greenhouse deteriorates, no one goes there anymore.

JOHANNA IN THE ROOM, IN THE EVENING, NOVEMBER 2006

THE AMERICAN GIRL in a snow globe.
She has taken it out again.
Solveig is not home, she has gone out.

•

Looks at the snow globe, she is alone in the house, in the darkness in her room, shimmering quiet, the light, the property.
Oh! Turns on the light.
Digs in a drawer and finds the book. *Architecture and Crime.*
The drawings in the book.
A blue girl on a cliff, above the water, she is screaming.

•

Ulla Bäckström earlier that day, at the house in the darker part of the woods.
About the Red One in the Winter Garden. *She talks about strange things.*
A completely different story.
Three siblings who were united by a secret that was supposed to keep them together but it drove them apart and turned them against each other.

•

Three siblings. Remembers Tobias's story. *The three cursed ones.* At a house, the stone foundation.
Rita, Solveig, Bengt.

·

Rita who left, never to be heard from again.
Bengt who died, burned up in a house—this house.

·

And Solveig who remained.
"I was Sister Blue."

·

The lifeguard, who saved a little girl named Susette Packlén from drowning.
A blue girl on a cliff, in the picture.

·

Three children at the foot of the hill. Rhythm. Rumba tones.
The three cursed ones.
They had a game called the Winter Garden.

·

The house that burned, Bengt who died in the fire, Solveig who built a new one, Solveig and the Winter Garden, *Rita's Winter Garden.*
"Rooms under the earth, Lille. The truth about everything."
There is a blue child screaming on a cliff.
Sister Blue.
Burned?
The outbuilding that burned. Fire on a stick. Solveig who tried to set fire to it.

·

Ulla with the mask, the Angel of Death Liz Maalamaa.
The Child, fluorescent, on the wall, the Red One, in the Winter Garden.
It's your MOOOM.

Ulla, who out of sheer devilry had imitated the district dialect that she does not speak unless it is needed on stage.

·

"She knew him. The Red One. They were adults then."

·

"And so, Lille, there was a completely different story, about two at a newspaper stand. Ha ha ha—"
"Who is my mother, Solveig?"
Solveig, never, does not answer.
The storks in Portugal.

·

Transcendence. Explosion. And suddenly Johanna sees like a picture a scene for the Winter Garden.
A man who is lying in a room, in a house.
It is winter, snow outside. Walk in snow.
But he is lying dead, shot. Blood everywhere, on him.

·

The Boy in the woods. And she knows. It is her father, Bengt. In the house, before it starts burning.

·

Mooom.
"You put balls into action, Lille. Come to someone . . . Maalamaa."
But Ulla who was afraid. At first. Before she put the mask on.
"I said I don't want to. Doing something else now. *Screaming Toys.*"
Project Earth. *You think you are going to get one story and then you get another.*

·

And now Johanna is afraid.
More afraid than she has ever been.

•

She is standing on the field outside the window.
The Red One. Maj-Gun Maalamaa.
The Child, fluorescent. Flames up on the wall.
But Johanna gets dressed, to the Winter Garden, and
to the Red One, out to her.

II

THE MASK, THE ROSE, THE SILVER SHOES

(An entirely different story, or maybe not?)

THE MASK

TO THE WINTER GARDEN, Liz Maalamaa's things:
The Angel of Death, Liz Maalamaa (a mask).

A mask that Elizabeth "Liz" Maalamaa received in a small package at the post office in her childhood during the forties. Came from Hollywood, she was pen pals with them. The movie stars. Ingrid Bergman, Ava Gardner. Really, truly. She received autographed head shots with letters at home. She took them and saved them in a scrapbook, or hung them on the wall in her room in the farm up north. And then the mask, one time. You could put it on and then you had the face of a movie star. Maybe Ava Gardner, Janet Leigh? Funny, as an adult she would not remember. Funny too that when you put that mask on, you did not look like a movie star at all. Just horrible, and frightening.

Did not go to the movies that much, there in the countryside, there was no movie theater. The movie theaters were in the cities. The movie stars, Hollywood, she had come in contact with them through a magazine, the *Film Journal*. An exciting magazine that she read, in addition to God's word, the latter of course increasingly more.

There were strange things in the *Film Journal*, you did not know much English back then. Readers who sent in letters and asked questions, how should that movie star's and the other one's names be pronounced? In particular she remembered a question like that, they used to laugh themselves silly about it, and the answer, her and her

97

brother, Hans, in the parental home. "Janet Leigh, but how do you say Janet?" Djanet was written out phonetically in the column, it was wrong that too. It should have been Djehnet.

She would explain this to the family she came to later, when she married a man from a society family in the city where she attended a training school for deaconesses. They would not understand. They would be absolutely certain that she was the one who had said Djanet, and in these circles they, skilled in languages, would correct her Djehnet Djehnet, in a well-mannered way. But first repeat her Djanet, so that the tone could be heard like a sheep bellow from the farm where she originated.

She would learn to hold her tongue in these circles.

She gave the mask to her niece and nephew later. She and her husband were childless.

THE GIRL FROM BORNEO, 1

SHE CAME FROM BORNEO, the little girl. Borneo's docklands, she dances there, the Happy Harlot. *Hamba hamba*, for her brother in the rectory. Maj-Gun Maal-amaa, or *Majjunn* as her aunt Liz calls her, the aunt who often comes to the rectory to visit, comes to "rest," in dark sunglasses, sometimes she has bandages. Maj-Gun, and her brother, Tom, who is lying stretched out on his bed in his room behind the closed door, peering through the fingers of his hands he is holding in front of his eyes, "Idiot, there aren't any docklands in Borneo, there's just jungle, an island." But then, he cannot control himself, he starts laughing so that he chokes, more and more, in the musty summer heat in the room—he sits up, stamps a beat on the floor with his feet, claps his hands.

Maj-Gun, *hamba hamba*, a dried dandelion in her mouth, it is supposed to represent the harlot's red rose. And her aunt's silver shoes, she has once again been into the guest room and swiped them from her aunt's bag without permission. The aunt does not like it, she gets angry.

"And now for the thousandth time: get out! Out into the fresh air!"

And then suddenly, of course, in the middle of the dance, the door is flung wide open and Mother is standing there or the aunt herself, yelling.

Two sweaty children, must go out into the summer day—wrinkled brows, still in high spirits from playing *indoors*, out out into the hot sun, the sunshine from the hazy high-pressure-filled sky is always stuffy in this childhood that is not unhappy, just the opposite. They do not know, these two siblings, what they are going to do, what they should get up to out there. On the other hand, the dance, there is no question about that either. A means of passing the time when you do not go outside. Not wanting to go out; these siblings have that in common. And a means of not fighting. Maj-Gun and Tom, always at each other's throats, it is almost comical. Like mama Inga-Britta says, dog and cat, dog and cat.

Sometimes when they have been chased outside, Tom will sneak back in. Locking the door behind him, lies there and reads the first best book, such as Gustav Mahler's memoirs, something like that. But then his sister is not allowed to come in anymore; she is going to stand there knocking on his door for ages if she also manages to sneak into the house again without anyone seeing her. Just silence on the other side of the door, dog and cat, she does not get in. As it turns out somewhat later, as teenagers, when her brother has his first girlfriend there. The Big-Eyed One, from the cemetery, who has grown up. The brother on the other side of the door, not talking, and Mahler's Ninth playing over and over again. Maj-Gun rushes to the cemetery and is *hamba hamba* the Happy Harlot, with everyone who wants to. The DAY OF DESIRE with the hayseeds, it is pretty and big and strong and everyone who wants to come—*hamba hamba*, dancing there, with everyone for a while. Imagines her brother at the window and the pale girlfriend at the window. And he is standing there, really: "The Disgust, Maj-Gun," you are Vile Disgusting Get Out of

My Sight, buttons the cuff links of his shirt, no girlfriend there then, just the two of them and a pale, icy mood.

The Big-Eyed One, the first girlfriend, from the cemetery, that is in other words where they meet her, Susette Packlén, both of them almost at once. Because sometimes on a frustratingly beautiful summer day it just is not possible to get indoors again. Then they take the mask with them and run down to the cemetery. The mask: the Angel of Death Liz Maalamaa—it is the unofficial name (if papa Pastor knew he would become furious of course). They had gotten it from their aunt, you see, and to do something with their time, which is now spreading out in front of them like an ocean, they run down to the cemetery and scare people, in other words. It is actually a mask that is supposed to represent the face of some stylish dark-haired old movie star, but the interesting thing is that in reality it is frightening, you can become scared of it·yourself, when you strap it to your face and look in the mirror in the bathroom when you are alone (yes, Maj-Gun has tried).

Buhuu, the Angel of Death! Liz Maalamaa! Which of course upsets papa Pastor when he finds out—and he *does* find out of course.

Maj-Gun first, Tom after, sometimes alone, often Maj-Gun just on her own too. Pastor's Crown Princess hangs around the cemetery gate, *tjiihit, tjiidit,* "Pastor's Crown Princess," she tries, "say the password to my kingdom." No one says it. Everyone walks past.

And there comes the Big-Eyed One with her mother, they are almost always there. Wildflowers picked on the meadows arranged in neat bouquets, several of them. Newly washed glass jars filled with water, bouquets placed in them to later be set on the graves, often the ones that no one else really looks after.

"Buhuu! I'm the Angel of Death!"

The girl fills jars with water in the stone grove where the water pump is located, a good opportunity; her mother somewhere else. Maj-Gun rushes up with the mask on. The girl looks up, confused but not afraid, not the slightest. And Tom Maalamaa behind Maj-Gun suddenly, says, "hi." To the girl, the girl answers, "hi."

And back to the rectory again, in her brother's room. Two siblings, dog and cat, throwing pillows at each other.

"Her big eyes," says Tom Maalamaa, who is throwing a pillow on his sister with the dandelion in her mouth and the silver shoes on her feet *again*.

"Her big *stupid* eyes," his sister clarifies. *Hamba hamba.* Throws the pillow back, right in her brother's face. But you can definitely see that she, the Big-Eyed One, has made an impression on him.

And later, after childhood: not so much anymore. Grows up. The family leaves the rectory because the father is given a position in another place. Tom Maalamaa moves away after high school graduation and starts studying law at the university, finishes quickly, becomes a lawyer. Maj-Gun, herself, in some way, the Girl from Borneo, takes her bag and baggage and moves to a rented room in the leafy suburbs below the square in the town center. Remains in the District, does not get anywhere for a long time. Works in the newsstand at the square, for many years it turns out, and moves from one rented room in the attic of one house to another rented room in the attic of another house. The years pass, Maj-Gun in the newsstand, sitting where she is sitting, on a bar stool. "Today is the first day of the rest of your life," it reads on a card on the back of the cash register. And then one afternoon in the late summer of 1989 Big-Eyed Susette Packlén, whom she has already gotten to know a little, separate from Tom and everyone else, comes walking across the square.

SUSETTE AND THE DARKNESS, 1989

Sometimes Susette Packlén imagines that she is a horrible flower that is about to bloom. But often, with Maj-Gun at the newsstand, she thinks about love.

MAJ-GUN, AT THE NEWSSTAND. Maj-Gun Maalamaa. On a bar stool behind the counter, among the newspapers and lottery tickets, tips and games. Sweaty, perspiring, in time a luxuriant creature. At some point maybe shiny letters on a yellowed card on the back of the cash register, the first thing you see when you come inside: "Today is the first day of the rest of your life."

Worn text on a grayish-blue landscape, rather abstract. Round, white moon in the upper right-hand corner and shadows of a spruce forest down to the left—an explicitness?

•

But first, they are still only children then, Maj-Gun is at the rectory, at the entrance to the cemetery, the old part. Nothing strange about that, of course: Maj-Gun is the Pastor's daughter and her mother works as deaconess in the assembly. Or *Majjunn,* that is what she is called back then, or at least the name she uses for herself.

"Say Pastor's Crown Princess," Maj-Gun yells, "that's the password." Hangs on the metal gate, it goes *tjii* this way *tjii* that way, back and forth in the wind despite the weight of Majjunn's large body. Not exactly a fat body but significantly larger than Susette Packlén's, which is almost as old. They go to the same elementary school, she and Majjunn, but they do not hang out, are not friends.

"Say Pastor's Crown Pr—"

You do not say it. You say nothing. You walk past. The gate is open even though Majjunn is hanging on it. But still, amusing, when you walk by, how that name Majjunn sticks in your head. Plays there, sometimes, in silence. *Majjunn Majjunn* you repeat silently to yourself; the name glues itself to your tongue, becomes stuck in your mouth.

You carry bluebells in your hands.

One bouquet and several, sometimes a whole armful that will be divided into smaller bouquets inside the cemetery; tidily organized in glass jars you bring from home. You: Susette and her mother, that is, who have a habit of going to the cemetery, just the two of them, together. Moreover, sometimes they have boiled the glass jars in water at home in the kitchen in their own house with a garden where they are living at that time in the lush suburbs below the square in the town center so that they have become really transparently clean. Not even just the two of them then, during her childhood, rather Susette and her mother and her father and two older brothers.

And they fill the jars with water from the buckets placed by the hydrant in a stone-covered arbor rather close to the entrance.

Flowers to place on the "Graves of the Forgotten."

You have been out yourself, picking flowers in the meadows above the town center.

With Mom. It is hard to explain this without sounding crazy: but seriously, nothing strange in that work at all.

Picking flowers, taking them to the graves in the cemetery that look decayed, abandoned.

"Say Pastor's Cr—" Into the cemetery as said, and Majjunn's voice petering out in the background. Later: at the gravestones, Susette knows some of the names by heart. Ephraim. Aline. Betel. Strange names, but still very pretty.

Scrapes the letters clean of earth and various bits of trash, weeds the ground in front of the stones.

And sets out bluebells and wood anemones in jars with water. Comes and replaces them: new flowers, fresh new water. They tend to laugh together, Susette and her mother: barely have time to wither and they are there again replacing them.

•

The Confession Grove. It is a bit off to the side. There is not exactly a sign with "The Confession Grove," but Majjunn who, as said, is from the Pastor's family, knows that sort of thing. Because she follows them sometimes, Susette and her mother, like a willing pathfinder even though no one has asked her.

"You'll see it down there. To the left."

And adds, rather pompously, "If you then wander in the valley of the shadow of death no harm will come to you." And, then, holding a hand to her ear. "Listen. Here at the cemetery you can say things that would sound completely cuckoo anywhere else."

Maj-Gun has a toy mask over her face. "Ho ho ho," she laughs. It *is* cuckoo; Susette's mother laughs, the mask reminds her of a movie star. "Ingrid Bergman? Ava Gardner?" Majjunn takes off the mask, wipes sweat from her brow, does not answer.

•

Maj-Gun has a brother, Tom Maalamaa. It happens that he comes up behind Maj-Gun at the cemetery, sneaking up so that the others see without Maj-Gun noticing. Points silently at Majjunn who is standing in front of him, twirls one hand a few times, as if to say "scatterbrained, idiot."

And smiles at Susette. And Susette smiles back, cannot help it. Only then does Majjunn turn around and discover her brother behind her back, becoming audibly angry at him. Tom Maalamaa: the Pastor's Crown Princess's big brother and, somewhat later, as teenagers, Susette's first love. They are together for a few months, not at the cemetery of course, but otherwise completely ordinary.

And later, gradually, when the first love is over the second love comes to Susette—a Janos—she runs away with him from the strawberry fields in the middle region of the country where they meet. And then, though really a lot of time has passed in between, Susette is already close to thirty, the third love.

"Confession." The mother, during Susette's childhood, at the cemetery, smiles a bit hesitantly. Susette thinks "confession" is a beautiful word and when Majjunn is out of earshot Susette wants her mother to explain what it means. Her mother has not felt like it, you can see it on her, it has made her feel ill at ease. Standing between the graves in office clothes—she works at the bank otherwise but lost her father in the war; she is of the generation that death for her has become at once a self-evident and vile thing—and hesitates for a few seconds. Then she laughs and whistles softly, almost a sharp whistle of the kind Susette's much older brother struggled to teach her when they were children at home in the house in the town center. And the mother shouts, with an almost endless tenderness in her voice:

"But what beautiful flowers you have in your bouquet, Susette."

Not: "What a cute little Angel of Death," which Majjunn later, when the mother is out of earshot, comes there to whisper in Susette's ear.

Or: *God likes the small, timid and defenseless.* Which she says sometimes when she suddenly appears at the water hydrant in the stone grove when Susette has gone there on her own to fill the glass jars with water.

The mask on: "It's not a movie star, it's the Angel of Death Liz Maalamaa, aren't you afraid of her?"

Susette busy with the water, the jars, shakes her head as if to ward it off.

•

"I don't want to play with her," Susette says to her mother when at some point her mother admonishes her and says, "You need to be nice to the little girl, maybe she's lonely."

"Don't want to." Susette sulks.

"But she is right about one thing," her mother continues, maybe pretending not to listen to her daughter, "some words really do sound beautiful here. Ringing the church bells for the weekend service, for example. Words like 'ringing church bells' I particularly, especially love."

But then later she adds in a somewhat softer voice:

"But I understand, Susette. You don't have to play with her if you don't want to."

•

But nothing more about that either. And that is okay too, perfectly normal. Because going to the cemetery and placing flowers on the Graves of the Forgotten is, as said, something Susette and her mother have a habit of doing, just because, when they are together. That is to say: there is nothing about it that is great or fatefully filled with meaning. A ritual in twosomeness that is only theirs sometimes, in the family. Nor was it a twosome fellowship, in the sense of excluding everyone and everything else.

Like cutting up old clothes and rags to take them to get woven into rugs by a woman they know with a loom. A real rug weaver, she lives outside the town center, somewhere far far away in the Outer Marsh. She is old too, probably has twenty cats, lives in a drafty old shack of a cottage, where it smells of cat piss and the loom is rigged up, almost always in motion, in the only room. It is big too, takes up almost all of the floor space. And, rather new: the Bankers' Employee Club, where Susette's mother is a secretary and very active, has bought it for her with money they earned by organizing bazaars and lotteries, and selling baked goods to each other, that sort of thing.

Beautiful rag rugs are produced, with many colors, beautiful patterns: the woman then sells them at the square or via the bankers' network and she can almost live off of it.

So, as said: in other words it is one other thing Susette and her mother tend to occupy themselves with in the evenings sometimes in the house in the midst of family life. Cutting up old rags, clothes, towels, their own or ones they have received from neighbors or others, sometimes they ask for them in the surrounding neighborhoods, go from door to door.

In the kitchen in the house or in the living room in front of the television. Just because, in other words not anything significant. Maybe you can describe it like this: that it is Susette and her mother partially in their own world that still, while Susette is a child, consists of so much more, so many other people too. There are, which has already been mentioned, two brothers almost ten years older who settle down somewhere else after finishing school; move away from the District in order to start families and work in another area. And the father of course who later, due to his work, is forced to be gone quite a lot. He is a doctor of engineering and receives an assistant professorship at a college in a city located rather far away in the eastern part of the country—and because of the distance and the expensive travel he comes home only on weekends and holidays. In other words, his profession is not that of a sea captain, which Susette likes to say at some point in school when someone asks her what her father does: but later, when Susette is in her early teens, he becomes ill, he spends a lot of time in the hospital. Not in the local hospital but in a larger hospital in the city by the sea, it is that serious. He passes away and a few years later her mother passes away: is hit with a massive heart attack and drops to the ground in the house in her own kitchen where she so enjoyed being.

But then, when it happens, Susette Packlén is already grown up and not there.

It is Maj-Gun who tells her how it happened. Maj-Gun Maalamaa, she knows everything. Has been living upstairs in the house as a boarder in the guest room for almost a year and a half already by the time Susette comes back after having been gone for three years.

Maj-Gun explains that her father, the Pastor, has during that time received a position in another parish, and she did not want to move with her parents to the new rectory. She explains to Susette that she has realized that despite everything she likes it in this municipality; and besides, she also had to prepare for all of the admission interviews and application interviews for the university. So therefore, and for practical reasons too, staying in the District has been a better alternative. And Maj-Gun has furnished a real attic study for herself in the guest room in Susette's absence: thick tomes of paper and compendiums lie in piles, drifts of paper on the desk and in the bookshelves.

And to support herself while studying for her interviews she has, in other words for a while now, started working full-time shifts at the newsstand at the square in the town center.

Susette has, as said, at this point in time been gone for almost three years; she has just turned twenty. "In Poland," that is what it is called, has been called, and will still be called. With her second love, but it came to nothing. And due to the poor telephone connections, the poor postal service, and poor communication in general . . . Susette has come home only when it has been too late. On the whole she gets to hear what happened when it is too late.

Maj-Gun Maalamaa is the one who meets her at the ferry terminal as they had agreed by telephone. "What a nice backpack, Fjällräven—" Maj-Gun spells out. "Is it new?"

Thick plastic bags filled with rug rags remain everywhere in the house, in piles on top of each other too along the walls in the kitchen (the old woman with the loom in the Outer Marsh has been dead for a long time already).

"What we did toward the end?" Maj-Gun stood there in the middle of the mess and the musty smell and asked herself rhetorically. "Cut. Rug rags. It was a calm and restful hobby."

"She was terrified of dying," says Susette.

"You can rest assured, Susette," Maj-Gun replies, "it was over in a few minutes. I called the ambulance. But it was too late."

"Can love make you crazy, can grief make you crazy, can regret, can—" Susette asks, no, whispers, because it can barely be heard. And her stomach hurts so badly, so damned much, as if her body is in the process of being cut in two, and her legs that collapse under her; then she has to go to bed and sleep, rest—remains bedridden for several days.

Maj-Gun, who hears, sees, says nothing. But she puts her arm around Susette: it is heavy, such a weight that holds on to Susette, almost like a vise. But in it there is, completely genuine: such tenderness, leniency, such comfort—

Later, Susette will remember that conversation with Maj-Gun Maalamaa in the home that day she returned, as clear as a bell, despite so much else being forgotten, also consciously, so obscure.

Maj-Gun, whom she has not seen since childhood, whom she quite literally does not know at all. Except for "Pastor's Crown Princess," a few scenes from the

cemetery that are buried in her from a distant childhood, and so, naturally, what you managed to see of Maj-
Gun in the rectory in her role as the sister of your first
love Tom Maalamaa whom you went out with for six–
seven months when you were about fourteen years old.
Though, in and of itself, you did not see a lot of Maj-Gun,
in the rectory, either. She was not home very much but
mainly it was that she and Tom Maalamaa spent most of
their time behind the closed door in Tom's room. And
listened to music: classical music, Gustav Mahler's Ninth
Symphony, always "Mahler's Ninth."

*A fantastic reconciliation with mankind's existential
conditions, a feeling of life so closely connected to a simul-
taneous consciousness of death.* As Tom Maalamaa used
to say, almost solemnly, sometimes.

•

What she said, what Maj-Gun said in response. Because
those have, so to speak, been the last sensible sentences
for a long time. She has not really been able to explain
why either. But also because a few months later when
that time in the house with Maj-Gun has passed, has
been over, it has been something she knowingly and wit-
tingly preferred not to think about after the fact.

The house is sold after these two months, Maj-Gun
forced to vacate her attic study on the second floor and
move away. And Susette bought a small apartment with
her inheritance from her mother and father, which was
divided in three among her and her brothers. A studio
on the first floor in a row of apartment buildings on the
fields on the north side of the town center.

And she started working for Businesswoman of the
Year Jeanette Lindström again: actually gone looking for

Jeanette Lindström on her own after a period of idleness when the money started drying up and more or less begged for a job, any job whatsoever. "I'll see what I can do for you," Jeanette Lindström had said. Jeanette whom Susette had worked for one summer once long ago, as a teenager after almost a year at the private nursing home in the District for the elderly and infirm. A few days in Jeanette Lindström's two-window Ice Cream Stand on the square in the town center, then the strawberry fields.

And a few years later Jeanette Lindström had added, stupidly jokingly so to speak but with some sort of warning in it: "But this time we'll let the strawberry fields go, right? Who knows where the butterfly might flutter off to this time and we don't want to be party to a flight like that again. Not to mention it gets costly and difficult for the employer to find a replacement on such short notice."

Where the butterfly might flutter off to this time. That is how she spoke, Jeanette Lindström, in other words like an allusion, that it was from those miserable strawberry fields up north where Susette had been sent as extra labor from the ice cream stand at the square where she really should have been working that summer three years ago that Susette ran away with a "Pole," Janos, whom she had met there, while working.

He was the one who had wanted to get away from there: he had not been happy or grateful in the least about this means of getting a visa to travel to a country outside the so-called Iron Curtain and then under controlled means, like a member of an official friendly exchange between the two countries, earn a *little* bit of money (actually *no* money, that is how it was for everyone at the strawberry fields, and Businesswoman of the Year was not exactly someone who drove up the wages).

Janos—her second love, dull and intense. And besides, he was not from Poland but Lithuania but everyone said Poland so it just stayed like that.

"Well, this time I was thinking of a real job that you can live on," Susette had replied, deathly serious, but now in this situation almost four years later, Jeanette Lindström has not grasped the sore spot rather let it go and actually offered Susette a job with a decent wage in her legitimate business activities, which found itself in an expansion stage at this point in time. And so it turned out that during the years that followed, Susette worked for her on different projects: shop assistant in the Little Gift Shop, assistant in catering and so on, up until the point that as a result of an argument she had with her employer, she quit her job and started cleaning for Solveig Torpeson in her cleaning business Four Mops and a Dustpan.

"With these words I'm transferring things to you, Susette," on Solveig's wedding day no less. Jeanette Lindström had pushed Susette Packlén in her server's apron up to the bride in a puffed-sleeved wedding dress at the bride's table after Susette, in a hurry and because Jeanette Lindström had been in the way the whole time, managed to drop a few plates from the fellowship hall's white bone china set on the floor so that they had broken. These words have become legendary, because afterward no one remembers what "these words" were, and in and of themselves, they were unintelligible because by that point Jeanette had pinched some of the wedding cognac. Of course, these types of stories were loved in the District.

•

But, as said, there was a time right before, before Jeanette Lindström, before Solveig, before everything: a short period lasting just a few months which, while it lasted, was still as long as an eternity, *perpetuum mobile*. At home in the house with Maj-Gun Maalamaa. Just her and Maj-Gun who becomes *Majjunn* again during that time. From the cemetery, the gate, *tjii* this way *tjii* that way. "Say Pastor's Crown Princess . . ." That Majjunn. A sound from a childhood, a name that has glued itself to your tongue.

Majjunn sitting on a kitchen chair in the house with Susette's mother's old sewing scissors. Cutting old clothes into rags. Long, skinny strips whirling down into a bucket at her feet. At their feet: because Susette has also been sitting there, on another kitchen chair, in her pajamas and she also had a pair of scissors in her hand.

Crehp crehp the scissors fly through the fabric, rags, clothes. Majjunn's scissors, and her own. Majjunn talking, humming.

Silk velvet rag scraps yes I have seen the most I have—

That song, which becomes Majjunn's song, like a strange refrain in a silence that when Majjunn does not speak, a humming envelops them in the empty house.

And the sound of the scissors, as said. *Crehp crehp.* How they flew through the fabric.

But then later it passed so to speak and when it was over—yes, why should you, why should Susette think about it then?

Life has gone on. And besides, it has at least been clear: these thoughts, feelings, they do not get her anywhere.

•

But this she remembers, despite the fact that so much else from that time becomes forgotten afterward: that the last thing she and Maj-Gun do together during that time in the house after her mother's death is go to the movies. Sitting perfectly positioned in the best seats in an otherwise empty movie theater. Maj-Gun ordered the tickets for them over the phone a few days in advance so they would be sure to get a seat. It is, Maj-Gun has been sure to explain, a very popular young adult film they are going to see. "A real young adult movie for young adults like us," she explains. "I got the best seats!"

Which, according to Maj-Gun, is important because they are supposed to be celebrating something. "That everything is over now," she says and not just that it is over but that they have made it out of "all of that" with "lives and youth intact"—that is Maj-Gun's own illustrious wording too, her emphasis on "youth" as well. Susette, for her part, does not say very much; in and of itself Maj-Gun is of course the one who talks the hind leg off a donkey the most even during that time but also because it actually is not necessary to talk because the house where they have been living together for a while is for sale and a reasonable offer has been made that Susette and her brothers, who are beneficiaries of the estate after their parents, have accepted and Susette herself has rather quietly placed a down payment on an apartment in the apartment complex above the town center and only when it is done does she tell Maj-Gun that she will need to look around for somewhere else to live. "You have to move, you'll certainly find something."

"But where am I supposed to go then?" Maj-Gun says, rapidly, unexpectedly pours out of her there where she has been standing in front of Susette in the kitchen, complete surprise on her face, almost on the verge of tears. Before Susette has time to repeat that Maj-Gun will certainly quickly find a better, not to mention more agreeable, room to rent, Maj-Gun's mood changes and she excitedly starts planning the farewell festivities that will take place as soon as the "moving work" as she calls it in that moment is "taken care of"—and these festivities will in other words, as said, be crowned with a visit to the movies. "As if," Maj-Gun says, "welcome back, in other words. The scissors on the shelf: TO youth, life, *an invitation.*"

When they get inside the movie theater that predetermined evening it is, in other words, empty; a long long time passes during the minutes before the film starts and no one is there. "Aside from the usual jack offs of course, *typical,*" which Maj-Gun loudly and expertly but with an awkwardly audible relief in her voice whispers to Susette as she is sitting there, squirming restlessly and glancing around furtively and then finally catching sight of some occasional losers of the male sex who trickle into the theater before the lights dim and the merciful darkness sinks and the movie at last gets started.

The film is called *Skateboarding* and is about a boys' gang in a run-down big city suburb in America, one of those against-all-odds-gangs united by its great passion for skateboarding and a lot of youthful complications along the way to the happy ending that is their own skateboarding ramp behind the apartment buildings and shaking hands with the mayor.

Not a film to write home about, in other words, and no one other than Maj-Gun and Susette stuck it out until

the end. But still, unforgettable. Susette will always remember the feeling of liberation on the bus on the way
back home to the District.

That it was over now, whatever that was: Mom, the
Pole, all the rest . . . Does not even need to be mentioned
in detail any longer—*AND Majjunn.*

Like a wave that is receding. And the feeling is her
own, private. Absolutely indivisible, much less with Maj-
Gun Maalamaa. Because that is also what the liberation
was about, a small decisive insight: they had not meant
the same thing when, before the visit to the movies, Maj-
Gun said that they were going to "celebrate" having gotten past "it."

On the one hand: yes, it was over. On the other hand:
for Susette it means, has meant something else, something more—beyond Maj-Gun too, all of that.

But: "Skateboarding, to life, then?" It is almost like
she is standing there saying it herself, Maj-Gun in the
rain after the movie, at a loss outside the movie theater,
alone on a rain-covered asphalt road where she suddenly, for a few seconds, just stands and dies. Maj-Gun
who is wearing what she calls "going-out clothes" for
the disco under her coat but Susette who just says, "I'm
going home now," and leaves.

Starts walking, rapid steps in the direction of the bus
station for the provincial buses. Maj-Gun who trots after
her, at a proper distance of course, maybe thirty feet, in
silence. Without calling out, without trying to catch Susette's attention at all.

Is just there, behind her.

And on the bus, Susette, got on before Maj-Gun, takes
a seat at the very front, in a row for just one person and

Maj-Gun walks past her to the very back without looking in Susette's direction. During the journey Susette gets up anyway and goes and sits next to Maj-Gun in the last row and they travel on in silence and when she and Maj-Gun go their separate ways at the bus stop at the square in the town center Susette understands that she and Maj-Gun will no longer be together as friends, or at all, for that matter. And it hits her too when she wanders home to her own, new apartment that she has not asked Maj-Gun where she has moved.

But she takes a shortcut through the cemetery that night.

•

And suddenly, there, she gets an impulse and turns off in the rain over to the new side of the cemetery, a few hundred feet away from the path where her mother is buried next to her father, even though her mother had said many times after her father's death, while Susette was still living with her mother, that she and father should "rest" on the old side where it was much more peaceful.

Her mother had thought that the new side was so deserted. Not much in the way of trees or leafiness yet either, from what Susette can make out in the darkness. But fuller now, though certainly none of the vegetation that provides a cemetery feeling of life and death, the passage of time—not seconds, days, but centuries, decades, "generations follow in the footsteps of generations," as her mother sang toward the end when they still went to church often, she and Susette, in black clothes, "from a house of sorrow," crowed loudly, her mother with a false and frail singing voice which, if you were not careful, was embarrassing; old silence, dignity.

But still, despite everything anyway, here now as well. Such a calm, at the cemetery, under a bright red umbrella in the pouring rain.

And in the midst of everything, all of that exhaustion that had been inside her, or whatever it is, had been, as if she could finally think, just herself, Susette.

". . . It only took a few minutes. I called the ambulance." Maj-Gun who had stood and said that in the house then, at the very beginning—and how Susette had lost her balance, had pain in her stomach. Maj-Gun's hand on her shoulder, but the tenderness in her grip too, which had held her. But still: no future—the feeling she had sometimes with Maj-Gun in the house, that they were two children playing while waiting for the mother to return.

When the mother would not be returning.

When she came from "Poland" her mother was dead. "Poland," she had not been there of course, it was just a designation. But it was not a secret or important, in and of itself. In contrast to what Maj-Gun had insinuated at the ferry terminal where she had met Susette, when she asked about the backpack. "Fjällräven, is it new?"

A long time, somewhere else. Did not come home. Did not keep in touch with her mother in the house in the town center on a regular basis. Cannot say exactly why, not even in hindsight.

And what has she been up to? Working in different places. Home help, care for the elderly, reading out loud for an old lady. Quite a lot of the type of work she had already done in the District—at the private nursing home for the elderly and infirm where she started working after finishing high school, before selling ice cream, and the strawberry fields.

And it had been good, nothing special about that either. She was used to old people, liked old people. But
then, as said, she called her mother at home one day
as she had a habit of doing and Maj-Gun answered the
phone. It perplexed her, she hung up. She called again a
few minutes later. Maj-Gun on the phone that time too.

"Where are you?"

"I'll be on the first ferry."

Maj-Gun's voice, calm and resolute: "Give me the date
and time and I'll meet you at the terminal."

She met Maj-Gun there at the terminal because they
had set up the meeting on the telephone, not because she
wanted to pull the wool over someone's eyes on purpose.

In reality she was coming from somewhere else, much
closer. But she stood there at the terminal and made it
look like she had come with the morning ferry. Brand-
new backpack, Fjällräven, on her back.

"Your mother is dead. You didn't make it to the funeral. My deepest condolences—"

She had been living in another city, in other places.
Would have been too complicated to explain. On the
other hand, explain to Maj-Gun, why did she have to do
that?

"It's not that bad, Susette." But there in the night in
the rain at the cemetery as if she suddenly heard her
mother's voice, she does not of course, not really, but—

*If you later come to wander in the valley of the shadow
of death no harm will befall you.*

And about the cemetery: "But, Susette, it will surely
be fine here too."

Now, it is crystal clear. Her mother was not, had never
been angry at her.

And when she had left home, not "run away," because of the strawberry-picking fields—how her mother had come into her room at night and kissed her on the forehead.

That kiss remained as well (Susette could almost feel it, in the rain, with her fingers).

"It will surely be fine here too."

And Susette cries a little, her own tears, just her own. Peaceful crying at the cemetery and then she walks quietly back to her new apartment in the apartment complex above the town center.

Does not need Maj-Gun anymore.

Several weeks after the visit to the movie theater, when Maj-Gun notices that Susette has pulled away, for example never has time to talk on the phone when she calls, retreats rather quickly. Stops getting in touch, stops suggesting a lot of things. "Don't we need to get out and get some fresh air?

And so has it become, without any accusations or talk of betrayal. And Susette gradually also realizes where Maj-Gun is living: as a boarder in another family home in the lush suburbs below the town center.

•

But then, it is seven–eight years until the summer of 1989 when Susette Packlén and Maj-Gun Maalamaa become friends again. Or if not friends exactly at least they start hanging out a bit again. In and of itself: they have not exactly lost sight of each other completely or anything during the time in between. During the years that have passed Maj-Gun Maalamaa remained sitting at the newsstand up in the town center. In the end she did not head off anywhere, neither to the admission interviews for various educational institutions nor to any other places. No. Sat where she sat.

"Sitting where I'm sitting." That is how she expresses it herself as well, an answer to a silent question Susette never asks her in the years that pass when they only exchange a few words about ordinary things in the newsstand when Susette is buying candy and chips when she gets cravings in the evenings.

Maj-Gun at the newsstand, behind the counter, the postcard on the cash register. *Today is the first day of the rest of your life.* Worn text, once a glittery silver? Buckled letters on a grayish-blue landscape, rather abstract. Moonlight, spruce forest.

An explicitness, in other words?

Oh! Susette does not think like that either. During those years when she sees Maj-Gun in the newsstand sometimes she does not think very much at all.

Maj-Gun, a doughnut on a tall, three-legged stool on the other side of the counter, the pork pouring over the edges of the stool: one obvious fact is that as Maj-Gun gets older, she puts on a considerable amount of weight.

And: she has started smoking. A particular brand of cigarette, which she also makes a big fuss about with her customers. How unusual the brand is, so unusual that it is not part of the ordinary selection but needs to be specially ordered from a place, the "Head Office" in the city by the sea from where all of the newsstands in the country are centrally run, something you can also hear her explain with authority in her voice, to whoever happens to be at the newsstand and will listen.

Maj-Gun standing, puffing on her cigarettes in the doorway of the newsstand, which is eventually turned into a small room with a window facing the square:

"Had to fight with the Head Office but at least NOW I won't get varicose veins until I turn thirty. Won't you be thirty soon, Susette?" she asks, if Susette is the only one there, but as if in passing, without waiting for an answer.

"Djeessus, Susette!" Maj-Gun sighs, whistling between her two front teeth. "The Head Office!"

Djessus. Remains in Susette's head for a little while on her way home.

Maj-Gun rolling her eyes, at the newsstand, "djeessus" this, that, and the other.

Maj-Gun on the three-legged stool, beads of sweat along her hairline, like an old woman.

Evaporated a few seconds later—gone.

•

It is sometime during the summer of 1989 that Susette Packlén starts seeking out Maj-Gun at the newsstand again, more than just as a random customer. In some way expressly to see Maj-Gun, talk about this and that, pass the time. And she often stays there, hanging out. Perched on another stool, "the customer's stool" as Maj-Gun calls it, a little off to the side of the counter behind which Maj-Gun herself is sitting. Or rather, standing in the doorway, as a smoking buddy.

Even though she really does not want to, or maybe that is the wrong way to say it because it is only when she is actually in the newsstand, listening to Maj-Gun talking the hind leg off a donkey (and it is always Maj-Gun who is jabbering away, Susette who is listening), that she simultaneously in some way regrets having come, almost does not understand why she is there, longs to get away from there.

But then again tearing yourself away without hurting Maj-Gun is not that simple.

Tearing yourself away at all. Which is a rather strange feeling.

And she would not have time of course. A bit later, in the fall, she gets a cat too, a white, long-haired abandoned summer cat from one of the houses she cleans, the beautiful Glass House on the Second Cape. Only partially purebred, has difficulty taking care of its coat properly, needs to be brushed regularly every day. And still quite the kitten: starved for attention.

And thus, of course, there is the cleaning during the day with Solveig. Susette likes her job, that is not it—just you get tired of being on your feet all day long, it sucks the energy out of you sometimes. And this particular summer and fall of 1989, Solveig has taken on, for her part and the company's, the final cleaning for the newly built residential area Rosengården 2 in the woods rather close to the Outer Marsh where Solveig lives, though to the south, closer to the sea. But still, far too much work for just two people, especially if there are already signed contracts for other places. Joint projects where Solveig and Susette regularly clean together, and individual ones, where each cleans on her own. During the summer, Susette has, for example, been busy with the summer guests on the Second Cape as well; they need to have cleaning done by the company that has been her special area of responsibility for a long time. Such as the Glass House, being rented by a French diplomatic family:

mother, father, and three children, two boys and a girl in their early teens, who have a habit of making music together on the veranda—the Winter Garden—in the evenings. A complete small chamber orchestra where all of the members are dressed in the same long red- or blue-and-white-stripped polyester blouses, the evening dress that they change into every evening around six o'clock, a domestic design from the best brand—but still . . . as if they were sitting there on the veranda in their pajamas, playing calming classical pieces, the sea behind them, wild, in revolt because it is very windy that summer.

White foam from the waves that crash against the windows and remains there as a stickiness, a hell to scrub away, something that is part of Susette's work: hang on the windowsill, try and get at the crap from the inside, rig up an A-ladder in the water along the beach, wedge it into place between the rocks, and climb up and scrub, scrub . . . it is really stuck as said, so you really have to focus, she does not have time to think about much of anything else, such as *hating* the sea for example.

Or going to the cousin's papa in the cousin's house, which is located right behind the Second Cape behind a copse of trees, farther in toward Solveig's former home, which Susette was immediately assigned as an individual project when Solveig hired Susette a thousand years ago and Susette had given an account of her work experience in which cleaning was not included but quite a bit of care work with the elderly and the sick, both at the private nursing home in the District and after that in other places.

"Can you take care of the old man?" Solveig had asked and added, "I'm going to say it like it is. I just can't be bothered. But that stays between the two of us and for Christ's sake, don't ask any questions."

And of course, Susette certainly said yes: she is used to old people, likes old people. And so maybe there was not anything particularly lovable about the old guy but there was not anything horrible or repulsive about him either. Tired, cranky, bulging from having drunk too much aquavit in the middle of a mess of shit and gloomy clothes and unwashed pots and pans and a sweet corroding stink of old sweat and alcohol and tobacco that hangs in the air in there. And of course, obviously, it must feel rather terrible to see that decay in person when it is your own home so she understands why Solveig does not want to go there herself.

But for Susette, who does not have any roots like that—mainly a job among others, and she has a habit of going there once or twice a week. Airing things out and doing the dishes and cleaning and what have you and when the weather is nice she quite simply forces the grouchy old man out into the garden so he will not be in the way while she was cleaning. He goes along with it most reluctantly of course, but in reality Susette has the impression that he protests mainly for the sake of protesting. Because he certainly must like having things cleaned up a bit and maybe he did not have anything against bickering with her; with a glint in his eyes too, "sweet tease," the loneliness becomes quite lonely, having a bit of company.

Once, in the very beginning, when she had gotten the cousin's papa out into the garden, she discovered a pistol lying on a pile of newspapers on the refrigerator. She took it, slipped it into her backpack, Fjällräven,

among her things for the sauna, because she is going to
the sauna later that evening, is planning on going there
right after work, but something else comes up, and then
the backpack is left hanging on a hook in her bathroom.

On the other hand, with Solveig, that old man the
cousin's papa is rarely brought up at all.

"How's the old man?" Solveig asks now and then,
mostly in passing. "Fine," Susette replies, adding, "Still
going strong. He seems to have nine lives."

But then he dies after all despite everything, several
years later, but still. Exactly in that year, 1989, when Susette starts hanging out with Maj-Gun at the newsstand
again. A Thursday in the month of August he is lying
on the kitchen floor in the cottage unconscious when
Susette arrives there by bus and she calls for an ambulance, calls Solveig, and the old man is taken directly to
the District Hospital where he dies that same night from
a subsequent heart attack without ever having regained
consciousness.

An old age regardless; he was eighty-two.

But then, that time, when she sees Maj-Gun again and
starts hanging out with her, in the middle of her life—
completely occupied with her everyday existence, work
and hobbies.

In her life. In *My Life*, which she also starts thinking about in a particular way when she starts hanging
out with Maj-Gun in the newsstand. Like a newspaper
headline or something to write down in "The Book of
Quick-Witted Sayings" (Maj-Gun's notebook that she
sometimes quotes from).

My life. With contours in other words, so nameable,
chiseled.

"What happened with your admission interviews, Maj-Gun?"

"I don't know." Maj-Gun shrugs on one of those late evenings when they are standing in the doorway to the newsstand, Maj-Gun is smoking. Tosses the cigarette away, a spot of ember lands on the dark sidewalk on the asphalt in the twilight.

"Lost steam. I guess."

"And then there weren't any good opportunities to study at the new rental place either. Concentrating was difficult, to put it mildly. Motormouths, motormouths in that family. *Djeessus*, Susette. If you only knew—"

"Well—." Maj-Gun holds the door open, they walk in again. "Moss is growing on our heads, years are passing— but, Susette, maybe it is just a way of saying something else. Maybe I'm sitting here . . . waiting. For, option one, the less likely: that my horrible godmother Liz Maalamaa will die so I can get her money. After having nagged her husband to death at an early age, he drank himself to death on the Sweden–Finland ferry, wasn't even fifty, maybe he just had to drink aquavit in order to put up with her . . . If he was DRUNK, Susette, then she has been SOBER all her life. My dad the pastor used to say that a little bit of wine made you NICE but she didn't listen at all.

"An old hag with lots of money, mercy me. Millions, you know.

"And then, Susette, I'll fly away. Far away from here.

"Flyyy," Maj-Gun, sitting on the stool at the newsstand, clarifies. "Fjuuh, Susette." And she stretches her arms out at her sides behind the counter, gliding in other words. "What a screamingly funny sight, Susette. With my extra weight—I know what you're thinking. A giant bee with helicopter wings flidderfladdering away. Djeessuss," Maj-Gun establishes and grows serious again.

"Doesn't seem particularly likely in other words. So, option two, *the other possibility*. And believe it or not the more realistic one, *because she'll never die of course*, for example. My only love, my greatest love. *The Boy in the woods*. That he will come. Back.

"And, Susette," lowering her voice, whispering, "a little crow has whispered in my ear that it will happen soon—the Boy in the woods. Bengt."

And Maj-Gun tries to make eye contact with Susette with a meaningful blink blink.

"I have always been the romantic type, Susette. Feel feel feel," placing a hand on her large torso. "How it's pounding. Inside. My heart. My blood. Love.

"Djeessusss—" she stops herself then when she does not really reach Susette in that way, gets new ideas, new clues, there are always new clues. Starts for example continuing the flight humor, since *that* association was actually funny, folding paper airplanes using empty lottery tickets, which she throws around wildly and then, more high-spiritedly, starts tearing pages out of certain magazines, *The Joy of Motherhood* that is lying on the counter in order to get them to fly as well. "Just a few sample issues, Susette," she shouts with excitement, "so don't shed a tear over them—"

Calms down again. "So many men, so little time, Susette. If I looked like you. With your looks I wouldn't be sitting here, rotting away.

"I mean," she adds more officiously, after a small, pregnant pause, "not the way you look *now*. But the *potential*. Come along and change. A bait for life.

"Your eyes, Susette. Those globes. A whole . . . world."

•

Though there are of course other versions of how things went when Susette started going to the newsstand at the square in the town center and hanging out with Maj-Gun again, Maj-Gun's own, for example.

The square, it is empty there in the afternoon and evening, in the summers too, on weekdays when the vacation period is over. An almost ghostlike emptiness hangs over it. Sometimes the only things that break the silence are cars that drive up, around around the square: three-four cars, often the same ones, hayseeds inside them. They roll down the windows, honk, yell, and if you happen to be on the square then you end up in the center, captured, for a few minutes, in a circle.

Susette ends up in the middle of the circle, maybe one of those evenings, possibly actually the evening after the day when Susette has been in the cousin's house on the First Cape and found the old man the cousin's papa beaten and unconscious on the kitchen floor. She cannot say for sure as said but it could have been that evening because it was fairly early after all and for once she was in no hurry to get anywhere.

She has a clear memory of it—because she had been working almost every day that summer from morning till night sometimes, at the usual places, with or without Solveig and then with Solveig in the afternoons and often later on overtime at Rosengården 2.

But this evening in particular they are free because they have not been able to go to Rosengården since the old man, Solveig's relative the cousin's papa from her childhood home, had died or is dying at the hospital and Solveig has to be there.

Susette who comes from the cousin's house after the ambulance and Solveig have left; it is Susette herself who has offered to clean up the house, suddenly felt so sorry for Solveig, which she still has not said directly to Solveig because she and Solveig do not talk to each other in that way and Solveig herself has also been as calm, almost unaffected as usual.

"I want to," is all Susette said when Solveig offered to give her a ride up to the town center.

She remained in the house for a while, but then later still without the energy to take care of anything at all after everyone had left, the exhaustion had suddenly rushed through her body. Left, her as well, walked along the road up to the main country road until the evening bus from the Second Cape came along and she jumped on it, empty that too, and rode it up to the square in the town center.

Got off the bus at the square, started walking to the other side in order to continue along the walking path through the small town center and then turn off on the pedestrian and bicycle path past the church and the old and new cemetery up to the northern hills and the apartment complex where she lives. But at the square, the cars that were suddenly there, had driven up and encircled her, around around for a few laps so that she had to stand still and wait until they finished.

Windows were rolled down, shouts, that she was cute, that sort of thing.

Stares in front of her, it takes time: suddenly someone else who is shouting, waving—from the newsstand on the other side, right across from her. That is of course whom she is staring at even though she is not even aware of it herself while all of the other stuff is going on around her. Maj-Gun of course. Maj-Gun Maalamaa.

Susette in cowboy boots, tight jeans, short jacket, her long hair hanging loosely—and big, big eyes. "Djessuss, Susette. You're *totally* spaced out. You don't seem to have a clue about what kind of signals you're sending out."

Naturally it is Maj-Gun who says it, making Susette aware of what she looks like from the outside. When Susette walks up to her after the cars drive off, Maj-Gun true to habit is standing in the doorway, smoking. "My God, Susette." Maj-Gun rolls her eyes, whistles. "*A small poor child I am* in farm pants, *boots*. Djeessuss, Susette. And those eyes. Your eyes, Susette. Like globes. A whole world—

"But close up like this you can see your age as well. And the fatigue, the wear," Maj-Gun adds, but Susette does not get mad at her, just the opposite. For a brief moment she thinks "so true" and that Maj-Gun sees it too. Fatigued feet and—so empty, suddenly. All the death, *fresh death*, the old man on the floor in the kitchen of the cousin's house, in her body, in her hands.

"Do you want some chocolate? I have a lot of samples today! Hearts, Susette. Small spirited trolls with truffle filling—"

Maj-Gun holds the door open, they walk in. And yes, it is nice coming into the newsstand, not like having wandered a long way and coming home, but just being able to leave the everyday for a bit. Step out of it, to the newsstand—Maj-Gun's stronghold, her kingdom.

"Those boys," Maj-Gun says, almost motherly, "*pistol awakening.* The hayseeds in the cars. Are a bit obtrusive but, Susette, you don't need to be afraid of them."

"Afraid?" Susette looks at Maj-Gun blankly.

But Maj-Gun is not paying attention, Maj-Gun at the newsstand, in the place "pistol awakening," what she wants to talk about for example and all sorts of other things she has been waiting to share with someone and now with Susette as audience, it pours out.

"My father the Pastor called it that. They drink milk and don't watch television and keep their wives on the straight and narrow having babies, strongly believe in Our Lord's Salvation but then they go out into the backyard and shoot at cans and bottles. They are TRIGGER-HAPPY, *pang pang pang.*

"Or however it goes. But when papa Pastor told me about it it was funny, but now, *djeessuss,* Susette, I've been sitting here so long, I don't remember anything from the rectory and all of papa Pastor's fun stories at the dinner table, or my brother's, the *human rights lawyer,* Tom Maalamaa.

"Don't remember anything. Empty slate. Tabula rasa."

In other words this is how Maj-Gun will stubbornly claim to remember how things were when Susette came to the newsstand for the first time.

". . . The fear, Susette. Your fear. How I saw it. Your big eyes. And I stood here and reeled it in."

"I wasn't scared—" Susette objected, but futilely, you have to give in, keep your mouth shut, Maj-Gun does not want to hear that either.

"Well, whatever you were," Maj-Gun continues, whistling. "When I saw your eyes I thought . . . like globes. A whole world. Something in them that reflects, so to speak. You can see yourself in them. That was a compliment, Susette. Hasn't anyone given you that compliment before?"

•

All About Animals in Nature, All About Relationships, A Hundred Years of Psychoanalysis and Personal Development, Everything About Being in a Good Mood and Everyday Interactions, The Nuclear Family and the Dog, Aquarium Fish in Four Colors, All About Dogs, Cats' World, Everything About the Underwater World of the Sea, and *The Joys of Motherhood.*

And then, Maj-Gun, at the newsstand, the fall of 1989. Maj-Gun among all of the magazines and newspapers that she lugs around and lines up on the shelves behind her and in front of her on racks and on both sides of the counter. Separates new issues from old issues that have not been sold; she gathers them in bundles and ties them with sharp ribbon in the back room to be returned to the Head Office from where a car comes and picks them up regularly a few times a week.

And reads them herself of course: new magazines and old magazines and certain particularly interesting issues she plows through from cover to cover during long, uneventful days before the evening rush hour and what she calls the "weekend whirl," the hours leading up to the weekly lottery ticket deadline that takes place on Friday afternoon.

So that she has them memorized. In any case certain sections. "The memorable ones worth remembering," she says and she writes down the particularly striking ones in her "Book of Quick-Witted Sayings," a small notebook with a black wax cover. "You never get a cavity in a clean tooth," "Test yourself if you're borderline," Maj-Gun quotes. Reads out loud, flidderfladder sentences from here and from there, *My statements.*

•

And yes, there is even a blank page in the notebook, in other words blank on purpose. "Tom's world," Maj-Gun has written at the very top in large letters with a blue ballpoint pen. Holds it up for Susette. "My brother, do you remember?" Knowingly, so to speak, not to mention with a silly, childish emphasis. Susette nods, of course, her first boyfriend, of course she remembers, and what about it? "The human rights lawyer," Maj-Gun clarifies later, suddenly rather bitter. "That's what he became later when he graduated from law school. And successful. All the raped women and children, *djeessuss.*"

But stops herself, something else suddenly catches her attention on the other side of the window on the square in the town center. And in the next moment she sighs, almost devoutly: "Think about what Madonna has done for fashion" because at the same time oneofthose girls from the high school or junior high is crossing the square in tight pants, short leather jacket with shoulder pads, curly hair in a ponytail, bow on her head, and a knickknacknecklace around her neck.

And then she says, in a tone new for the moment, serious, so tender that it is suddenly impossible not to like her: "So many men, so little time, Susette. If I looked like you. With your looks—I wouldn't be sitting here rotting away.

"I mean," she adds more obtrusively, after a small pregnant pause, "not how you look *now*. But *the potential*. Come along and change. A bait for life. *To life, an invitation*."

And then she takes her makeup kit out of her purse that she keeps stored under the counter, takes a hand mirror and lip gloss from it. She has several sticky colors in round plastic cases sealed in small crackling plastic bags that she has carefully, so that there certainly would not be any marks, scraped away from the cover wrapping around certain women's magazines with a knife before setting them out for sale on the shelves. And starts daubing the sludge on her pale, cracked lips, several shades at once. "*Starling darling kiss-ready for the evening enjoyment*," then she hisses and smacks wildly at the pocket mirror that she holds up when she is finished.

"*Kiss kiss kiss*."

And calms down a little, looking around roguely. "Or maybe you just need to color your lips because you're going out for a smoke. A woman of the world, Susette, *always* leaves lipstick on the end of her cigarette." Grandly, quoting from "The Book of Quick-Witted Sayings." "SO," Maj-Gun explains with an eternal poker face because of course she knows that what she is going to say next is sly, "you can see in the ashtray that a Real Woman was here."

"Stop." Susette is laughing so hard she almost chokes. But *today is the first day of the rest of your life*. Maj-Gun sits up straight, there is a customer walking across the square toward the newsstand, and she takes her position on the customer serving stool again, meek as a lamb.

"Look, Susette," she says just before the door chimes. "Who we have here! Now we're going to have some fun!" In other words it is that customer, an older gentleman with a lot of lottery tickets. And when he has taken the three steps up to the counter with three quick youthful strides Maj-Gun is sitting ready with a quote she has randomly chosen from "The Book of Quick-Witted Sayings" (which, in other words, is the point of the hobby: saying to the first best customer exactly what happens to be on that page in "The Book of Quick-Witted Sayings" regardless of whether or not it sounds stupid or crazy).

"Just because you're a count doesn't mean you have the right to walk in and out of my life as you please," Maj-Gun says to the man, with her softest and most beautiful customer service voice.

And he, the man—incidentally the Manager of Susette's apartment building—stands there speechless for a moment without knowing how to react. Certainly not angry my goodness, just the opposite. Hums something cheerful, suddenly almost embarrassed because he has a hard time hiding what a good mood this girl has put him in, and most of all, for a second you get the feeling that he might like to stick out his chubby hand and pinch Maj-Gun Maalamaa on the cheek.

And it is entertaining, of course, both of them laugh heartily, Susette Packlén and Maj-Gun Maalamaa, when the Manager has gone on his way. "Now I seem to have gotten one of those gaffers on the hook again," Maj-Gun determines, and adds with a bit more irony: "As you can see, Susette, I really am surrounded by a crowd of admirers," wiping sticky lip gloss from her mouth with an almost ill-tempered sweep of the back of her hand.

But then she shrugs. "Bother! Forgetabout it. That isn't love, it's a hobby. What do you know about love, Susette? And, Susette, what do I know?

"Love is something bigger . . . Oh, Susette. Now I'm suddenly getting nervous. Come on. I need a smoooooooke!"

And she hastily snatches a newspaper to use for holding open the door.

All About Animals in Nature, All About Relationships, A Hundred Years of Psychoanalysis and Personal Development, Everything About Everyday Interactions, Cats' World, All About Dogs—and of course *All About Love.*

Susette and love.

Because suddenly the magazine that Maj-Gun has stuck under her arm slips from her grasp there where she is standing in the doorway to the newsstand, in the process of lighting her cigarette with a lighter. Falls to the ground, opens to a column, it is just too fantastic, they both stand there staring.

"Do you see?" Maj-Gun says after a few seconds, in total genuine surprise and for a moment without her usual sweaty excitement. "Your story, Susette. And what it's called. Oh, oh, oh, Susette. 'Your Love.'"

Susette and love. A black-and-white sketch of a woman's face illustrates the story, a car, lanterns, a few trees, and broken fog—and behind her face, in the background but in the distance so to speak, a man. With sideburns, wearing a polo, a blazer.

"And what is love?" Maj-Gun continues, once they have come inside. "Sharing the everyday and not forgetting to take turns washing the coffee cups?

"Oh no," Maj-Gun immediately determines. "That isn't anything other than ordinary everyday *servility*. You can have different kinds of arrangements, with or without *legal validity*.

"Or a marriage between friends. Two bank directors in a mixed Lions Club who found each other through their mutual interest in charity."

And so, Maj-Gun who dives into her book again, "The Book of Quick-Witted Sayings," her statements.

"More like this . . ." Skims, skims until she comes to a suitable place. "'*He* taught me to walk' . . . '*She* made me see' . . .

"'*It is a terrifying thing to fall into the hands of the living God. Love means doing everything for love.*' Even dying, *not just for show but PANG truly.*

"*I* am more romantically inclined than you, Susette. In other words, it is just as I suspected—

"I don't mean it in a bad way, but . . . now. I see. That we—might be two. That maybe YOU were also created for a greater love."

"My God, Maj-Gun." Susette Packlén laughs in a girl-friend sort of way. "Isn't it enough already?"

"Can you imagine dying for love? Yes, Susette, when I look at you. These globes, Susette. Your eyes. A whole world. I feel it. That your love is great, Susette. So great it can overturn houses. *Duel in the sun*. Life and death.

"So that later, afterward you can say that there were two of us who loved. Though," Maj-Gun adds elatedly, thoughtful, "of course if it happens to go that way for us then afterward, in and of itself, there won't be so much for us. But"—brightening at the thought—"*the memory* of the two of us will remain.

"I remember when I saw you come running across the cemetery, Susette. To the rectory: like a romantic heroine from a movie. A movie with deserted plains, clouds and rain and hard winds. *I love you . . .* her *whole* body screaming, the loneliness inside her, the heavens opening, church bells.

"It is a terrifying thing to fall into the hands of the living God. It is love, Susette.

"To the rectory. But yet, it has to be said, love's representative in that story looked a little pale, so to speak," Maj-Gun determines with reference to her own brother, Tom Maalamaa. "So the question is," she says thoughtfully, "Susette and love. If *I* am going to love the Boy in the woods then who are you going to love—*now*?

"Well." Maj-Gun shrugs after a brief pause. "Should I tell you another story then instead, as an illustrative example? A true story?"

"I have to go home now, tomorrow is another workday," Susette says but Maj-Gun anticipates her. "But listen to this now and then maybe you'll understand me better, Susette. We were at sea, so to speak. *Life is a cruise*, so to speak, that's how *she* said it. And she took out her flask and poured out 'her medicine.' Then she also said, 'My flask.' Held it up. 'My medicine.' A small cute bottle, as it were.

"You know who I'm talking about. My godmother Liz Maalamaa who had become a widow and wanted to head out to sea and invited me to come with her as a female companion. Didn't want to travel alone, she whined, and I was a child then and I guess she thought that I needed some entertainment in the sea of balls for example.

"But the same miserable routes Susette, Sweden Finland Sweden Finland, which her husband, of blessed memory, had often traveled alone in his spare time until his heart, liver, kidneys just exploded inside him and he was found dead under some berth under the car deck by the cleaners when the boat had reached port.

"The buffet room, the shrimp shells, milk glasses; her talking and her talking; swans in the archipelago that filed past on the other side of the window. TWO swans, that was what she saw even though there were several of course, black swans, white swans, but in other words, she had to pause at just the two of them. Dick and Duck, her and her husband, and crying over the shrimp shells . . . and how you can long for someplace else, Susette, despite being so young! So I left the restaurant and ran ran out through the ship back to my own normal childhood as it were that I suddenly didn't know where it was at all, but the sea of balls then, like a hypothesis; to drown myself in the sea of balls, I wanted to DIE! And I tried, I swam in and under the balls and squeezed my eyes shut but nah nah there was no nice sister in a blue bathing suit, for example, who wanted to come to my rescue.

"There was just one—an older woman: one *single* lady in the universe. My aunt Elizabeth 'Liz' Maalamaa, in comfortable sandals size ten—a reminiscence from her happy childhood on the farm up north where she and her brother dreamed about becoming missionaries, and sometimes you need to walk a long way if you're going to save heathens, Majjunn, which she always called me, she explained sometime during her bedtime stories for me and my brother Tom when she came to visit at the rectory in order to rest during the time her husband was still alive. Sometimes on unruly ground, Majjunn, and there in the jungle, the conditions and laws of the jungle prevail, looked a bit like she had come from that wilderness herself, bruises on her wrists and a black eye on the left side . . . But yes, it was those sandals I saw in the sea of balls when I opened my eyes that I had squeezed shut because I thought it would make me invisible like when an ostrich sticks its head in the sand. On the other side of the windowpane that separated the children's playroom from the ship's corridor while *chubby girl on the run chubby girl on the run* echoed from all of the ship's loudspeakers. I WAS not exactly fat then, Susette, just big.

"But, no escape, *pjutt* spit a ball out of my mouth and back to the dining room, the buffet tables from which all of the other people had already excused themselves and we were alone: the swans, Dick and Duck, her and the husband . . . while darkness fell, Susette. Over all of these lies too. And the archipelago, on the other side of the window. The only thing that could be seen, one solitary lighthouse. A white light, at a distance.

"And then, Susette, it disappeared too—

"Do you think this is funny, Susette?"

Maj-Gun stops in the middle of her story.

"I don't know," Susette replies truthfully. "I don't think—" She tries, does not know how to continue, she wants to say that she does not really believe what Maj-Gun is saying, that maybe Maj-Gun should not exaggerate so much, but suddenly Susette sees the tears in Maj-Gun's eyes behind the counter and it pains her.

"Then I saw hell," Maj-Gun says and big, shiny tears run down her cheeks. "A life I never want to live.

"That marriage which wasn't much of a marriage but she pretended to sit there and miss it when in reality she was just embarrassed because she was drunk."

"But you said she never drank."

"But, Susette!" Maj-Gun shouts impatiently through her tears. "Don't you understand anything? Djeessuss! Those three–four thimbles she poured into her milk glass, her medicine, it was her big secret. And it's her, never me, who talks big. 'A little bit of wine makes you nice,' papa Pastor said at the rectory and I say so too. But I had caught her red-handed." Calmer now, she is no longer crying, dries all the snot and tears from her face with the back of her hand just as determined as she had been with the lip gloss on her lips, sits up straight. "But this is what I want to say, Susette. That the life lie—" Maj-Gun starts with such seriousness that all of the issues of Positive Consciousness she has ever studied pour out of her. "That. The end. Fuck. The end. Never. THERE. Djeessuss. That you can long to get away!"

And she grows silent again, determines later, thoughtfully, but with great emphasis. "Her life. *Her damned shit of a life, Susette Packlén.*"

"Well," Maj-Gun says then after she has caught her breath, "now we come to the little turn in this idiotic story that happens to be true, to boot. *Sorry*, Aunt Liz suddenly says there on the boat. In the restaurant where we remain all alone except for the servers because by that time it's really late. And she looks at me and says that, at exactly the same moment as I get a burning liquid in my mouth that looks like regular milk because what has happened, which she has realized before me even if it was too late for her to do anything about it, is that I have gotten thirsty and taken her glass by mistake instead of my own.

"Sorry. But she, Liz Maalamaa, is like me—unfortunately we aren't related for nothing and what belongs to the genetic material we seem to share is that you are never allowed to have a pause in the conversation regardless of whether there is something important to say or not. Babble, it just continues, especially if someone unmasks you, or even worse, you unmask yourself. SEE the life lie shit life: *she never loved him after all.* And he, yes, he wasn't nice to her anyway—but she immediately has to jump over to the absolution that happens later.

"'Majjunn,' she says accordingly, taking that babble in her mouth. If Majjunn doesn't tell anybody about this then when Auntie dies, Maj-Gun won't get the prince because Auntie doesn't have a say about that but she will get the *whole* kingdom.

"And then, Susette, we go down to the cabin and she writes her will. *After my death all of my earthly possessions will go to . . .* and so on.

"And it was for real. I get to inherit everything. Including the apartment in Portugal where she spends her winters these days because of the varicose veins that also run in the family.

"Djeessus, Susette. Tom Maalamaa. HE isn't going to believe his eyes. That miser. That He. Will Be. Left With Nothing.

"But, Susette, she'll never DIE of course, and then, well"—Maj-Gun grows quiet as if she has run out of air—"we were back in port again."

And at the newsstand now, Maj-Gun who is drumming her fingers on the surface of the counter and suddenly it is really quiet and dark, after closing time, a good while, because neither of them has looked at the clock.

Dark over the square too: only one solitary streetlamp is lit. A cat who is leisurely moving across the empty square, not even black, an ordinary gray tabby, a fat barn cat.

"Everything ,can happen here," Maj-Gun finishes. "Just that . . . that . . . do you think, Susette, that anything happens here at all?

"You can say anything here. That's how it is, at the newsstand. In general."

•

"It's late." Susette clears her throat, now she wants to get home right away.

Maj-Gun sighs, gets up as well, is going to start closing up.

Counts the register first, opens the cash drawer, *PLING*.

"Wait, Susette," Maj-Gun calls when Susette is already at the door. "I think. About your mother. I understand, Susette. More than you know."

"What do you mean?" Susette asks quickly, almost spitefully.

"What I'm saying," Maj-Gun calmly replies, "your mother. She was for real. Not like my aunt or . . . like someone else. Your mother, Susette. Was as healthy as could be. In some way healthier than everyone else in the world who is healthy. Does that sound like a cliché? But still, what I want to say. It was just a logic. To go along with."

"Maj-Gun. Don't bother—" Susette says, but still, she cannot pull herself away, in some way wants to hear more.

"Life like a room, Susette. That's what she said, maybe to you too, there at the rag-cutting bucket in the kitchen—a special mood that never leaves you once you've been there. Room after room after room that you enter and leave and then go on to the next one. That house, what it looks like on the inside, you don't feel but you know . . . suddenly you've just ended up there . . . Not in a basement or in some dusty attic.

"But maybe just somewhere where it is . . . empty.

"Brown. Nasty. She spoke like that. Cut up her office clothes, they were like that shade you know, you remember. Worn woolen fabric. We cut. For the most part she cut and I listened. I really *listened*, Susette, because it was touching for real. Listened like I had never listened before and maybe will never listen again either because it hurt, and continues to hurt too.

"Is that death? *It is a terrifying thing to fall into the hands of the living God.* Is that it? Maj-Gun? Susette? Questions like those. The most terrible or the most comforting, because that is where life and death cancel each other out, laughter grief same thing, there is no answer of course.

"But she remained sitting there cutting, didn't give in.

"She remains sitting there, doesn't give in.

"It demanded respect. But on the other hand I understand that you can't live in it."

"Maj-Gun. CAN we stop talking about this now?"

"Yes, Susette. But you don't need to be jealous. It was, it IS, your mother. My occasional affinity with your mother, Susette. Originates from there and only there.

"She didn't pretend. You could see it in her. A logic. I mean, also in the most absurd of contexts, at the rug rag bucket and among all of the rags."

"Be .quiet now!"

"Sorry, Susette," Maj-Gun says again, one of the last things she says that night but then Susette is already outside. "I mean something else.

"When you don't pretend. It isn't like it is at the newsstand. That you can say anything. But it isn't like that.

"You can't say just anything and yet, even though you think so, it is so beautiful and right when someone says so—so you still keep going, the words pour out of you.

"I want . . ." But Susette is already halfway home on the pedestrian and bicycle path, when she really takes it in, the normal, fresh air, the autumn night. "I want something real.

"A love for example. Which is greater than death. Which overcomes death. It is . . . if nothing else . . . then my . . . readiness.

"The Boy in the woods. Someone who loves despite everything, Susette. That's me."

And Maj-Gun who calls out after her: "Sometimes I have the feeling that *we* are the Angels of Death. The two of us. In the same timelessness.

•

But otherwise, Susette in the everyday, ten thousand miles away from that. Cleaning with Solveig, traveling with Solveig in the company car to different places, joint cleaning projects and individuals ones, where they clean, each on her own. They have a good collaboration, get on well together, even if they are not friends in that way.

Solveig is Susette's employer, has her own life as well; has a five-year-old daughter, Irene, lives somewhere in the Outer Marsh. In a room on the top floor of an old house, not a single-family home exactly, Solveig laughs sometimes when she is in a good mood, but a shack with "room for many generations" that flow freely over all of the floors, small fry, cousins, sisters-in-law and in the midst of it all the mother of the clan, Viola Torpeson, with a can of beer and Benson & Hedges cigarettes and the apple of her eye Gossip Queen Allison, certainly full grown by now, who comes and goes, on "beauty trips," as she says to the kids, they worship her and several kids crawl across the floor when she comes home.

At some point Solveig says she would like to move away with her girl: her husband, Torpe, who comes from that house, has traveled to Germany with his brother Järpe and some cousins, is doing construction work there. Move, not to Germany but to someplace that is just hers, and the girl's, Irene's, of course. Should not be impossible, business is booming, this year in particular has been great, with the assignment in Rosengården 2.

On the other hand, the Outer Marsh, it is okay: the girl gets on well there and does not need to be on her own very often, there are, as said, other kids to play with and always someone acting as babysitter: Gossip Queen, the sisters-in-law, Viola Torpeson.

Besides, Solveig can also say when she is in one of those moods: the Outer Marsh, an interesting environment. The marshiness, stinging sand in the air, fires on opposite beaches at night. Often someone is burning something there: at night when you cannot sleep, stand at the window on the second floor that faces the marsh, look at the fires, something a bit magical about it all, so to speak, comes close. And then sometimes, when Solveig talks like that, in passing, it whizzes through Susette's head too: a rug weaver in a small cottage next to a body of water filled with reeds, she was there once. She, Susette, with her mother and the rug rags in sacks, loads of them, which they had cut up at home, brought them by taxi from the town center. Thousands of cats, the stink of urine, and a massive loom in one single room. Solveig shakes her head, no, did not know that woman, knows nothing about it. On the other hand, she is not originally from there. Has, as mentioned, grown up next to the First and Second capes, the cousin's property, closer to the sea, which she also says as if it is in some way nicer. Still, without having gone into detail, you understand there is a lot of shit in that life: orphaned early on, a twin sister, Rita, who left the District several years ago and has broken all ties with her sister completely.

Rita, *Sister Red*. And Solveig, her twin sister, once upon a time they were inseparable, she was Sister Blue. In the swimming school for the District's children on the Second Cape, a long time ago, where they were the teacher's assistants for Tobias the swim instructor, who is still a good friend of Solveig's, because they were skilled swimmers even from an early age. Were going to become swimmers, trained hard: there, at the Second Cape, and later, for a while, when the public beach was moved from the sea bay out to the woods, to Bule Marsh. Sister Blue, Sister Red, they were called that based on their bathing suits because otherwise it was quite impossible to tell who was who, especially in just their bathing suits and with their hair wet. But sometimes at the swimming school they changed bathing suits on purpose in order to confuse everyone and especially Tobias who stubbornly insisted on calling them by their first names, claimed that he definitely saw the difference, which was not true of course, he mixed them up all of the time too.

But "I was the one who was Sister Blue." Solveig has been able to carry on with Susette in the company car sometimes, these hundred years later. Because an episode that Solveig remembers very well but that Susette has almost completely forgotten belongs to the time in the swimming school when Susette was also a student once when she was really little. That one time at swimming school she, Susette, had ended up too far out at sea and almost drowned, but then, in other words, it was Solveig who had been the attentive one and thrown herself into the water and crawled out to Susette who was sinking already then, Solveig and no one else got hold of her and pulled her to land and gave her CPR there on the cliffs. And later, that same fall, Solveig was awarded the Lifeguard's Medal, at the Lifeguards' Club's yearly banquet even though she had not been able to be there herself. Was at home in bed with the mumps, but got the medal by post.

"I was the one who was Sister . . ." with Susette in other words, in the company car, she insisted on it and could sometimes get really agitated too. If Susette, for example, in order to tease her tossed out the idea that what IF the one who had saved her had been her sister Rita who happened to have Solveig's blue bathing suit on that day.

"I mean. I don't *know*, of course. You two looked so much alike." Though in reality, it *is* just for fun, because

Susette really does not imagine for a second that Solveig could be wrong.

Not because she has any real memory of it, just something blue flickering before her eyes, she was so little after all, long before Majjunn, the Pastor's Crown Princess, the loom, the rug rags, that is how it feels anyway. Apart from in general, what it had felt like to sink, lose her breath, *blubb blubb* . . . she can certainly recall that in her consciousness but mostly in situations when she is not thinking about it, it rises up, a discomfort and then of course the fact that she *hates* the sea so vehemently that it is almost a secret, at least it is not something she discusses with anyone. Besides, she has her job to do. The Glass House, the Second Cape, she cleans there in the summer after all, one of her cleaning projects, the individual ones. Is being rented by a French diplomatic family during these years: they play music on the glass veranda in the evenings, the whole family, mother father children, in floor-length polyester shirts, it becomes a complete tiny chamber orchestra, freshly squeezed orange juice in icy frosted pitchers on a small glass table for refreshment when they take their breaks. Looking in through the crack in the door, on the way to the second floor with the ammonia bucket—the music, the orange juice, and the sea in the background, in protest. High rolling gray waves, white foam, *a hellish roar from the sea*, which is thrown up against the windows.

And becomes stuck there. And you, if you are Susette, the following day, alone on an A-ladder wedged in between the rocks on the beach right next to the bay where she once swam out and almost drowned. The Frenchman's white summer cat meowing on the cliffs, hating the sea, but high up on the ladder, not thinking, scrubbing, polishing the windowpane clean, not looking back—or down.

But otherwise, Solveig, Rita: it is obvious that it was Solveig and not Rita who came to the rescue in the swimming school, no doubt about it, seriously.

Back then she had not needed more than a few seconds in Rita's company to realize it. Businesswoman of the Year's two-window ice cream stand on the square where Susette and Rita had worked together for a few days before Susette was transferred to the strawberry fields in the middle region of the country by her employer.

Rita Rat with higher prospects: would never have lifted a finger to help anyone without thinking about what was in it for her. Could clearly be seen on her face. Rita's sullen silence, a mute rage in the air, tangible like an approaching thunderstorm. A trembling point of power, collected energy. Certainly *fascinating* but it had not interested Susette any further, she was preoccupied with her own problems. Some pangs of conscience for having quit her job at the private nursing home for the elderly and infirm where she had a full-time position. "They will be so sad, the old sick men and women, they are so attached to you," the manager's farewell words echoing in her ears and a certain disappointment, which she had had her hands full trying to hide. The ice cream stand, was this it? The J.L. kerchief and Rita Rat grumbling beside her: is this what she had longed for in the quiet hospital corridors where she had stood in front of the window and looked out over the square on warm spring days, scoops of ice cream on cones, sweet tastes, wild strawberries, pears, and chocolate?

Had not really made heads or tails of those thoughts either, so what she had done at the ice cream stand with Rita Rat was what she had already been good at, at the time: making it look like she was sleeping. But she was *not* sleeping, was as alert as could be, conscious of everything going on around her. A peculiarity she in other words still has, and Solveig in the company car can sometimes get annoyed about it. Some mornings in the car for example when they are heading into the city by the sea and need to get an early start and Solveig picks her up at the first bus stop by the main country road outside the town center, where Susette has walked all the way from her apartment in the complex on the hills on the north side; how she then sits there and dozes next to Solveig who is driving and playing the radio or one of her old cassette tapes. As they approach the city, how Solveig turns the volume up to an insufferable level in order to *wake the bear who is sleeping*, as she says. But completely unnecessary, which is proved by Susette who, several hours later in the middle of the working day, suddenly just starts rambling loudly about the high water level from the weather forecast or singing some song, *and the girl she moves in the dance with red, golden ribbons*, which Solveig was playing in the car that morning.

But in the car Susette is startled by an unpleasant surprise, the sound buzzing through the front of the car, she straightens her back, says grouchily, "Thanks for saving my life Sister Blue. I am so damned grateful."

"And with these words I give you Susette Packlén," Solveig says in turn and then you are supposed to remember what no one remembers, what "these words" were, that is to say what Jeanette Lindström had said when she and Susette got into an argument while catering and Jeanette pushed her employee up to Solveig in the middle of her wedding.

But joking aside. Sister Blue, Sister Red—or Rita Rat, no more about her. *I was Sister Blue.* Except one thing. Susette can certainly understand exactly what it is like to be the shapeless one of two who are so alike on the outside.

The other, the one off to the side, whom no one has any real memory of. Because it is true after all, also for Susette. You do not remember Solveig, you remember Rita.

And then to just be left behind alone when the other has left for good.

Left at the childhood home, the cousin's property, just that old man, the cousin's papa, whom Susette always cleaned for and visited and looked in on sometimes as part of her work responsibilities and who had died in the late summer before that fall.

"What are you going to do with the house?" Susette asks Solveig after some time has passed. Solveig shrugs her shoulders, answers that it is not hers. The old man left everything to her brother. *The whole shitload*, Solveig clarifies, spitting out the words, poorly restrained wrath bubbling under the surface, Susette has never seen her so angry so angry. "That *property* still has a certain value after all."

"You have a brother?" Susette asks in surprise while at the same time realizing how stupid the question is. Of course she knows, has always known. Just had not really thought about it.

"Of course I have a brother," Solveig hisses impatiently. "Bencku. Don't you remember anything?"

"Djeessuss!" rushes out of Susette's mouth, because in that moment something else has occurred to her of course. *The Boy in the woods.* Bengt. *My love it is pure and true.* Maj-Gun at the newsstand. Susette just cannot, even though it is unsuitable, hold back a little laugh.

"What are you laughing about?"

"Nothing, sorry. But shit, Solveig. Seeing as how you've been stuck with everything."

"I'll be fine," Solveig says, cutting her off, collected again. "Business is good. There are loans from the bank."

"That brother," Solveig asks carefully. "Where is he now?"

Solveig laughs shortly. "Djeessuss. Who knows? And I *don't* mean anything mystical by it. To hell with him. That's it. And don't ask me where it started for him. Nowhere, everywhere. Being adrift, more shit. He is drawn to it, so to speak."

And that has almost been the most Solveig has ever said about herself in that way, in the company car, or while working.

Because Solveig and Susette, they do not exactly talk about personal matters, whether they are cleaning or riding in the company car together. So, seriously, they do not talk about anything really. Ordinary things and that jargon they have, isolated observations from various cleaning projects. Susette about the Frenchman on the Second Cape, for example. Not about the sea or the music on the veranda and all that, but about the floor-length polyester blouses that the entire diplomatic family,

mother father and three children, change into every evening when it is not about representation but having spare
time, whether or not they are making music. The French
family's idea about how a real summer archipelago life
should be lived, *running around in pajamas on the cliffs.*

On the other hand, with Solveig, in general: it is good.
Stories; old stories, been there done that, it blows away.
Traveling with Solveig in the company car—that year, the
last year Solveig and Susette clean together and in general,
Solveig gets a new car, a Volkswagen Transporter, marbled
gray, four-wheel drive. And Solveig who plays the radio,
the news, the weather forecast or her old cassette tapes.
Folk songs, *Micke's Folk band, And the girl came from her
lover's meeting,* the volume higher, less exorbitant.

With Solveig during the day, but actually, how do you
know a person? How do you get to know them? By talking, endless arguing about this and that, stories, stories
about life and death and success and adversity and all
the experiences you have had? Nah. That is not the
only way, Susette knows. Because with Solveig, despite
the fact that they never share information about themselves—when Solveig says something for real, something
important about herself, it comes in passing—but still,
Susette knows exactly who Solveig is. And that both of
them, she and Solveig, in some way are alike. Not like
twins, but parallels so to speak.

And besides, does everything *have to* be attributed to
something that has happened, something in the past?

Because later, with Solveig, in Rosengården 2. Walking, running down the avenues, in such a pounding
NOW, sunshine.

Tabula rasa. Being nothing, and new. That possibility.

•

As mentioned, it is early fall, they are in Rosengården 2 almost all the time when they are working together. Vacuuming, washing windows, polishing so that the houses will be ready to be lived in. Those who have bought the houses and are going to live in them are rarely seen, you do not know who they are of course except for the fact that they have a lot of money and most of them come from somewhere else, not from the District. A mother-in-law or wife with girlfriends with an eye for color and good taste who show up sometimes, give good advice. My grandmother this, at Marttorna we learned it this way . . . and so on, though of course they do not grab the polishing rags personally, but they know exactly how they should be used.

But for the most part Solveig and Susette alone, in Rosengården, in the empty houses: all architectonic masterpieces, different from one another but certainly at least three floors in each one of them. Enormous spaces, millions of feet up to the ceilings, the floor space. Furnishings like landscapes that in some of the houses should be completely ready when the residents arrive. Curtains hung up, beautiful patterns, material, paintings along the walls, sculptures, art. An exquisite family of rabbits, for example, made of heavy and transparent glass, in countless pieces. Two larger and two smaller ones that for several weeks have been standing ready on a podium on one of the landings outside the door to a room that presumably will be the nursery: washing machine–friendly jungle animals on the wallpaper in there.

These rabbits collect dust: need to be dusted, *crrrrfllll* Solveig hisses all the time.

Moving inside the houses, a bit like a thief. With endless care, of course, no Solveig is needed in order to point that out. *Tippytoe.* But a certain thieflike merriment amid the respect.

Or, then, outside: on the lush avenues cutting through Rosengården 2, which is going to be fenced in with high walls and have an electronic monitoring system at the gate so that the area can be kept closed off from outsiders. "This is the future." Solveig laughs, there on the avenues, silly maybe, though when you find yourself in that exact place, it is not at all.

Walking in the future with Solveig, in Rosengården 2: on the open asphalt roads where the trees are already growing tall. Full grown from the beginning, symmetrical and richly branched, as if they have been standing in the same straight line in the same places in straight rows and are not, as they are, newly planted.

"Tobias would say that it's cheating," says Solveig. "Tobias would say that you can't *buy* history and experience."

"But, Susette," Solveig says later. "Forget about Tobias. You don't need to think so much—

"There is also that possibility, Susette, that all of the old stuff can disappear. And it's not silly. Doesn't need to mean obliterated or forgotten. Just that you don't need to walk around and see with the same eyes, the eyes of the old people."

And right after, something else, something about herself. "It was hell for quite a while but it's good now. It took a hundred years before I got my child. I had so many miscarriages."

Susette nods, she understands exactly. No more words are needed, no words spoken from the heart, nothing *that big.* Just walking with Solveig, in that openness. A clear day at the beginning of September, thinning, blindingly white clouds racing across the sky.

Here you are nothing and everything disappears. The possibility of new. A great laughter grips Susette, remains a few steps behind Solveig, spins around and around on the spot. Dizzy. The empty slate. Tabula rasa.

"She was terrified of death. Everyone around her just died."

There was a time, they were cutting rug rags.

But "love," stated Maj-Gun, sitting at the newsstand reading from "The Book of Quick-Witted Sayings," "is partly. To create yourself, and new."

There among the tall buildings, on the avenues: "Is your love like my love? So great that it can overturn houses?"

My life. NOW—*Susette and love.*

So yet, inside Susette. There is a small seed. Of love. Baby bird under your jacket, at your chest. Small heart, small sparrow. Bird. Baby. Starts growing—

"Come on, we're in a hurry, silly!" Solveig is already at one house, in the yard, has turned around and yelled.

And Susette stops spinning and jumping and acting like an idiot and runs as fast as she can to catch up with Solveig and bumps into her playfully, like a small dog.

"*It is a terrifying thing to fall into the hands of the living God,*" she chants, with a dull and solemn voice, imitating Maj-Gun Maalamaa, right in Solveig's ear. "*Duel in the sun—*" And then she adds, as usual, "Solveig, do you know Maj-Gun?"

"Nah. Which Maj-Gun?"

"*Today is the first day of the rest of your life.* Her. In the newsstand."

"Nah," says Solveig. "Do you?"

"Not . . . really," says Susette. "Or—well. A little. She's . . . okay. Just talks a bit funny. Says strange things."

Simultaneously: it is hard knowing with Maj-Gun and your connection to her what you should say. There are not any of those coherent, real memories to reproduce. If she were for example to say, "We were classmates in elementary school," then it is also true that she does not remember anything from that time. The Pastor's Crown Princess? Cuckoo. Good evening. "Say the password." Or: "The sister of my first boyfriend, Tom Maalamaa." What do you mean first boyfriend, saying that when you are almost thirty years old? But then it starts burning somewhere again. *My* love. But: a damned preparedness and no candidates.

"Strange things about what?" Solveig asks.

"All sorts of things. *Just think if there is someone inside you who is dying for love?*" Susette yells out, laughing into the happy day.

"Ha ha ha," says Solveig. "Stop dawdling now. We've got work to do."

And they go inside the house.

•

Susette in landscape. It is a little while later, in that house, Rosengården 2, the one with the glass rabbits on the podium on the third-floor landing. She has gone up there, and suddenly that merriment from outside on the avenues fills her, a bit thieflike too, upward upward, three and a half floors, in this house, to the very top floor. A small staircase, a door, she opens it and comes out.

An empty landscape, and how large. A wide wide space, warm wooden flooring and a window at the other end, enormous, reaching almost from the floor to the sloping roof, probably fifteen–eighteen feet at the highest point. Walks up to this window, there is, so to speak, a door in the window, there is of course some sort of artistic idea behind it. A glass door that leads out to—everything.

And it is fantastic, what is revealed. The sea in the distance, and the woods, the capes. Everything exists in there and then the sky as well, the clouds, everything— that space. And to stand there, like on a stage, as if someone had thought about it. Because heavy curtains are already hanging at the sides of the window, curtains made of velvet, soft, like theater curtains.

Tippytoe, carefully, hop hop, Susette walks up to the window. And stands there, alone, in the emptiness, the silence, with everything in front of her—it is dizzying.

Tabula ra—

But suddenly, at the window, where she is standing there at the window, the handle on the door that most certainly cannot be opened even though it looks like it can, and yes, steady on her feet, is not afraid of heights, not afraid, not—but suddenly, exactly right there, an- other thing. Which comes back.

Silk velvet rag scraps—I have seen the most I have. Maj-Gun, her stories, at the rug rag bucket. The rug rag bucket. The scissors. *Crehp crehp.* Mom.

Maj-Gun, again, again Maj-Gun. That strange time eight–nine years ago, mother was dead, they were cut- ting rags in the kitchen in her childhood home. Silk, velvet . . . Maj-Gun's conjurations, like refrains. And her stories, or just that she talked, talked all the time. My horrible aunt Liz Maalamaa. The Boy in the woods.

Not important in and of themselves, not even then; it was just the purpose of them: to lighten the grief in an otherwise rather sorrowful and confusing time.

And at the same time, silly too. The Boy in the woods. Maj-Gun's great love, for example. This Bengt, that is, Solveig's brother—whom you had never thought about, and you do not think about in any more detail now either. Just a boy, of course you remember him—even if Susette never knew him at all, just known in the way that everyone who grows up at about the same time in the same place knows each other.

Somewhat older, the kind the girls in the District had crushes on: looked pretty good, drank a lot of beer already back then. But in an interesting way, so to speak, celebrated, and could be attractive at a certain point in life, a short period, but nothing more.

Maj-Gun's: "My undelivered love, it is pure and true." So yes, there was already a lot of forced comedy around this at the rug rag bucket in the house. Something Susette had understood back then already despite the fact that she had been rather dazed there, sitting in her pajamas, listening. That there was not much truth in Maj-Gun's story, that *he* would have been interested in someone like Maj-Gun, who had neither the looks nor the manner about her, was rather unthinkable.

Of course in addition to the fact that maybe he had been there and "helped himself" there at the cemetery for a while as a teenager, according to rumors that Maj-Gun, who no longer was the Pastor's Crown Princess, had "received."

But at the rug rag bucket Susette had not said to Maj-Gun that Maj-Gun's love was a fantasy-fetus born of a lot of wishful thinking, and she was not planning on saying it now either.

And besides, what did she know about it anyway? She had not been with the girls and had a crush on some Bencku in her youth, or had a crush on anyone at all. During that time she kept company with Maj-Gun's brother Tom Maalamaa and when she had not been with Tom Maalamaa in his room at the rectory she had been at the hospital with her father who was suddenly dying and when he died she had not been able to be with Tom at the rectory anymore so she and her mother remained alone in the deserted family home in the lush neighborhoods below the town center. Far away from all the ordinary youth life in the District, far away, in some way, from everything.

"The Disgust." An empty page: "Empty world." And suddenly again here at the window in Rosengården, an old memory: Tom Maalamaa standing at the window of his room in the rectory that faced the cemetery where his sister Maj-Gun Maalamaa, the self-appointed *Pastor's Crown Princess*, wanted to hold court, but with little success. "My kingdom," she said that too. But Liz Maalamaa the Angel of Death mask (not scary, just idiotic) or without the mask, had hung on the metal gate *tjii* this way *tjii* that way . . . and you had, everyone had, walked past. That cemetery, which a few years later, as teenagers, had been transformed into a place where it was whispered that his sister "received." "The Disgust," Tom Maalamaa at the window who said that and Susette standing next to him nodding in silent agreement even if they did not talk about it with more words than that when they were alone in Tom's room at the rectory. Behind the closed door, just the two of them, in the music, Gustav Mahler's Ninth Symphony, always "Mahler's Ninth—"

That you could escape to the music from the Disgust. "The Disgust." In these moments in the room at the window with the view that otherwise is so beautiful: trees and hills, the church with its bells ringing on the weekends, six o'clock on Saturday evenings. Isolated words that had been thrown into the air, when the record, "Mahler's Ninth," on the record player had ended.

As that relationship with Tom Maalamaa had also, in other words, gradually ended. Nothing dramatic about it either: they parted as friends of course and lost touch with each other as a matter of course. Tom Maalamaa who, according to what his sister Maj-Gun said at the newsstand, had finished high school and moved away from home and started studying law at the university and after finishing his studies became a human rights lawyer for an international charity.

And Susette herself who had finished school after high school in connection with her father's death and started working at the private Christian nursing home for the elderly and infirm in the town center. She worked there for almost one year: kept watch over the dying ones, which the manager maintained Susette was good at and maybe it was true but suddenly she had enough and quit and gone to the Businesswoman of the Year and begged for a normal summer job instead. Which later, as said, after a few days of working at the ice cream stand in the two-window shack on the square in the town center, had continued at the strawberry fields in another part of the country, to Janos, the Lithuanian, the second lover, what later became "Poland," all of that.

But Tom Maalamaa's voice, how it pushes its way through her memory. Speaking "softly," says, "the Disgust," at the window in his steady but soft voice. One spring evening, March–April, big and bright. Tom who is speaking, Susette who is nodding, the quiet understanding around a feeling that they share without needing to formulate it into words.

Afterward, in that other life that was not "Poland," which she had said to her mother, to Maj-Gun, which had gone on for a while, three years in other words before she returned home again, she had been able to recreate that feeling many times. A feeling that became inseparably glued to the District in particular, the entire district, what had happened to her personally, her mother's death, everything mixed together. "This Disgust" over everything.

The cemetery, the death, all death, her father's death. "No, Susette," her mother had said admonishingly when she let go of everything, "it's not easy living in a house of sorrow." And Maj-Gun, *Majjunn*, the Pastor's Crown Princess, "say the password" . . . a metal gate *tjii* this way *tjii* that way in the wind . . . and Maj-Gun older, receiving: Maj-Gun's bleeding teenage bottom in the sleet between the headstones.

And at the nursing home later, the lonely dying ones on whom Susette, according to the manager, had a favorable effect: to these beds in particular where both nursing home cats were often already lying at the foot—they had a habit of sneaking in just before death came, jumping up onto the beds, had a nose for death.

Sitting there on a chair at the bedsides, holding hands, saying good-bye.

The Disgust. Instead of the beautiful and the normal. Which had been exactly that, no descriptions. Her mother at the cemetery: "What a beautiful bouquet, Susette!" "Listen! They are ringing for the weekend service. Listen how beautiful it is."

The Disgust. In relation to the District—her youth, her home, everything. In relation to herself with: the memory of it—padding steps, soft and meek, down those corridors. Did not say much, almost mute, but stick thin and with those big eyes, bulging globes that greeted her in the mirrors of the nursing home. Padding over shiny waxed floors: were seasons, summers, springs, falls, going on anywhere?

Looking out through the window, the square, the life, the movement.

"Kitty, kitty come to me." *Scchhhh hisssss*: the nursing home cats who saw red at the mere sight of her and ran for their lives down the corridors.

The Disgust in relation to time, to herself, to everything.

Which had also been a reason why she remained in the city by the sea, in other cities, in other places, a long time. Sporadically getting in touch with her mother at the house. Called from "Poland," just a designation, no camouflage for anything tremendous.

Because Janos, *her second love*, the Lithuanian, from the strawberry fields, there had not been much to it. The story had barely started when it ended.

And gradually undeniably, you came up with a way to talk about it and think about it, with the comic points as well. How they had "escaped" from the boardinghouse in the middle of the summer night where all of the strawberry pickers were lying, sleeping, packed their things, headed off. Out into the woods—but the woods in the center of the country are bigger and more deserted than those in the District could ever be. And getting lost there.

She had found her way out again a day and a half later, suddenly found herself by the side of a road on which cars passed now and then. Hungry and exhausted she set herself up by the side of the road in order to bum a ride: it had not gone very well and she had been so tired she had not been able to stand and had to sit on a rock to rest. She had fallen asleep on the rock and when she woke up there were some boys in a car that had stopped by the side of the road and they asked her if she was feeling all right, if she needed a ride.

And she had been allowed to hang out with them, they gave her food and she slept in the backseat the whole way and when she woke up again they were in the city by the sea and she stayed there with the guys for a while, somewhat older, nice guys, had been their "mascot," but no one was allowed to touch her, they were very kind.

Everyone had been so nice to her: "mascot." But then she left and got a job and her own place to live. And stayed in the city awhile, and then traveled to another city, and so on.

Janos, her second love. A few days there, then—the whole time, gone.

But here, now. *My life.* How it is flying by. An opportunity exists. Be nothing and new. The Disgust? Of course it was, of course it is, so beautiful here. The open spaces.

•

But still, Maj-Gun. At the cemetery, one April evening as a teenager, Susette who happened to come by, on her way home from Tom, the Disgust? It had not been like that. Indifferent, almost in a bad mood, told Susette to go away. And Susette had gone away, home. They had not spoken about it either, ever.

Maj-Gun at the rug rag bucket—no, that was something else. Maj-Gun at the newsstand ... "I was standing there, reeling in the fear." But she had not been scared. In the middle of the square, Maj-Gun waving.

As if there was a connection between them. Invisible threads, rags, rug rags. Moss that was growing over their heads, moss like a fungus from the earth, old folk songs.

Maj-Gun with a mask over her face: Liz Maalamaa the Angel of Death.

Oh. Up here in the empty room, it blows away, so beautiful, open.

"Overturn houses?" Nah, standing firmly you know, on the ground.

Tiny love, tiny baby bird under your jacket, tiny seed— *I love you*. And running over plains.

"SUSEEETTTE!"

Solveig's voice blasting from one of the lower floors, through the house. Have to go.

•

But then *CRASH*. A glass rabbit that splits into a thousand pieces, raining over the hard, stone floor. Susette has left the attic, *polishing rabbits* half a floor down, has returned to her work.

This house: partially open plan living divided over three floors, ceiling height and space and Susette at the railing on the third floor: high above the ground level where Solveig is polishing the hard floor made of expensive Italian granite way down below, and Susette who is supposed to be dusting, but that strange thieflike merriment in her again.

Susette with polish on her rag is polishing the rabbits, my love, your love, finding a tiny seed, tiny baby bird under your jacket, light heart little sparrow hopping crow hopping sparrow. "Look, Solveig!" Cannot resist rollicking a little. "Look look!" Holding a rabbit in her hand, over the railing, Solveig far down below, Susette pretending to juggle the rabbit, pretending to throw it dangerously up into the air. Look, Solveig! "Gråhara northwest nineteen, Bulleholm northeast thirteen..." starts rattling off the weather forecast from the company car that morning, it echoes through the house, sings the song, *but dearest my little girl don't tie the bands too hard,* "the folk song has many verses, the same thing happens in every one, over and over again, an eternal repetition, look, Solveig!"

"You're crazy!" Solveig yells loudly too, through the house. "Crazy idiot!"

And then: "NO! Susette!" because it is in that moment that Susette loses her grip on the little glass piece, slippery from the polish, and it slips out of her hands and they both understand what is going to happen, it cannot be stopped. The rabbit that is falling, falling through the whole house and breaks on the floor into millions of small, hard shards that fly everywhere and Solveig is forced to run run away, is barely able to take cover behind a door.

Then silence, a fall day that has come to a standstill—and Solveig is furious of course.

Is silent the rest of the working day, they leave together in silence. On the avenues, the sun that has been covered by the clouds, Solveig walking a few steps ahead, quick, jerking steps, toward the car, Susette who is sauntering after her.

But then, in the middle of everything, Solveig turns around, and you can see that everything is okay again, the anger has blown over.

"Come on now you damned dreamer and idiot. We have to hurry home."

"Now I remember her," Solveig says in the company car as they are leaving Rosengården 2 behind.

"Who?"

"Maj-Gun. Maalamaa. The Pastor's daughter. Because a long time ago, when I was little. She stole an apple. From Doris Flinkenberg. The biggest apple in the fruit basket that Bengt won at the bazaar in the fellowship hall and gave to her. She was stubborn, Doris, had to have everything, though it was a shame about her."

Maj-Gun Maalamaa, stuck her hand through the cellophane and took the biggest apple.

"They were both very greedy. She did not give in to Doris." Solveig laughs.

"Then you remember all sorts of cuckoo. Which Doris?"

"This Doris. On the cassette."

And the girl she walks in the dance with red golden ribbons on Solveig's tape player in the car. The folk songs.

•

A few days later Susette picks up a white cat at the Glass House on the Second Cape. The French family that had been renting the house as a summer residence have left and Susette is there on behalf of the cleaning company to help with the move: air out bedclothes, dust and roll up rugs, and wrap things in silver paper and pack them in moving boxes for transportation back to the winter residence in the city by the sea. But their summer cat, long haired, white, mixed breed, which the diplomats had adopted from the animal shelter in June, has in some way or another been forgotten.

It is sitting on the kitchen stairs of the locked, abandoned house when Susette returns a few days later: as if it had been waiting for her when she, as if led by a sixth sense, suddenly got the inclination to take the bus from the town center out to the Second Cape one Saturday morning. The wonderful white cat. And what a different cat in comparison to other cats Susette Packlén had, up until then, come across in her lifetime: both of the nursing home cats in the ward for the elderly and infirm where she had worked as a teenager, her very first job. Two peevish cats, siblings with shiny coats, who snuck around the corridors, so calm and at home where they spent their days padding from room to room, bed to bed, from dying person to dying person, but got out their claws and hissed at the very sight of her, "little Susette," which had been the nursing home manager's nickname for her.

The white cat is hungry, almost emaciated. So it eats, eats when she comes home with it. "Damned animal torturer," Maj-Gun establishes at the newsstand about the French family in the Glass House when Susette comes to the newsstand to buy more cat food that same night because all of the grocery stores are already closed and she tells Maj-Gun everything in broad strokes.

Personally Susette does not care that much about the summer family on the Second Cape having abandoned the cat: actually, deep down inside, she is happy. To suddenly have the little white kitty, it is almost like a gift and at the newsstand with Maj-Gun she is suddenly gripped by a great eagerness to show it to someone.

"But come and see it then!" she exclaims and before she knows it she has, in other words, invited Maj-Gun to her home. And then Maj-Gun immediately forgets everything else, lights up and says, almost devoutly, humbly, yes. "You have to give me the address," she adds later with a small laugh, but still happily so that it does not sound like it would sound otherwise, like a dig because Susette has never asked Maj-Gun to visit her before, during all the years she has lived in her own apartment on the hills north of the town center.

"Oh! Are you still in your pajamas!" Maj-Gun howls when she rings the doorbell that following Sunday, during the morning, not particularly early, certainly at the appointed time, Susette has slept through her alarm. "I've come to look at the kitty! Here is my contribution!" Maj-Gun, who purposefully pushes her way into the apartment, has a chocolate swiss roll and ice cream with her and a one-pound package of coffee as well as some family magazines from her newsstand, throws herself down on the love seat in Susette's tiny living room and immediately starts speaking expertly about everything she knows about various cat breeds and their particular oddities in accordance with what she has read in some magazine "Cat's World" despite the fact that she is, after all, which she still gets to point out in the same sentence, "really a dog person."

•

"Must have a little bit of rag doll in it," Maj-Gun determines. And clarifies: "Rag doll. A rag doll. One of those soft ones. Loose joints. Can easily be confused with characterlessness." Lifts the cat up into the air in order to demonstrate: and yes, indeed the animal hangs limply and loose limbed, folded double in her grasp. But so, finished with that demonstration, she throws the cat away again, back on the floor with it—as if done discussing this and moving on to other things, things that are more important, more important things that she has on her chest and that certainly, in her opinion, are the real reason for her visit, naturally, in addition to, *as a guest you don't diet,* drinking coffee and stuffing herself with as much chocolate swiss roll as possible.

Like, for example, the magazines she has with her then. *"Family magazines."* Which Maj-Gun underlines so you can hear that she has thought out everything she is going to say ahead of time and cheered herself at the shrewdness in it:

"Magazines for *the entire family.* It can be informative to read about what the rest of mankind is up to, don't you think?"

With reference, of course, to their mutual solitary situation in that regard.

Humorously said, but still, the smile that Susette has had ready at the corners of her mouth freezes, ebbs out, and she suddenly stops in the middle of everything. Because in exactly this moment it is as if it hit her with full force. That *humbug.* Maj-Gun, everything. And not because of the talk or even because of the cat, which Maj-Gun pretended to be interested in at the newsstand but which she is now barely paying attention to when she is actually here, rather everything she knows about it. You understand that THAT is not meant so seriously, as usual Maj-Gun's know-it-all attitude of the well-known type that, in and of itself, could sometimes even be entertaining to listen to at the newsstand.

Maj-Gun who knows everything, so to speak, and establishes: the one with the other and the third. *My statements*, and notes, chosen pieces in "The Book of Quick-Witted Sayings" that she loves to quote from. Urbanely, as it were, occasionally superior too—and very sure of herself even if often later, *almost always*, it turns out that she was wrong.

And *how* wrong Maj-Gun is: it did not start in the newsstand or even with the skateboarding film that did not turn out to be a *young adult blockbuster* either, which Maj-Gun persisted in claiming when they were going to go out and get some fresh air among their peers after a difficult and strange time in the house in the town center. Nah, simply originates from the beginning of time, that incorrectness, from the cemetery, the Pastor's Crown Princess, all of that.

Everything with which Maj-Gun had gotten hold of the wrong part of the stick. About her and her mother for example, the flowers on the Graves of the Forgotten, as if there had already been something crazy about it to begin with. Stood and hissed "the Angel of Death" at Susette at the water hydrant in the stone grove when her mother had been out of sight, wearing that silly mask, "Buhuu aren't you afraid of me?"

But if you then much later, so to speak, when the water had flowed under the bridges and you had more of a will

of your own, for example in the newsstand, personally
ventured to hint to Maj-Gun about everything she had
been wrong about, just something completely normal,
even in joking, then Maj-Gun would instantly become
grouchy and snap:

"Well! You're probably lying too." And of course put
you on the defensive. "What do you mean?" Maj-Gun
has started tallying. "First, The Sea Captain. Your father.
Back in school. When we were little. YOU said that he
was a sea captain. AND second . . ." And then of course
you were forced to stop listening, it is not possible to discuss things with Maj-Gun when she is in that kind of a
mood, putting her own spin on things, it just gets worse,
leads nowhere.

But still, *nothing* of that NOW, here, in the apartment,
not even important. Just the following, so simple. That
here for once you have gone to Maj-Gun as one friend
to another and been beside yourself about a cat you had
just gotten as your own and wanted to share your happiness with her, with someone. But Maj-Gun who, as soon
as she has commented on her commonplace knowledge,
"rag doll," has just brushed the cat aside as if what was
coming out of her mouth was so much more important.

Humbug. And Susette feels the anger pulsating inside;
so angry so angry like she has never been before.

Even if you cannot see it on her, because she does not
say anything, does not move a muscle.

But it has become quiet for a few minutes during
which Maj-Gun, with her feelers, registers that her joke
was not appreciated, maybe she can hear that it is not as
funny as she thought it would be. But immediately, in
the next moment, she pulled herself together and so to

speak discovered the cat anew. Carefully lifted it up in her arms again, burrowing her face into its fur. "Joking aside," blinking a bit roguely, eyes narrowed through the cat hair, "you can find a lot of *almost* fat-free recipes in them, for single people too."

And it is a little bit funny after all, cannot be helped, Susette cannot help but break into a smile. And she softens, the hot fury disappearing almost as quickly as it came over her.

Ventures to ask too: "Something from 'The Book of Quick-Witted Sayings'?"

"Oh," Maj-Gun answers, squirming a bit in her seat, but of course she cannot hide that she is happy again, about the appreciation and the attention. "Just something I made up. By myself, so to speak."

•

"But now, Susette, for the remaining entertainment," Maj-Gun continues then, the afternoon that passes, the chocolate swiss roll eaten, the ice cream melted into slush in the bowls on the table, the cat fallen asleep in Susette's arms, heavy and sweaty on her pajama-covered legs, still in her bedclothes, wearing just her bathrobe. "Shall I tell you about something else? Something about myself and my life? Things are happening there too even though it may not look like it from the outside. But a little bird has whispered in my ear: that *I* may not be here for very long. It is starting to burn, Susette . . .

"You know, Susette, as I have a habit of saying. I'm flying away. The two alternatives . . . money or love, you remember. And now I'm *not* talking about the former. My aunt Elizabeth and all of her money that I'm going to inherit and that will provide me with the opportunity to live an independent life as a single person with loads of financial freedom so that I can leave this joint . . . I'll be able to have a nice apartment too, and certainly be able to get started on the right diet right away, so that *my life*, oh djeessuss how I'll be able to say it, *my life*, like an architectural monument, white and airy and with high ceilings . . . so that my life—well, it won't be any story about Fat-Dick and Fat-Sally who found love together, 484 pounds of true love and then they lived happily ever after with only vegetable fat on the table, Susette—ha-ha." Maj-Gun laughs at her own joke but then she suddenly grows quiet and, "where was I?" Looks around Susette's cozy little living room as if she had just woken up, a living room that is such a different environment from the newsstand where she otherwise sits and tells her stories, everything sounds so different here. A few seconds' pause, and then she has found her place again. "Well HERE I was: that, the jump in the lake, Susette.

"The old bitch will never die, believe you me. It never becomes evening there—nah, always morning in that life. Early morning hours, a hysterically bursting dawn particularly in the company of someone with her healthy fluids who would love to lie around in her pajamas and lounge around until the afternoon. And *five* glasses of water every morning to not feel hungry and she doesn't feel any hunger, I promise, before her morning aerobics and the long morning walks that occur daily. But—what do you get out of it, Susette? From those kinds of healthy habits? Hallelujah, Susette, you get eternal life.

"But now that wasn't what I was going to talk about rather it was the other alternative: a small bird has

whispered in my ear that the Boy in the woods is back.
Love, Susette. That possibility.

"Yes, in other words," she adds. "I haven't actually
seen him. But I know. There is so much you know that
you don't know. Can you explain it?

"A criminal returns to the scene of the crime. That's
what I mean. I love him. Because he ... loved so much
he killed—'*Nobody knew my rose of the world but me.*'
It was a tragic story. The American girl who died at Bule
Marsh. Do you remember?"

Certainly, of course, an old story from the District, Susette shrugs her shoulders: "And what about it then?"

"Well. HE. Loved her. The American girl. So much
that he killed—"

"Sorry, but who are you talking about again?"

"Djeessuss." Maj-Gun rolls her eyes, opens them
wide. "I'm talking about the Boy in the woods of course.
Haven't you heard? Djeessus, Susette. If you weren't so
curled up in your own suffering," Maj-Gun continues,
but not at all as exaggerated as she sounds. "And now I
don't mean you personally but *for example* you—

"Or *me* for example. Because that's how it is with all
people. Your head is filled with so many other things,
so many other things, your own things, that you aren't
attentive. And then of course you need—protection. To
protect yourself, protect each other.

"Like you at the rug rag bucket when we were young,
in the house. You were in shock after your mother's
death and you had such a terrible stomachache and of
course I talked about my love then too but I couldn't just
tell you everything because you were so unwell. What it
was really like. With him and the American girl.

"Well, anyway. What I want to say is that there is a suffering which, even if you see and hear it, regardless of how obvious it is, you don't bother with it, not out of meanness but because you're so preoccupied with your own things. So. For example me. I should have been more aware because that girl went and shot herself. *Pang.* A bullet through the head. Also at Bule Marsh. The same place where the American girl drowned."

"What are you talking about? What girl?"

"Doris. That was her name. A year or so older, the folk band girl. The soloist in that band, Micke's Folk Band . . . Micke Friberg whom all the girls had a crush on because he was good-looking and musical and so *deep*, something big was going to become of him, do you remember? Oh, well, Susette. I don't either. The two of us are just as forgetful. There are lots of golden boys with prospects and there isn't room for all of them on Olympus or whatever it's called later in life. Well. Anyway. Doris Flinkenberg was his girlfriend for a few weeks that fall and Micke Friberg was in love with her and she also tried to love him but it didn't work out because she was in love with someone else.

"We, Doris Flinkenberg and I, in other words, had raked the cemetery together the summer before. Of course, she was the one doing the raking because it was her summer job but I had summer vacation, long, free vacation days at the cemetery, my hangout in the world at that time. And as I said, it would turn out, her last summer but you couldn't know that then, not even later in the fall when she came back to the cemetery once and I met her there a few days before she took her own life.

"Maybe it was like this. That she knew something about all of that with the American girl that made it so she no longer wanted to live. Something really awful. But I thought about that later when it was too late so to speak. Maybe we should have brought everything out in the open while there was still time, so it wouldn't have been just a few sentences she had spoken in passing. Just think if *I* had been able to help her. I saw that she was depressed, of course: the fear, the anxiety that stank around her. Still, oh hell, I didn't understand—not then.

"And I was so angry at her too. Thought she was proud. During the summer, at the cemetery, she just walked around and talked about everything she was going to do *later* when her summer job was finished. Travel to Austria with her best friend and all of the fun things they would do there. Rather dismal for an outsider to listen to in the long run. But in and of itself, it's understandable in hindsight too: you know, how you can pin all your hopes on a trip like that to anywhere, just escape, when you don't see any other way out. Because there wouldn't be any trip later, with her friend. It was probably just daydreams and bragging.

"In other words, we didn't really get along. And in some way, I had certain expectations of her. Her and her friend: I had seen them wearing the same shirts with the writing LONELINESS&FEAR on the front and thought that maybe there was something a bit different there, something with spice for real, in some way. And yes, it can be said in passing even though it isn't important in this context: it was of course her friend, Sandra Wärn from the house in the darker part of the woods, whom she was really in love with but the two of them ended up fighting in the end and it broke Doris's heart; Micke Friberg whom she was together with later, regardless of how he tried to make her forget, oh no, Susette, Doris didn't forget.

"Because later, in the fall, at the cemetery, in other words she came there again once the way some people come to the cemetery in a fateful mood, was so upset, beside herself, you could see it. But then I was angry at her, as it were, because during the summer she had gone to the caretaker at the church and complained about me. Said she couldn't do her summer job properly because I was following her all the time and babbling and babbling about myself. So she had arranged a gag order with the summer workers and papa Pastor he was mad because the bit about the Liz Maalamaa mask that I had started using again had reached his ears. Just for fun, of course.

You remember the mask, which Tom Maalamaa and I used to run around with at the cemetery when we were little, you were there of course, you and your mother, with the flowers by the graves. Papa Pastor had to deal with a lot of complaints, not from you and your mother, of course, but from others who had business at the cemetery and he forbade us to take the mask with us there. He detested that mask because we called it the Liz Maalamaa mask after our godmother and aunt who was also his own sister of course—"

"Maj-Gun, wait a second," Susette interrupts her then. "Were you wearing that mask when you saw Doris at the cemetery?"

"Yes. At some point. Why?"

"But—isn't it ... I mean ... you weren't a child anymore you know?"

"Nah, Susette, that's true. At the very beginning, in the summer, for the most part I definitely wanted to make myself interesting too, in some way, show that I could have some interesting stories too. Later, in the fall, I guess I just wanted to scare people. WANTED it to have an effect on her. Well. It did.

"She got scared. Quite simply damned disproportionately shitscared. But, Susette, it was never my intention to scare her for real. *Here is the Angel of Death Liz Maalamaa.*

"But, Susette—" Maj-Gun gets ready again out of her contemplativeness and says with emphasis, "Actually. I didn't care about *her.*

"All the time from the beginning. NOW I'm going to tell you what it was like: that *the reason* I got close to her at all during the summer was her story. That is to say, what she had been through. Everyone in the District knew about it, it had been in the local papers. That it was her, Doris Flinkenberg from the cousin's house, who had found the corpse of the American girl. FIVE years after she drowned at Bule Marsh.

"She had died back in 1969 but her body didn't surface until five years later. It's true, no fraud about it there, no sir. But a strange body of water there in the woods, currents, deep and ice-cold. Like a refrigerator. She must have gotten stuck at the bottom in some way, everyone *knew* the whole time of course that she was there somewhere in the mire, the deep. And she had a red raincoat on; that is what Doris Flinkenberg saw. A red spot somewhere in the reeds . . . and yes, in and of itself, not much left of *her* then, of course.

"The corpse itself I mean. But the plastic was whole, plastic doesn't decompose. Think, Susette," Maj-Gun suddenly exclaims, "all the plastic that's still going to be here when we're gone—

"So, Susette. That was what I had in my head when I first tried to get to know Doris Flinkenberg that summer at the cemetery. And I had summer vacation, I had time to do a lot of thinking, so to speak.

"About a corpse in the marsh, for example, and what it would be like to find it. What something like that would feel like, as it were. That was what interested me. That experience, in general.

"But when I brought it up with her—well, yes—

"She really didn't want to talk to me. She got scared. I understood it later, in other words. What she got scared about.

"And in the fall, a few months later. *Scared shitless.* She was shaking—

"Then the fear in her had grown, a horrible flower had blossomed inside her. Or, like an island. Late one night, as I said. In the darkness, under a solitary lamp there at the cemetery. Just a few days before she shot herself. But no one could know it then, of course, not me either. I was completely defenseless.

"That revelation. You couldn't imagine there had been only a few months in between.

"Not everyone saw it, of course, but I've spent a lot of time at the cemetery, Susette, and grown up in a pastor's family and I have special eyes for that sort of thing.

"So beautiful on the outside, in the midst of every-thing—but it was her appearance that was deceptive.

"Wanted to sing. The folk song had come to her. *And the girl she walks in the ring with red golden ribbons. The girl came from her lover's meeting.*

"Cute. You might think.

"But, Susette, not at all. Because in the eyes of some there is—like there is age in my eyes, or timelessness. The weight, Susette. The eternal repetition. The idea behind the folk song. You walk out into the woods and there comes the wolf and tears your throat open. In all of the verses, over and over again, and the folk song has many verses, Susette, in time and space.

"And it should have happened then, Susette, between me and her. It should have been like in one of those stupid movies when after a brief conversation during which a lot of repressed feelings and aggressions you've had toward each other finally get aired and you actually get to talk, for real.

"Well. It didn't happen.

"Idiotic. I was just thinking about how angry I was."

•

"Wait a second, Maj-Gun," Susette says suddenly. "So you were standing there at the cemetery with the Liz Maalamaa Angel of Death mask on in the darkness and you scared her?"

"I already said that I regretted it!"

"And *how* may I ask do the American girl and the Boy in the woods fit into all this?"

"If you would have a little patience, Susette, for once," Maj-Gun says leisurely, "we'll get to it, we're almost there. The fear, her fear.

"I know interesting things about all sorts of things, Susette.

"And the fear then, for example the following. That it is a common feeling, like a state, which in the beginning has in and of itself been set off by something specific. But the fear itself, once it has been woken, doesn't disappear. It is separate: a latent state that just exists inside someone. Once scared, always scared. And you can, if you see it, draw it out.

"Call forth the fear in someone who is scared to begin with. Hold the one who is scared captive that way. So yes, as I said and I'm up front about it but I'm not proud of it no sir; I wanted to scare someone. Irritated at first when she just ran away from me and was busy with her own business. And then later in the fall when I was angry because the caretaker at the church had spoken with papa Pastor about my disobedience when he was there, demanded to have the extra key to the old, beautiful side of the cemetery returned, the one he had given me in secret.

"So yes, I told her about my horrible aunt Liz Maalamaa. The Angel of Death, with the mask on.

"But, Susette: this is where I wanted to get to. Her reaction was not in proportion to how scary it actually was. It was silly of course, she wasn't a child anymore, sixteen years old already and it was in the middle of the day.

"Later in the fall, *then* she was in and of itself so far gone in everything that if you had touched her with your pinkie then *fjutt* she would have sunk down to the ground. I didn't, of course, just asked a few questions about all sorts of things, the cousin's house, the American girl— which I had been going around, pondering about.

"But it was crazy, Susette. I just didn't understand the extent of it all. The gravity. It was only when I heard about the suicide that I understood.

"That she knew something about all of that, which made it so she didn't want to live any longer. And that was where the fear was coming from, its specific origin, so to speak. Maybe something she had always known but kept hidden, also from herself. But her friend, it had been just the two of them together, those two against the world and that had been a protection against it as well. And when it was gone then there was nothing.

"And the folk song. Came pouring into her."

"What everything did she know about?"

"Well, of course, the American girl. What really happened. She knew who killed her. And she couldn't live with the knowledge—

"Because it was someone close to her, a cousin.

"All of them were from there, of course. 'Cousins' from the cousin's house."

"What are you saying actually happened? There wasn't anything mysterious about that, was there?"

"Yes, Susette: that's where the problem lies. When the American girl died people said it was her boyfriend, who was jealous, who pushed her into the water from a cliff at Bule Marsh, and when he realized what he had done he became desperate and went and hanged himself.

"That boy. Also a 'cousin' in the cousin's house. There were several there. The three siblings, *the three cursed ones*. Rita, Solveig, the oldest brother Bencku, the Boy in the woods, in other words. And then Björn, who had come to the house together with the new mother. And when Björn was gone: Doris Flinkenberg.

"But, Susette, there was also *someone* else who loved her. And she, yes, she loved him too. Maybe even more than her real boyfriend. Despite the fact that it was impossible. The age difference alone. She was nineteen, the Boy in the woods was only thirteen. She had promised him something, but then later, she was leaving."

"Did she TELL you all of that? Doris Flinkenberg?"

Maj-Gun squirms a little. "Something like that, Susette. But, Susette, I *know* . . . *Nobody knew my rose of the world but me.* That is like the melody to the story. The rose in the wound. Which no one, no one suspects.

"And when I started the conversation about that then, you could see, she felt terror.

"The Boy in the woods. He was also her 'cousin' in the cousin's house you know. And brother to the other 'cousins.'

"Pure fantasies, Susette. I see what you're thinking.

"But she spoke about three siblings who shared a dreadful secret. She said that. And that everything was spinning, she didn't know what she should think or believe about anything. So just sang, folk songs.

"Yes. And then—" Maj-Gun hesitated a little. "Then she died. And when I heard about it . . . that was when *I* really fell in love with the Boy in the woods.

"I put two and two together and then it hit me. My love. Was cemented."

"But, Maj-Gun," Susette starts. "If you now know all of that for certain, shouldn't you go—to the police? Or should have gone, a long time ago?"

THEN Maj-Gun pays attention. Then Maj-Gun looks at Susette again, like at a ghost.

"The police? What, the long arm of the law?

"The law's long *fucking* arm I say. Don't you get *anything*? Djeessus. I'm planning on fucking.

"*I* love him, Susette. That kind of love. Like a fate you don't choose yourself.

"I want it to take possession of me. Want and want, moreover. Just as if love . . . were my will.

"Love him because he died for the sake of love. It's for real. Something that has happened. And the only salvation."

"Yes, you've said that."

"But don't you understand, Susette? Love like a conversion. Like when the princess kisses the frog, the spell that is broken. Or the white cat in the folk song that says to the prince 'cut my throat' and I will become your princess and the prince does and she becomes one.

"You have to be careful. You have to come to love. New."

"You've said that too—"

And silence, when it zooms through Susette's head of course that fundamental silliness in everything Maj-Gun is saying about the Boy in the woods, again: in other words, one Bencku in a barn where people partied and Bencku partied the most and for a while in his youth that made an impression, plus the fact that he was good-looking and the girls in the District had taken their bikes out there just in order to sit, lined up along the walls of the barn in the darkness, slowly becoming DRUNK too while waiting to be seen and some were cuter than others and then they were seen more often and so on. *Starling darling kiss ready for the evening entertainment.* It must be Maj-Gun Maalamaa in order to get something meaningful out of that.

But at the same time, on the other hand. Something that effectively obscures all desire to laugh for example. The three siblings. The cursed ones. Bencku, Rita—and Solveig. And Doris Flinkenberg, with the folk song. Not because Susette had not known, but she had, so to speak, not thought about Solveig that way. Solveig in the company car, Doris Flinkenberg on a cassette tape. Nah, Susette does not know anything about Doris, that fall when she killed herself, Susette had not been in the District any longer. And the cousin's house, where Susette had cleaned, cleaned, the old man, the cousin's papa. Who had died—and not that long ago either. And there, in the cousin's house, after the ambulance had left she walked around with death in her hands.

And so, still, how all of that is also suddenly obliterated because of another image, another scene.

Just: a terrified girl at the cemetery, Maj-Gun with the mask, the Angel of Death Liz Maalamaa.

"Damn it, Maj-Gun! You scared her! With your damned mask! And do you HAVE to say the Boy in the woods all the time? He's probably a hundred years old and his name is Bengt!"

·

Damp. Down on the ground, reality. Maj-Gun grows quiet, does not say anything, looks down—at her hands, her nails.

"My bladder is about to explode," she says then and gets up. "I have to go pee."

And she walks out into the hall and into the bathroom. Susette gets up off the couch too, opens the window slightly and fresh air pours into the room. Starts picking up empty coffee cups, empty ice cream bowls and carries them into the kitchen and turns on the hot water and puts the dishes to soak in the sink.

A relief, as if something had let go, no fury, nothing is pounding now. No "What does Maj-Gun want from me?

What is she doing in my apartment?" No feeling of connections, rags, fungus.

But just ordinary, normal. The cat is purring at her legs now, begging for food because it is hungry. Susette takes a can of cat food out of the cabinet, looks for the can opener but as usual does not find it, takes the old pair of scissors instead, uses the tip to make a gash in the lid of the can and bends it up, ladles the food out onto a plate and sets it on the floor in front of the cat who starts eating.

Hears Maj-Gun behind her, coming from the bathroom, and in the midst of everything Susette thinks of something funny, which is also an ordinary way of finishing a conversation.

"Maj-Gun!" she calls. "Maybe you're right. Maybe you don't need to wait so long. The Boy in the woods. Bengt. He inherited the whole house."

But then Maj-Gun is standing in the doorway with a pistol in her hand.

"Damn, Susette. What are you doing with a revolver in your sauna bag?"

•

On the other hand, still, at the newsstand, a few evenings later. "More cat food?" Maj-Gun in the doorway, puffing on a cigarette that she tosses away half smoked when she catches sight of Susette who is approaching across the square, holds the door open, bows. "Just because you're a duchess—" Susette shakes her head, Maj-Gun does not finish the sentence, they go in.

"Think about what Madonna has done for fashion! It's crazy! Djeessuss!"

A girl is crossing the square, they see her through the window where they are, as always, sitting on either side of the counter among all of the magazines, lottery tickets, games. The same girl as all the times before: hair teased, bow in her hair, medium-length leather jacket, knickknacknecklaces. And Maj-Gun who yells what she has yelled a thousand times before, and lacking just as much irony in her voice—the opposite, almost filled with reverence, esteem.

Susette who laughs, Maj-Gun who stares at her, and speaks so that it sounds like an accusation:

"You're so spaced out, Susette. Don't know anything about what is going on!

"If I looked like you, Susette. Not exactly what you look like now, but *the potential.*

"Come along and change!" Maj-Gun calls out. "With you as bait, Susette. To life, an invitation. NOW we're going to the disco."

And that is what they do the following Saturday when Maj-Gun does not have to work: go into the city by the sea and buy clothes and then they go to the disco. Only clothes for Susette, because there is nothing in large enough sizes in the regular stores for Maj-Gun, something she cheerily points out. She is wearing what she calls the tiger blouse party shirt: an ill-tempered leopard mouth with red sequins that swell over her stomach.

And Susette in the fitting rooms in the stores, in the junior department: Maj-Gun who is lugging clothes between the fitting room and the department, fitting room and department, serving as fashion adviser, choosing and deciding. Dresses Susette up for all she is worth, like bait. Broad-shouldered yellow blazer, aviator pants with creases, and in front of the mirror in the restroom at the train station Susette's hair is combed back into a curly, poodlelike hairstyle with a ponytail.

The disco is enormous, an ash-gray hall; Susette is sucking on a Blue Angel, which is a blue drink with an umbrella stuck in the glass with white foam on top. *"It's stardust,"* Maj-Gun explains when they take a seat on a group of couches suitably close to the dance floor, *"stardust stardust,"* stirs her finger in the whiteness, sticks her finger in her mouth, "mmmmm." Raises her milk glass—Maj-Gun never drinks anything stronger—says cheers! One Blue Angel, two Blue Angels, and a few more: Maj-Gun picks umbrellas out of the glasses as Susette finishes them, one after another, places the umbrellas in a row on the table. Maj-Gun orders new drinks from the waiter or goes to the bar herself and brings more when the hall and the sofas fill with people; "you can't yell *waiter* because then they'll get offended!" Maj-Gun drums her fingers on the low coffee table in time with the music and Susette is drinking, later dancing—drinking, dancing, boys are asking her to dance. One boy after another, boys boys how they crowd around her: "She has good luck!" Maj-Gun laughs when Susette returns to the sofa between the dances only to immediately have a new boy there who is going to lead her out onto the dance floor. "Luck, luck." Maj-Gun laughs until she stops laughing, new people sit down on the sofas, lots of people, strange people, forcing Maj-Gun farther and farther into the corner. Susette too, of course, but then she is not really there but on the dance floor, on the dance floor the entire time, and gradually Maj-Gun grows quiet, just sits, does not say anything at all anymore.

But Susette on the dance floor: under the blue, white lights, in the smoke that comes from the floor and whirls around the dancers under the disco ball turning around around silver and glittering on the ceiling. Susette who is dancing, dancing—and sees Maj-Gun at a distance, on the sofa, among all the unfamiliar people, squeezed in between them, in the corner. And not that Maj-Gun is looking in Susette's direction any longer, does not try to make eye contact with Susette in order to signal an understanding like she did earlier in the evening. Now, is sitting, *is sitting where she sits*, among all the ordinary girls and boys who are swelling in every direction on the group of sofas, pretending not to notice Maj-Gun, not bothering about her, Maj-Gun is like air to them. But yet, it is still Maj-Gun who, due to her size, is the most obvious of them all. Is shining, fleshy white around the arms, paler than ever: Maj-Gun like a beacon through the gray smoke and silver light, a leopard mouth adorned with sequins exploding over her enormous bosom and a half-filled glass of milk on the table in front of her that she no longer touches.

Rag doll. "Dance my doll while you are young, when you become old you'll be no fun." No, Maj-Gun does not sit there and hum that rhyme now anymore either, just sits, Maj-Gun, alone. *I'm more romantically inclined. The Boy in the woods will come soon. And all my longing will be enclosed in my dream of love.* Maj-Gun's stories about love, Susette suddenly finds herself thinking on the dance floor: Why can't Maj-Gun get them, fantasies or not?

•

But Maj-Gun disappears there, no thoughts any longer, out of sight in the sea of all the people on the dance floor. Susette who is dancing, dancing, with boys boys, *all* the boys and they do not call her *the Angel of Death* even though it feels that way. Because it is like this and it is inexplicable: "Such a beautiful little Angel of Death." Her mother, her voice in Susette's head in the midst of everything, and cuckoo of course because her mother who in and of herself had death on her mind those last years *never* spoke like that. But now, in any case, like from a dream: glitter glitter in her head in time with the *stromblights*, which Maj-Gun earlier in the evening had for sure incorrectly informed Susette that was what those blinking lights at the disco were called. Her mother, in a memory that in other words is not a memory even though it could have been one of course because in reality, during Susette's childhood and also as a teenager after her father's death when Susette had quit school and been working full-time at the nursing home for the elderly and infirm, she and her mother had done the same thing. Picked flowers and taken them to the cemetery, set them out there. On *the Graves of the Forgotten*: that is what her mother used to say and Susette thought it was beautiful. All of these graves that no living person took care of aside from the general grave maintenance of the parish.

"If you later come to wander in the valley of the shadow of death no harm will befall you." Her mother had also said that. And in the church later, during Susette's teenage years, *her mother and funerals.* Suddenly they had been there, for real, she and her mother at the very back of the church, together, her mother had sung along with the hymn. And afterward, at the funeral reception in the fellowship hall, organized addresses on the funeral table in alphabetical order, in neat fans *with a grave and dignified hand* about which her mother used to preach to Susette in silence. "The grieving have their own sorrow to think about." These dead ones then, not exactly strangers but certainly often ones they had not known directly—for example, former patients at the nursing home, which was Susette's place of employment at the time.

Her mother, glitter, at the disco: Susette small again, during her childhood. Her mother who suddenly, in the middle of picking flowers on the way to the cemetery, looks at her daughter and does not say what she says in reality, "What beautiful flowers you have in your bouquet, Susette," but:

"What a beautiful little Angel of Death, my Susette."

•

And it IS true: the essence of a development. The normalcy that disappeared and was obliterated. And she, Susette, could not say when it happened, just a peculiar transition from the one to the other.

The rug rags that suddenly piled up in the kitchen in the house: garments, garments, old garments and towels and worn-out sheets, you cut and cut but could not keep up. "It's not easy living in a house of sorrow." Her mother's words, at the rug rag bucket, and later: all the death that was suddenly everywhere but rug rags were to be collected and cut up and wrapped in spools that would be placed back into the bags for weaving even though the weaver had been dead for a long time already. Her father who, while he was still alive, had built houses out of balsa, *a fragile structure*. Measured and cut out teensy pieces from paper-thin wood with a small saw, glued the pieces together carefully, and Susette had liked watching. One of her father's hobbies in the living room in the evenings in the house during the time when everything was still normal and ordinary. That house, it had been standing there on the living room table later—

And buried in rags, crushed by the weight of rug rags too.

"Where is the weaver, Mom? And the loom, where is it?"

Gone from door to door, she and her mother, in the picturesque suburbs below the square where ordinary families lived in beautiful single-family homes, a lot of family noise and dogs and cats and neat gardens; apple trees, plum trees, and cherry trees in the gardens. Her mother and her, pushing a wheelbarrow in front of them over the cobblestones, over asphalt and on sandy paths. Rung doorbells, knocked and asked for, begged for, *silk velvet rag scraps*, everything that could be woven into rugs instead of being thrown out. And Susette who had been ashamed, gradually anyway: when everyone knew that the rug weaver in the Outer Marsh was dead and there was no other loom anywhere. Transported plastic bags home and washed garments, or not washed them, started cutting right away, long scraps that were called loom lengths, to roll up onto the spools later. But still, away from everyone's eyes, easier to be there, in the house, the kitchen. The mother and Susette, just the two of them, each with scissors, each sitting on a stool at the bucket . . . and Susette who left her first love because of the grief, the death, her mother—or not left exactly, just walked away from the rectory once and then never went back. Her father's death, which got in the way then; maybe she thought he, the boyfriend, would arrive as her savior, take her away from the house, her mother, all of

it. On the other hand, furthermore, she had not thought
that way at all: she knew of course Tom Maalamaa was
not like that.

Her mother with the better scissors, the textile scissors, her dearest possession, you might think. Were kept
stored in their own case in a kitchen drawer and were
not to be used for anything other than cutting fabric so
that the edges would not become dulled, her mother had
been very careful about that. Her mother who had asked
Susette to sharpen the scissors before using them, her
eyes were so bad.

So no, you could not have lived there. Understandable.
Gone away and stayed away too long, and Maj-Gun on
the telephone: "Your mother. They buried her. Mydeep-
estcondolences. When are you coming home?"

"Calm down now," Maj-Gun said again, when Susette
had returned, her hand on Susette's shoulder. "I understand completely."

"Understandable." The mess in the house when Susette returned after having been gone for three years. Her
mother who had been a "collector" due to the war, that
generation. And in the mess, Maj-Gun who had stood
and said exactly that: "It's the war, she told me. Understandable." All the old rags in the plastic bags along the
walls, everywhere, cut, uncut—and when Susette became
better they had gotten the house in order. Thrown things
out, dragged out black plastic bags filled with clothes,
rags, glass jars for flowers, plastic yogurt containers for
the flowers . . . which her mother had collected.

And so, still, in the midst of everything, in the middle
of the cleaning, sat down there again. At the rag bucket
in the kitchen, with the scissors.

"Your mother. She was for real.

"She didn't give in.

"Such a cute little Angel of Death.

"We cut rug rags . . . we talked about you.

"Silk velvet rag scraps—"

Each on her own stool, Maj-Gun's stories later, cloth in long strips that whirled down into the plastic bucket between them.

Who was Maj-Gun?

•

Still, so easy to blame it on Maj-Gun. Her silliness, stupid talk. Maj-Gun had been friendly too, for real. Comforted, in her own way, as best she could. And not held Susette responsible for her lies. Lied, could not stop lying, had to have another story, coherence, there has to be life.

"Poland." And a stomachache.

". . . the black Madonnas, the incomprehensible language . . ."

"You were never really there. And certainly not pregnant? Take it easy now, Susette. I understand completely."

Still, Maj-Gun, who was she? Majjunn, like a sound in your mouth?

"Hell, Susette, what are you doing with a revolver in your sauna bag?"

And suddenly, something she had forgotten, even though it was not more than a week ago. Maj-Gun had been standing in the kitchen in her apartment with the pistol in her hand. "Djeessuss, Susette." As if she had not known up or down, what she could have said otherwise.

Then put the pistol to her heart.

"Maj-Gun!" Susette shouted. "It could be loaded!"

How Maj-Gun looked at her then. "Take the pistol and put it away, Susette."

Snip, nothing.

As if nothing had happened.

CAN you actually go on after this as if nothing happened?

Answer. Yes. You can.

Maj-Gun in her childhood, the Pastor's Crown Princess, at the cemetery. Stood and pointed at the Confession Grove.

"There it is. Shall I show you the way?"

"I'm fascinated by the Death in her." Her first boyfriend, Tom Maalamaa, had spoken that way once at the cemetery. To his sister Maj-Gun: the two siblings, who otherwise were always at each other's throats, could, you had discovered, have certain very close moments just the two of them. Like that time in the cemetery back when Tom Maalamaa was her boyfriend and she had been on her way into his room where his sister also was: they had not noticed her at first and Susette had stood in the doorway and heard them talking to each other like that, certainly not about her but it still felt that way.

Two children at the cemetery, with masks, Liz Maalamaa.

Answer again. Yes. You can. Because those were just images, scenes.

All of that darkness, the death, nourished by guilt from longing, fear of yourself, not from Maj-Gun but from herself.

The whole time with Maj-Gun, as if that was exactly the point with Maj-Gun. How she calls forth those things in you. Intensifies them until they roar in your head and dunk dunk become more real than the original scenes, what actually happened.

More real than the real. Maj-Gun in the kitchen, how they were cutting rug rags, Maj-Gun's laughter, Maj-Gun's panting laugh, the sweat running down her face. Maj-Gun at the newsstand . . . the ordinary that became strange all of the time. *In the midst of life there is an instinct to death.* She wanted to get away from there, but still, had to stay, motionless on the stool.

You thought you could see horrible slimy underworld-fungus hanging from Maj-Gun's head as if it were hair.

Something held them together, but what? Maj-Gun like a message she tried to decipher.

Something held them together. In the midst of life . . .

And neither of them wanted it, as if both of them were fighting it. *Starling darling,* to life, an invitation.

Still: "a logic you have to go along with."

From room to room, they were in the same room.

Maj-Gun, her, and her mother.

Crehp. Crehp.

Maj-Gun, a figure, *silk velvet rag scraps* in her head.

"I was standing there, reeling in the fear." Susette in the middle of the ring on a square. Cars driving around. Nah. She had *not* been afraid. Other than, then, of a destiny. Had wanted to blow up the ring, Maj-Gun, everything else in the way. *We are two Angels of Death, Susette, in a timelessness.*

•

Still. Susette. She is not there after all, on the square. She is here of course. Has been here the entire time, dancing, on the floor of the disco.

"Little" Susette, big earrings and a lot, even though you cannot see it, of death inside her head.

•

She becomes aware of everything again: the smoke, the sweat, the people.

Blue Angel. The nausea wells up inside her, she has to run to the restroom, push her way past the whole line and puke and puke in the stall and when she is back in the hall she searches for Maj-Gun but does not find her.

The sofa where they had been sitting is filled with other people. Four umbrellas are neatly lined up on the table. Among the cigarette butts and stickiness from a milk glass, half empty.

"Hey." A hand on her shoulder. She is standing face-to-face with Tom Maalamaa.

In a blazer, some sort of beard, and a polo shirt.

•

And Susette Packlén, a bait for life, has run, is running running away, has left the disco.

The cat meets her in the hallway in her little apartment when she comes home.

Then she is completely calm, takes off the horrible new clothes.

The avenues, running in the avenues.

Overturning houses.

Houses made of balsa. A fragile structure.

Buries her face in the cat's fur.

"Mom. I have the feeling that I want it to be over now. Everything."

•

Susette who is sitting on the sofa in her little apartment and cutting up the garments that had been bought that day. The parrot jacket with the shoulder pads, the creased pants.

The cat deep asleep in the corner of the sofa, in the light of a solitary floor lamp.

With the "textile scissors," an inheritance, one of the few things of her mother's Susette had taken with her from the parental home before it was sold. Long strips, loom lengths.

SUSETTE, MAJ-GUN, AND THE BOY
IN THE WOODS, 1989

THE NEXT MORNING SUSETTE PACKS her back-
pack and takes the morning bus out to the capes to bury
the white kitty.

Sunny day, few clouds, tepid. No one on the bus except her. She gets off at the last stop at the grove of trees
where the Second Cape and the sea are, on the other
side. Roaring, wind in the trees, is felt, is heard.

She walks back on the road toward the mainland,
onto the cousin's property from the left, where it looks
deserted as usual. To the barn, which is never locked,
across from the house where she is also going to leave
something, but it will have to be later, the other thing is
more important now. Takes a shovel from the barn and
continues into the woods on the path that starts on the
other side of the road below a high hill where a half-
burned house gapes with a large, dark hole in its side,
like always. Otherwise it is quiet, no people anywhere.

Into the woods, to a place where the ground is soft
enough to be dug into. Not particularly easy to find, she
has to walk quite a ways, backpack heavy on her back,
shovel in her hand. Turns down on the path to Bule
Marsh, which reveals itself, still, shiny water, between
the trees. Does not continue all the way down because
she discovers a pretty glade a few feet off to the side of
the path. Hardwood trees, soft mossiness. Shovel in the

205

ground, yes, no bedrock there. Carefully takes away the whole layer of moss first.

When the hole is deep enough she takes the package with the dead animal out of her bag: has wound it in terry cloth towels and in thin light blue plastic bags used for cleaning. Lays the bundle in the ground, hears a noise behind her, turns around. He is standing there on the path looking at her. She becomes a bit nervous but not scared; not because of him, he is not a stranger after all, but the surprise.

He asks her if she needs help. "Nah." How thick and strange her own voice sounds, in the midst of everything. Together they cover the bundle with soil and place the layer of moss on top.

Later she is going to tell him about the beautiful small white cat she took from the Glass House on the Second Cape where she had cleaned during the summer, about the French family, the diplomatic family, that just left it behind. About how she brought it home and how she had it for only a few weeks when the night before she met him she found it dead on the floor in the hall in her apartment. That she did not want to take it to a cemetery for animals, or to the veterinarian, but put it in the earth, out in nature, where it belonged, where it came from.

Now they were walking in silence back on the path toward the road, she with her backpack in hand, he with the shovel. He says he saw her from the cousin's house. Saw her take the shovel from the barn, became curious. She says quickly that she only wanted to borrow the shovel, she knew there was a shovel there since she used to come to the house and clean when the old man was still alive, she works for Solveig's cleaning company. And then suddenly it also occurs to her *who* he is. Here. *The Boy in the woods.* Solveig's brother. Bengt.

How long had he been here, in the cousin's house? He shrugs. A while. Then Susette thinks he looks the way she had imagined based on Solveig's descriptions. Like someone who has been here and there and at some point stopped accounting for anything, even with just a little bit of effort, placing anything into some sort of context, coherence. "Completely washed up." Which Solveig had also said, in the company car. "Gone to hell."

He takes her hand on the forest path. Strange. She squirms out of his grip and when they come out of the woods she keeps going, alone. Along the road, in the direction of the main country road and the town center. She walks for several miles, then the bus from the capes comes, she gets on.

We can leave her here, Susette Packlén. Wandering forward along the road, one fall day in the sun, the Fjäll-räven backpack dangling over her shoulder. Small poor child I am, in cowboy boots, *boots.* Or on the bus, where she is the only passenger on this Sunday morning. Gets off at the square in the town center, walks home.

Arrives at her apartment, it is well cleaned. Hangs her backpack on the hook in the bathroom, again. Yes, she has forgotten the pistol; it was going to go back to the cousin's house of course. At the bottom of the backpack, wrapped in a towel, that too, as always.

At that point she is so tired that she falls asleep with her clothes on, on the sofa in her tiny living room. Sleeps for a long time, without dreaming.

And in the evening, he is there. At her door, ringing the bell. "Hey." *Newsstand toppler.* She invites him in.

·

Newsstand toppler? One evening, a weekday a few weeks later, Maj-Gun Maalamaa is at Susette's door. She has two trays of cat food, in cans, 2×24 in each, which she bought at the wholesale store where she actually should not be allowed to shop, not even for the newsstand, because all of the acquisitions at the newsstand are dealt with centrally by the Head Office. But Maj-Gun has been to the wholesale store anyway, with her wholesaler's card, on the newsstand's budget, in and of itself, on the Head Office's behalf. Something in the stockroom that had run out, needed to be restocked quickly. Chewy ducks, small sweet troll hearts filled with truffel or the like which there is a rapid consumption of in certain seasons at her newsstand on the square in the town center. You barely have time to fill the minimal plastic bags in which the sweets are sold, five or ten in each, tied at the ends in knots, and they are sold out. So Maj-Gun has, in exceptional cases, been driven in the Head Office's truck to the wholesaler in the industrial area on the outskirts of the city by the sea, from the newsstand and back.

The cat food she had probably paid for with her own money at the wholesale shop: a whole load to drag around, the apostle's horses, from the square almost half a mile past the new and the old cemeteries to the apartment complex where Susette lives in the hills above the town center.

Filled with anecdotes from the day and similar days and the past days—it has been a while since Susette properly visited the newsstand in the evenings—Maj-Gun rings Susette's doorbell in the D-block.

Susette opens and Maj-Gun walks in, "here," giving the cat food cans to Susette and luring *kitty kitty kitty* but then she is already in the tiny living room and there is the Boy in the woods, he says "hi."

"The cat?" is the only thing Maj-Gun gets out, she is standing in the middle of the room. Susette, behind her, says that it is not there anymore, "It got run over."

There is a language that is called the Winter Garden. Pictures on the wall, soiled water colors and a sweetness in the room, stink, tobacco, sweat, beer.

My love, *pure and true.*

The surprise, the heartbreak. Maj-Gun, speechless, stumbles out.

We can leave her here.

•

Maj-Gun and Susette, November 1989. They meet again, it is about a month later then, at the beginning of November, in the boathouse, the American girl's hangout on the Second Cape. Snow is suddenly pouring down: in the morning, or maybe it was early afternoon, when Maj-Gun came down there to the boathouse, the ground was still bare, the hard wind, the waves were crashing against the other side of the pine forest grove. Cold, yes, but the freshness, the openness, coming there.

To the boathouse, that is where she is, Maj-Gun Maalamaa, sleeping on the floor in the middle of the room among old junk; nah, nah, not exactly the leftovers of some old story, no remains like that either, meaningless now, so long ago. But things from the sea, fishing tackle, the like—a broken outboard motor that someone had thrown an old rug over. It is the rug Maj-Gun pulls over herself on the floor. Falls asleep, sleeps deeply, does not dream about anything in particular, about the square maybe, hayseeds at the square, *pistol awakening* with their revolvers, how they shot the empty tin cans. Not a dream you have been longing for either; one of these hayseeds had, earlier that morning, picked her up when she was wandering around in the town center and driven her out to the Second Cape and gotten rid of her after a brief exchange of words a few miles from the cousin's house where she had later walked, and been there, before she came here.

And when she wakes up on the floor in the boathouse it is almost with a smile about her dream, then she becomes aware of where she is, and the snow that is snowing now and—a dark shadow on the terrace. She crawls up, Susette turns around, and they discover each other at almost the same time, on either side of the window. Both of them just as surprised, it was not the intention after all, in no way was it arranged.

Susette comes into the boathouse. Words are exchanged, maybe no words. But Susette who is just standing there, with her big empty eyes and Maj-Gun who attacks her, suddenly, hits and hits and hits. *Things to add to the Winter Garden: Young man against a background of flames, 1952, was it in Rio de Janeiro? But in any case, that place, a hotel room, where Liz Maalamaa hit the wall for the first time, hamba hamba, the Girl from Borneo, she had bought one of those statues at the market, the one that flew out of her hand when she flew in the room, on top of the bed, the last thing Liz Maalamaa saw before she lost consciousness, everything went black, a portrait: young man against a background of flames, on a wall. Or did she see? Because in reality, when she came to again, there was only a bouquet of flowers in a vase on the wall and her husband was remorseful, bought her silver shoes, that was him.* But Maj-Gun Maalamaa in the boathouse in the month of November 1989 who hits and hits: and Susette Packlén, little Susette Packlén, who does not put up a fight really, loses her balance, falls backward, hits her head on an anchor and just lies there. Already dusk now, Maj-Gun who leaves and walks out into the snow.

And up in the cousin's house, on the other side of the grove of pine trees, *the Boy in the woods.* He is lying on the floor in a room as well, in blood.

Walk walk in whiteness and walk in whirling snow that shrouds you, walk walk walk in the snow.

THE ANIMAL CHILD
AND THE LAW
(THE GIRL FROM
BORNEO)

(Maj-Gun Maalamaa, November 1989–
January 1990)

LIZ MAALAMAA AND THE ROSES

TO THE WINTER GARDEN: a rose, a type of rose. Flaming Carmen/Carmen in flames.

One of the types that Tobias Forsström is going to try. to cultivate in the greenhouse.

Liz Maalamaa did not like roses. Or maybe "didn't like" is too strong.

But she had no relation to roses.

Sometimes, of course, she thought about roses. She had a romantic side too, of course, don't we all?

But in reality, not roses either, in that way (there had been lilies of the valley in her wedding bouquet, she had liked the simplicity). But when she thought about roses, this is how she thought about roses:

The roses had the look of flowers that are looked at, that is how she thought, on the one hand, like T. S. Eliot (in later years she read a bit of poetry, but in other words not much, scant).

Liz Maalamaa was more robustly inclined, her dreams had been concrete ones. For example, comfortable shoes, and China.

On the other hand, a proverb. *Life is also a dance on a bed of roses.*

A strange proverb, because roses, they prick of course, whether you sleep on them or not.

And in time, because she had thought about it mostly when she was young, she understood that it was a rather universal wonder. She was not the only one who had thought about it either.

But roses, in general. *Carmen in Flames.* Flaming Carmen. Would have been altogether *too* . . . for her.

SHE CAME FROM BORNEO, she dances there, in the docklands. "The Girl from Borneo," it was an amulet, that was where Maj-Gun had gotten the idea to call herself the Girl from Borneo in that *hamba hamba* Day of Desire dance. Woman with slanted eyes, dark hair, and flamenco skirts. A gift to her niece, her goddaughter Majjunn, from the aunt sometime when Maj-Gun was younger too. A souvenir from Rio de Janeiro where the aunt and her husband went on their honeymoon, a round-the-world trip with some cruises, it might have been 1952 (the silver shoes were from Rio de Janeiro too).

So she, the amulet figure, was not from Borneo at all. Maj-Gun had made the name up. Inspired in turn by another story that in turn will inspire her a great deal later, later in her early twenties when she leaves her parental home, her possessions in a seaman's chest a third of a mile from the rectory down to the town center where her first rented room is located—she has the amulet with her then as well. She is, in any case, thinking like that, then. A story like that, so amusing . . . but it does not turn out like that of course.

It is, in other words, that story, a story about two houses, down in the town center. In the suburbs, below the square where she later starts working at the newsstand. Tall, white houses, "colonial architecture," a bit of the American Deep South style, so maybe not very much of the Southern Pacific in them really. But the South Pacific houses is what they are called, Java and Sumatra—those are their names too. And at some point in her childhood, Maj-Gun and her brother Tom have in a passing sort of way spoken about those unusually beautiful houses. "Twin houses" because they are identical in plan and construction—and completely different from all of the other small picturesque buildings around, which come later.

Probably a hundred years old, two captains lived there. They were brothers, confirmed bachelors, who had sailed the seas to strange countries and had gotten to see so many strange things. Like the South Pacific islands, Java, Borneo, Sumatra. Come home, leave the harbor, try and relive their beautiful memories here. It does not really work, there are just occasional photographs, black and white, barely that kind even, and if they exist they are rather meaningless. Function mainly as documentation; *I was there* but otherwise no real life or real feeling in them. But *Negro in Sunshine*, hanging breasts on dark patinated native women, almost naked, next to *White Man in the Tropical Hat*, pulled down properly so that you cannot even see the eyes.

It wasn't like that. So the captains built these houses instead and lived there for the rest of their days, each on his own hill across from each other. They had been confirmed bachelors, both of them, had no blood offspring, but one of them got married to his housekeeper in his later years, a Ms. Lindström who was a widow with her own children, and when the captain passed away the Sumatra house went to the Lindström family—and Göran Lindström, one of the sons and eventually also a teacher at the school, would later, in addition to his wife Gunilla and their children, take it over.

It turned out that the other captain had been a bit in debt, so after his death the Java house had to be sold at a compulsory auction; it was purchased at the end of the '50s by an engineering family named Packlén.

The Girl from Borneo, that is where the journey leads, from the rectory to Java and Sumatra. First to Java, later, as it turns out, it is not planned but is a coincidence, in reality to Sumatra. The seaman's chest with her possessions loaded onto a wheelbarrow that she pushes a few blocks over the cobblestones, from the one house to the other.

And of course, it should have been a nice story to tell, rather amusing too, even beautiful—because those two houses really were beautiful, white with bright attic rooms that would become her room in each house. And nice people there too: Packlén who cut rug rags in Java, and Lindström, the teacher's family, in Sumatra. So, in a way, she really would have been able to get on well there.

But it was funny. Because at the same time as she was supposed to be in this funny story, the Girl from Borneo—not the Harlot anymore, but the Seaman, with the seaman's chest—it started falling apart for her. But not so that the story itself would betray her; it would go on as usual, Borneo and Java and Sumatra—but her personally. Suddenly there was no room in it. Or another room—but which one?—other than the one she had planned for herself.

It was in the attic room in Java where it all started. She had come there with her books, compendiums, was going to study for the entrance exams at the university.

There turned out not to be so much studying after all, and the letters she wrote to her brother who was eagerly studying and dynamically interested in his major—these letters where she vividly and humorously was describing *her* journey, from Borneo to the South Pacific Islands and yet it was still just ha-ha-ha the town center, the District! Just that way—*think, Java, now that I've arrived here* . . . yes, they had rarely, gradually never, been finished, and besides, she had very quickly stopped writing to her brother altogether.

All of that in and of itself might be meaningless, but still funny, which only her brother, she thought, would be able to understand. Was forgotten. Even the interesting information that the woman, who often sat in the kitchen on the ground floor in Java, was the mother of the big-eyed Susette Packlén from the cemetery, *your first girlfriend!*, which when she figured that out, she really thought she would be able to take pleasure in it— to be able to write that, to Tom!—yes, even that started feeling meaningless before she even had the energy to get out her light pink stationery.

But still, despite everything: it was meaningful anyway, what happened in Java, even if from the outside, it looked liked nothing was happening. A slightly crazy woman who cut rug rags and talked about things like death and grief—but in a particular way, which was absolutely impossible to recreate or communicate directly afterward, just a feeling of something real, almost completely revolutionary in Maj-Gun Maalamaa's life. And it had such an effect on her—in addition to the fact that she and the woman who would die just a few years later became good friends—that everything changed. She threw away, stopped thinking about—in her head that is—everything, all stories, all amusing things, anything smart, all the thises thats from her fantasy, rather started writing, something simple, honest, real. And that is what she did in the attic room, summers, winters when she was not at the newsstand or with the woman on the first floor, wrote and wrote and it was to darkness and to light it was to everything and back and forth, but *there it was*, worlds opened. And were imposed with meaning, another light—her personally, about her, everything she saw—

And did not see. The woman died, the big-eyed one came home, Susette Packlén, then they almost became friends. A while, something with Susette, always with Susette . . . yes something, something called forth in Maj-Gun . . . something she wanted to get to and was frightened by . . . no, it could not be explained, but a driving force . . . to that in particular, *there it was*, like with the woman with the rug rags in the kitchen, Susette's mother, entirely real, realistic.

But then she was in Sumatra, and for many years already. And had lost a thread, a rag, while at the same time she had all the threads, rags in her hand—wrote and wrote, further, but all of the stories just multiplied in her head. And at the newsstand and in "The Book of Quick-Witted Sayings" where she sometimes wrote down this and sometimes the other, "useful," *my statements* or whatever it was—it multiplied, but *there it was*, I am without space, it did not exist. And she had to get to it, could not live without it.

And then Susette was there again, a big-eyed one, who was a connection, because among all the stories she had in her head, everything she had dragged out of herself, all of the this and that and the Literature, the Critics, with the new landlords, Gunilla, Göran, *art was suddenly happening here, in this house* like starry-eyed listeners in the house, so that was what she gradually started telling Susette, the rag cutter woman's daughter, which was the only real thing—and yet that realness did not exist in what was told. Strange? Yes? Because she would become angry at Susette later, and kill her.

Out of love, another story, which suddenly, even though it was not real, also was. All the feelings, everything that flew past, just sitting . . . Because it was also like that with all of these stories, even though they were a façade for what was real, *it was there*, so they started, like the story about the Girl from Borneo from Java to Sumatra, to affect her too.

Anyway, confused. Anyway, she got on very well in Sumatra. Better than anywhere else, after the rectory—she loved the children, and Göran and Gunilla. That is what it was like—well. Maybe this should not be investigated further here, it just was like that. Strange. But in the end, a confusing fall, it is this fall 1989, led up to the horrible, the horrible thing that has now happened and that is irrevocable, thus she has been sitting there in Göran and Gunilla's kitchen serving them stories about the Girl from Borneo as if on a silver platter, and they have been enjoying it so. How beautiful, the seaman, the seaman's chest . . .

And of course how beautiful. But what would she do with that story now? And everything else, which she has, as it were, gotten herself mixed up in? Nothing worked. Yes, except maybe. Follow the story line to the end, in order to find the beginning of another story, her own, if afterward—a story that is about losing everything and winning everything but then not knowing what you should do with any of it. Complicated? Metaphysical? Maybe. "We aren't much for the metaphysical," as her brother Tom will tell her later in life when they, after a great deal of shilly-shallying, renew their brother-sister bond for real, and then Maj-Gun is able to start a future, become a lawyer, the Red One, become skinny, *after the Scarsdale Diet, anything is possible*, and have her own life, with her own independent rooms to live in.

Well, follow the story line to its end. And then this is not the least bit metaphysical. Just the Girl from Borneo, the Happy Harlot, or the Seaman (and she threw that amulet away somewhere a long time ago of course—does not exist). Because in the final chapter of that story the following now happens: the shipwreck.

And if you have been shipwrecked then you have been shipwrecked, you have come from nowhere to nowhere, are no one—someone who is clinging to a nearby piece of driftwood and lets go.

THE SHIPWRECK

Experiences from the apartment. She becomes the Animal Child. Peering into the darkness. In that apartment, an apartment complex on the hills above the town center. November 1989. Three–four days maybe, does not keep track of the time when she is there. The Animal Child is timelessness, notime.

She is alone there. The pictures on the walls.

"The Winter Garden." That "exhibition." At one point in time this was a lovers' nest, abandoned now, has not been taken down. She does not see the pictures. Was in a story once. *The Boy in the woods.* There are no stories here, nothing and notime.

She has turned off all of the lights. She is in the dark. The Animal Child's peering eyes. Dark dots in a darkness. Waiting, different kinds of waiting, rumbling in the pipes in the building, the building is an organism.

Snowfall, slush, rain, snowfall, rain, decay.

Tear apart, "I'm fascinated by the Death in her," "the manuscript of a life." Tear, rip into pieces, and "The Book of Quick-Witted Sayings."

The wolf, the folk song. A cassette tape from another room. From room to room to room.

Tearing to pieces. Time. Cat food. Sirens, ambulances, police cars, blue lights, waiting, different types of waiting.

•

Later she is in another apartment. Music surges there in the evenings: *Carmen. Ratata.* Lucia di Lammermoor's aria of craziness, it is eight minutes long. At a low volume, in the background, but the walls in the apartment are thin, all noises can easily be heard. The Manager—it is his apartment—has carried his stereo into the room next door: a simple gadget, a small portable record player, two plastic boxes for speakers. He is the one on the other side of the door, which is closed in the evenings, reading, working. Using his small nightstand as a workspace since the desk is in the other room, or his bed, a lot of papers, books, spread around him. She has glanced in.

There is also a dining table in the room she is in, a television, and a sofa bed where she sleeps in a sleeping bag at night, on top of clean sheets. A bookshelf with many books. *History and Progress, We Are the Future, Architecture and Crime*, a lot of titles fly by. *Nordic Family Book*, an encyclopedia, several volumes, "half French," a funny term that pops into her head, from the rectory, another context. Pushes it away, or pushes, does not push—however it is, not consciously. Gardening books, books about butterflies, insects, birds, a herbarium for collecting plants.

They eat their evening meals in this apartment at the dining table at five thirty in the evening when the Manager has come home from work. Watch the news. At quarter past six and eight thirty, both newscasts.

Sometimes the Manager is on the telephone out in the hall, the door is closed, the music in his room is playing. He speaks softly, she cannot make out what he is saying.

Sleeps. A lot. She falls asleep as soon as she rests her head on the pillow with its fresh pillowcase. To the music, *Carmen, Lucia*, faint in the background. Sleeps calmly without dreaming, long nights, like a child.

The Manager moves carefully around the apartment, does not want to disturb her. "Have a good rest." She rests.

But the waiting. On the television police cars can be heard, sirens—ambulances. Susette's empty eyes. When are you coming to get her? Justice. The law. She has no plans to escape.

She does not ask because she is mute, but the Manager just says in general that she does not need to explain if she does not want to.

The waiting. Time is passing. Nothing happens. You get used to it. The waiting. Becomes more abstract with time.

•

She is alone in the apartment during the day. After a while she discovers that it resembles the other apartment, the one she was in for several days. Rather quite the same, but where you had a wall in the other one here there is a door that leads to a room where she is now allowed to stay. The very biggest room, with the bookshelf and the sofa and the television. And a balcony facing the town center.

The building is located on a high hill, the apartment is on the fourth floor, you can see quite a ways.

When she gets more energy, she huddles on the balcony, wrapped in blankets, smoking. Cigarettes the Manager gives her: he has a pack, Marlboro, which he bought on a cruise to give to guests, he explains, he does not smoke.

"And now it is coming in handy."

Smokes, looks through the railing on the balcony on the side, the church with the rectory, the cemetery, the old side and the new side, a ways away.

And straight ahead, as said, maybe a third of a mile, the town center. The jumble of buildings, houses, shops. The square in the middle, a square, well lit.

Cannot be seen, but it is there.

And she does not look toward the town center, sits, as said, on the floor of the balcony, keen on not being seen, not seeing, wrapped in blankets, smoking, huddled.

But the square. It is there after all. The square that is empty for the most part, sometimes a car drives up on it. Hayseeds, "the pistol awakening," in their vehicles, farmers' Mercedes-Benzes, all of the fathers' rusty Toyotas and the like. Driving around around on the square, in wide circles, or tighter ones.

And at the newsstand then. Her personally, on the stool behind the counter in the middle of her busy business. Among the lottery tickets, magazines, and games: not many customers came, especially not during the "wintertime" which included all but three months during the summer.

And then: Ciiiiigarette break! Took the pack of cigarettes from the shelf under the counter where she kept her own things: "The Book of Quick-Witted Sayings," makeup bag, wallet. Three steps down to the entrance, pushed the door open, lit up.

Hayseeds, if they were still at the square, honking, giving the finger. And she, if she was in that kind of a mood, flipped them off too. Windows rolled down, impertinences, and she, sometimes, yelled back.

The cars disappeared, the sounds of the engines died out; though sometimes, a while later, they were back.

Someone who came walking across the square. A girl from the high school, in fashionable clothes and who, when the cars were suddenly there again circling around her in wide circles, around around, came to a standstill, like Madonna, *think about what Madonna has done for fashion Like a Virgin heavy crosses around her neck*, in the middle. Nose in the air, eyes looking up. As if: above all of this, toward life, the future whatever, which was around the corner anyway if you just finished grade school, high school, and *got out of this hole*.

Someone else. Her with the big eyes. The globes. Susette Packlén. Not that young either, your own age. Still, at a distance, so small, minimal. Jeans, cowboy boots—*boots*.

Surrounded by the cars too. Stood and pretended nothing was happening so to speak. But frozen, not invincible.

And Maj-Gun, suddenly gripped by a feeling of recognition, liked what was inside her so much. And remembered: they knew each other, youth. Rug rags.

Susette who was looking ahead and straight at her. Maj-Gun who waved, "Come." Or did she wave? In any case, the cars left, Susette came. The one did not follow the other, that the cars would have left just because of that, like cause-effect, but in some way, that was what it felt like.

"I reeled in the fear." Reeled in Susette. And the quotes pouring out of her mouth.

"A small poor child I am, in cowboy boots, *boots*. Wow, Susette. The way you look. Do you have any idea what kind of signals you're sending out?"

A big smile, neither of them could keep from laughing. And how the quote had just plopped out of her, cracked lips, dry mouth, as if she had not spoken for a long time, maybe she had not. And all of the rest suddenly, the stories, were brought to life.

Susette's round eyes, lifeless in the middle of the laughter. Or empty: you had to fill them in yourself, quite a lot. Those globes. A whole world.

But then, on the balcony. The next memory that rushes in here exactly now, nothing else in between. Susette in the boathouse on the Second Cape. The American girl's hangout. The same eyes that just stared at Maj-Gun. Stared and stared, surprised but so to speak confirming. As she, Maj-Gun, hit and hit. And Susette who fell and fell and fell.

And snow. Whirling. Her there later, slipping on the cliffs. And beyond, out into the whiteness.

•

It was from there, from the Second Cape, that she had come to the first apartment. Opened the door with a key she had begged off the Manager somewhat earlier. From this Manager. Perhaps several days beforehand in real time, but still an eon. Spoken about a friend who was away and Maj-Gun had promised to water the plants. Stood outside the Manager's door in the Manager's building, this complex where the apartment she is in now is located, and showed off like she had a habit of showing off to him at the newsstand, she knew that he liked it. "Just because you're a count doesn't mean . . ." Dot dot dot. Or whatever she had said, picked a page at random from "The Book of Quick-Witted Sayings." "Susette! Look here!" and the old man with his lottery tickets had been delighted. He had also known they were friends too of course, she and Susette Packlén from the apartment complex where he was the Manager. He had seen them together at the newsstand.

But then that evening, when she arrived at the other apartment straight from the boathouse, it was, as said, another time. No time, not even the Animal Child's, because it began to be born there again, later, in the darkness. There, in the apartment, where she had waited. First waited in one way, later in another, but both ways had effectively kept her from making a reality out of all the wild plans she had. The "Getawaybag" she had packed in her rented room before heading off, *killer rabbit on a killer journey* (that was how she had felt, but not at all amusing). A few blouses, makeup stuff, two pairs of underwear, and the Gombrowicz journals that a book editor thought she should read at some point, "how you can use self-pity productively, carry it to the extreme," but what was this now really, *travel reading?*

What was in her bag was forgotten. The bag was forgotten. Rug rags. Discovers a multipurpose knife in this bag later, a knife with many uses, for example as a can opener. Useful.

When she was there, in that apartment, the telephone had rung a few times. She only answered once. That was the first evening, or maybe it was already night.

Susette's employer, Solveig Torpeson.

She had said loud and clear to Solveig that Susette was sick. Angina. Throat was swollen, could not come to the telephone herself but her friend Maj-Gun was there taking care of her so there was nothing to worry about, "she's sleeping now," and they had an appointment at the clinic first thing in the morning so that Susette would get medicine for the streptococcus and a doctor's note to present to her employer regarding her statutory sick leave.

She had also said that Susette would call when she was feeling better.

It surprised her how the words were formed into lies and how the lies carried her. Carried her voice also, how, from speaking, it became that much higher and more definite, climbing to a story. Statutory sick leave. In another situation she would have laughed but now there was nothing to laugh about.

She never wanted to hear that voice again.

Scenes to add to the Winter Garden: Susette lying on the floor in the boathouse. Blood running from the corner of her mouth.

"If you weren't so curled up in your own suffering, Susette."

She had hung up the phone and stood in the darkness in the apartment for a while and looked out the window. The snow had turned to rain and she suddenly understood exactly what it was she had understood in the moment she told Solveig on the telephone that Susette was "sleeping now." Hey. Impossible. Susette.

She would not be coming back.

She had turned on all of the lights in the apartment. The Winter Garden. That Winter Garden, "the exhibitions" on the walls.

The hacienda must be built. *Kapu kai*, the forbidden seas, a blue girl on a cliff, a scream. But she had not looked at it. The Boy in the woods. My great love, pure and clean, et cetera. Not that either. Turned on a lamp, turned it off, on off, blink blink blink.

Finally, she turned off all the lights and did not turn them on again the rest of the time she was in the apartment.

The Animal Child peering into the darkness. And did not open the door when the doorbell had rung and stopped answering the phone.

•

Drank water, lived on water that flooded out of the faucet. And when she got hungry she ate cat food: there were two packs of unopened cans, 2 × 24 cans in each, still wrapped in plastic that she tore open, hacking the lids open with a knife—the rag scissors, rusty blood with white hairs, were lying on a shelf in the pantry, she got it on her hand when she was looking for a weapon to open the cans: could not be used, she put it in her bag, get rid of it.

Bent open the lids and ate with her fingers directly from the can. Tasted like shit, of course, but when hunger struck hunger struck. There was a hunger that could not be checked, the one that came in fits and needed to be silenced despite the fact that it turned into nausea right after. She had *not* thrown up. Strained in order to hold back the gagging, hold back the food in her. More water, that helped.

But: it had been surprising, this unruly seed of life that existed inside her, like an instinct. Had not really been able to relate to it. Though, naturally, that she had started reflecting on it at all was a sign—then some time had already passed.

The telephone rang. The pictures on the walls. A body of water reveals itself in the woods. The Winter Garden. The hacienda must be built. *Kapu kai.* Words that went inside her, meant nothing. A blue girl on a cliff. Hand over her mouth—a scream.

Sirens, ambulances, shouts, from outside.

Justice, according to the Law. She waited. Nothing happened. It did not come.

At some point she started cleaning a little, took the pictures down from the walls, placed them in her bag in the hall, just away. That getawaybag, it was as if she had discovered it again, properly. Put the pictures in her bag. Not for any particular reason, just not to have them there in front of her eyes. Because it was upsetting.

And when she saw the bag in the hall it hit her. That it had been there *the whole time*. It had just been a matter of opening the door, heading on her way.

Right then the doorbell had rung again, voices could be heard on the stairs, a key was in the lock, and she ran ran back into the apartment. Huddled in a corner of the sofa.

That was how the Manager found her. The Animal Child. The surprise, the disgust. But he had immediately come to his senses there out in the open, returned to the stairwell, she heard how he spoke calmly to some grumpy hag, everything was in order, shooshed the woman away—later he would tell Maj-Gun it was a neighbor who had complained about the noise in the bathroom. This week in particular the building's super was on vacation and the Manager was filling in and when no one answered the telephone or opened the door when she rang the bell, the neighbor had gone to him.

The Manager had closed the front door, come back into the room and taken her away from there. Spoken to her calmly, carefully, and wordlessly, she allowed herself to be convinced, followed along.

To his apartment in another building, next door. And there he had gotten some real food into her, gotten clean clothes on her. Men's boxers, men's socks and washed-out overalls, green and wide, but made of jersey cotton, comfortable and soft. Her own clothes thrown in the washing machine.

But the very first thing had been to run a hot bath for her in the bathroom. And then she lay there in the tub and listened intently to all of the sounds outside. On the one hand, all of her senses on alert, the Manager's low voice in the hall, he was talking on the telephone. The police? Lain there and imagined scenes, how she would give herself up. Just the handcuffs on. Guilty, guilty. On the other hand, nodded off in the warmth, the water. Woke again when the Manager knocked on the door and when she came out of the bathroom in the overalls he had made up a bed for her in the sofa bed in the small living room that had become hers.

In a sleeping bag, clean sheets beneath.

NAH. Tobacco, the balcony, the square in her head, "the square, the square"—this huddling in blankets on the floor of the balcony, suddenly she could not stand it.

•

When the Manager comes home from work that day she says she is thinking about quitting smoking. Marlboro, it is not even her brand. But does not matter. She has been thinking about quitting anyway. He becomes happy, he smiles.

"Senseless to ruin your health when you're so young." She shrugs. "It gives me a bad taste. And I'm not young. Soon it will be Holy Innocents' Day. I'll be thirty."

These have been the first sensible words to come out of her mouth in that apartment, after days, maybe more than a week, a sentence with coherence. And "djeessu—"

automatically following it, whistling it through her teeth, she stops herself. And grows silent.

A fraction of a second, how the Manager's mouth twitches. As if in laughter, as if he actually, here and now, in this situation, a long way from the newsstand, likes what she has said.

"Now you're starting to become yourself again." As if he *wanted* to say it. Like in the newsstand, all of those times she had said something funny to him when he looked like he wanted to pinch her cheek. But naturally, he does not. Tousles her hair, lightly, when he walks by, turns on the TV. "The news is on."

"I give up. Unconditionally." She is on the verge of saying it to the Manager—

Police cars, sirens.

They watch TV, the news.

Two newscasts. The one a little past six, the one at eight thirty.

But the Manager, justice, the law, where is it? The Manager plays on his side of the wall, *Carmen, Lucia di Lammermoor.*

Current events, sirens. The waiting. More abstract. Weeks which pass; it has become Christmas.

•

A small plastic tree with plastic balls and glitter and electric lights in different colors. The Manager retrieves it from the basement where he keeps it stored and the two cardboard angels with hair made of yarn in a cardboard box marked CHRISTMAS THINGS.

Places the Christmas tree on the desk, the angels on the television set. Homemade angels, the work of kids, you can see *that*, not very nice at all.

"Do you have kids?"

"No."

"Have you been married?"

"No."

His "almost" goddaughters are the ones who have made these angels, he explains, and gave them to him for Christmas. When they were little, they are grown up now. And they have names as well, the angels, that is: Sister Blue, Sister Red, or if you want, the Astronaut, the Nuclear Physicist. "Which one do you think is which?" the Manager asks jokingly as if it were a particularly interesting thing to ponder and answer, it is neither, just idiotic. AND you cannot see a difference anyway. Both are just as ugly, the empty toilet paper rolls benevolently camouflaged in water color, but she does not say that, Maj-Gun shrugs her shoulders, says nothing.

They eat ham and turnip casserole for three days. And listen to music, the same opera, during the day too. She says that he can leave the door ajar, she likes music.

On the television, the news, the third day: a dictator and his wife have been shot. An old couple is lying dead under a wall on frosty ground—the image, black and white, opens the newscast. Thick winter clothes, fur, do *not* look peaceful, or wretched, just dead. Terrible people, terrible regime. And soon fresh earth and sandy earth, that serves-them-right-earth will soon be shoveled over them.

But "djeessus!" comes out of Maj-Gun's mouth then, loud and clear, whistling between her teeth, it is also a surprise. From *Carmen*, *Lucia*, small electric lights to this. The first image from the first real newscast since the highlights on Christmas Eve.

Maj-Gun puts her hand over her mouth—

Then the Manager turns the TV off in the middle of the news.

They sit in silence on either side of the dining table.

And the Manager suddenly speaks, softly. Says serious things to her. She should not be ashamed. Regardless of what has happened, life must go on. Also her life.

Then he adds, word for word, and calmly: *that he liked her so much there in the newsstand.*

When she said the kinds of things she said, who she was. She was not like other people, like *no one* else. She should not misunderstand him when he says this but there is so much *life* in her.

It becomes quiet again. So much life, and suddenly, just because he says it: everything she once was comes pouring into her—

But stop now. Because in the following and immediately: Susette with the big eyes, the globes, a whole world.

"If you weren't so curled up in your own suffering, Susette."

Her own voice from somewhere—had she actually said that, had she personally really said that? Yes. And it comes back. Susette falling in the hangout. Her eyes during the fall. The emptiness in them, not even surprise. Before she came to lie there, dying and dying.

And Maj-Gun, what is she doing here? Justice, the law. Why doesn't anything happen?

Later, in the Manager's living room, she has started crying. A big child's big tears: screaming and shrill and insistent, and then, while she is crying, it comes out of her. She left her friend to die in the boathouse. And everything else too, pell-mell: the Boy in the woods, the jealousy, Susette, the fight, the meeting, the boathouse—and the snow, the cliffs, and the snow.

Why did Justice not come? What is so wrong with it?

And now when the crying, many weeks after, in the Manager's apartment, Boxing Day 1989, is set free in the quiet apartment, how it sprays out of her eyes, nostrils, mouth, all orifices. Tears, snot spray over the rest of the ham, the mustard, and turnip casserole on the plate.

At first the Manager does not say anything. He lets her cry. Does not come to her to give her a hug, comfort her or the like. Nor does he put the TV on again, or some other record in order to drown it out, does not leave but goes to the kitchen to get more paper towels, which they have used as napkins during their meals, and tears a few sheets from the roll that he gives to Maj-Gun to snuffle in.

Then he sits down on the other side of the dining room table, clears his throat, and says, "Maj-Gun. Should we start from the beginning? Your friend, Susette Packlén. Right? She isn't—dead—"

At first Maj-Gun is so absorbed in her crying that she does not even hear but then it forces its way inside, she stops crying, everything stops, stop—and a desertlike silence follows.

The Manager's mouth is moving. In a state of shock she only sees his mouth moving at first, but the anesthetic slowly eases and she hears as well.

"And is in good health. She has been tired and upset. They traveled to Portugal during Christmas to rest. She and her fiancé."

Fiancé?

But, the Manager adds, "of course it's a tragedy," and then he tells an amazing story that does not match up with anything at all.

There has been a fire, in the cousin's house, the whole house has burned down. Bengt, Solveig's brother—yes, they're good friends, Solveig and the Manager, have known each other their entire lives—had fallen asleep with a cigarette in his hand. The fire truck came, but it was too late.

It was burning. That house is located pretty remotely, the Manager says, and the weather was bad, it took some time. And when the call came in, there was nothing to save. A tragic accident, even though he was "an alcoholic, washed up," says the Manager.

"I've understood that they were close in some way." The Manager is talking about Susette now, about Susette and Bengt, though it takes a while before Maj-Gun understands this too. *I* was the one who loved him. On the other hand, right when she is about to say it, like a real objection, a type of reflex just like all of the millions of "djeessus" that come out of her mouth as soon as she does not pull herself together, it hits her again again again: *but it was just a story*. And in the same moment, how that story leaves her; it is almost terrible.

The Boy in the woods. Bengt, and at the same time. She had been there with him. She, Maj-Gun, that exact same day, beer (he had been drinking) and cigarettes she had brought with her and then yes . . . dot dot dot . . . this and the other but damn it, "What are you babbling about?" how he had looked at her like a crazy person and laughed at her, but then everything was already over. No one came, she was alone with him, a complete stranger whom she did not know, and in some way was afraid of too.

But: she had been in that room, that house. And he: so alive. And he: lying on the floor in the room.

•

But why, Manager, why why had he not said anything earlier?

The Manager says that yes, he *should* have said something, he knows that. In particular, he should have asked when she had gotten more energy and become more herself again. Says that again, herself, with almost happiness in his voice. But then . . . in the beginning. She was so weak. And the other apartment: had been such a shock to him too. He had not understood very much, first lately, in this apartment, it had started dawning on him that it might be a question of a misunderstanding.

But he had known that they were friends after all, she and Susette Packlén who had had Bengt in her apartment. Not living there, Susette had explained to the Manager several times. It was the neighbor lady who alerted the Manager to the fact that Susette had Bengt there, and that if he *was living* there then a notice of change of address should be filled out. So the Manager had asked, but of course he knew what stories like that could be like, here today, gone tomorrow. But Susette Packlén had flat out denied it and held her ground.

And yes, he also knew of course what it could be like between girlfriends, if jealousy was playing a role, or otherwise, discord, sadness over the other one having left. He had not been able to imagine that she, Maj-Gun, had gone around brooding in another way.

And yes, that mess in the apartment, and—yes, he had been shocked too. Thought about asking about it too, when she got better, but on the other hand, had not wanted to bring it up. He had thought, yes, has thought, that it was so nice seeing her get her strength back and become . . . hersel—

This is where the Manager stops, as if he had suddenly become confused. That it was absurd.

But he tries to explain, as businesslike as possible. He has enjoyed having her in the apartment. The days that have passed, and celebrating Christmas . . . which there was not anything really special about . . . but, in any case . . .

•

SO he has gotten it together again, gotten a grip and told her everything he had de facto set about doing for her during this time. Contacted her family, spoken with her father the Pastor on the phone, the old vicar whom he knows and has in confidence, between two old men, been able to tell him a little more about the situation, her condition, and kept him updated the entire time: to the others he said that she has severe angina, but everyone has been worried about her. And her brother Tom Maalamaa had personally been in touch.

He had also been in touch with the newsstand, the Head Office, been connected to the correct personnel department via the operator . . . and her landlords down in the town center whom he is acquainted with too. Said that she is recovering at her parents' home, with the Pastor's family, who live in another county. Her landlords, Gunilla and Göran, sent many warm greetings to the patient and are not worried at all about the rent being paid. Maj-Gun has always been a hundred percent exemplary boarder. It has been easier that way, this white lie, the Manager explained, referring to himself as well: for example his job as a teacher at the school where both Göran and Gunilla are his colleagues and Göran a Lions brother, outside of work.

"Angina!"¹ A breeze through Maj-Gun's head, something she once said on the telephone. To Solveig, Susette's employer, the only conversation in that horrible apartment which, in that moment, and for always, seems like a million years ago. Then it dawns on her, so she does not need to ask anything else about the matter that is for certain. The angels on the television set. Solveig, Rita. "My almost goddaughters, friends for a long time."

And maybe, a little, Rita, Solveig—and Bengt. Three siblings, the three cursed ones. Something she also always knew but had not thought about in relation to anything in reality, so to speak. Exactly because it still has never been real to her, a story.

The Boy in the woods. "The one who killed out of love."

"But what are you babbling about?" That is what Bengt said, she will not forget it, when she, on that horrible day, had actually said that to him. *What are you babbling about?* He quite simply had not understood a word.

But WHERE is Susette Packlén? It was almost ridiculous later, because in the midst of everything Maj-Gun has known the answer to that question too, before she even finished thinking that thought.

"Portugal." The fiancé. Djeessuss! Djeessuss! Tom Maalamaa who spoke with the Manager, about his fiancée.

But djeessuss too, which cannot be said either, not to the Manager, not to any one at all.

The polo shirt, the blazer, and the disco. *Susette and love.* Oh God. "The Book of Quick-Witted Sayings." A blank page, "Tom's world." Djeessuss.

She remembers herself at the disco. Sitting, squeezed onto the sofa, in an unbearability, though nothing compared to later unbearabilities, but out of whack, Melancholy. Susette dancing on the dance floor. Rag doll. *Dance my doll.* For a while it had been a bit entertaining. As if that which connected them—rug rags, long strips, loom lengths—made it possible to control her, Susette, as it were. Perhaps stated exaggeratedly, but still. "You are so easy, Susette," which she had also said once.

Susette who was dancing, disappeared, slipped away on the dance floor. One among the crowd, bodies, bodies, smoke. And then, in that moment, how Maj-Gun had suddenly thought, a pang inside her. A pistol in the bathroom, in a bag. "God, Susette, what are you doing with a revolver in your sauna bag?" The utterly incomprehensible.

That which had become so clear when Susette slipped away, disappeared, on the dance floor.

That Susette was a stranger. That she, Maj-Gun, knew nothing about her.

"I'm fascinated by the Death in her."

And then, at the disco, she caught sight of her brother. Tom Maalamaa, in the throng at the disco, on the dance floor. Like *a fish in water*, the blazer, the polo shirt, and those crooked idiotic cones that were running down along his cheeks. Then she immediately got up, careful so that her brother should not see her, and left the disco. Because it had first been, at the sight of her brother in the crowd that she had, there in the throng, squeezed onto the sofa, been gripped by . . . not shame, but some type of hopelessness in her that was out of step, fat or skinny, it was not important, but so *old*. And not on her life had she wanted her brother, who immediately would have understood, the only one in the world who would have understood, to see it.

Goatee? she asked him roguishly on the phone when he called a few days later. Rather unexpectedly, and despite the teasing tone, she had been a bit happy, certainly. He had not understood what she was talking about. She said that she had seen him at the disco, he sounded surprised, oh, she had been there. Yes, she said, with a big group of young people, other shop assistants and the like, from newsstands, and they had so much fun, so much so that she only caught a glimpse of him in the crowd, but was so caught up in the music then, the young people, the dance, that she lost sight of him and when she looked for him she could not find him.

She also said, as if in passing but certainly oh so meaningful, that Susette had been there, and he was rather surprised about that too. And she knew her brother well enough that she could tell when he was lying and this time he was telling the truth.

"Hee hee hee . . . maybe you want her phone number?" she chirped on the phone. "Do you want to get in touch with her? She's quite lonely." Because that had been before she brought the cat food to Susette's apartment and everything had fallen apart for her.

But he took the phone number, Tom Maalamaa. That he had.

And my God, they HAD gotten together, and oh God, everything about Susette—what you did not know about her. Scissors in the cabinet, dried blood—

But *the Boy in the woods*, Bengt, what was he to her?

"I don't know anything about anything." Again, Susette in the hangout. No, unavoidable. It had been real. And when Maj-Gun had hit, not even then had Susette been unsympathetic.

And it IS for real, cannot be talked away, pushed away. "If you weren't so curled up in your own suffering." Everything else disappeared in the presence of this attempted murder, a concrete action almost carried out. Susette's big eyes, the boathouse, the snow. It happened: and she, Maj-Gun, *had to* remember it, carry it in her consciousness, it always had to be there.

"I was so angry so angry so angry . . ." she says to the Manager. "Probably jealous too. I thought I was . . . in love with him . . ."

"Maj-Gun, I've understood that she has had a difficult time," the Manager says. "But she is going to therapy. Some great sorrow in her past. Unresolved," the Manager determines and it is probably true, very true, because that is also what Susette, many years later, in the future, will say. "Like being in a forest. Not finding your way out."

I love you. Running over the plains. All stories, and blood. "Can you imagine killing out of love?" Susette. Duel in the sun. Bengt. *Djeessuss*. Oh God. Tom.

Someone in a polo shirt. Tom Maalamaa came and got her. *And behind her it was burning.*

"But it's better now," says the Manager. "Everything is better now. And now it seems like she and all of us are ready to move on. You too, Maj-Gun—"

Yes. But first. Bengt. She has to say it anyway.

"But Bengt—"

"It's very tragic," the Manager says again and though it can seem indifferent there is still nothing sugarcoated about it.

The angels on the TV. Rita, Solveig—and the third one, the brother Bengt.

Pictures on the wall. His pictures, drawings. Blue pictures. "The Exhibition." *The Winter Garden.*

"Did you know . . . him?" Maj-Gun asks carefully.

"Of course. Were very good friends, the three of us. The kids had no real childhood. I knew them since they were little. Tried to help them as best I could. Especially the girls.

"But," he adds, "it can, well . . . you know, sound . . . the way it sounds. But, it *wasn't* exactly unexpected, what happened. But, dear Maj-Gun. You need to think about yourself now. You have so much inside. So much life."

And then he catches his breath, stretches, and asks her about the future, what she is planning on doing now, on becoming "when she grows up."

•

"I am grown up, Manager. I don't know. I—I wanted to become a pastor once, I think."

And then she starts relating an episode from her childhood, at the rectory. That childhood, that rectory: one Sunday at the dinner table, her brother Tom Maalamaa,

who was a pompous brooder as a teenager and this particular Sunday he brooded a bit more than usual and
realized what he decided to "proclaim," to his gathered
family this Sunday in particular, his word that too, wearing a blazer, which he always did back then, despite the
fact that he was only fifteen or sixteen. That HE did not
have a calling to become a pastor and would, for that
reason, unfortunately not be able to pass on the family
tradition from father to son.

"I'm sorry, Father," he added, like in an old-fashioned
movie. One of those brooding films that played nonstop
in his head at that time; they had in common that it
was always his alter ego in the lead role that, after long
scenes in an inappropriate childhood, youth, ended
the same way: with the alter ego becoming "famous,"
something "successful," Gustav Mahler, Ingmar Bergman, the like.

On the other hand, Tom Maalamaa had on this Sunday
afternoon explained that he understood that he could
"serve humanity" in another way and had in other words
come to the conclusion that he would become a lawyer.
He had already mail-ordered the compendium for "the
preparation course" for the admission exam at the law
school.

"Where is your girlfriend?" was all papa Pastor asked
with a small roguelike glint in his eyes, when Tom Maalamaa had stopped speaking, because that girlfriend with
the big eyes, cuute, who never said a word, but who, during the past few months, had been present at all of the
Sunday dinners at the rectory, was not sitting at the place
at the table where she usually sat despite the fact that the
place had been set for her: the chair was gaping emptily

for a quiet and big-eyed Susette Packlén, poking at her food, in tight jeans, boots.

"She's gone. Ended things," his sister willingly and helpfully prompted loudly after a hasty destructive look at her brother Tom—Tom in the sense of TOM, seen as a world, in that subjective perception of reality that no one other than the two siblings in this family shared.

A world where the Happy Harlot in the middle of the DAY OF DESIRE, which had been great and wonderful (in any case, it should be mentioned, like a hypothesis), has been transformed into the Disgust, a world where it was "a shame about," there . . . there . . . and Maj-Gun had almost stammered internally out of anger *and here here here Tom Tom you'll get for this.*

"And to be honest," his sister added in a steady voice, "you can have some understanding for it. *I love you* over the plains. Love's representative, a bit *pale* in that perspective." This too like a silent reference to something that only the brother and the sister in the family shared: then, a long time ago, before Tom Maalamaa started hanging out with his first girlfriend, he had certainly enjoyed himself when his sister Maj-Gun, when talking about that mother with the big-eyed girl Susette at the cemetery, had grown quiet at the mere thought of the name, "CAN you be called that, Tom?" Asked humorously, rhetorically so to speak, and added, "nah I don't think so. Newsstand toppler. Susette. *I love you over the plains—*"

"We are SEPARATED," Tom Maalamaa, with poorly restrained anger, personally declared out loud at the dinner table, though somewhat paler in the face. In and of itself, possibly, not entirely wrong either because in reality his sister did not know the details surrounding the breakup of his relationship—that Susette Packlén's father was ill, dying, both of them knew that, probably papa Pastor too, who looked after the members of his congregation but that was work, nothing to touch upon with great seriousness during these pleasant Sunday dinners when the whole family had the opportunity to get together in peace and quiet for once.

So it could just as well have been Tom Maalamaa himself who had slowed things down, because in some way, the Weakling that was hiding under the Ponderer's cowl that he had invisibly put on and that did not suit him very well, significantly less well fitting than those woolen mantles of quality he would use later in life . . . that Weakling was not prepared for illness, death. Unthinkable, for a thousand reasons, also because quite simply if it affected someone else more, then that person's rules applied, there would be another main character in the story, so to speak. Following that sweet girl who says nothing to the very darkest, Death's landscape, no, that had not occurred to him. But he was afraid of death too, in that blunt, naked way that healthy youths, who are not dragging themselves out into war and dying the hero's death, are—the difficult, lengthy illnesses, death as violent but relentless decomposition, death as a physical utterance too, and handling the dead body, the whole *coffin hell*, quite simply, should be handled by deaconesses, mothers, wives, girlfriends—that was their role in life, which would come to show itself in practice later.

But it was not exactly something you wanted to endure. Your fear. That kind of "disgust." And then the contemplation came in situations exactly like that and it existed so that it would come to you in situations exactly like this, with messages like the following: that you were young and had your future ahead of you, a boy with prospects, a purpose in life. Do something, for, like, *humanity*. And Gustav Mahler, but regulated, not like it had surged at the worst moments in your room with your girlfriend, in order to soften the anxiety in the presence of a disownment—because, say what you want to about Tom, maybe he was empty but not stupid. His sister in her capacity as the Happy Harlot as a *happy* appellation, not fresh, but *hamba hamba*, in the openness of childhood, without boundaries, who was not let into his room, but was left outside, pounding on the door.

"Well, well, let's not quarrel, children." Mama Inga-Britta finally jumped in and as always, when she stepped in, it became calm around the dinner table, even a relatively nice mood again.

"I have the church's calling," Maj-Gun explains to the Manager in the apartment on Boxing Day 1989, that she had carefully whined at the dinner table on that Sunday. *That* is in other words what she says: not about Tom Maalamaa and Susette Packlén and her father, or about the Happy Harlot and so on—or about her own shortcomings with her brother, in general, the metaphysical violence in them, that does not belong there. Brave but determined, this whine, she points that out here to the Manager now, since there were drawbacks to coming with a similarly brave announcement in this Pastor's family, which was Old Testament–minded.

"The woman in the congregation is silent," the Pastor, who was gentle despite his religious indomitability and strictness, which unfortunately unfortunately still had to come before everything, sorrowfully determined in the presence of his daughter but looked at her with an endless gentleness and started speaking about the work of the deaconship as a true challenge to her . . . um . . . femininity. At that point he had some difficulty again because she was just a teenager after all, almost genderless in her own eyes too. That DESIRE in her from the DAY OF DESIRE, for example the Girl from Borneo, was not Woman's Dawning Sexuality that would gradually lead to a balanced marital sensuality that could then be stimulated further with sex tips from all the magazines and regular childbirth but that was mankind's happy horrible amoral physicality, wonderful on the one hand, but no show-off, also terrible and dangerous as a-moral is, but crossing all boundaries: wanted to enjoy enjoy, caress, play . . . feel . . . her life, her life force without all the boundaries. Without gender, a life force unpersonified and so on, but no more about that now—there is also something here with the Manager now, the mood, during all of these days, which makes it so that it is important not to travel forward with too many words, move carefully, with caution.

But papa Pastor had, in other words, become a bit shy in regard to femininity, which implied certain things, not to mention at the dinner table, as it were. Maybe he was also thinking about the fact that his beloved daughter was in the process of growing up, going out into life, away from him. "Deaconship." He got hold of himself again . . . which had been such a . . . um . . . challenge and source of happiness for his dear sister Liz and his dear wife: dear dear Shadow Inga-Britta who always smiled so pleasantly—it was true!—at all of the amusing phrases at the dinner table, considerately poured more brown gravy over new pieces of steak on everyone's plates. With rowanberry jelly, mmmm, made from berries she picked herself.

The Manager, when he hears that, listens amused but quickly gets a rascallike glint in his eyes, familiar from other places, it strikes Maj-Gun. Of course the newsstand, and in some way, despite everything that has happened, how wonderful, what a happy recognition. And then says in a sober tone of voice that maybe we should have a *small* bit of snuff. "I knew your father when he lived here in the District." He chuckles. "We were brothers in the Lions Club," and ho ho ho, "at that man's house, who is one of the nicest people I've met, there was a lot of open-mindedness. Oh, Maj-Gun, you're a good storyteller, so lively, self-willed, enticing. But, unfortunately, your father, he probably isn't fundamentally inclined at all."

He was right of course, but in some way, what Maj-Gun could get irritated about at the newsstand, especially with Susette Packlén, was when someone did not believe her, when she was questioned about her stories that she liked to tell when there was an audience, does not bother her now.

Rather it was a bit nice not to be steered onto the right road but still, within this framework, *I am not without space*, can it be like that, with the Manager, that, *here*?

And the feeling, like a seed, the beginning of one, do you even dare say it—a rose, so powerful inside you. Back to reality again, it is not the newsstand, not the other apartment, the rooms in the attics, the rectory—but here?

"Maj-Gun," the Manager starts, but then he does not really know what to say.

"Well, it was just a story anyway," says Maj-Gun. "Manager, I like telling stories. And in some way, Manager, there is still a grain of truth to what you say. Or it should be like that. You carry something to its point in order to make it clear. Though sometimes in the newsstand I got the feeling that you can tell, say, whatever, as long as it sounds good, has flow so to speak. But it isn't like that, Manager. You can't say just anything.

"I mean, becoming a pastor. It was just a thought ... among many others. At the time.

"And, Manager," she adds after a little while, "we were a family, at the rectory, that liked telling stories ... not my brother Tom of course, he would rather hold speeches and lectures. Reason. He can reason, he can. About almost anything. But I don't want to reason about just anything. I want to say something I believe in.

"But we had quite a lot of fun together sometimes, there at the rectory." And then, in the midst of all the emotion and warmth inside, she comes to the almost most important thing of all: "And how is Father doing?"

The Manager smiles, says just fine and that he has been worried about her, of course.

"You know what, Manager," Maj-Gun says, the last thing she says that strange, perplexing evening. "I think I've always wanted to become a lawyer too."

The Manager smiles, tousles her hair, and then they go to bed—and that night, is it not as though he played *Carmen*, a rose you threw at me, a little bit louder than usual?

FLAMING CARMEN

ON HOLY INNOCENTS' DAY, the twenty-eighth of December 1989, when Maj-Gun turns thirty, the Manager gives her *The Law Book* as a present. Bound in red, unbearably heavy and in small print, wrapped in glaring red silk paper with a similar indecently colored bow around it, which Maj-Gun tears apart in an attack of birthday girl happiness that knows no boundaries, as if all of the happy birthdays she has had that have lived their quiet lives inside her flame up in one moment, and she throws her arms around the Manager's neck.

Remains clinging. A few seconds. An eternity. The Manager carefully but gently loosens Maj-Gun's hands from his neck.

"Now I finally get to read articles," Maj-Gun adds but softer, because both of them are a bit embarrassed. "At the newsstand I mean. Maybe the newsstand really *is* my calling."

The Manager does not answer, does not look up, he is suddenly completely and entirely occupied with transferring the birthday cake from the cardboard box from the bakery in the town center to a cake plate that is really just an ordinary plate. But he has put a paper doily with edging under it so it will look extra festive: an Enormouscake, with green piping and a sugar bud, a small pink rose on top. And then there is coffee in the kitchen that must not be allowed to boil over and all the cups and saucers need to be set out and the silver spoons that

254

he has six of in a special case, stored in a special cabinet in the living room.

Maj-Gun grows quiet, in other words, sits down on the chair and neither of them says anything for a good while.

I love you sweet child never change! But the Manager, who *almost* said that a long time ago in the newsstand and *almost* put his hand out over the counter in an almost irresistible eagerness to pinch Maj-Gun Maalamaa on the cheek. So overwhelmed by who she was, who she is, all her pretty quotes too, from "The Book of Quick-Witted Sayings" and otherwise, all her oddities. "I love you don't ever change!" Or, now, two days ago, that evening when Maj-Gun found out about everything, for example that she had not murdered her friend as she thought and would not be spending the rest of her life in prison, and they had spoken about the future, what would become of her, later: how the Manager, when he had gone to his room on the other side of the wall that night, played *Carmen* like always, at a low volume, but still a little louder than usual. Or? And, as if in the midst of everything it had been a message to her, Maj-Gun. *The rose that you threw at me*—a seed that had been planted, the Manager, was it imagined? A seed that had grown during the night and the days that followed. Even if new music played on the record player, in the middle of the day too, *Old Men's Choir Singing in the Fellowship Hall,* a choir in which the Manager as well as her own father, papa Pastor, had been members, sung the highest part—her father, "with true pastor's vibrato in his voice," as her father had said at the rectory once. Maj-Gun suddenly remembers how her father had said it, rascal-like, as it were, because regardless of how much her father liked singing, he had never really had much of a singing voice but he had, in other words, never made a secret of it either. More than generously admitted to himself, among others, the following: that the Manager had been as right as anything when he soberly claimed in the middle of Maj-Gun's somewhat free-flying story where the Pastor had the lead role in another way that no, no father certainly had not been strict, not the least bit "Old Testament–minded" at all. Yes, of course, so right, for real. At papa Pastor's there was, there is, a lot of open-mindedness. And Maj-Gun may have wanted to say that to the Manager too when they were listening to the men's choir, but *drag father into this now*, in this mood during these days, full days, where everything that has been said, and not been said, all the silence and all the music have become one peculiar hidden message about the will to and the longing for touch. *It is a rose blooming*, but Manager, don't you hear WHAT they're singing? All possible invisible threads between them, and the Manager has, without a doubt, felt it too because in the middle of everything he cleared his throat and started, in an extra-objective tone of voice, to lament the lack of men in the District who enjoy singing, resulting in that the Men's Choir, shortly after Maj-Gun's father quit as vicar in the parish and received a new post in another municipality, had to be put down altogether. "He was a *real enthusiast*," the Manager tried to explain further and the social life in the municipality in general owed so much to her father too . . . but then he suddenly grew quiet in the middle of that thought and that sentence, stopped. But the music, undeniably, roaring about roses, played on on the record player.

I love you over the plains, church bells? Nah, no. Rather, like this: a road like a path that hesitantly reveals itself in the woods, out of a fog that scatters, for a while. But it can disappear, the fog can thicken again, at any moment. So—hold on to it, the road, the image of a road, carve it into yourself like a map before it is gone.

A rose, *your* rose, which is thrown at you, *your* Winter Garden. Take the golden ribbons, Maiden, go into the dance—

And here, now, the birthday. The Manager has finally gotten everything on the table, clears his throat. Ceases with all other business as well, sits down, like her, on a chair, on his chair, on the other side of the dining table and neither of them says anything. They just sit there on their respective sides of the table: saucers, coffee cups, the Enormousbirthdaycake like a half coconut, turned upside down, swollen with a pink, wartlike bud on top. *The Law Book*, the red silk paper fallen under the table, the bow. Maj-Gun looks down between her legs, picks up the bow, the ribbon, winds it around her fingers, damp, shiny. "Just because you're a count, Manager," she starts, looks up, around her, in the room. Two hellish angels with golden stars, bodies made out of empty toilet paper rolls, standing on the television set, weak wings painted with water color, Sister Blue, Sister Red, or whatever it was, The Astronaut? The Nuclear Physicist? *Guess which one is which? But HOW interesting, Manager, couldn't care less.* "Just because you're a count, Manager," she tries again but it does not work, suddenly the sentence has gotten stuck in her head, the words that were grinding inside her. But at the same time, in this attempt and that sentence which artificially starts running out of her mouth, from "The Book of Quick-Witted Sayings," the newsstand, which goes on and goes on, because it is so long, Count, then it changes and is transformed into a seriousness that is—enormous. "Forget it, Manager," she mumbles because she does not get any farther, "just forg—"

"Maj-Gun," the Manager says then, almost pleading. And Maj-Gun looks up at him lightning quick, meets his gaze, a bird in my hand? "Shall I tell you something?" she asks quickly, heatedly suddenly with an urgency that surprises even her.

The Manager brightens, another story, and you can see he is also relieved. "I like your stor—"

"Something I read, in the newsstand, once." Maj-Gun cuts him off. "Magazines, informations, Manager, every-thing was there. About this and the other, quotes, ideas, this and that from here and from there. Something about reincarnation, Manager—

"About people who were convinced they had a life be-fore this one. Famous people everyone had been prior to this life, princesses and the right-hand man of kings, Vincent van Gogh and the like.

"You know what, Manager?" Maj-Gun grows quiet for a moment before continuing, more carefully, hesitat-ing. "I think . . . about myself . . . that I—was a relatively lonely person in my previous life.

"Someone who—was in the Lions Club and who liked spending time outdoors, for example. Picking rowanber-ries with the Nature Friends, collecting plants in a her-barium, catching butterflies. At least in theory, seen as an idea: you could never get away forever, not to mention that the days were long, and you were often tired. But someone who watched the news every evening, quarter past six, eight thirty, both broadcasts. And listened a lot to—music, opera music, for example.

"Had management as my great interest. On the side of course, in addition to the daily tasks during the day, at school.

"Later then . . . yes, he met someone. Someone who, let us say, might have been from . . . the Lions Club. Another lion, one of those newcomers. Certain people . . . *other* people I mean." And when Maj-Gun speaks now she is not speaking in a rascal-like way, but hesitantly, her voice filled with seriousness. "Other people who don't devote themselves to that sort of activity under the guise of friendship and charity, think that only *they* have interesting lives. They are the only ones who have creativity and personality and a thousand and one wines to taste before they die, a lot of quality in their daily lives and jogging . . . They, these people, are wrong, of course.

"And how do I know that, Manager?"

Maj-Gun pauses, a few seconds and then, NOW, she looks at him. Stares at him, her whole life in that moment, *a bird in my hand*, don't give way now.

"*I* know that because I have been old my entire life.

"For ages, Manager.

"And sometimes it has been. Strange. Lonely, of course. At this age.

"I thought it would help to, for example, meet people the same age, go to the disco.

"There is so much we think, Manager. Which later, when reality forces its way in, turns out to be wrong.

"A bird in my hand, Manager.

"It is a rose, blossomed. It didn't help."

And the words that catch in her throat, but he gets up, he comes to her.

Maj-Gun in the bathroom later, brushing her teeth, looking at herself in the mirror.

Walks out, opens the door to his room. Walks in, crawls into the bed, he opens his arms to her. The Animal Child and the Animal Tobias meet, in the darkness, all walls come crashing down.

·

The nausea starts immediately the following morning. The Manager has gone to school in the middle of Christmas break to prepare his teaching for the spring semester; "fresh air," "snuffle a bit at the everyday" . . . He said ahem, and the door shut after him and a Giantbirthday-cake has been left sitting on the table since yesterday, alongside *The Law Book* with its bordeaux red spine and the crumpled-up fire-red silk paper under the table as well as the red ribbon bow, curly and streamerlike at the ends. Invoking seasickness, all of it; the nausea has been intense: Maj-Gun rushed to the bathroom and threw up but despite her birthday and the other extenuating circumstances, no avoiding it, she knows immediately what it is. Quite right, it will turn out: the next morning and the next and the next the nausea is back. "What are you babbling about?" The Boy in the woods, in that house that room, *with the men in the fields.*

No immaculate conception in other words, Jesu Maria Annunciation, a funny word that can be looked up in *The Nordic Family Book* if you are in that kind of a mood, but Maj-Gun is not in that kind of a mood, will not be either, push it aside, do not think about it at all for a while. "Some bug," she says to the Manager who is suddenly back that first morning while she is in the bathroom. He has been gone forty-five minutes at the most, stands and counts the minutes out loud in the hallway when she comes out, *could not keep her thoughts collected*. Out of breath, panting, thin hair wet from the rain, it has been raining hard out there but he has run the whole way and he comes to her.

And then, yes, it is, has been, possible to set aside all thoughts, exist right here, nothing else, nowhere else. Just here. In the woods a body of water reveals itself, the third possibility, like a hypothesis. Appears in the fog, a path, it clears—becomes almost two days during which *Carmen* is played in the apartment, *Lucia di Lammermoor*, but most of all an old Christmas hymn that sounds the way Christmas songs usually sound when you are still listening to them on the days between Christmas and New Year's. Discarded, a bit past their prime, but that is exactly why they draw you in. *It is a rose, blossomed,* words and melody that emit other meanings too, reveal themselves to what is most personal and you get to be part of it. Some kind of excitement also, in the apartment, listening to Christmas carols this way, because the weekend is not over just because of that.

Carmen in one room. A room of love, where she has shut herself in. With the bullfighter who was with her, who was in other places, who had his bulls, his fights, his . . . everything. Carmen in the room of love (maybe in a hotel), jubilation at first, but at the same time a destiny, she was trapped, had locked herself in.

A bird in my hand. The rose that you threw at me. A body of water reveals itself in the woods. A moment, closed in the fog, imperceptible.

•

It becomes New Year's, *clingclang* the clock at city hall
rings in the town center, New Year, a new decade, they
drink nonalcoholic wine from plastic champagne glasses
that the Manager conjures up at midnight. *One* glass of
wine per person, cheers, Maj-Gun laughs, the bubbles
rush to her head. And are cast in metal; Maj-Gun's "happiness" is a weak clump with knobbles that are money
and when you hold the Manager's up against the wall in
the kitchen in the light the shadow of a pretzel stands out
against the yellow wallpaper, which means: even more
loneliness—and suddenly, pain in her stomach, it hurts
so damn much, all of it, everything. But she does not say
so, she says "sugar pretzel," tastes, stretches out her red
tongue. *Hamba hamba.* The Long Afternoon of Desire,
dancing in the kitchen. The Manager laughs, maybe a
bit insecurely, *The Long Afternoon of Desire*, one should
look it up in *The Family Book* whatever it was that faun
was now called. But he does not walk over to any bookshelf, there is no time—says afterward, when they are
lying naked, entangled like streamers on the sofa bed
in the room, as the District's mainstay, which he also is,
grade school teacher and mixed school teacher and *ped-
agogue* all sorts of things, with that voice in other words,
that he has a *little* weakness for Cookies certainly, even
if it they contain, as it were, pinching Maj-Gun's naked
bum, "quite a lot of carbohydrates."

Maj-Gun sits up in the sofa, laughs, the docklands
in Borneo, the Happy Harlot, gathers her hair in her
hand at the nape of her neck and lets it fall, so to speak,
shakes her head, her hair flies, stupid angels, the TV,
straddles the Manager, on all fours above him, hisses,

Starling, darling, ready to be kissed, like she once had in the newsstand.

"Come." The Manager pulls her down on the sofa and they do a little more of that and later when they are lying in the darkness taking a breather the Manager asks Maj-Gun how she ended up at the newsstand anyway.

·

"The newsstand?" Maj-Gun asks, dazed with sleep, does not really know how she should relate to the question, if she even likes it. The newsstand, the last decade, this is new, and now. But in order to say something she starts talking about her godmother Elizabeth "Liz" Maalamaa and all of those years that maybe in the big picture were not so many: a miserable childhood, youth for example, which she was never really able to get away from. In contrast to her brother Tom Maalamaa who had shared the misery with her for a while, without the siblings still being able to, or maybe exactly because of that, have this misery in common. Which was not exactly unhappiness, just a type of restlessness, out of place. Her brother left it behind but she personally, in some way, remained behind with it. But is that how it should be said? In any case, the godmother, Aunt Liz, who became a widow early on, "husband drank himself to death on the Sweden–Finland ferry," and she and her aunt on the Sweden–Finland ferry later, *life as a cruise*—as an image of it.

The aunt who retired and had not really known what she should do with her time at first. But *the freedom* she had spoken about loftily, "I am so happy and free!" But she was sad in the very beginning, turnedupsidedown. And during that period she had been busy spending time with her only goddaughter, Maj-Gun Maalamaa, whom she invited along for company on the cruise, to rewrite a marriage with an, in and of itself, appallingly wealthy but violent and alcoholic husband who was not exactly someone to write home about, to a story about belonging despite everything and the love that never died. Dick and Duck, two swans among other swans; "climb into a story, Manager, you need it." Maj-Gun interposes as a moral here, seems to fit, but otherwise she does not know. And as mentioned, it had of course been a passing phase in her aunt's life: she took her maiden name back later and bought a house in Portugal where she spent the winters because of the hereditary varicose veins that Maj-Gun personally also suffers from. "Cottaage," the aunt has a habit of saying about the place in Portugal in order not to sound rustic; the reason is due to her "country origin," on the farm in the north that her husband's good family from the higher burghers of society indirectly heckled her for in the city where she and her husband lived while he was still alive; it has never truly left her. But it certainly is no cottaage but a château. Has sent pictures: the house, the dog, Liz, and the sunglasses.

She had a dog for a while, a real pet dog, an ittybitty-dog under her blouse. Handsome, Ransome: from the beginning they were two but one of them died as a puppy from some sort of canine disease while the other one died in its sleep of old age after ten years of happiness with its master. "That kind of little dog, Manager, they don't get very old." *Handsome*: named after some movie star, whom the aunt had loved in her distant youth, who had a dog of the same breed with almost the same name. "Come and see my gallery," in other words, she sent these pictures to her goddaughter from Portugal. Liz and the dog on a patio, the sea behind them, the horizon.

Come and see my gallery. Written cards and letters. "But I didn't go, didn't answer either." Had been busy with, well, all sorts of things: admission exams, compendiums, a book that needed to be written, The story of my own life . . . cutting rags. Rug rags . . . which she still does not have time to delve deeper into because suddenly the Manager is paying attention, truly alert: "You *write?* That's what I thought. Maybe you're going to be a writer? You have so much, life, all of your clever wordings—"

"Come and see my gallery, Manager," Maj-Gun reiterates because if there is something she does not want to talk about then it is that. And besides, for once, to remain in that other right now, which is just as important. About her godmother, her aunt, who is still as alive as could be. That she had thought *get old now old hag and die* and she had that and she stills feels bad about it—maybe it will improve if she says it, but it does not help very much. "But, Manager, Aunt Liz, she's okay, even if she has her quirks . . ." Dreams from her childhood of being a missionary, which she has nagged about more and more as she gets older, walking in the jungle in comfortable shoes, searching for heathens to save . . . "But, quirks, Manager," Maj-Gun adds, so to speak, philosophically, "don't we all have them?" And isn't that the delightful thing about us? Everyone? Everything we have that is not written in the family chronicles and the magazines and in Everything about the world, *you can say anything here as long as it sounds like something* . . . not very much has been written about it anywhere at all, and maybe there won't be either. Because a lot of it doesn't make you feel good, you just become cuckoo, from being written down in pretty formulations.

And well, later, the whole time, she was, so to speak, in the newsstand and the moss was growing over her head, living with Susette Packlén's mother for a while as a boarder while Susette was away and her mother was, during the final years, not really right either. "Rug rags, Manager, she collected them. *Crehp crehp*. Had to be cut, cut—

"But we had fun together, I really liked her." And the mother died and Susette came back and the house was sold and suddenly Maj-Gun became a boarder with another family in another house there in the same neighborhood below the square in the town center. A normal family, Gunilla, Göran, a pair of teachers; moreover the Manager's colleagues at the school. "But shhh, Manager, they aren't, no one is allowed to know about this relationship . . . I respect the Count, the charm of the office manager and maintaining the façade in your capacity as the District's mainstay." Maj-Gun stammers, suddenly in the middle of the story about something other than the intense indignation that pours into her, an appallingly bad mood.

"Maj-Gun"—the Manager takes her hand in his—"it isn't like that."

"With, then, Manager," Maj-Gun continues with the Manager's hand in hers, it feels better, "a thousand cranky kids on the ground floor," and there at the new boarding place she fattened up for real. Not because she had eaten that much; "it wasn't a feel-good problem, Manager," or a hormone imbalance or Femininity, which was exploding, uncontrolled inside her, swelling over

every orifice and border, but a condition that was given
form: "I am without space.

"This isn't very coherent, Manager." Maj-Gun suddenly interrupts herself, but in a new way. Because in
the midst of everything she realizes maybe it is the Manager's hand in hers, *a body of water reveals itself in the
woods*, the fog disperses entirely, right here, in the open,
New Year's night: the possibility. That she might be able
to. Can. Tell, everything. Both everything that is clear
and everything else, less clear, more incomprehensible.
Images, scenes, that she does not know what she is going
to do with. About Susette Packlén. The revolver in Susette's bathroom. And the cat, which all of a sudden was
not there. "It got run over."

And also. That which in some way belongs to what
is obvious, though it was a fantasy fetus, but not any
less because of it, it was real too. She has to beat it into
her head: not *the Boy in the woods*, but Bengt. Maybe
she would be able to say something about that too. In
some way. That she had never known him. It had been
her story, a story that has gone on and on in her head.
And that received a continuation in reality, at the newsstand, with Susette Packlén on the other side of the
counter. And flowed out, unchecked, ran away—like
"The Manuscript of a Life," a novel she had been sitting and writing in her rented room. "Promising! Short!
Kill your darlings and tone down the self-pity." Sometimes she opened the leather-bound folder where she
kept the comments from the book editor on a first draft
she had sent to the publisher a long time ago. As the
years passed, she had opened the binder more often,
and those comments and how they sounded had grown

inside her head too. Had, in and of itself, almost become a monument and that is where the talk had come
in, about Literature and all of the interferences that
should be done to it, regardless of whether or not the
Critics would have any understanding for it; a topic of
conversation she had introduced in long monologues
she held in the kitchen, with her landlady Gunilla as a
willing, respectful listener because more was happening
here in the house now than "1,001 Castles to Furnish
Before You Die," recurring purchases of new curtains
for the kitchen that never turned out right regardless
of how you tried. In other words Art was happening
here in the house. And no, it was not as though she had
stopped writing, not even in secret. No, she sat in her
room and wrote and wrote, it surged and surged, the
more Gunilla and Göran, her landlords, moved around
on *tippytoe* in the house, shooed away the children who
wanted to play with the renter, "Come out now Terrible Animal Child and chase us!" But "Shhh, kids, get
away from here," could be heard from the other side
because the Writer should not be disturbed during the
"working&editingphase" of the "great manuscript"—
that word "great" had also come about with time—
Maj-Gun herself when she was not in her room had,
with importance in her voice, led the landlords to believe that was what was occupying her behind the door
in the boarder's room, which always needed to be kept
shut so "the creation process" could proceed.

So yes, she wrote, but the more she wrote, that was
strange, the more she took notes and took notes in "The
Book of Quick-Witted Sayings," "collected material," the
farther away she got . . . yes, that was strange.

But something had existed for real, in earnest, a place where everything had started. Something terrible and great that pulled, had pulled her toward it. Rug rags. The Animal Child's peering eyes in the kitchen of a single-family home, among rags. A woman who was cutting, cutting, Maj-Gun who was cutting, but it was no image, it was for real, not one of those similes, metaphors.

Rug rags. Which need words.

Silk velvet rag scraps I have seen the most I have . . . Yes, "raw, unworked," which the book editor had also written in his comments. But still: honest.

The writing that had carried her there, from one room to another room, an empty room despite the fact that there was a lot of paper there, a lot of dreams, stories, tales, feelings, jealousy—but her, personally, somewhere else, *I am without space.*

Talk about it, in some way. And about Susette. Rug rags, Susette. What was it about Susette?

"Sometimes that you are two who are one. I sought that in her as well."

Susette in the hangout. Her eyes. Maj-Gun who was hitting, and blood.

At the same time. She *had wanted* to kill her. She wanted to kill her.

And Bengt. *The Winter Garden.* "What are you babbling about?"

And another image. Which was not an image. A scene that was hanging, pulled loose, but was still true.

Him lying in the house, the room, and blood—

Talk about Bengt. The Love that was no love. But he died, despite everything, anyway.

All of this that could be explained—is not, after all.

•

Because *PRRRR*. There, in the middle of the night, the phone rings.

The Manager jumps up from the sofa bed, runs out into the hall, closes the door, and when he has finished talking he comes back.

"I'm afraid, my dear girl, that it's bad news," he says carefully. "That was your father. Your aunt, Elizabeth. In Portugal. She's dead. He asked me to give you the news.

"Well." The Manager stands there in the doorway and it comes out quickly, as if he were ashamed. "He said that he would very much like to speak to you personally but we agreed I wouldn't wake you since you had already gone to bed—

"She'd been ill. She went peacefully. Your brother and his fiancée were there. Good that she has found peace."

The Manager suddenly looked so old: his beer belly, his nakedness. Lions brother. The old men's choir.

And that night, when everything is over, Maj-Gun says the most beautiful thing she knows about Love.

The newsstand again, what it was like there, all of the magazines she had read. How they were filled with such a language, like in "The Book of Quick-Witted Sayings," which existed everywhere, made itself superior, you could not keep up, regardless of how you printed and printed the best bits. "You can say anything here": everyone who went around and "expressed themselves," outside the newsstand, everywhere, all the people who were saying the same things to each other.

"But Love," says Maj-Gun, and *that* is the beautiful thing she says so that the Manager will have it in his head his whole life, despite the fact that in a few weeks they will not see each other again. Ever.

"Is. Searching. A unique language.

"That is the urge to Love. *The Winter Garden*. A Winter Garden—language."

Kapu kai. *The forbidden seas. The hacienda must be built. Silk velvet rag scraps*—

And the Manager who is listening says, softly. "Dear child, lie down here. Time to sleep now. Tomorrow is a new day." Takes Maj-Gun in his arms, they fall asleep.

But Maj-Gun not Maj-Gun, it does not work, she is awake. More awake than she has ever been her entire life. An Animal Child's dark eyes peering out into the darkness. "Your brother, his fiancée were there, she went peacefully."

Liz Maalamaa. "I didn't understand what connected people, Manager. Now I guess I've grown. Been slapped in the face."

The rose—which you threw at me. It is Carmen, who is walking into a room that is the most terrible room of love, and the most wonderful—there is only seriousness there, and she becomes locked in there. Locks herself in, it was just a matter of opening the door and walking out, really.

And love, the rose, an abstract room: love is the bullfighter who is dancing with her. And everyone died and Carmen died. But she had already died: died for love, a rose. Love is the bullfighter who is dancing with her—

But how does it help to think?

•

Because now: sirens, blue lights, an ambulance, pulling onto the property. Maj-Gun gets up in the night, stands at the window. Someone is being carried out on a stretcher from another building. It was, she will find out later, the neighbor, the lady from the other building who had complained about the noise in the pipes, but nothing too serious, an asthma attack, the old woman will get better.

Blue lights that fall in, blink blink, light up the room that so far, just a few days, but still, has been a whole world.

The Animal Child, in the window, stares out into the darkness, peering. Out into the night, a panting blue light.

But cannot be kept hidden.

"Can you see yourself killing for love? Or dying?"

"A love that is greater than death, Susette."

"Maj-Gun, you have said that, yes."

And farther back in time. A girl at a cemetery: the folk song. The same thing happens in the folk song, in every verse, over and over again. A repetition. That girl, her eyes. She could reinforce fear. The mask. Her art.

Susette's eyes in the boathouse, when she fell. Kill her.

Walk in whiteness, in whirling snow.

And later: standing there on the cousin's property. Looking in through the window, cupping her hands. He is lying there. *The Boy in the woods.* Unmoving, in blood. And she in the snow. Blood on her hands.

Blue lights. Sirens. Justice.

"What is it?" the Manager asks behind her, heavy with sleep, blue blinking over him too.

The nakedness.

Only a Manager's testicle can look like a small pink bebé tart when blue light falls over it in the darkness.

Djeessuss. And just a hellish Animal Child Maj-Gun Maalamaa can be so hopelessly idiotically elephant pregnant that her stomach turns over, because a great Nausea just cannot be held back, has to rush to the bathroom, *in the middle of the night.*

"Some bug." The Manager tucks her into the sofa bed in that sleeping bag, puts fresh, clean sheets under it. "Dear child." Cold towel on Maj-Gun's forehead, the Manager kisses this forehead before he leaves the room, closes the door, goes back to his business.

"A WILD PAIN"

MAJ-GUN IS WALKING across the square in the town center. One of the first days after Christmas and New Year's, freezing in her fall coat, is not wearing any mittens, lugging things that have fallen out of a just-broken plastic bag, her hands slowly turning to ice cubes in the cold. On her way to the old rental place in the attic in the neighborhood below the square, in order to settle accounts with the landlord family and empty the boarder's room in the attic, because she has terminated her rental agreement via telephone. Is going to leave the District, move now. Is coming from the newsstand where she collected some of her remaining personal items that have, in other words, been in the plastic bag that broke just after she left the newsstand for the last time; the new shop assistant is the one who packed the bag and had it lying on some shelf in the back room.

The new shop assistant. Just an ordinary girl, nothing special about her. After having worked for only a few weeks, has her own system for everything and has cleaned properly too. A good, not to mention *exemplary*, organization everywhere. Maj-Gun had almost thought of saying it to her too, "exemplary," like a compliment, but let it go. Besides—what does it have to do with her, Maj-Gun, anyway? And her contacts with the Head Office too: *the Head Office*, which the new girl pronounced with almost the same respect in her voice that Maj-Gun recognized from herself, from when she had been working at the newsstand.

"If there's anything else then you'll need to talk with the Head Office. Even though you, seeing as how you're no longer an employee, cannot be in direct contact with the section, the operator can certainly help you."

The Head Office, once such a *central* place in the world. Maj-Gun also, for a brief moment, wanted to say something friendly, a bit humorous, about it to the girl, in general. Maybe add something personal to it too: about her own experiences from this newsstand in particular and give some good advice that the new girl might find useful. But this girl was not exactly talkative. After she reeled out the bit about the operator and the direct line, Maj-Gun had suddenly been like air to her: during Maj-Gun's continued presence on the other side of the counter, "the customer's side" (there was not a customer's stool anymore either), in what was now her "place of employment" she had practically strained to be demonstratively unaware of Maj-Gun altogether.

Hummed a pop song while she energetically sorted magazines: old issues from new issues that she had collected in bundles to return—bundles to tie strings around, hard, sharp plastic strips and Maj-Gun was suddenly almost able to feel the burning and tearing in her hands from working with them.

Maj-Gun looked away and tried to maintain some distance. From the newsstand, everything here—in general too, as it were. A short moment from inside the newsstand, where she is never ever going to return, looking out over the square. The square that, during many years—djeessuss, how many had there been?—had been her place, her place here in the world. Just hers too. An empty square, but a space where so much could happen— *the potential*, but where, in reality, not much had happened at all.

And then, since this is over on her part, experience some sort of superiority in relation to all of this. In relation to the new stuck-up shop assistant who did not want to have anything to do with her, and also, in some way, in relation to herself. The one she once was but is no longer. NOW when so much had happened and a new page had been turned in her story: new life in her stomach, *The Law Book* under her arm (figuratively speaking, hell, no one goes around lugging that tome around out here on a cold day like this!). A change had arisen, which could, for example here and now, also be seen in that she had actually managed to keep her mouth shut when necessary. Despite the fact that her tongue had undeniably been itching to speak, she refrained from beginning any form of sarcastic dialogue filled with ambiguity with the new one here; but of course you have seen that, one of those girl shop assistants who can be knocked over with subtleties in three seconds flat—all of which Maj-Gun was once so good at.

But, then, had not felt anything at all. Just looked out over the square, that possibility, and suddenly completely unrelated to everything Maj-Gun understood that she could easily be here again. Stay in the newsstand, continue being here. Would not need many days, not even one, not more than a few hours and everything would in some way be the same again, that timelessness. Going back. Difficult to explain maybe but not mystical, not a bit. Just calmly established so to speak, as it was, is.

"You can say just about anything here." All of the tips, coupons, and games. "Everything about . . ." all the magazines. *Be happy every day* and "Are You Borderline? Test Yourself!" Sticky lip gloss under the counter, a hundred miniature plastic containers originally prepackaged in small crackling transparent plastic bags glued to magazine covers but carefully pried off with the use of a paper knife, *when I wanted some!* Various hues, Blue Anemone and Pearl Rain and Champagne—

But at the same time, at exactly that moment, Maj-Gun understood something else as well. Whether it was with the life after this one or whatever it was, for example all of the phenomenal views in it—and she will have them . . . from the window at the law firm in the dapper southern area of the capital city's center, from the Municipal Legal Assistance Bureau in the northern part of the country (a square again, but rather small), even by the sea, the wild sea as it will appear from a patio in Portugal from a house she will inherit from her aunt. At the top of a mountain that falls right down into the sea. Yes yes, fantastic, three thousand feet below: breakers, the foam, the salt, the birds, and the horizon, all of the nuances in it . . . still all of this, all of these views, in the end rather interchangeable after all. In any case that is how it was with the future, law, all of the houses she is going to live in and own, all of the properties—she knows NOW that it is *this* view in particular, the view from behind the counter at the newsstand, or from the newsstand's door where she had a habit of standing and smoking, the same square, this square, in the District, the town center she has stared at the most in her life, that will come to live inside her the most. Be her most, regardless of whether or not it means anything.

"Where are my things?" The girl has stopped humming, shuffles lazily toward the back room but hesitates immediately, because she does not want to drag a former shop assistant in there either really, not to mention a complete stranger. On the other hand she also wishes Maj-Gun Maalamaa would leave and in other words quickly disappears behind the curtain to the back room and is back a few seconds later with the stupid plastic bag that she pushes over onto the other side of the counter. Maj-Gun takes the bag, peeks inside: sweaty tiger blouse, half a carton of cigarettes of an unusual brand, "The Book of Quick-Witted Sayings."

Today is the first day of the rest of your life. The card? The girl shakes her head, shrugs her shoulders, but the card has undeniably been removed from the cash register; there are not even any tape marks left on the aluminum, that girl really has scrubbed and polished and had many things to do. "Forget it." Maj-Gun takes the plastic bag, goes on her way—it was not really that important anyway, the card, it was not even hers; had been there from the beginning when she had started, but certainly thought she would like to have it with her as a memento, in some way.

"Wait!" the girl yells when Maj-Gun is already almost out on the street. "THE POISON STICKS from here! *I* don't smoke!" The girl with her fingers like a clothespin over her nose and . . .

"Yes yes yes." Maj-Gun Maalamaa lumbers back up the three steps. An opened pack of cigarettes from some corner on the shelf under the counter, cigarettes into the bag and Maj-Gun hurries out, never returning to that newsstand in her life! Across the square, toward the boarding place in the house "Sumatra" in the lush neighborhood to the right with the plastic bag that ripped at the bottom after only a few feet, the contents spilling onto the ground. Picks up "The Book of Quick-Witted Sayings," shirt, carton of cigarettes, and with more or less all of this in her hands continues and then there comes Solveig Torpeson walking toward her.

•

They meet in the middle of the square, as if they had arranged to meet in that exact spot. Of course they have not, they barely know each other. "My deepest condolences," Maj-Gun says in rectory language, a language that resides in her bone marrow but she despises how it automatically pours out of her in that moment.

Because what she sees: "a wild pain." In that face, in those eyes, in some way the entire posture. Winter jacket is buttoned halfway, no hat in the bitter cold, scarf wound too tightly so that glimpses of thin white skin shine through the knitting—indefensible. No. No façade here, no rosy nights or birthdays, nothing. But— accidents. *The folk song.* Has many verses. Same thing in every one. Pearls on a necklace. An eternal repetition. Over and over again.

"Such a different way of looking at time." An old cassette tape in an old room, the renter's room, played and played, a few months back in time. Maj-Gun suddenly hears it NOW, in her head, and so clearly: a whole story rolled out, again.

The Boy in the woods. Susette in the hangout. And again: "What are you babbling about?" Freeze that picture now. It does not help.

"I love you because you killed for love."

"What are you babbling about?"

The Boy in the woods. A stranger. She did not know him. Except as someone in a story, her story. No idea who he really was. But he, who he was later: in the room, the cousin's house, before she had gone to the Second Cape and the boathouse and before a hellish snowstorm had started outside while she was lying, sleeping in the boathouse, dreaming about the hayseeds who were shooting on the square, and before she was awoken by a shadow outside the window, on the veranda.

But her in that house. "What are you babbling about?" She had already wished then that she said what she was first inclined to say, aside from all of the stories, everything: "But dear friend. Regardless of who you are, you can't stay here in this shithole, the cold, come away now. I'll lend you money, we'll buy you a bus card!" But she had not said that. Instead, that other thing.

"What are you babbling about?" He did not say it once but two–three–four times and he was already cuckoo drunk. And she was smoking cigarettes, smoking cigarettes and then, case in point . . . dot dot dot what had happened had happened, not much else to say about it.

But: the alienation. There is no story. And the terrible: she knew nothing about him. Had never known.

"A wild pain." But what had happened had happened, cannot unhappen, that is true as well.

·

Like the realism here now, on the square, almost takes the wind out of Maj-Gun despite the fact that maybe it is not visible because Solveig does not say anything. Not, "He fell asleep with a cigarette in his hand," as the Manager had said, or something similar. Or about the funeral, which the Manager had also mentioned to Maj-Gun: the cremation, the simple memorial service, no one else present except Solveig, her daughter Irene, and Tobias. A sister, Rita, who was supposed to come but never showed up.

But then, when the Manager told Maj-Gun this she had mainly focused on the angels on the television set: how ugly they were, those angels, Manager, CAN'T we get rid of them?

"Maj-Gun," Tobias said then, movingly. "Tobias," Maj-Gun replied. And then, they carried on for a while, "Maj-Gun," "Tobias," "Maj-Gun," "Tobias."

•

"Have you started working again? Wasn't it the newsstand?" THAT is what Solveig asks now, as if in passing, the only thing she asks Maj-Gun at all.

Maj-Gun, a shake of the head, a mumble, almost inaudible. That well . . . she is going to move, probably. Start going to school, probably, study law at the university.

"I've heard," says Solveig. "Tobias told me." And yes, the angels again, remembers the Manager's, "my friends, goddaughters." As said, that connection is so familiar but suddenly, here now with Solveig in front of her, in the middle of the day, truly fresh information, like a scoop.

"Tobias is kind," Solveig says without any particular feeling, as if it was something she has said a thousand times before. "What would we do without Tobias?"

"Tobias." How Solveig says it, that self-evidence, that right to ownership. *It was a shame about those girls*—no, it was never hers, Maj-Gun's, could never be.

The Manager, the Tobias Animal: *that* was hers, that closeness. And, of course, it is some sort of gilded story about the future, how it would be like that, regardless of where Maj-Gun finds herself in the world, the connection would remain. Letters, phone calls, "How's it going?" "How are you doing?" and so on. But it is only a story because it does not turn out like that. When Maj-Gun, in about five and a half years from this point in time, becomes a board certified lawyer, she is going to invite Tobias to her graduation party, but he kindly replies by letter that he will not be coming—something to do with school, something that prevents him from coming, insurmountable. But he sends flowers, some kind of orchids, no roses.

And yes, it will also happen later in life that she calls the Manager herself. Late in the evenings, nights, farther in the future, from her rooms. Dials the number, but for the most part it rings emptily. Of course, then she remembers that the Manager sleeps in the bedroom with the door closed or has the music on, and if he is sleeping he sleeps like she sleeps when she sleeps, and it is still for the most part, deep, without dreams. And if someone answers, she becomes mute. Though he must know that she is the one on the other end of the line: "Maj-Gun" he will get out only once after a lot of silence on his end. But then suddenly she does not know what she should say and hangs up and later she stops making these strange phone calls in the middle of the night. And then in reality that story ends, the one about the Animal Child and the Tobias Animal—the story about it from a certain perspective, *the only* closeness that existed.

You cannot step into the same water twice. But you *still* have to go there with your foot, dip, dip, move it around, over and over again.

Which also is, quote, "mankind's predicament." Her own exceptional formulation, one of them. For example from all of those appeals for trials she is going to write for work, for the defense, at the law firm—though fewer there than at the Municipal Legal Assistance Bureau in the north.

In and of itself, most of those speeches that she writes she never gives at all—in contrast to her brother Tom Maalamaa, in the service of the international organization, *him*, on well-paid podiums, he can talk. She just sits at home in her rooms and writes them: walks from room to room to room, different kinds of views to look at in order to find inspiration for the task at hand. Thick, fantastic woods, as said, broad views, horizons, perspectives.

Walks there and if she is in that kind of a mood and is thinking, writes as a means of passing the time.

And it is not that bad. A bit lost. Has lost something, but it is not very dramatic, just as it is, and she is not particularly lonely either.

Djeesss . . . nah. *Tass tass* in feng-shuied spaces, on warm wooden flooring, in rag socks.

Because otherwise, during those times: has toned down the "offensive" in herself a long time ago, which she would get criticized for already at the beginning of her college career. "Maj-Gun, you don't need to attack like a hyena, going right for the jugular.

"There is nothing wrong with strong opinions, a strong belief in right and wrong is the backbone of all legal proceedings, the fertile soil from which the judicial system originates . . ." blah blah blah ink squiggled in the margins of her notebook, talk talk . . . while she looks up, smiles, at the lecturer whose name is Markus.

"A hyena does not go for the jugular, Markus," she says. And djeessus, it sometimes still whistles silently between her teeth.

Sanded away. And in reality, her imbalance during that first period at the university is due to a long period of loneliness and sun and sea, and the child—like a want. Also a physical want. How she milked her breasts, read true stories about surrogate mothers. *True Crimes*. Because nah, there really is not a single experience in life that is just yours.

Come and see my gallery. Read for her entrance exams, walked around in rooms, whitewashed walls, admired landscapes, views, the sea in different ways, the foam on the waves, the horizon, the patio.

"After the Scarsdale Diet, anything is possible." It was a lasting expression during her college years, afterward. "My transformation."

Otherwise: age has been an advantage. Partially the visible, that she had been circa ten years older than most of her classmates. Partially the other, the timelessness.

He became her lover later, for many years, the lecturer, the corporate lawyer Markus.

•

"Solveig," Maj-Gun suddenly bursts out here on the square in the town center in the month of January 1990, with a sudden urgency that almost makes her stammer. "I don't know how much you know," she starts, does not even know how she is going to continue but, regardless of what is has been and is like with everything, after all she, *someone*, has to get something sensible out. "I would like to say something. That I—liked him very much. Your brother."

Solveig grows stiff, stares at her.

And again, fleeting, such a *need* in Solveig's eyes.

But she has pulled herself together in the next moment, cuts her off. "It'll pass, Maj-Gun. You have your whole life in front of you. And I have my girl, Irene. I'm planning on building a new house at the old place.

"There must be life," Solveig adds, like a conclusion. Which is of course something you just say but suddenly, exactly when she says it, Maj-Gun feels as though she is staring at her roundish belly.

This year I have something kicking in my stomach.

"You think you're so important with all of your secrets. Your damned songs. But shall I sing a folk song for you?" The girl at the cemetery, the lass with the folk song, Doris Flinkenberg, the last time she was there. But it was not Doris who was singing that time, that song, it was Maj-Gun herself, with the mask on. *The Angel of Death Liz Maalamaa*: Maj-Gun who wanted to tease her, get back at her, angry because Doris had not wanted to talk to her during the summer and had gone and tattled on her to the church caretaker who, furthermore, had gone to papa Pastor and told him everything.

"Last year I walked with the boys in the field. This year I have something kicking in my stomach!" Maj-Gun had sung, she had not wanted to hear any of the girl's secrets at all at that point. "What do you do if you know something terrible, something everyone has known, all of your cousins, everyone but you?"

Doris, who had been so depressed and spoken so strangely, had, in other words, not gotten any response from Maj-Gun at that point, just a ridiculous song that of course did not exactly make her any happier in any way. But all of her fear of Maj-Gun had, in that moment, fallen away from her anyway; she had just wanted to turn away bam, run away, you could see that, but Maj-Gun had been standing in the way, singing and preventing free passage in the solitary glow of a cemetery lantern in the otherwise compact October darkness.

Until Doris Flinkenberg herself in the middle of Maj-Gun's stupid song hissed, angrily, almost disgusted: "What the hell do you want from me you damned idiot?"

Then Maj-Gun lost all interest and Doris Flinkenberg left and that was the last Maj-Gun had seen of her because Doris killed herself a few days later. But from there, when Maj-Gun had known that and had all the time in the world to think about Doris and what had been said between them—most of all, everything that had not been said but insinuated in passing,—from there, in any case, a crazy story was born. *The Boy in the woods*, which here, now in the middle of the square with Solveig, ends.

Like all stories end.

Here again, in absolute reality, realism.

Though the song does not stop because of that; Maj-Gun's own little folk song, it keeps playing in her head and her body, like a mockery.

And Maj-Gun, on the square, fingers like ice cubes: all of the things she is carrying that slip from her hands, fall down on the ground. "The Book of Quick-Witted Sayings," the shirt, the carton of cigarettes, the opened pack of cigarettes among others. Because suddenly she has known, an insight that becomes formulated clearly first somewhat later but it comes to her exactly here and now. She cannot keep the child. She cannot. It was never hers.

"Here, the cigarettes." Solveig helps her pick things up off the ground.

"And good luck with school!"

They go their separate ways, Maj-Gun and Solveig, each in her own direction on the square.

•

"You look fresh. Pale. But fresh. Have you also started dieting?"

"After the Scarsdale Diet, anything is possible. Strong character and discipline. Starting anything is difficult. Then it becomes a habit."

And just a few minutes later Maj-Gun is sitting at the table in the cozy kitchen in the Sumatra house, where she lived as a renter for several years up until the beginning of November, stuffing down Danishes that her former landlady Gunilla had purchased expressly for this afternoon when she has a free period from school and Maj-Gun, as agreed, arrived to settle business. Pay the outstanding rent, empty the room, say good-bye. "Oh, sweet Maj-Gun we're going to miss you, and the kids will miss you too! They're at school now. Look at what they drew for you as a farewell present!"

A drawing representing a large monster sitting in a recliner: "Good-bye Terrible Animal Child!" it reads under the drawing in straggling middle school handwriting followed by a red heart, and it cannot be helped, Maj-Gun is moved to tears; she likes those kids so much, the kids who would often stand at the door to her room with the desk and the Thinking Chair upstairs despite the fact that their parents, "Gunilla," "Göran," often rebuked them with *shhhh, the genius is working, don't disturb!* "*Grrr*, Terrible Animal Child, come out and play!" The

Animal Child, that was Maj-Gun's own name she used with the kids, she had come up with it herself.

•

"And how *was* it at the rectory?" Maj-Gun replies "fine." As usual she cannot hide how much Gunilla also always appreciated that Maj-Gun Maalamaa, that she in particular, their renter, was the daughter of the former, very well-liked vicar. In the beginning, to the point it was almost uncomfortable.

Not to mention, what a transition. From the other rental place, Java, the rug rags, Susette Packlén, to Sumatra, *here*. Suddenly being someone. How Gunilla, otherwise a robust woman, a math teacher at the junior high school and the high school, rather round as Maj-Gun herself had gradually become here at the house, but partially due to other reasons, *without space*, it was true too—that Gunilla was almost embarrassed in front of the old pastor's daughter about everything that perhaps was not "proper" enough in this house. Not only that the classics were missing and all sorts of good literature on the bookshelves, bookshelves were missing altogether in that sense, instead filled with other knickknacks and record collections, but everything with the furnishings was always turning out wrong wrong . . . probably had something to do with her senses of color and taste not being as they should be, in a fundamental way, so to speak. Regardless of how she approached the business of furnishing the home, buying wallpaper, paint samples, different types of knickknacks, and other things to place tastefully here and there.

"Maj-Gun, do you think this is nice?" she had a habit of asking anxiously, as if Maj-Gun, just because she was who she was and not to mention was sitting upstairs in her room, "with the Literature," which Maj-Gun already at that time, in other words, was writing that Book. "The Manuscript," which Maj-Gun later, with a growing irritation that was not dependent on Gunilla though Gunilla thought so, had corrected her.

"Maj-Gun, do you think this looks nice?" Maj-Gun had replied: "'1,001 Castles to Furnish Before You Die,' Gunilla, I don't know anything about home furnishings." As was the case but it was also an amusing line from "The Book of Quick-Witted Sayings," at least she thought so herself, but Gunilla had not understood the verve in the quote, had only become sadder. Sighing, uncertain: "Well, maybe one should find another hobby." And flipped through to a new page in the magazines Maj-Gun tended to bring home from the newsstand and of course she did not have to flip through for very long before, quite right, a new possibility had revealed itself. *Inga and Petrus have wine tasting as their hobby.* "Maybe that could be something?" But then quickly changed her mind again: "Yes, of course, I know you don't *drink*, if you're going to create something then you need to do it with a sober mind, right?"

And Maj-Gun had smiled mysteriously, like a real sphinx, because at that point she had of course quite simply started hating that word, "create," but could not show it, she liked Gunilla, after all, did not want to make her sad. "Yes, for a while now I've been in the working and editing phase in close contact with the Book Editor, then what is known as the finalspurt remains."

"And may I ask how it's going with the Bo—" Had, like always with Gunilla, come back to the same thing.

And Maj-Gun's angry shrug of the shoulders, which had given rise to even more misunderstandings. "Yes, sorry, I'm walking along like an elephant in a china factory."

But Maj-Gun, with regard to her size, had laughed loudly. The Book, the Manuscript. Or whatever it was called, Authorship. That was in a way what was wrong with everything after all, or had started to be, there in the cozy house, the cozy family life. *I am a dwarf in these rooms*, Maj-Gun tried to say to herself, but it did not fit either really. Because otherwise, if it were not for "the Book," which had started taking on mystical proportions at that kitchen table, "go upstairs and work, write," then Maj-Gun would have been able to spend time sitting in the kitchen with Gunilla whom she really appreciated and talk chitter chatter about just about anything, "One should really start dieting."

"Listen to this, Gunilla, what your stomach fat says about your character." A funny thing she had also written in "The Book of Quick-Witted Sayings." But the talk, which there was not anything special about, still fun, relaxing.

And Göran and the kids too, of course, when they were in the kitchen. "Maj-Gun is walking around here like a Poet in Bourgeoisie," Göran could say, with a funny tone of voice, and then all of them could actually laugh, a bit relieved.

On the other hand: "I should probably go up and write some now," because right then, in moments like that with Göran and Gunilla and the kids in the kitchen, Maj-Gun had once again been reminded in some way about something she should have. Like flipping through to find a new page in a magazine. Get something like that for herself. Become *hungry like a wolf*, go to the movies, the disco, out and hunt.

"No, now I really should go up and write." So Maj-Gun, book-pregnant elephant girl, girl, gradually the only gracious thing about that creature, had removed herself from the warm, bright kitchen.

I am without space. Up to the room. The novel. Djeessuss. The Thinking Chair. The Book. Authorship, the Animal Child here and paper there, in all places.

Paper paper, between her, the world, everything. Had been working "in tight connection with the Book Editor for a while now" who had certain "minor" changes, that hellish word which always entered her mouth when she was standing, hanging by the door, wanting—certain "minor" suggestions for changes and comments . . .

The room, the Thinking Chair, the desk. But the truth was also the following: at the very beginning, ages ago, when she had come to this house, from Java to Sumatra, she had "the manuscript" with her. But it had not been "the manuscript" then, in any case not in the same way, but at that time this writing had in other words been real.

Where she had started writing, in the other rented room, with the woman on the first floor, rug rags. Suddenly, amid the rags in that kitchen in Java, she had seen the Animal Child, peering into the darkness. Demanding. So close. She had almost been able to touch it and feel the raw, slightly damp fur with her fingers. Unexplainable, but not crazy; it became crazy only when you tried to explain the Animal Child. Here it is. That closeness.

But then, the woman died, the talk. All of the talking. Became vaporized. Rug rags. Susette.

Search for it in Susette as well, in Susette's big eyes. But djeessuss, still, every time she had become so disappointed with Susette.

"And may I ask how it's going with the boo—" Gunilla has asked her one last time in the kitchen now during the farewell coffee. And then for once Maj-Gun does not look moody instead she says that she is thinking about putting the book project on the shelf and starting to study law at the university. Which, she still has to add out of loyalty to something she once was, may be bad news for the Literature but good news for the kids—they worship that typewriter, that is why she is giving it to them.

Gunilla cheers up, whether or not it is the typewriter, she seems a bit relieved otherwise too.

"Oh, but I'm sure it must still have been nice to rest up at the rectory. You looked, to put it mildly, a bit worn out."

•

And in the room for the last time, and alone. Gunilla had to go back to school: "Don't worry, we haven't touched anything, no one has been in the room since you left!" The key in the lock, pushing the door open carefully, almost sneaking in. The mess. Almost even worse than she imagined. There was paper here, paper everywhere. "The Manuscript of a Life," ten thousand pages, swelling over the desk, the floor, the Thinking Chair, and the bed, "all the shortcomings."

"The true story" and that and that and that . . . one of those thousand working titles in horrible glittery red letters, solidified nail polish, red and mother-of-pearl, which she and the children had amused themselves with by coloring together when she let them come in at some point, also wanting to play, not be alone.

And other papers: the letter from the Book Editor, which she still, before the appointed evening that had been the last evening in this room when everything had overflowed, neatly stored in a leather-bound folder in the top desk drawer and taken out and hastily glanced at sometimes, reading a few lines: "Promising in places, kill your darlings and tone down the self-pity . . ." And periodically it had given her a calm feeling of confidence but she had not been able to follow the advice, had not toned down but up. All of the humiliations, everything that was done to me and me and me, in a thousand scenes, "characters," an ocean, billowing waves that could, from the Thinking Chair, be heard like a satisfied clucking from her mouth sometimes when she thought she had been able to jot down a few particularly good parts. Sometimes not written at all, just thought things out, because she would gradually become so inspired that she did not even have time to write anything down, ideas, impressions that rushed through her head. And the jealousy. And Susette. MY love. A new story that came pouring in. Had not exactly improved matters any.

But now, as mentioned. All of that. Foreign. Gone.

Despite the fact that everything is exactly the same as when she left the room almost two months ago, turned off the lights, *click, click,* taken the getawaybag, and headed out.

In the morning. Early. Susette, on her way to work, was going to be picked up by Solveig down by the main country road, she had known that. Had waited for Susette in the darkness, stood in front of her on the walking path a bit past the town center. "I don't know anything about anything."

Had she said that? Could not remember, maybe she had not said anything. Just stood there and stared ahead, with her big dumb eyes.

"You're so easy, Susette." And Susette had become frightened, pushed past her.

They were going to meet up later in the day. On the Second Cape. Neither of them had known that then. Then, in the morning, Maj-Gun still had no idea that she would be heading out to the capes, not at all.

In other words, they had not arranged to meet at the American girl's hangout in the early afternoon. "Come down there, and we'll settle things." Nah. The Killer Rabbit had not said anything like that on the walking path that morning-night, it in no way had any plans. Killer Rabbit. That was namely how she had felt, as well, somewhere. Like a terrible black rabbit who, because it looked so horrifying, was called the Evil Rabbit, not the Killer Rabbit even though that was the word you thought about in that context, the context of the children's garden, and in other words for that reason, the rabbit had been considerately placed on the highest cabinet where it could not be reached or seen in order not to scare the life out of the kids in the children's garden from where it was now on the run.

A fictive children's garden in other words, of course she did not know anyone who would have or had such an experience from their own children's garden and Maj-Gun did not have any memories like that either. She and her brother Tom never went to the children's garden, in their own home; it was always looked after by Mama

Inga-Britta, or by Aunt Liz who came to the rectory and "babysat" sometimes when she needed to rest. No, nothing less than the novel writing again, the Book, again an "interpretation," and "tone down the self-pity."

And: she had, as usual, not toned down but toned up and stood there on the walking path right between the church and the main country road that morning-night in front of Susette who had, in any case at first, looked so sleepy—the Killer Rabbit who, in its violent fury, had practically cried out of exasperation. My love, the Boy in the woods, and so on.

At the same time as the Killer Rabbit's urge to kill was completely intact. And it could be felt: Susette had suddenly been one hundred percent on the alert. Like an animal who has met another animal: wide awake, and, in the midst of everything, also scared to death in those big eyes.

So alike. The Angels of Death. The likeness.

"Go away." Though Susette had done her best to hide her fear. "I don't know anything about anything."

Call forth the fear, reinforce the fear. But there had been no time for that. She had attacked immediately.

"Go away!" Susette's pathetic whining.

"NO!"

And then, just as fleetingly, the situation was over, as dreamlike as it had started. But if a Nightwalker with a dog had not come along on the walking path, Maj-Gun certainly would not have gone away.

A compass through Susette's eyes. It was night in the world for the Animal Child, the clock had stopped, five in the morning.

Left unfinished. But later.

Susette had suddenly arrived down at the boathouse on the Second Cape, in the middle of her own working day which she seemed to have left, of her own accord, and alone.

Why? You did not understand. You did not understand anything. Parallels. Rags.

But there where Maj-Gun has found herself anyway: just as much to her own genuine surprise, at exactly that moment. *The American girl's hangout*, filled with all sorts of junk, nothing nice about it, sleeping. Lying on the floor there, barely enough space, the getawaybag under her head. Some old rag pulled over herself, among the boat motors, fishing equipment, and a large metal anchor. Slept heavily and deeply.

Awakened by a shadow on the veranda. Sat up, dazed with sleep. Susette had not believed her eyes, it had already started snowing then.

Lots of snow. And Susette, a dark figure in all of the whiteness. And Susette, had seen her through the window, eyes met. What a resignation in her. As if: walking toward a destiny.

Rug rags. That was how it was going to be. Death's Angels.

Is that what had spurred Maj-Gun on?

Susette had opened the door, come inside.

"What are you doing here?"

She was going to the sea, she replied, like Susette in love, *Susette and love*. And Maj-Gun suddenly assaulted her.

Hit hit hit.

And Susette had fallen and while falling hit her head against the anchor and Maj-Gun rushed out. Into the whirling snow, onto the slippery cliffs. Struggled through the snow, up and away from here and farther.

The cousin's house. Which she had left a few hours earlier. That was where she had been. But Bengt. Not the Boy in the woods: it had disappeared, right there, when she was in the house together with him.

Because that was suddenly where she decided she was going to go, from the town center. That morning. Had in some way lost her sense of direction after the meeting with Susette on the walking path. Killer Rabbit. Its power inside her. It had not become light. That time of year when it almost never became light.

First around nine o'clock. Then she had already been on her way to the Second Cape. In a car. With a hayseed, in a rascallike mood: wanted to set up a time to meet. Some movie at some movie theater that just had to be seen.

She had also been in the other apartment. Susette's apartment. Empty. Susette at work; Maj-Gun had an extra key, which she had begged off the Manager. Walked around there in the Lovers' Nest. Alone. The pictures on the wall, the Winter Garden, the "exhibition." Blue-bluepictures. Many strange words. *People float freely from themselves.* Otherwise. An appalling mess, but *I don't know anything about anything*, at least it had been true in that moment. He had not been there.

Gone on his way. In reality, she would have liked to have gone home and slept. But home, an impossibility. No space. Across the cemetery and the walking path again, and out toward the main country road, the bus stop. Away. Was going to run away, at least fulfill that intention. The bus stop. No buses. But a car. The hayseed, all fathers' Toyotas, one of those. The window was rolled down, "Need a lift?" And why not?

Where? *Have an objective.* Mushy. The capes. He drove her there. Small kid who had actually been embarrassed about driving around and around this morning when everyone else was at work, not able to sleep.

Well, long story, cut it off here. Slammed the door shut, ended up on the side of the road heading toward the capes, a few miles from the house, had started walking. In which direction, did not matter. But THEN she had gotten the cousin's house on her mind for real. The Boy in the woods. Her love, her purpose. Maybe he was there, he was.

Come to the house, cold, ice-cold, beer and cigarettes, syrupy.

She had wanted to say, actually, if she had been in full possession of her senses: "But come away from here now, you can't live in this shit."

But still. Her dream of love. The only one. Pure. Hold on to it. Instead spoken like a ghost about the other things. I love you because you killed out of love.

"What're you babbling about?"

That was the lasting meaning. He had not understood one bit.

But keep on to the bitter end. Her end.

Ha-ha. Realism is here.

What do you do with your dream of love the second after you know that it has been forfeited but you want to hold on to it anyway? Answer: if you are Maj-Gun newsstandess, you tackle it. Programmed to *kiss* it back to life again.

And it had allowed itself to be kissed, indolent, without resistance, without interest as eroticism is, and what had happened had happened and on the floor, in an old parlor where she was lying, through the window she had seen: the wind, the cloudy sky, the dirty gray of mid-morning, the trees.

Had removed herself. He was sleeping then. Not like a child, but sawing wood.

That was the last she had seen of him alive.

The sea, clean, smelled good, wind and freshness, and then such a tiredness in her. To the hangout, through the pine trees, the cape, the openness.

Snowflakes had started falling, so tired in the hangout— snow snow snow. While she slept, dreamed about the hayseeds, the pistol awakening, snow and more snow.

Susette. And the anchor.

•

Hours later. The whirling snow, the cliffs, bloody. The road again, the house was there, called for help, ambulance, police.

Gone to the house. First. Like a Peeping Tom. Looked in through a window.

What she had seen was indescribable.

She had lost everything, all purpose. Run run away from there. In the snow, the slipperiness, the zero visibility. A thousand miles forward, but on the same road, the same Toyota, the same redneck.

"Do you want to run away with me to the ends of the earth? We're going now?"

He had shaken his head, hesitantly. Nah. Nah. Time to eat. *Homeandeat.*

•

But over now. Here in the room, never think about it again. If she were to think then everything would just start spinning again, an old folk song.

Now. Here, on the desk, in the room that will be left behind. "Hungry like a wolf." Folk songs. The cassette tape on the desk with all the paper.

Doris. A demo tape that a boy named Micke Friberg had sent around to various record companies back then. *Micke's Folk Band.* Back then Maj-Gun had gotten a copy off of him, Micke, granted "for compensation." Pulled out into a long, brown, small curly strip.

How nice: what a cassette tape later becomes when it gets tangled in the machinery and you have, in the end, lost all patience, and torn at it, who cares if it breaks.

Magazines. One particular one, open. Wrinkly. Glossy photo. Woman's face, big eyes. The compass, with the needle that poked through these paper eyes. Maj-Gun's compass, her needle.

Through Susette's eyes. Not Susette of course, a look-alike. How similar. One of those *young women*, a dime a dozen, an article. Which had been about just that. A serious magazine with a socially critical spin. How stupid that girl was, clueless, that *was* the message. Was not written out clearly, what was the art of formulation not good for? But, should be clear, based on the descriptions. Her stupid everyday existence, her stupid life.

That girl had been upset later. They met her at a café after she read what they wrote in the article that was going to be published—this meeting was also described in the article. "That's not me at all," she cried, otherwise defenseless, they chased after her with their camera. On the last photo, big-eyed in a wood, a small dog at her legs. She who had been crying and crying. "I'm not at all like that . . . *and stop taking pictures!*" Of course they had not, they became interesting pictures. As if in harmony with a revelation. *Don't know anything about anything.* Even about herself.

•

Maj-Gun hastily cleans everything up. The papers, the magazines, the cassettes, the compass, pens, and so on. In a black garbage bag that she drags down the stairs and leaves it next to the garbage can by the door. She puts the room key on the table in the hallway, the house is empty, glances all the way into the kitchen, cannot help herself.

The distinguishing feature about this house, Sumatra, is, as said, that on the inside it is exactly like the other house, Java, the same blueprint. The same view in other words, out into the kitchen. In Sumatra like in Java, when you come down the stairs from your rented room on the upper floor. The woman at the rug rag bucket. She had thought it was a dream at first; it was not.

"Can you help me with this?" The woman had looked up from her work, among the rags, the bags in the kitchen, piles of them. In half darkness in the middle of the day, the window shades pulled down.

"An office rat on the lower floor." Maj-Gun had started a letter to her brother Tom about life there in Java. "In gray clothes, all of her gray."

A letter, among others, that was never finished.

Because she had liked that woman, they had become friends, for real. "Susette, she didn't give way." Whatever she had meant by that, Maj-Gun, then it was one hundred percent true and real.

But now. Gone forever. Giving away.

So: here in the house, Sumatra, everything is normal. The table wiped clean, coffee cups and saucers in the sink, lemons against the dark blue bottoms of the curtains, really nice, fresh. A dull January afternoon light.

And left, left the big, black garbage bag by the garbage can. Everything from the newsstand in it too, except for "The Book of Quick-Witted Sayings," which she still did not dare throw away, keep it, like a memory. But the cigarettes, the blouse, and so on. She puts the remainder of what had been hers from the furnished room that she had rented into the seaman's chest that she had brought with her when she moved in many years ago.

There is room for a lot in the chest, everything she has. A few weeks later, after her aunt's funeral, right before she travels to Portugal, she transports the chest to a storage space in the industrial area on the outskirts of the city by the sea where it will remain until she returns one year later, buys a little house in another part of the city, a lush suburb, where she will live during her university studies.

She puts some other things in the chest as well. Red bow, a piece of wrinkled silk paper carefully folded, everything from the getawaybag that was hanging around forgotten in a closet in the Manager's hall for many weeks. It was close to being left behind altogether. The Manager, from the stairs, came running after her with it when she was already seated in the passenger's seat of the rented delivery van next to the delivery man. Tobias in the slush, temperatures above freezing again. Maj-Gun had taken the bag, good-bye, they never see each other again.

•

The drawings were also placed in the chest. Bengt's drawings from the walls in the other apartment, which she put in the bag while she was there. Blueblueblueblue pictures, watercolors, which she has not inspected more closely, will not end up doing so either actually. That "exhibition." That Winter Garden. Which may come to exist in the Winter Garden later, the one on the Second Cape.

She gives these drawings to Rita, some years later. Rita, Solveig's and Bengt's sister, from the Rita Strange Corporation. They do not know each other, cross each other's paths during a legal dispute. Maj-Gun is the lawyer, recently graduated from the university where already in the final stages of her studies, which she completes quickly and "brilliantly," she is offered a good position at a law firm with a good reputation, which has its reliable offices in the nice southern quarter of the city. A law firm where the lawyers occupy themselves with inheritance law and the like. Rita is the client. In her capacity as party in that corporation, *Rita Strange*. An elegant context for wild elegant ideas. Advertising people, artists, architects, gladly calling themselves "avant-gardist." Those kinds of dreams, which can be taken seriously thanks to their financial solvency, "the backing." Feasible, you can dream big.

And it is back then, in the wake of a recession, when dogs are eating dogs and some have become full even if it is not spoken about publicly.

Build. The Winter Garden. Architecture. The Second Cape. An idea on paper that has been born out of all of this? Maybe. But it is not interesting, in any case in the perspective that Maj-Gun cannot muster any interest in it, not even enough to pay more attention to it than she needs to for the purposes of her job, not in the least.

Market transactions, inheritance and gifts, and so on, the kinds of things that can be bought with money, and the kinds of things the law is there for, plus the money, to secure them. The Glass House on the Second Cape is owned by a friend, Kenny, who is also a member of the corporation, she inherited it from a relative she once lived with. And Jan Backmansson, who is Rita's husband, has the hill on the First Cape, but some sister Susanna is being obstinate, and so on. Several transactions, legal obstacles, but those kinds of obstacles are there to be overcome. An idea. Which may be realized. But what is just as true is that the Winter Garden, a few years after it has come to be, is transformed.

Has already aged then. An idea that was an idea, a thought, but when it was realized: well, not what you had thought. Not a lot of added value either, a bit clumsy too.

Is sold, is bought by someone else. As a physical place, the Winter Garden can be seen as a process, that light is transformed and transformed.

But the brochures will remain. Kapu kai. *The hacienda must be built.* That, for example, and other things.

•

Lengthy? Diffuse? Maybe. Maj-Gun thinks so in any case while she carefully, and down to the last letter, becomes acquainted with all of the details in the matter, she is being paid for it. But *My God when it comes to the business matters that person cannot stop babbling* she thinks, which could be an interesting observation since Rita, cool as a cucumber, is someone who de facto *does not* babble. At all. Puts forth facts. Papers on the table. One of those, could have been fascinating.

She gives the drawings to Rita during the final stages of the proceedings. Says, "I knew your brother." And adds, after a brief pause, "We had a relationship."

Rita looks at Maj-Gun Maalamaa, one moment, takes it in, so to speak, what does one say: the revelation. She is wearing red clothes. Expensive skirt, expensive small jacket with discreet and solid buttons, and slim, that stomach fat like all of the other fat she dieted away of course. Attractive. Shrugs her shoulders. "Bengt," Rita says later, as if it were nothing, shrugs again, "had many relationships." Tragic? Neither of them says so, nor "he was washed up" as Solveig said once a long time ago on a winter day on the square in the town center, "a wild pain," which for Maj-Gun settled everything, in one moment, but—in and of itself, the pain, the words, for Rita's part does not mean that it does not, could not, exist there.

In some way, perhaps it is audacious, it makes an impression on Maj-Gun. Reluctantly. No nonsense. Rita's attitude.

Rita just takes the drawings and puts them in her bag. Nothing more about that. And maybe, if you had been in another mood, or in some way, in relation to everything, could have sat on your high horse, you could have hissed, *You could actually call Tobias now and then, someone who did so much for you too.*

Two angels on the television set. The Astronaut, the Nuclear Physicist. Sister Red, Sister Blue. But that is something Maj-Gun no longer thinks about every day. Been there done that. But giving the drawings to Rita is no whim, no impulse.

Rita. She sees Solveig. Rita might as well be Solveig, no difference. That twin likeness, still.

Getting rid of an old story. Which still, seen as a story, possibly as a crime, never really stopped following her. "Countryman Loman covered things up." One of her classmates at the university had been fascinated by that kind of information. Gaps, holes, misunderstandings, when the law had seen things through the fingers, *women and crime*, men and crime, these people without legal rights. Information she does not gather or think about, but to which she will return, like a refrain.

And maybe when she gives the drawings to Rita she thinks for a moment about Doris Flinkenberg, at the cemetery, before she died, the folk song. Just a breeze, through her head.

The Winter Garden. The idea for the Winter Garden was not born there, *Rita Strange*, those contexts. It has existed for a long time. Whole long lifetimes. A game on a hill, three siblings. *The three cursed ones* in the eyes of others, *rumba tones*. She knows that, and does not know.

But she thinks about other things too, which she does not think about of course but which exist nonetheless. The Child. Solveig. The Child.

Sometime later, in the middle of the 1990s, she quits her job at the law firm, leaves a brilliant career that has picked up pace on the private side and gets a position as chief legal assistant in a small city in the northern region of the country.

THE FUNERAL

MAJ-GUN IS REUNITED with her family at her aunt's funeral in January 1990. Elizabeth "Liz" Maalamaa— she took back her maiden name when she became a widow—has passed away at a respectable age; after a brief illness, quietly "fallen asleep," literally, died in her sleep. A peaceful passing, the best you can think of, in her Portuguese winter home. And avoided being alone at the end. Her nephew Tom Maalamaa and his fiancée happened to be visiting, and after her death they took care of all the practical details. All papers, documents and, naturally, the repatriation of her remains to the homeland and the funeral in the little city her husband was originally from and had, for some time now, been resting in a spacious family plot where, during his lifetime, a spot had been reserved for his wife.

The whole family, in the church, and at the reception afterward. Relatives and a large circle of acquaintances and friends and surviving relatives of the many old and sick whom Elizabeth "Liz" Maalamaa, during her career within the deaconry, had cared for with a big heart and tireless effort.

"She made the last days for our loved ones so bright."

Flowers, telegrams, and loads of addresses that later, during the memorial service in the nearby fellowship hall, were read aloud by Tom Maalamaa in a loud, steady voice.

And before, in the church: Maj-Gun's father the pastor emeritus ministers the ceremony, speaking devoutly about Elizabeth "Liz" Maalamaa's exploits during her career. And, next to the coffin below the altar, he wants, before he takes a small shovel and pours sand over the white coffin, grains of sand on folded, white silk fabric with beautiful white- and lilac-colored flower arrangements, *from the earth you came, to the earth you shall return*, say something personal too.

About his own sister, the dearly beloved. For example: there were once two siblings, Elizabeth and Hans (the Pastor himself, that is), who found God early on, on the farm, up north in the country where they had grown up. Both siblings, and God: wandered in the woods that were large, like China, the wonderful Middle Kingdom. They decided they were going to become missionaries when they grew up, picked pinecones off the ground and lined them up neatly in a row on a rock and the pinecones were the Chinese to whom they preached the joyful message of Christianity that had come to them, Elizabeth and Hans, already at an early age. Almost like a miracle, their *own* revelation, in an environment that otherwise was not more than normalpiously religious.

And when Hans, who was two years younger than his extremely more patient sister, sometimes grew tired and allowed his eager playfulness and his own rascalness take the upper hand, and started throwing the pinecones around—his sister did not get angry at him, she never did, but led the small, high-spirited boy back to their serious business with a gentle hand.

"But with an affectionate hand": it became a lasting childhood memory. And a character trait that would stay with his sister throughout her life, the affection, how it would just grow inside her.

"A large and hardworking heart that would find many outlets later in life." And of course, as it is in life, endure many trials.

But also had a wonderful sense of humor, and when she became older she was able to laugh heartily at the somewhat exaggerated melancholy of her childhood. Because a playful humor existed inside her, even though she did not always let it out. And here in the church papa Pastor urges forth the image of a girl with hair braided far too tightly who became a young woman and let her hair down; swooned over film stars from the movies, wrote letters to them in Hollywood and received autographed pictures in return, greetings from Ingrid Bergman, Ava Gardner.

So the small "missionaries" in the woods, the wonderful Middle Kingdom, the pinecones grew pale with time. Plans for the future under that cloak, but not God—not for Liz Maalamaa, never God. Just life, which got in the way . . . "and young women have their own dreams as you well know." Papa Pastor pauses here where one can, at least if you are his daughter Maj-Gun Maalamaa, hear the ellipses hanging in the air. And it is and remains there in the church, where even several members of the upper-middle-class family that the dead husband belonged to are present, the Pastor's only reference to the childless and not particularly happy marriage that followed.

"On the other hand," papa Pastor reasons—and yes, maybe this speech becomes long and certainly personal, it is often the case when Father gets going, but the devoutness and his own evident emotion make it so that all thoughts one could possibly have about a tiresome choice of words fail to come. The wordiness that the Pastor could devote himself to during ordinary Sunday sermons too and for which he sometimes had to endure certain criticism for; mild criticism, in and of itself, because on the whole the Pastor was a respected vicar in all of the congregations where he has worked. But there had, in other words, been those who at some point in passing had said that when the Pastor was speaking in church it could, quite simply, sometimes become a bit too much *of a good thing*; maybe also a small reference to what was not said out loud, oh no, my goodness, but about the Pastor's "country upbringing," which perhaps made it so that he did not have the same well-developed mind for "the simplicity in the heaviness," "the elegance of the unsaid," and similar things that certain other people had gotten from their mother's milk.

"I just get carried away so easily," papa Pastor used to say in front of the family at the Sunday dinner table, apologetically as it were but with a rascally glint in his eyes because in reality he did not care what people said about him when he was preaching in church and the following Sunday he would, if he was in that kind of a mood, carry on the same way as always.

Rascallike. That was a reminiscence for Maj-Gun as well, here and now in the church, of something old, not forgotten, but something she had not thought about very much for a long time. Her beloved father, how he is, was, and could be.

"On the other hand," papa Pastor continues as it were, pulling himself together. "The foundation that exists in everything," Elizabeth "Liz" Maalamaa never lost it.

Faith like a mountain. A child's belief in God, innocent and self-evident but as an unspoken demand. Belief as something to answer to.

Belief places certain demands on us when we have left childhood, become older. These demands *can* be formulated into words but should not be answered with words, but with actions. Belief is activity.

And many times, papa Pastor remembers again, and when he speaks, the tears glimmering in his eyes, and no, it does not need to be said, he is not embarrassed about them, not in the least. When he personally, the brother, failed in his belief. For example during the difficult years at the theology department when he was beset with heavy doubts, pondered and pondered, fallen and fallen. Of course some of this brooding was the normal brooding of youth of the kind brooded on during a certain period in life, a passing phase. You understand everything, understand nothing, know a lot, lack experience, the experience that comes from the heart, the blazing core of faith and life.

But there had also been a great, alarming question which, since he had left his comfortable and cozy childhood home, had been assaulting him: in the form of images, scenes of loneliness in a student room at a boarding school for "country boys," made him defenseless. So, suddenly, he felt as though he had lost all contact with the living, with mankind. And with God: that *if* God— that question, so simple, but struggling with it was like walking on hot embers, about God—*where* was he then in this world?

I call to you from the abyss, Lord. But then, how his sister Elizabeth, "Liz," student at the deaconess school, had come to see him at his student dormitory. Time after time, spoken to him, as in their childhood, in the woods—and gotten him to see. All the grace. The Light.

"The Lord is my shepherd, I shall not want."

And finally, here in the church, now, papa Pastor says that *the innocence of our childhood is the best thing we have.*

Maj-Gun, the warmth swells within her. And: how proud she is. Her father, there, in front of her, everyone. His words, his endless love.

And how he personally, just in the moment when he has spoken about the grace the light, looks up, over all of the people in the church and at Maj-Gun, meets her gaze there where she is sitting in one of the back rows.

The lost daughter who has returned. "On the other hand": it was never like that. "On the other hand," in some way, in that moment, as if father and daughter both, like in a mutual silent agreement, in some way want it to be like that. Inside both the father and the daughter there is a certain rather well-developed feeling for the dramatic, to take the opportunity and reinforce the drama, but not just because. But because of something obvious, and maybe that is the essence in the story about the lost child's return. Something that has been murky and therefore impossible to say out loud.

In the daylight. *That it is over now*, Maj-Gun. Beloved. Regardless of who you are, and that, whatever you have done, I love you and forever.

The hymn in the church later. "Glorious here on earth."

Maj-Gun in the next-to-last row, the very end. She had to sneak in and take the first best possible seat because the memorial service had already started when she arrived and that is why she is not sitting at the front with the rest of the family. She was running late, nothing particularly special about it. Just taken the wrong bus, gone the wrong way.

But then gotten on the right bus after all. "As it often is in life." Maj-Gun smiles at the memory, in the middle of the memorial service.

Something her father also said once, at that dinner table at the rectory, during her childhood. With a certain humorous emphasis too, but with the same good mood as always. Speaking of some of the new pastors who wanted to make use of modern analogies and *the language of our time* when they were preaching. Simple everyday similes and words besides, as easy to understand as possible. *The way it is in life.* Getting on the wrong bus, the right bus, remembering to stop at a red light, go when it is green, and brake for all of the pedestrians in the crosswalk. Sometimes you made a mistake, did something wrong, *everyone* does, but Jesus, who was forgiveness, forgave you.

And the whole family had laughed at the dinner table, not harshly, because there, at the dinner table, there was no meanness. Just as the Manager once pointed out when Maj-Gun had let things get out of hand when she was talking about the future, "the pastor's calling" that she still, just like her brother Tom, had never actually had, then her father papa Pastor that open-mindedness, he was not fundamentally minded, not the least bit. But just did not want to have "the language of our time," everyone's everyday in the church. Not because it was wrong but these trifling rules, concerns which were just concerns that had nothing to do with the great, life, death, both extremes. Which all of us in some way are affected by and which can be felt in church in particular.

Everyone's life that is, as it were, larger than that, and it needs to be taken seriously, not be diminished, just because it may not immediately be comprehensible.

So not that, in the church. Wanted, in church, to have God's holiness because it was what it was, almost in Esperanto. Have that space, that glory. And the words, the melodies, the words and the melodies that brushed against the unspeakable, the tremendous. *We go to paradise with song.*

These words, not because they were supposed to be "solemn," as it were, but because it was exactly these words which were felt in your body or which, in some way, already existed there. Set down inside you and when you heard them, came close to them here, how they were brought to life: something great, a glimpse of what is time but not directly history, rather time as an archaeology inside oneself, and inside other people, inside people in general. To feel that for a moment as well, such a participation. That all of us are also in some way the *same*: we carry ourselves in the same landscape—and time. That there was, is, another time, we carry ourselves in time that is not seconds minutes days years decades, my life, the story of my family . . . but time in the sense of *"generations follow in the footsteps of generations."* A greater time, a landscape, everyone's time.

Wander inside God in time, in a landscape that we share, we have a share in each other, can see a glimpse of it sometimes. A woman who is cutting rug rags by a bucket, long strips, *silk velvet rag scraps*—

There was room in that language. For everything. *I am not without space.*

And there in that time then, a moment, a fragment of your own life. A fragment in a landscape with fragments of other landscapes inside it, the landscape of others. Across all borders, in time and space. Across narrow family borders too of course: mother father child inheritance beyond these inheritances but also these. And how obvious that the DAY OF DESIRE is housed in this landscape too. Something old that is not you but has come up inside you. The Happy Harlot, the Girl from Borneo, whatever; they are of course, were of course, just denotations. The Disgust as it were, as it was called for a time after childhood when there had been a built-in sense of *that which was yourself but yet so much bigger than.* But the Disgust then, devastating so to speak, so termed by Tom Maalamaa, in royal supremacy, Gustav Mahler behind his back. The Pastor's Crown Princess who was the heiress to the words, and the words existed for him and became his and that pathetic girlfriend who quietly rolled her eyes next to him. Prompting, nodding in silent support, as if on order. Though, it was easier to agree of course, no resistance in it. Be in his landscape that was given limits the more he spoke, the limits of his words, became secured as the only landscape.

So that you became, if you were his sister Maj-Gun, an extremity. Some sort of comment, the other. The Harlot, that is, with a capital letter suddenly *hamba hamba*, she came from Borneo—at least it was effective. Something in your eye then, if nothing else, because the brother who was standing at the window in his room in the rectory was suffering the view over the cemetery in a grand way. The Disgust still would have been a little tantalizing if not for the fact that this Happy Harlot was his own sister.

But djeessuss, if you were the sister, you were supposed to be all of that to a T, you received. In order to *prove a point*. The Day of Desire. *Don't give way.*

But on the other hand, all that was just as true but that she, the sister, had not wanted to bear: first, the jealousy. The brother and the girlfriend behind the closed door in the brother's room in the rectory and Maj-Gun on the other side, alone. Without her brother, rather much alone, regardless of how the siblings had been like cats and dogs with each other during childhood.

"What do you see in her?" Maj-Gun could go into her brother's room and ask when the girlfriend was not there. "I am fascinated by the Death in her," he would have been able to say then, while he, as it were, was preoccupied with buttoning the cuff links on his starched shirt. But all of it was just silliness really, a slight becoming feeling of the "metaphysical" (he had loved that word for a while too) because later, when death showed itself for real, the girlfriend's father who became ill and was suddenly dying, Tom Maalamaa had pulled away or maybe she was the one to retreat but one thing was certain: that when she left the rectory for the last time he had not exactly run after her. Let it be. Ordered *Reader for the Preparatory Course for Future Lawyers* as COD "papa is paying," and became engrossed in it.

Second, *We go to paradise singing.* The Day of Desire. An experiment—or whatever it had been. It had drained off of her rather quickly—that is to say the Desire in all of it. Partly for the obvious: that it had not been much fun. Standing with your freezing bum among the

headstones and that girlfriend who naturally happened
to come running from the rectory just at the moment
when she truly realized it was rather shitty, all of it, and
out of resentment Maj-Gun had, in other words, cried.
In other words cried NOT because she was ashamed or
because it was a pity about her. In any case not in the
way the girlfriend with the saucer eyes had seen it, *poor
poor thing what have they done to you?* Which of course
had made Maj-Gun even more frustrated and in combi-
nation with the jealousy that also always came to the fore
during that time, in the girlfriend's immediate presence,
she had suddenly been standing there, howling about
the WONDERFUL in all of this . . . about the Desire
that was great and strong and ct cetera. Djeessuss. The
girlfriend, who had not understood a thing, had looked
at Maj-Gun, frightened and suddenly so unhappy, confused, alone (her father was very ill then too), who Maj-
Gun had, many times afterward with Susette, developed
even more of a bad conscience from it.

But as said, not amusing. Something violating about
it too, there among the headstones, "receive." That is to
say, completely private. *The innocence of one's childhood.*
The boys who had come to the cemetery, the hayseeds
often with some religious affiliation. Well, she had not
really bothered about it actually, but afterward they had
not looked at her and those years later, on the square,
they seemed to have completely and totally forgotten
that it was her, the Happy Harlot, the same person as
the fatty in the newsstand, "today is the first day of the
rest of your life." The Happy Harlot had just been an
idea to them. They drove cars around around the square,
but around others "just think what Madonna has done

for fashion," girls like that, or that hollow-eyed one who had suddenly been there again—Susette Packlén, "I am fascinated by the Death in her," *silk velvet rag scraps* rug rags. That one.

At their level given Maj-Gun the finger from the cars; ordinary fingers, nothing special about that. And her personally, of course, if she had been in that kind of a mood, flipped them off in return.

And at the same time, on the other hand, again again: *he* had been nice, that hot-rod farmer who had driven her from the square to the capes in his car that terrible day in November, just a few months ago when she was going to . . . yes, what was she going to do, kill, die? Who had carefully asked about "meeting." "Go to the movies?" In other words, one of those kinds of meetings, youthful, normal. And nor was there in that question any apology for anything that had taken place at the cemetery in the past, he had possibly been one of them, but been there done that, in this situation, a question only, from a boy to a girl, perfectly normal. "Don't have time. First I'm going to do something terrible. Then I'm going to run away to the ends of the earth. So." Naturally she had not said that because she could not have known what was going to happen ahead of time, but still, she had that feeling, transparent in exactly that moment, an imminent catastrophe, like a fate, *because you were the catastrophe*, not for any other reason. And then not drag some other outsider into this: then what she had de facto said in the car had been that she *might* be busy, did not have time to chitchat, and fired up by the catastrophe that was pounding inside her right when everything could have been normal shot off as a closing remark, "and now there have been quite enough of these advances, you can let me out here!" "Here?" They had in other words been in the middle of the woods, or in the middle of nowhere, on this road out to the capes, but a whole two miles there and almost as far to the cousin's property where she had consequently ended up in the following.

"Can I call you?" had been his last question before he drove off the side of the road and stopped but *hmptt tjjjmp* she slammed shut the car door, a powerful existential slam that echoed in the silence, in the entire world. And the car, the hot-rod farmer inside it, had driven off.

But that fate had an irony: after everything, hours later, he had been there again. The same lout, the same car, the same road, roughly the same place, whirling snow. Terrible road conditions. The car that suddenly showed up just right in front of her in the middle of the road where she had been plowing her way through the snow just falling and falling, in an unbearable state of terror and shock, inexpressibly that she never wanted to suffer again. Bloody hands in her pockets, no mittens. The car had stopped, the door opened again, and she had been grateful then, gotten in.

"Shall we run away together? To the ends of the earth? See. I have the getawaybag with me." She had said, or something along those lines.

"Nah," the hot-rod farmer had replied, and added, a bit legendarily: "I dunno. Can't. Homandeat."

So: back to the square again, they had skidded their way there, slowly slowly. To the middle of the square, the familiar square, despite the abundant snow that was walling up everything there too. But suddenly, when she stepped out and the car started with a *vroom* and slid out of view, Maj-Gun, bloody paws even more well hidden in her pockets, had not had a clue about where she was.

Started walking, up to Susette Packlén's apartment above the town center. Justice. The sirens.

•

But now, in church, as if she had awoken from a dream. To reality. HERE she is after all, now. Has gone through everything, to this, to the middle of the hymn, the church, *to her father's house.* A fragment of everything, in everything, others, her own, inside her. And her father who is looking at her: "Welcome home." And suddenly, she knows exactly how she is going to introduce herself to her father again when they have the chance to talk after the funeral, just the two of them. How she, with a glint in her eye, will go up to him and say to him that unfortunately she came late to the memorial service because she had, by mistake, gotten on the wrong bus a few times on the way there but then she had gotten on the right bus after all. And arrived. And how he, her father, now she knows this too, will look at her then with yes—he knows how he would look at her regardless of what she says to him. That dearest Maj-Gun, we have all missed you, welcome home. Open-mindedness. *We go to paradise with song . . . but*

OWWW in her stomach.

An intense pain, like a reminder, she almost folds over double inside on the church pew because she can control herself after all: but that is the memory, *this year I have something kicking in my stomach.* Unpleasant consequences . . . how could she forget that? And at the same time, exactly at the same moment she becomes aware of it: something that she, of course, in some way had been aware of the entire time, has been said to her besides, should not come as a surprise. But still, like a bombing. The gaze that traveled over the pews in the church, over the people in them, naturally also to the family in the first rows. Her brother's erect neck that is sticking out of the stiff shirt collar, his neck sunburned—and another neck, the one next to his. Hair in a ponytail, gray shoulders, skin shining, despite the great amount of sunshine in the south where it has also been—white.

Maj-Gun remains staring.

It is Susette Packlén. Who turns her head slowly, looks back in the middle of the hymn, eyes meet Maj-Gun's eyes, big eyes.

Suddenly, during a few seconds, which will later slip away, for a long long time, Maj-Gun has understood exactly everything.

On the other hand, of course, the obvious though nonetheless fantastic for that. *Susette and love.* Polo shirt, blazer, sideburns. Susette from the underworld, under the disco ball, gray, glittering. Susette on the dance floor, through the cigarette smoke. At the other end of the dance floor: polo shirt, blazer, sideburns. Tom Maalamaa. Her own brother.

Rag doll. "Loose limbed." Dance my doll . . . Susette and love: like a story to dance to.

"Sometimes I have the feeling that I planted things inside her, Manager." The Manager, who has not really understood, but on the other hand, she had not really been able to to go into detail or explain what she meant. But: all stories. The Boy in the woods. Duel in the sun. Dead. For love. The boy in the house. Susette in the hangout. When she was falling and falling—

Rug rags.

On the other hand, this is the landslide, something she will keep hidden for a long time in life because it is so amazing. That Susette, *a stranger*. She knows nothing about Susette. Has never known anything.

Her head spins, her stomach turns. Her stomach. OW! OW! OW!

Her stomach. *This year I have something kicking in my stomach.* Solveig on the square: "a wild pain."

"What are you babbling about?"

The Boy in the woods. A violation.

•

She cannot keep the child. It was never hers.

•

So after the memorial service, the burial. At *this* cemetery, another place, another city, the little town where Liz Maalamaa's husband had come from. This is where she will now be lowered after all: in this earth, for her not the earth of home but foreign earth, though no more heartfelt singing about this either. The swans, Dick and Duck, her aunt on the ship, maybe there was some truth in all of this too. "I didn't understand what connected people, Manager. Though now I guess I've grown up. Been slapped in the face."

A lush cemetery, picturesque, you can see it despite the fact that it is a dull and snowless January day, no leaves on the trees, gobs of old, dirty snow on the ground. The temperature is above freezing again but there is a biting wind that goes down to your bones and it makes it feel like fourteen degrees at least. Maj-Gun has been freezing in her new red winter coat with a silky soft lining during the roughly thousand feet she and all of the

other funeral guests wandered from the church behind
the creaking black cart with the white casket on top—
three male descendants on either side, Tom Maalamaa at
the very front on the right, the most important spot, like
oxen pulling the hay wagon along behind them.

The cemetery grove itself where the family grave is
located is particularly nice: so if one had the desire to say
something nice, something that could be said in the presence of all relatives from both sides of the family, then it
would, for example, be exactly what Maj-Gun herself is
going to say afterward at the reception, mainly in order
to put an end to a certain burial ecstasy that has caused
some of the closest relatives on the dead husband's side
to start getting out of hand.

"God knows everything," Maj-Gun is going to say, "but
the grove is beautiful and that Aunt Liz Maalamaa would
have appreciated resting in that place is something we all
can agree on.

"A childless marriage but God gives and God takes
away and that sorrow which lasted so many years only
brought the two of them closer together." Afterward, consequently, some relative from the husband's side suddenly felt the need to determine this despite the fact that
there had not been a single person at the table for the
closest mourners who would not have known exactly
what the married life between the two, now dead, people in question had been like. If not the "family doctor"
himself—a cousin who is enthroned at one end of the
relatives' table instead of at the cousin's table where he
actually should be sitting but has apparently received a
better seat due to his respectable age in addition to his
task as "physician in ordinary," which they say in that

family, to that family. He is ninety-four years old but clear as a bell, possibly a bit *loose tongued* in his old age; that is to say less restrained with what he in company as company might happen to allow to come out.

That "doctor" whom even Liz Maalamaa was forced to see many times while her husband was still alive for a neck brace and bandage and grogginess-inducing calming tablets as a result of what, of course, did not exist, something everyone was well aware of—her own cowlike clumsiness that caused her to fall down the stairs all the time. Which is, in other words, what her husband had pointed out in public where still no one had spoken out against him: that his wife so to speak *had to* stumble, fall, or come tumbling from the second floor to the first floor in that beautiful house, which was in everyday language called a "shatoe," on comfortable sandals where they lived. But "ssshh," even "the doctor," just like the entire family, put his finger to her lips. "Ssshhhhhh," had not even needed any form of extra request to "the doctor," he was bound to confidentiality in any case and then of course it was decorum too. But then in any case, with great sympathy—because he was no wild animal of course—generously prescribed all of those calming medications that sometimes made the aunt float forward so to speak, under the influence. Not over the ground, but in her head, where a lot of strange things—China, memories from a life as a missionary that had never been lived in reality—started welling forth.

But that is, consequently, when "the doctor" here at the reception after the funeral suddenly starts speaking like that, in small print over the sorrow of childlessness and about some sort of despite-everything-union between the two partners, that Maj-Gun is going to look at her own father, the dead one's brother. And notice for once that he has a hard time keeping his own council; his hand that is gripping the coffee cup—fine Chinese porcelain, *a fine china*, they had to drag the most exquisite family china to this exhibition as well—starts shaking unreasonably and you suddenly understand for once that he is not planning on being the country boy from the boardinghouse in the company of these people, which he is in all other places except for in the church where he is so keen to stay on good terms with everyone; *too* good terms, he has just realized now and now in other words, readiness, he has decided for the first and the last time to say things as they are, speak, shout out.

Accordingly, this is when his daughter Maj-Gun quickly jumps in and states that bit about the grove which, despite everything, is so lush in the summer of course in any case. And her father then, when he hears that, how he comes to his senses again and relaxes and places his warm pastor's hand on his daughter's hand on the table.

And THAT IS HOW Maj-Gun, after a period of absence, introduces herself to her father, with that line, not as she had imagined in the church during the service. Though before she has the chance to say anything else here in this situation her father will personally say something, wink with one eye and say softly, just to her: "Came too late? Maybe you took the wrong bus?"

A warm smile spreads over his daughter's face then, and her father's warm hand in hers, and her warm hand in his—and hands, in general, everyone's hands will, for a little while, become warm. Even Tom Maalamaa's paw that is pounding his sister's back, exaggeratedly brotherly.

"Hey, Sis," with a painful pluckiness that rhymes poorly with his impeccable exterior. As if he, for one moment, when he sees her again after a long time, finds himself in a childhood where he and Maj-Gun never were, either alone or together, for the same age exists in him as in her and that was always what united them—and divided them—actually.

But Tom, there at the reception, otherwise brown like a gingersnap next to his fiancée, white and pale in the face, in the middle of all the warmth, she is beaming as well. One of those, a few seconds, a complete moment, in reality. "Ahem": Tom Maalamaa who is going to clear his throat and get up and with his future wife in his wake will walk up to the table where a photograph of Liz Maalamaa is standing next to a tea light and a large pile of telegrams and addresses. Which he consequently starts reading aloud with his fiancée's help: she, next to him, hands the addresses to him one after the other and then she carefully arranges the read ones in a perfect fan on the table. Susette Packlén, a glorious light around her. Those eyes, like globes, a whole world, *silk velvet rag scraps*—so filled with life and meaning now. The engagement will be made official later in the spring in connection with one, in a line of her brother's many appointments, that he is also casually sitting and talking about at the table with relatives from the husband's side of the family without it sounding like boasting.

And what are you supposed to think then, about Susette Packlén? Love. *Susette and love. My life.* That there had ever been another lover. The Boy in the woods. A *newsstand toppler*? But that is just absurd.

A long, LONG time later, many years, hundreds from this point in time, Susette Maalamaa like Maj-Gun Maalamaa will, who otherwise will not have any contact at all over the years, explain it like this:

"Do you know what it was like with him, Bengt? Like being in a wood. Getting lost. I didn't understand what he was saying. Like with Janos, the Pole, or the Lithuanian, which he actually was. From the strawberry fields. Just went on and went on, I didn't understand a thing. That's how it was with that."

Mrs. Maalamaa, which is what becomes of her later, for many years. Susette Packlén from the District who cleaned for Solveig at Four Mops and a Dustpan, got a white cat for herself for a while, and walked around and did not get anywhere in the District.

Susette at the window. It is high there, above everything. A window in a room in her own house in the outskirts of the city; there are parts of cities in the world, does not matter in which city, these neighborhoods, exclusive outskirts, by water if there is water, they all look the same. Tom Maalamaa with family will come to live in neighborhoods like these in the cities where the international organizations he works for have their headquarters.

Tom Maalamaa. You will be able to read about him in the paper sometimes, hear him speak from well-paid podiums, see him in pictures. "Improving the world"— unpretentiousness. "The wife in the background." Can be recognized by her large eyes. *Cute.* Three children. Karl-Olof, Mikael, and Elizabeth Ida. No pets due to the allergies in the family. The aupairgirl, Gertrude.

"This," Susette will suddenly say at the window in her home in the living room, second floor, view over a bay, "reminds me of Portugal. Death in the hands. I had it then as well."

•

But STOP, here now, stop. Right here, NOW, still, the inevitable. The cemetery, before the memorial when Liz Maalamaa receives many dear greetings filled with memories from the past, before everything: as if one wanted, through these jumps in time forward backward, to get away from the unavoidable in front of you. The GRAVE. The coffin with the aunt being lowered down, roses falling on the coffin in the hole before the wooden lid is placed on top and wreaths with flowers rain over it.

Two roses, no more. From both godchildren, Maj-Gun's, Tom's. Maj-Gun's a small, simple pink one that the Manager helped her pick out at the flower shop in the town center where they had gone together in public that last day they had been together. The rose, which had already been standing in a vase in fresh, nourishing, lukewarm water, a few delicate slits with the knife in the stem, on the counter in the kitchen in the Manager's apartment during what had been the last night.

And Tom's rose: dazzling, huge like a sunflower, dark red, becoming in the way it matches his cashmere scarf. *Pjutt*, drops it, an unnatural gesture, which is exactly why it cannot, with that movement, avoid etching itself onto the retinas of the audience.

But it does not help. *My child my child, I am going to make you so happy*. The dead one, Aunt Maalamaa, gulping on a ship with her goddaughter a long time ago, a will. It has not been fun, as it will turn out.

Because Maj-Gun Maalamaa inherits everything, the entire estate—"the whole kingdom," including a winter home in Portugal. In her brother Tom Maalamaa's face who had the entire *coffinhell* to deal with personally in Portugal, which he, in the moment he grows pale beneath his sunburn, hisses at the lawyer's office when the will is opened and read aloud which, according to the wishes of the deceased, takes place first thing after the funeral—these, the aunt's final requests, which have been quite a few and had mostly to do with the funeral and the shape of it, meticulous instructions, right down to the china that should be used during the reception, *a fine china*, were neatly written down in a notebook in the nightstand drawer next to the aunt's bed in Portugal. And Tom and Susette have followed these to a T, with the exception of the seating of the family doctor because, in regard to him, there has in Liz Maalamaa's notes not been a single mention.

Coffinhell. Tom Maalamaa has given the show away, but only for a few moments, then he pulls his act together again—and forever.

Maj-Gun gets everything, right in front of the noses of the husband's side of the family too, who have been putting on a show for the aunt since she became a widow. Dick and Duck, amusing maybe, because against the good advice of his relatives' and his family's lawyers her husband had refused to sign a prenuptial agreement so everything he owned went to his wife. Properties, stocks, and what in inheritance language is called "loose money," cash in other words.

The significance of this inheritance for Maj-Gun should not be underestimated. Not due to any malicious pleasure in the presence of the relatives or her brother who had hidden his greediness well with his smooth walking and talking: things like this pass, are evened out. And besides, those differences of opinion they had during childhood, they really were not that bad: mutual frustration and irritation as said, like *dogs and cats*, which Mama Inga-Britta always used to say.

Not to mention that Maj-Gun is going to give her brother a portion of this "loose money," including a share of the revenue from the aunt's home in Portugal when she sells it a few years later.

But Maj-Gun Maalamaa is going to become *respectable*. A word she quickly learns to master during her law studies, which she starts a year and a half after her aunt's passing and finishes brilliantly and quickly, with family law, inheritance law, and the like as her areas of specialization. And she finds daily use for it during those years after graduation when she works as a family lawyer at a distinguished law firm in the city by the sea.

But financially independent, *djeessuss*. It will provide her with a certain freedom—and space. She will have many rooms, rooms upon rooms upon rooms. Will not have to live in an apartment, never live in an apartment again.

•

"Susette, wait!"

But, still, at the cemetery, the burial: the wooden lid and the flowers, the wreaths, a sea, the ribbons: "wonderful is short," "a final farewell." One thing, the most important.

Maj-Gun in a red coat, like a stoplight alone by the grave, she has stayed behind. A few others, a couple, also dawdling on the gravel path. Susette and Tom.

"Wait! Susette!"

Susette obeys, turns around, hesitates.

Tom Maalamaa one step ahead of his fiancée, scarf flapping in the wind, also stops, looks back. Susette says something to him, speaks softly, he shrugs, waves to Maj-Gun "so long"; they are going to see each other at the reception. Removes himself with determined steps, perhaps a bit relieved.

Maj-Gun and Susette. Susette on the gravel path, Maj-Gun who walks up to her. And again: *how long ago*. The newsstand, all the stories, an apartment, a cat. Susette, *to life—an invitation*, shoulder pad wearing, in smoke, at a disco. Susette now: her big eyes, eyelashes covered with mascara, but only a bit, and on her full lips, a little lipstick, coral colored, "discreet." In nice clothes. Gray winter coat, ankle boots, dark gray suede, heels just the right height, elegant.

Rug rags, *silk velvet rag*—something unexplainable that bound them together. And the District, the marshiness. Maybe it can still, faintly, be discerned, like from under layer upon layer upon layer: the smell of a winter day. Rain that became whirling snow, her wet mittens, fingers frozen anyway, blocks of ice. Wind and tight jeans. That thing inside Susette which made it look like she was always cold. And cowboy boots, *boots*.

The defenselessness. And: Susette in the hangout. One moment, gone. *And nevermore.*

Because now Maj-Gun says: sorry. A few times. And, well, she knows it does not make things better by saying it but is there something she can *do* now?

Susette is silent, picks at the ground with the toe of her boot, globs of snow, earth. Starts, "It turned out . . . wrong . . ."

Looks up again, as an introduction to something else, so to speak, longer. Maybe that she, so many years later when they meet again by chance, is going to mention, in passing. How depressed she was, had been. For many years, the Sorrow: over and after her mother—the words she does not have now but will have later. Has had the common sense to get therapy.

Or maybe she, Susette, actually thought about saying something else.

But she has grown silent again, lowered her gaze again, toward the ground and then says softly but clearly, audible and determined: "Maj-Gun. Now you have to promise me something. That you, we, will NEVER talk about this again."

And before Maj-Gun has a chance to answer, say that she promises because she does of course (she promises something else at the same time in silence: that they, she and Susette, will never ever again under any circumstances whatsoever hang out in any way shape or form), Susette has looked up again and pointed at her stomach. Smiling, in the midst of everything, brought her finger to her mouth: "Sshhhhhh . . ."

And Maj-Gun, who idiotically, but almost as a reflex, thinks in that moment about pointing at her own stomach as well.

Oh no, still not. Remains an idea and then Susette says, "It is more than a month now. Tom and I. We're going to get married and have a baby."

Tom. That rascal—

But at the same time. Maj-Gun remembers. Solveig on the square. In Solveig's eyes. "A wild pain."

"Djess . . . Wow, Susette," Maj-Gun quickly corrects herself, *now you can say whatever you want*, came pouring out like from "The Book of Quick-Witted Sayings," almost grotesque but still. "Moving fast. At least he shaved off those awful cones on his cheeks, what were they—sideburns?"

Susette laughs. Yes yes, her suggestion, terrible, she has to admit.

And then in the middle of everything, an even bigger smile on her face, and it comes suddenly, almost like an exhalation.

"Oh, Maj-Gun. I remember you in the newsstand. Starling darling. How cuckoo so to speak." She never forgets, she adds, with delight. As if it were a thousand years ago—"And how did it go again? Just because you're a count—"

Maj-Gun thinks, hardened. *She* had reeled Susette in, on the square. Did not know what she was going to do with her. "It turned out wrong."

"The Angels of Death," "I'm fascinated by the Death inside her." Tom Maalamaa, the rectory, their childhood. Then—rug rags . . .

She does *not* answer. What should she say? *Cuckoo?*

"Maj-Gun you could. Say everything so well. Starl—"

And then there is not much more, Susette suddenly grows quiet, they have started walking.

"My deepest condolences," Susette says later, serious again.

"Me too," Maj-Gun replies. "So Susette," she has gotten ready, because the bad conscience has hit her again and hindered other thoughts, "you remember—how I could carry on. But I just wanted to say. That she, Liz, my aunt, was actually quite okay."

"You've gotten thinner. Red suits you. I'm going to sell the apartment—"

But then they were already at the gate, had left the cemetery behind them.

And her brother there, Tom Maalamaa by his dark car in the parking lot. Regardless of how stupid it looked when he leaned against it, Maj-Gun is not able to contain herself; in the middle of everything she runs away from Susette, up to her brother, and practically throws her arms around his neck. "Congrats congrats, she told me," whispered this, as if for that reason, that is, in other words, what the hug looks like.

"Hey, hey, Sis, careful . . ." But in reality, something else. Maybe like this: that both siblings, Maj-Gun, Tom, suddenly know something else too. Two children from the rectory, siblings, ruffled hair, uncomfortable wrinkled brows in the sun, pulled from inside the house, a summer day. Recently pulled from their activities inside the house. "Out into the fresh air, out out!"

After *Hamba Hamba*, the docklands in Borneo, hey Harlot there aren't any harbors here, *Hamba Hamba*, anyway, clap clap, the Girl from Borneo—

Like a farewell, an end to childhood, farewell to this: that childhood, it stops here.

And Liz Maalamaa, the mask, it belonged here. Death, the Angel of Death, all of it. But still, is Maj-Gun the only one?—maybe, leads over into something else—

At the same time, a feeling, inexpressible: away, do not look back, pushes her face against Tom's throat so long that it almost becomes cuckoo.

"Are you coming with us?" Susette is suddenly asking, is standing behind them.

"Nah," Maj-Gun jumps back, shakes her head.

"I'm going with . . ." Whom is she going with? She will certainly get a ride from one of the other relatives and friends and so on to the reception in the fellowship hall.

"See you."

"See you."

And Maj-Gun is standing alone in a pretty much empty parking lot.

On the other hand. In a way too: idiot. Everyone has already left. But of course there is always, as her aunt Liz used to say, "the apostle's horses."

The apostle's horses. Comfortable shoes. Missionary boots. You certainly get around that way too. Half a mile to the reception, the fellowship hall, she has started walking.

•

A few weeks later Maj-Gun travels to Portugal where she gives birth in September. She calls Solveig. Solveig comes, with her daughter Irene. She cannot keep the child. Solveig gets the child.

Come and see my gallery. A white wall in Portugal.

And then she studies law and is accepted into law school.

THE GLITTER SCENE, 2006

(The new songs)

The new songs had no humility. They pushed past the veil and opened a window into the darkness and climbed through it with a knife in their teeth. The songs could be about rape and murder, killing your dad and fucking your mom, and then sailing off on a crystal ship to a thousand girls and thrills, or going for a moonlight drive. They were beautiful songs, full of places and textures—flesh, velvet, concrete, city towers, desert sand, snakes, violence, wet glands, childhood, the pure wings of night insects. Anything you could think of was there, and you could move through it as if it were an endless series of rooms and passages full of visions and adventures. And even if it was about killing and dying—that was just another place to go.

(MARY GAITSKILL: *Veronica*)

The Glitter Scene, "Ready to be gone"

Ulla Bäckström has now opened the door to the Glitter Scene, the drapery, which is like a curtain, has been pulled to the side.

She is standing on the edge, white skirts, swaying.

In the wind, her hair, her teased hair, insects glittering.

In the wind, glittering in the glow from the Winter Garden, the darkness, the fire, the wind

THE SILVER PARTY SHOES

To the Winter Garden (*Liz Maalamaa's things*): the Silver
Party Shoes, made of strass, with a brooch. Purchased
in Rio de Janeiro, 1952. She loved the shoes. Her party
shoes. Liked dancing too. Sometimes.

Come and see my gallery. A white wall in Portugal.
Liz Maalamaa's gallery. Everything she held dear on the
wall. Photographs, a brother, a family on a farm, a map
of China. Portraits of her idols, black-and-white pictures,
with autographs. Ingrid Bergman, Ava Gardner.

A postcard, two swans among other swans. Dick and
Duck. And the godchildren, her brother's children, several photos. Maj-Gun on a boat. Majjunn, as Liz Maalamaa always called her niece, in a sun hat, dress, laughing,
looks happy. A child's drawing. A woman with a mask.
Represented her, the children's aunt Liz. "To Liz from
Majjunn." The dogs of course. Handsome, Ransome: she
had two. Expensive lapdogs, the first one died almost
right away from a congenital condition, the other died
ten years later after securing a happy life and old age
under the aunt's jacket.

The silver shoes on a podium. They are a memory,
not even particularly worn. Liz Maalamaa, who comes
from simple circumstances, is careful about dealing with
things carefully.

TO ROSENGÅRDEN 2
(*Tom Maalamaa, 2006*)

THERE IS A CAR on its way into Rosengården 2. It has stopped at the gate, the chauffeur rolls down the window, punches in a code on the keypad, the right number, they are expected guests, okay okay, green light, the gate opens. Entrance road, November 2006, dark car, strong headlights that light up the deep, dark fall night.

"Courage." Tom Maalamaa is the one who is driving, his wife is sitting next to him, just the two of them. Both children who are still living at home are home, with the aupairgirl Gertrude. In the new service residence on the other side of the city by the sea, a suburb, the diplomats' area. They have recently arrived, just a few weeks ago, back in their homeland again. They are going to stay for a while, maybe even a few years; this appointment. The family has not lived in the house for many days, yet the husband, who is otherwise always a pillar of patience with his wife and the family in general, despite the fact that he has a lot on his mind when it comes to his job, had time to get irritated about the fact that the unpacking was taking so long, going at a snail's pace, mess everywhere.

So it is nice to get out a bit, away, on an invitation. Maybe Tom Maalamaa says "courage" to his wife in the car for exactly that reason. His wife does not always like going out, spending time with other people, acquaintances, strangers, "keeping up appearances" or, like now, meeting some of his friends from way back when, during his time at university. Peter and Nellevi, both architects, whom it will be really nice to meet up with after so many years, now, here in the homeland where Tom Maalamaa with family has not lived in seventeen years. Even if it cannot be seen on her, the wife, that is. Susette Maalamaa never complains; that she can feel uncomfortable in the company of others is something only he, Tom, her husband, knows. Or feels, because they have not spoken about it very much.

Actually, Tom Maalamaa thinks in the car in Rosengården about his wife Susette, that there is a lot he does not know about her. But that is okay, as it should be. There are mysteries, air between people, especially the ones who are closest to you. He has a habit of saying that to his wife sometimes. She agrees, nods, smiles, looks at him, her beautiful eyes. Which he cannot "read"; her look. Still, even though it was many, many years ago, he can remember the time she came to him in his tiny bachelor pad in the center of the city by the sea. It was that year, 1989, when they met again after having been together for a short period as teenagers when they were both living in the District. That fall, somewhat earlier, he had, after many years, run into her anew at a disco in the city by the sea. Actually that time he had only seen her at a distance but it stirred something old in him to life. Strongly.

He called her a few times that fall and they had seen each other, fleetingly, at a café. She had been evasive, distant, and he already had time to think: disappointment. But then in November, that same fall, November 1989, one night, a telephone call from her: "You have to come." And he had come, he had found her, picked her up. So still, because she was the one who had called, because of that attraction in her, in the end it was still she who had come to him.

Moving. Those eyes, of course. But also something else. There was, in other words, in all of her something *appealing*, in general. Had been there from the beginning, as a teenager. And at the same time, when you thought about it, with that word, determined it in that way in your head, it still turned out wrong. It was *still* something else.

Which maybe was something that could not be expressed in words, and it had always existed between them.

She and he, Susette and Tom: what had really started as a game during childhood, and not even an innocent game, one she really had not wanted to get involved in. But a game he had played with his sister Maj-Gun, in the rectory. A restless childhood, not on the outside, but maybe exactly for that reason, in peace and quiet, a certain frustration. They were two children who had, in some way, not really done themselves justice; there were growing pains of course, because it passed later. But there are children who are not in step, not with other children or with their childhood in general. In step with their childhood the way they expect it to be: often intelligent children, sensible—because only intelligent and sensitive children clearly sense such expectations from their surroundings. Especially unspoken expectations, and they can, these children, if they are keen, receptive, be petrified by them. Not difficult children, but calm ones: children without all that energetic spring inside them that would make it possible for them to rush away from all thoughts, feelings, revelations.

"That old age in us," as his sister Maj-Gun said on the telephone later, when they had gotten back in touch with each other a bit. No intensive socializing, but sometimes telephone calls, sporadic. "Old age." Hm. His sister Maj-Gun had, in and of herself, always been the older of the two of them, and far more dramatically minded. In that childhood, youth, she also had a way of going whole hog, trucking on until the bitter end. For example, a chapter, which the siblings had not touched with a single word afterward, also belonged to that time. The Day of Desire. The Happy Harlot. *Hamba hamba.* How his sister danced for him in his room in the rectory, hot summer days, inside, where it had been quiet and pleasant and cool alongside the hot, taxing summer day. Been the Happy Harlot from the docklands in Borneo. "There aren't any docklands in Borneo, it's just jungle," he had of course soberly, precociously pointed out to his sister then already but still played along: clapped his hands in the dance, whistled, "like a sailor," *hamba hamba.*

As a game it is silly, especially described in this way, in hindsight. But on the other hand, children, even siblings, sometimes play lightly erotic games with each other, that is normal. But he had, of course, felt ashamed afterward even back then, during his childhood, youth. And actually sometimes already while the game was going on thought it felt good to leave it behind and get out into the summer day—even if he later did not really know what he should help himself to there. Consequently, since an adult had literally chased both obstinate siblings from the room out into the fresh air: their mother, sometimes

Aunt Liz who was often visiting at the rectory during that time despite the fact that she was married and living with her husband in another city. But her husband was violent, had drinking problems, and the aunt sometimes needed to get away and "rest." The mother or the aunt would tear open the door to his room where he and his sister Maj-Gun were spending their time: "and now children out into the fresh air!" Well, as said, the irresoluteness continued out there in the yard but it still was not entirely stupid leaving the game and he had even been able to enjoy carrying out some punishment tasks he was allotted if he snuck in again, which he often did. Back to his room, alone, with a book. Closed the door, even for his sister then. Wanted to be alone, read Gustav Mahler's biography. Cuckoo. He had not understood a bit of it of course: *Mahler's music says more about the nature of emotion than all philosophers.*

But the aunt had often caught him red-handed and as a punishment for his disobedience he was forced to scrub the sink in the bathroom with a dish brush and detergent. Small, horrid paper edging to glue on the tiles above the same sink. "Remember to wash the washbasin after every use!!! That goes for Tom too!" That strip was taken down when the aunt went home again; Mama Inga-Britta had not wanted to hurt the aunt's feelings while the aunt was there but she thought the paper edgings made the furnishings look terrible. And yes, maybe they did.

But *the Day of Desire, the Happy Harlot.* For Maj-Gun, his sister, the game had not remained in the room, at the rectory. She *had to* take it with her. To the Cemetery. And how Tom, her brother, had been ashamed, disgusted, been angry, angry at her—because at that time they had not even been children anymore, teenagers. His shame, his fury, had naturally just egged on his sister even more, though he truly understood that only afterward, as an adult. And how everything had become even worse for a while, combined with his sister's jealousy when he got his first girlfriend and she, the sister, who in and of herself was always at loggerheads with him otherwise too, still had, as it were, become more alone and kept to herself. Had been a peculiar one among the teenagers in the District, a rather quiet one of course, nothing that reached the ears of the adults. How Maj-Gun Maalamaa "held court" at the cemetery. But inside her, no shame. It had been her idea from the beginning, she had held to *that* when he, her brother, in various ways, tried to explain to her the disgust he felt.

In any case. Gone. And they, he and Maj-Gun, as said, have set it aside, a long time ago. Nothing to talk about. And she is someone else now, a lawyer like him, and he can, for example, admire her because she left at the beginning of a brilliant career; quit her job at one of those awful family law firms, one of those with "a good reputation" that tend to be the very worst, and started working with law and justice for real, as the director of a legal assistance bureau in the northern region of the country. His sister, Maj-Gun. Another, but still the same. Because the Disgust. No. When he thought about it later sometimes, as an adult, he realized that it had for the most part been about him when they were young. That he had been ashamed and irritated on his own behalf. Because still, always, his sister: such a purity in her.

But despite everything, this should be interposed in the context: Tom Maalamaa has also sometimes felt a

certain relief and gratefulness that his own children
do not seem to take after either his sister or himself in
that respect. Children *completely* of their time, in step
with everything. The oldest, Karl-Olof, sixteen years old,
badminton champion and fencing champion and soccer
player and popular among his friends at the boarding
school in Canada where he goes to school; *like a fish in
water*, here, there, everywhere, and it is not hard won—
is planning on beginning his studies in international relations and political theory at some esteemed university
in the United States or England. And Mikael, the middle
child, who when he was younger you might have worried
a bit about: trouble concentrating at home, at school, not
far from an ADHD diagnosis at one point—had suddenly
on his own found an outlet for all of this extra energy
and restlessness. Computer games. Now earns money
from his hobby even though he is not more than fifteen
years old: plays and tests games for a large gaming company. Yes yes, too good to be true, you can almost laugh,
but it is true, is completely true. And then the youngest,
Elizabeth Ida, named after the aunt, twelve years old but
seems young for her age. How calm, how sweet, with her
stuffed animals, her dolls, her small friends who visit her
and whom she visits. Elizabeth Ida: not the center of the
party but always invited to them, Little Miss Friendly,
that type. Crawls up in her father's lap in the evenings.
He tells her stories. She, big eyed, listens. Well. They
outgrow you too, the kids. Because the stories, Tom cannot help but break into a smile when he thinks about it
more deeply. Stories: despite everything it has been quite
a while ago now with Elizabeth Ida. How she, all of the
kids, are growing, outgrowing you.

"I just want our children to be happy and well-balanced people," his wife has a habit of saying sometimes. And Tom agrees. Small individuals, all of them. To see your children develop into that, a privilege. "Well-balanced." Tom Maalamaa particularly likes hearing *her*, his wife, say that. Has always had a certain forgetfulness about her, a kind of absence, sometimes, like ... not with major things—but the worst in that respect was when the children were younger and she forgot them in a park in Rio de Janeiro. Just forgot, came home, but there was something she had forgotten. After that they hired an aupairgirl: Sonja, Anna, and the last in a line for a few years, Gertrude.

But she cried after that, his wife, and *how* she had cried. It was that Sorrow which existed in her too that he had never really understood and gradually he was able to admit that to her openly as well; in the beginning he had a guilty conscience. "You don't need to understand," she once said, with that endless gentleness that exists within her. And it had been a relief, as said, and in some way, even though it sounded like the opposite but it was not, had brought him and his wife, Tom and Susette, even closer together. And she has gone to therapy, many years, and it has, according to herself, helped her.

But maybe it belongs to her character, to sometimes go somewhere else, as it were, to Sorrow's Room, or whatever it is, maybe it is a part of their life together—of that unnamed bond that exists between two people who neither can nor want to live without each other. An integrated part of their way of being with each other, but unnamed—quite simply because there are no words for it. Like in Portugal, in the month of December 1989. They had spent a few weeks there, with the aunt who became ill and happened to pass away while they were visiting.

It was that month of December that they had started being together again, had found their way back to each other. She had cried then too, in Portugal, not come out into the sun where he had been, on the patio. But taken care of the aunt like an angel those last days, so in that way certainly been present in situations where presence is required; she had cried in spare moments and at night.

But when the aunt died there were other things to think about: everything that needed to be done, repatriation of the body, all of the practicalities, and then she had livened up again, jumped into it whole-heartedly. And when they had come home again she took a pregnancy test, it was positive, they have always spoken about their first child, Karl-Olof, as a love child who came to them, in Portugal.

But the Sorrow inside her—that was her word, though it is highly likely that it originated from the therapist, the therapists. Or "long-term depression," but in that case he preferred the Sorrow, a sorrow with an element he referred to as appealing, which moved him so deeply it was almost terrifying.

"We met at the cemetery," she would sometimes say, but with a laugh, because she could joke about her melancholy as well.

Which could of course still stir certain guilty feelings in him, even if his wife was not aware of it, even needed to be aware of it, all of the details surrounding it. In other words, that game which led to him getting to know her, during childhood. And *how* messed up he had been at that time. The game that started everything, another crazy one he and his sister Maj-Gun had, out of frustration, devoted themselves to as children, like dogs and cats they had been, running around together when they were not allowed to be at the rectory and he had not been able to sneak in again because his sister had pulled him with her, down to the cemetery, and had a mask with her—they called the mask "Liz Maalamaa," "the Angel of Death," or "Liz Maalamaa the Angel of Death." Many names, though rather alike and secret. But papa Pastor, whom they needed to be kept hidden from most of all since the aunt was his sister, had of course in some way found out about them anyway and become furious. As if the complaints that reached him via the caretaker at the cemetery had not been enough: that his children were running around scaring people with the mask.

They had received the mask as a gift from the aunt, from there the nicknames. It was supposed to represent the face of a movie star, probably Ava Gardner, dark haired, sharp facial features, but the special and terrible thing about it was that when you strapped the mask to your face you looked terrifying—would become afraid if you saw yourself in the mirror.

Not the least bit funny, actually. Not the mask, not the secret names for it. So to speak when the aunt came up, he and his sister, lying on the bed in his room talking about all the money they would inherit from her, whose godchildren they were, after the aunt's death; her husband had died at some point during that childhood, they had no children of their own and the husband had been tremendously rich.

As luck would have it no one had listened to him and his sister THEN. No one in the world because IT had been the height of childishness, a true manifestation of killing time in the musty summer day, without energy: that aunt, she had been okay, both siblings liked her despite her fervor for cleaning toilets when she came to visit the rectory and that she was so determined that instead of reading real bedtime stories she would sit on the edge of their beds one after the other and paint stories about various imaginary missionary exploits in China, "the wonderful Middle Kingdom"—where she had, as said, never been, despite the fact that the couple had traveled around the world several times with various fine cruise ships. *Life is a cruise*, she used to say; but then toward the end it had really gotten soiled, her husband's final years, his spare time spent going back and forth on the Sweden–Finland ferry where he drank himself to death.

But Tom's future wife, Susette born Packlén, had, in other words, been at the cemetery as a child, come there accompanied by her mother and brought flowers to the graves. Those eyes back then too—and somewhat later, as a teenager, she became his first girlfriend and he the first boyfriend for her too.

But wait now, first this. *The Angel of Death*. That was what they had called her. He and his sister Maj-Gun, when they were together. The girl who came to the cemetery with her mother, with flowers they had picked from the meadow that became the new side of the cemetery later on. The girl who filled jars with water at the water hydrant, placed the flowers in them. Big eyes. "Have you seen those globes?" he asked his sister. "Should we scare her?" And she galloped ahead, his sister, and he followed after her. Wearing the mask—but the girl was not afraid. Maj-Gun said to him later, "Death is not afraid of Death," and they laughed. That is why she had for a time in private been called the Angel of Death by the two siblings. But he had of course too, in private, alone, without saying anything to his sister, immediately taken a liking to the girl with the big eyes. Not because of the Angel of Death, but because of who she was. Calm, a bit lost. Something steady in here, anyway. And a few years later he started dating her.

"I'm fascinated by the Death in her," he had admittedly solemnly recited back then for his jealous sister, which he actually had not meant a word of. Because he had been embarrassed of course, shy. In the presence of everyone. In the presence of himself. The infatuation. Which there had been no words for. Then not inside him in any case And, dear Lord. What an unbearable person he had been, in public. What could be seen of him. As a person. "Old age," which Maj-Gun talks about. Yes, yes, certainly.

Had gone around wearing a suit and a tie in school and a bow tie at festive occasions and cuff links and the like. God knows why. It had not exactly brought him closer to "friends" his own age at school for example. Not rejected, bullied, just off to the side. As if he wanted to, in some way, *prove a point* about something, but what this *point* was would be unclear, completely *hidden in the mist*, which would have been completely clear if someone had pushed him up against a wall and asked about it in detail—or "interrogated," which is how he certainly personally would have described the matter at that time. No one had done so, none of his classmates exactly enjoyed getting into a discussion with him: he could debate, follow a line of reasoning, already then. In a way that was truly overbearing too, an overbearance that he would consciously eliminate when he got to the university. It had been easy. On the other hand, he found his place then and was so much more content with life and with himself, in general. Was incredibly interested in his studies from the beginning, it was also something that swallowed him up. So the smugness had disappeared; he knew what he was going to do, and now instead perhaps a bit exaggeratedly but still, almost a humility, a leniency started revealing itself in him. He could move and carry himself in company, deal with people which, granted, had carried and would continue to carry him far in his career.

But "I'm fascinated by the Death in her." His solemn words to his sister at the rectory. He could barely think about it now. Of course he had not said it to poor Susette personally, not then and not ever. *That* would certainly have scared the life out of her from the beginning—or no, incidentally, despite that appeal, that Sorrow, whatever it was, there was something in her that did not yield. But it would without a doubt have called forth a coloring in their relationship from the beginning, transformed it into something it was not.

There as teenagers in his room at the rectory they had listened to music. Gustav Mahler's Ninth Symphony. He remembers that, truly, even if he does not want to. Those pretentions in him. During the pauses he had spoken when the record was finished playing. Not many words as luck would have it, which quite simply also depended on his rather great shyness and strong timidity. He had not known, of course, what he should say to her, *just wanted to be with her, so much.* But what had come out of his mouth, however spare, insufferable. "Consciousness of life" and "consciousness of death," which were united in an "intricate way" in Mahler's Ninth, which was playing on and off on the record player. "Gustav Mahler's music says more about the nature of emotion than all philosophers." Elegant? Terrible. And maybe she had understood that intuitively, nodded (but submissively), absent as it were but still agreeing, in other words. But sought to be closer to him, his body, like a kitten.

Was this romantic? "All of us were young once." And that fumbling, clumsiness. Yes, he could think like that. But he has still never been able to listen to Gustav Mahler after that.

And will never—incidentally—listen to Gustav Mahler again. With Susette they do not listen to very much music, have never done so. Sometimes they go out dancing. Just the two of them, she and he. Tango, salsa, Latin. Transformed in the dance. Good together. And the nights afterward.

That night 1989, seventeen years ago, when they started being together again, for real, in reality, she had called him. He had driven through the darkness after her, the same time of year, the same darkness, as now. But in snow. Here, now, no snow, just black black on the ground, everywhere. An appalling whirl of snow then and she had said on the telephone that she did not know where she was, but was on a road, and had been very upset, he *had* to come after her. Had been difficult to find out exactly where she was, but he had not hesitated for a second. Borrowed a former classmate's car—Peter Bäckström's, incidentally, the one they are going to visit now, and his family in Rosengården 2 where they are driving down the avenues to the right address—and yes, he, Tom, had found her in the end.

That night when he had picked her up in the snow, on the side of the road, in this area (as said, she was also from here, so that was not strange), and seen her, a small figure with a Fjällräven backpack on the side of the road in the snow, in the light of the headlights, he had known not only that she had been found, but he as well.

And not many words were needed after that, that had been clear. She had tried to speak, said, "I'll do everything for you. I'll—" Repay? No, she had not said it like that, not that word, there were no complicated words like that inside her, had never been, and also, for that reason, how he *loved loves* her.

But that had been her message, she was worn out: bloody, beaten, but appealed quietly and determined for a promise that he would *never* ask about it—but, she pointed out, *no one* had done anything *to* her. She would go to therapy, never talk about what happened, otherwise. Otherwise she would not be able to . . . live?

She had not needed to say that. He had promised, just as silently. And it had been clear. He had thought it would be good for her and for both of them to get away for a while. Thought about his aunt, in Portugal, who often wrote and invited him but he had not visited, had not had time; in and of itself had not had time then either, but he had been able to arrange the leave from work. The aunt was also sick, of course, needed help. "I know where we're going!" he said to his fiancée Susette Packlén who was going to become a Maalamaa and have a child with him already that next year at the same

time and then they would be living in New York, his first
lengthy foreign assignment. "We'll go to Portugal!" And
she became as happy as a child too because she had
never been abroad really and the aunt had also sounded
happy on the phone and immediately wired money for
the airline tickets, and shortly thereafter Tom and Susette were sitting on a plane, flying above the clouds in
the beautiful clear air, her pale skin, her tired eyes—but
held his hand, as said, those attacks of sorrow and melancholy were not over, of course, it would periodically be
difficult in Portugal as well. But the main thing was the
direction, the will, the approach, and he had not needed
to say it out loud like when he held a speech for work, lay
out the direction, the approach—this was without words,
she knew. "*Ja sieltä ei sit tuoda mitään ruumiita Kotiin /*
and then no corpses are brought home from there,"
someone in the row behind them on the plane had said,
vacationers in a vacationing mood who were describing
how they had been let off by friends from their home-
town when they were going on their first *charter*, country bumpkins among country bumpkins who had never
been anywhere who clapped their hands when the plane
took off, cheers!, in red wine and beer and sangria! No
corpses. Ironic maybe, amusing, because it turned out
that way when, roughly a month later, Tom Maalamaa
and Susette returned to the homeland it was in connection with the repatriation of a corpse: the aunt who had
died while they were there visiting her. A difficult time,
a lot to take care of those final days in Portugal, so it
had not exactly turned out as they thought it would. But
Susette, his future wife, mother to his three children,
had been invaluable, and still, also, as if the hardships

involved with everything that needed to be arranged down there in Portugal and later with the funeral in the homeland only brought them closer together.

•

And—this is becoming long now, when Tom Maalamaa is driving with his wife down the avenues of Rosengården 2, this November evening 2006, a Thursday.

"Courage," he says to his wife, takes her hand in his, maybe thinks she is nervous about tonight, his old university friends . . . or maybe he takes that hand because he has a bad conscience because he has, the entire afternoon, earlier in the evening, up until now, been rather grumpy and cross. About the mess at home, and the new workplace, chaos there too: that is what it is always like arriving in new places, he certainly knows that, should be used to it after so many years. But he had shouted and carried on, and that is why they have been quiet the entire drive from their home to Rosengården 2. For example not spoken about any "dear" old memories that both of them, together, separately, could have from these places, the District, after all they are both from here. Here, where Rosengården 2 now exists, it did not exist back then. This striking, luxurious—almost absurd—development in the middle of what once was a wood where Mama Inga-Britta used to pick mushrooms and cloudberries, lingonberries, rowanberries with the Nature Friends. And possibly somewhat exaggerated this peachy keenness, but "architectural dreams are architectural dreams," which, for example, is something that Tom Maalamaa under normal circumstances certainly might have said here in the car, with a small bitonality too, though well-balanced because the Bäckströms and

certainly many of the others who live here are his friends
of course, if not now, then they will be; he has that kind
of a job, lives a lot on "contacts." Still, it is something grotesque, something almost frivolous, amoral. No, not because it would have been showing off—a lot of, as it were,
too much of a good thing and Dallas, money&poortaste,
but exactly because it is not that, PLUS the money that
exists but cannot be seen cannot be seen cannot be
seen . . . the style, all of the *good taste*, so perfect AND
being enclosed, fenced in. Seen as a metaphor the irony
of all this had of course not been wasted on him either.
These people, these enclosures, these people inside their
personally staked-out borders—people just like him,
who always have the best, as well as education and class
and taste and civilization and the best schools and uni-
versities and the power, on their side—how, for example,
they can still carry out *good deeds* there, as he does in
the service of mankind. And in contrast to those who
have only money, he also has the power of language: can
reason well, about almost anything, also their own shortcomings and this grotesqueness which, after all, it is. But
with his own quick phrases he can also win people over
so that it sounds not only plausible but also something
worth striving for. "Here you can say anything as long as
it sounds good." That feeling.

The irony naturally also applies to what he sees in his
job: the other, "the other side," those lacking legal rights.
So too, him personally. And in contrast to what his sister
Maj-Gun once thought, he takes his job seriously, what
he does—the difficulty then is that it always becomes
pompous when you are talking about it. He actually does
not like hearing his own voice at all, going on and on

about justice and equality in the world. But he likes what
he gets accomplished, what he does.

•

Well, philosophers. He, Tom, can get carried away too,
like papa Pastor in the church when he gets started and
talks, talks. As luck would have it, his wife Susette Packlén does not have a predisposition for philosophizing,
either to philosophize or to listen to the outlays of others. So it has therefore always been nice to come home,
to her, the kids, the family, and just be something else,
turn things off. And sometimes, as said, the two of them
go out dancing.

But this day in particular he, in other words, became
furious when he came home—or had already been before, at work, but he lost his self-control first at home
and quite simply made a racket. And therefore, as a result of just this mess, Tom Maalamaa has, this afternoon,
this evening in particular, not had his telephone on and
not been able to take the phone calls, the phone calls
from his sister Maj-Gun who tried calling many times—
and who is now, without his knowledge, right here in the
area, exactly right now, this evening, at this point in time.
In the Winter Garden, or on the field, or in the woods.
The Boundary Woods—below Rosengården 2, its large
enclosures, at the edge of the woods, below the Glitter
Scene, with her daughter, which he also does not know
she has, her name is Johanna.

On the other hand: if he had the opportunity to speak
to his sister, then you can ask yourself, would anything
have been different as a result of this conversation in particular? Highly unlikely, because his sister Maj-Gun would
not have been able to say anything about everything she

needs to say to him on the telephone. They would most likely have arranged a meeting, later. Met for example the following day—it is important but too terrible to speak about on the phone—at some café. As soon as possible, but not soon enough. Because then, in any case, everything that will happen this night would already have happened, it would already in all ways be too late.

His sister will know that as well, certainly. Because what she has to say almost takes her breath away, it is so great.

But as said, Tom Maalamaa has not had his telephone on. He usually always has his telephone on. But earlier that day there was something with the telephone lines at work: the new telephone system, the computer integration in it—one big chaos there and chaos when he came home: moving boxes, cardboard boxes everywhere. Of course these urgent phone calls for work are not directly connected to his own separate private telephone but the problems today have certainly affected his attitude toward telephones in general so that he, after a day of working, in one moment of fury and complete frustration, angry at his phone, turned it off at home in his own bathroom.

After he has, in other words, yelled at his wife, screamed at the aupairgirl Gertrude and even at twelve-year-old Elizabeth Ida, who *unlike* his wife does not answer back, just looks at him with her big eyes, in contrast to Gertrude, who produces long shrill harangues in French, German, and with assistance Italian as well, if *she* gets insulted. Which she has been this late afternoon and develops a cacophony of everything, and Tom

Maalamaa from his Service of Mankind stood there and battled with the Swiss she learned at the nice private schools and secretarial institutions (oh no, there aren't any Sri Lankan domestic servants in this household) with complete self-control. And *handle things with great care*, it does not say *things* or *great* on the boxes with the sherry glasses that he fumbles down from the dining room table, *craaasssh*; it says HANDLE WITH CARE, but he sees the sentence in his head in that way, for some meaningless reason. Well, glass like glass, sherry glasses, wineglasses, china cups, *a fine china*, can always be bought new but then it has already been way too much, over the edge, and he felt ashamed inside like a dog on the one hand, on the other hand he still barked like the same dog on the outside. For a while. So. *Away from here*: such an impulse and he went to the bathroom. Where the telephone in the pocket of his blazer started ringing and the name on the display was not the name of one of his golf buddies (he does not like golf, but sometimes you have to play golf, go and *bond*, he has golfed with cannibalistic dictators and played cricket with terrorist leaders in India; well-brought-up boys from good schools too, besides)—rather from the Head Office! Not the one that is his superior in this country, but another one, the *only* other one—the Head Office that was and is the entire goal and direction of his career, that *level*, which he thought he still had a ways to go to get to, now wanted to get in touch with him. But he stood in the bathroom in his own home, overwhelmed by his own rage, and looked at that, stared at it, *damned telephone*, angry angry at it because he suddenly understood not only that he should answer but that he WANTS to answer but cannot due to the fury still pounding at his temples, it is too great, he is not capable of getting himself together, which rarely happens, he is usually always able to get it together. So he did not answer, it stopped ringing, he turned it off, put it in the pocket of his blazer, and then first calmed down, took care of business, and carefully washed his face with ice-cold water for a good while.

Ashamed like a dog and mellow mellow. But that energy inside him: if there had been a *fresh* brush set out ready in the bathroom, which there had once been in the rectory and the Coral washing powder in a glass jar "Goes for Tom too!" he certainly, out of regret and frustration, would have scrubbed and scrubbed the sink shiny with it.

But, the avenue now, Rosengården 2, they are almost there. "Courage." "I'm not afraid." Her hand. In his hand.

Handle things with great care.

This turned out to be long.

But it has to be, long, this. And still, these thoughts, ideas, maybe only a distillation of an *entire story* too long to fit into the few minutes between an entrance gate to a large house in a fantastic location just a third of a mile away. Of everything possible, everything, he had wanted, wants, should have said to her. Which he will always think about, the rest of his life, afterward.

It has to be long. Eternally ongoing. It is, has been, his explanation of love for her.

Her eyes, "I'm not afraid." The Sorrow, an appeal? What it is. In her. No, he cannot find the words for it. Cannot. But he has loved her, he loves her, for it. The unknown in her, because of the question mark. And, in contrast to what his sister once thought, he is not very preoccupied with fine-tuning pretty formulations that run out of his head like water, a tap, or like diarrhea, when he is going to hold a speech, debate, he can certainly debate, "You can say anything here as long as it sounds good."

The opposite. Here. Susette. His wife. A love that simply makes him defenseless, and mute.

Later, he will wish for a great deal, about talking, in the car, that bit to Rosengården 2, that that night some kind of dialogue between him and his wife had played out, a dialogue that could have gone something like this:

"What are you thinking about?" she would have asked suddenly, since they had been sitting in silence the entire car ride.

"I'm thinking," he would have replied, "about us. About everything."

"What do you mean?" she would have said but with poorly concealed happy surprise. Despite the fact that she usually does not engage in disputes with him, she has always been good at sulking and keeping quiet and then, when you are going to make up, he has always been the one who has started speaking, spoken his way forward the entire way—but then, despite the fact that she does not want to show it, she has of course become happy.

And then he would have placed his hand on her hand, which he had also done in reality, despite the fact that he had not said any of it, here in the car, on the avenues in Rosengården 2, and she would have taken his hand, held it, as she also does, for real.

"I like it when we dance together," he would have said.

"Yes," she would have answered. "I do too."

And as if it were . . . or it is, this snippet of a conversation

that was never held but that existed anyway, silence between them, which makes it so that despite the fact that
he, in the entire future, will have facts and laws and justice against him, there will always be a figure inside him
who will never believe what they accuse her of after her
death.

•

They have arrived now. At the right address. Get out.
He discovers the small shoe bag with the silver shoes in
the backseat, the party shoes, she *has* remembered them.
Liz Maalamaa's party shoes, strass, with a brooch, fifties
model, small heel, which he and Susette had taken with
them as a memento from Portugal, seventeen years ago.
He liked them back then already, how they had fit her
perfectly.

"Don't forget—"

He will always remember the shoes, the silver sandals
in the backseat, and her, her eyes, all of her, when he
handed them to her.

"Courage," he says. She laughs a little, everything is
okay. And how she takes the silver sandals he hands to
her, he has loved, loves her.

THE GLITTER SCENE
(*Susette in landscape, 2006*)

THIS, FIRST, is shorter. Suddenly on the avenues, in Rosengården 2, in the darkness, in the car after the entrance and the gate that has closed behind her, she recognizes where she is.

Maybe it is something with the trees, the same trees in straight lines along the road, as if they had always been there. And the tall houses, several stories, despite the fact that there is a light on in almost every window, which there was not then. Remembers. Tabula rasa. Being nothing, and new. That possibility. Spinning around around in the avenues, one fall day, sunshine then.

My love, *my life*, around around, nothing and new.

She remembers a feeling, a body, her body, her skin, the skin on her wrist, patinated by the summer and the sun and the scrubbing of windows on a veranda called the Winter Garden in the Glass House, the French family's summerhouse, on the Second Cape. Standing high on a ladder wedged between rocks on the beach, scrubbing scrubbing, hating the sea like a secret, not looking up not looking down, a cat meowing on the cliffs, long haired and white.

"I'm only twenty-nine after all": pulling her nails across her dry summer skin, white powder stripes on the skin.

Twenty-nine years, she never became any older. Has never become. And: as if she has never been anywhere else but here.

Jump, jump, in the avenues. A small baby, a baby bird under her jacket, love, life. *My* love, *my life*, hop crow, hop sparrow—

"You have arrived at your destination," says the woman's voice on the navigator, the engine stops. The navigator lady has a name, Gertrude, named after the aupairgirl. "Oh, Gertrude." They have a habit of saying that, she and her husband, in the car sometimes, even though that lady on the navigator actually has a different name, now she does not remember what it is.

•

But: a private joke they have, because Gertrude, their Gertrude, can undeniably maintain order and *navigate* the family's sometimes chaotic life filled with children and many residences around the world and a great deal of keeping up appearances. *What would we do without Gertrude?* is the question they often seriously ask them-selves and each other.

Gertrude who steers and arranges with the same calm voice as the navigator in the car—except when she gets angry, of course; then she roooars, and she has done so today, the aupairgirl's terrible scream that Susette still has ringing in her ears. Despite the fact that it has not been anyone else's fault but hers, Gertrude's, that a bunch of fragile glass was sitting in an unpacked box in an open box in the wrong place in the new residence where the family had just moved from abroad and that Tom, who had been in an unusually bad mood and had come home earlier than usual from his job, managed to knock down on the floor by accident so *CRASH*, a lot of invaluable drinking glasses broken into thousands of pieces.

So Gertrude, she does not always find the right path, does not always navigate correctly. And she has that in common with the lady in the navigator: suddenly ending up in the middle of a winery somewhere in Germany just because she has directed you there—it must have been the previous summer? "Oh Gertrude, Oh Gertrude." Tom had laughed in the middle of the jungle of vines and suddenly the embittered German wine farmer with the rifle on the little road in front of them, *"an auf hinter zwischen wir sind turisten,"* pretended not to speak the language so that things would not get any worse. *"Grüss Gott."* An amusing family memory, pointing with the tip of the rifle, *but* they had gotten out in one piece.

"Make a U-turn," Susette says out loud in the car in Rosengården 2 suddenly alarmed by the strange merriment growing inside her. Hop crow, sparrow, *CRASH*, tabula rasa. But "courage," her husband Tom said a little while ago, while they were still driving down the avenues, he had taken her hand, it had calmed her down and calms her, a little, now. But she has not been afraid, and besides, he certainly wants to make up after the scene at home earlier. And of course: when she says that about the U-turn Tom does not hear it, even as a joke. He has already gotten out of the car and is on his way to the other side to open the door for her. Then, briefly, almost simultaneously, it quickly rushes through Susette's head that she has forgotten to tell him that surprisingly his sister Maj-Gun came by the new home that day for a visit. And that Maj-Gun sends her greetings to him—or does she? Now Susette does not remember exactly how it was, also not exactly what was said between her and Maj-Gun, so to speak. Just a bad feeling, and a complete feeling of alienation, nonconnection. Red and slender, *after the Scarsdale Diet, anything is possible,* a person like that, new.

But Susette did not have the intention of hiding from her husband that Maj-Gun had stopped by that day. There just has not, during the afternoon and evening up until now, been an appropriate time to mention it: Gertrude and Tom had been shouting at each other.

And now. No turning back. They are there, here. And Susette: *never anywhere but here.* Never more than twenty-nine; there. Tom Maalamaa opens the door, she steps out.

"Don't forget." He discovers the shoe bag with the silver shoes in the backseat. "Thank you."

And then she drifts away again. Forever. Everything else disappears now. Never anywhere but here. Never more than twenty-nine. The silver shoes. Tabula rasa.

To the house that is beaming; they have stepped into the house.

·

Also here she has recognized where she is, but no longer a surprise. Italian granite on the ground floor. And *crash!* Yes, *that* house. In other respects, foreign.

"Peter, Nellevi." Laughter. Naturally your name cannot be Nellevi nor can it be Susette either. A name from a tabloid, a serial *Susette and love.*

"So nice."

A daughter. Ulla. Talented. Oh oh oh. "The theater, the dance, the music . . . a band called *Screaming Toys.*"

Headstrong. Does not come downstairs.

"ULLAAAA! Ulla is sulking. Temperamental. Artistic temperament—ULLAAA!" resounds through the house.

"Peter also has a good singing voice," the wife, Nellevi, laughs.

ULLLAA! Susette's ears temporarily become deaf.

"Oh well, to the oysters. When she's done sulking. Ulla loves oysters."

·

"I CAAAAAN HEEEAAR YOU! LAAATER!"

A voice from upstairs. The voice cracks everything. Absurd, immense. Like from the abyss.

"Ulla *is* talented."

"Are you cold?"

Tom Maalamaa puts his arm around his wife's shoulders. Nono.

The living room, the kitchen . . . beautiful view. You see: the Winter Garden. Like a blaze of light, strong, farther away. Light over the trees as well, part of the road.

The Winter Garden. *The Rita Strange Corporation.*

In the living room, the sofa.

"We knew each other. From the Rita Strange Corporation. The Winter Garden. Was going to be magnificent. Wasn't. An idea. Became something else."

"Architectural dreams."

"Ho-ho, Tom." Peter Bäckström laughs. Tom, like himself.

These people, Peter and Nellevi, are also in the "business," of course, architects, both of them.

But she, Susette, as mentioned, actually, she is not listening. Is not really even there. Twenty-nine years old, never got any older. Rosengården 2, her Rosengården. Recognizes and recognizes.

·

She gets up.

"The bathroom is upstairs, one floor."

I know. She mumbles, quietly, to herself. Already on the stairs then.

"The American girl." A black-and-white poster on the wall in the bathroom.

The girl on a cliff, her hair flowing, flying. She is going to fall.

Black-and-white photography on the poster, matches the decor. White tiles, black trim. THAT was what it was like then. Otherwise she does not look at the picture. An old story. Neither it nor the old theater poster says anything to her.

She steps out. Not back to the others, but up the stairs, landings. The third landing. *There they are.* The rabbits.

She is *here*. Has never been anywhere else.

And farther, quickly up the small stairs, to the attic room. The door is slightly ajar, but she sees, before she sneaks in, THE GLITTER SCENE in glittery letters, on a plaque on the door.

•

And Susette in landscape here again. The same room, the empty room, fall 1989, before everything. The duality NOW, still, full empty full empty, the old new at the same time, everything here: *Susette on the Glitter Scene.*

And it is windy on the Glitter Scene. The door has been standing open as said, but wedged fast with a small piece of wood, because you notice the draft when you come in. Because of the glass door at the other end, the one that was part of the large window and could not be opened, is open all the way. Cold late fall weather wells into the room.

The girl is standing in the opening. Not far from the edge, many feet of open fall down. All the openness.

The girl, the daughter, Ulla Bäckström, in white, with her back facing the room. A great mane of hair falling over her shoulders, long white skirt flapping around her legs.

Does not notice Susette in the door opening.

Susette who has taken off the silver shoes, left them at the door to the room. And tippytoe, an old thieflike merriment now completely unstoppable, tippytoe tippytoe, sneaks onto the stage carefully, into the room, the greatness.

The empty landscape/the Glitter Scene. A room where there is nothing and everything.

And EVERYTHING. Theater things, books, papers, manuscripts. Musical instruments and clothes, more clothes, ordinary clothes, dress-up clothes, on racks along the walls or in piles on the floor, notes, bags, shoes, and things, things.

Pictures on the wall, art, posters: *Screaming Toys*.

And: the American girl, the same poster here too. And other posters, theater performances: *Singin' in the Rain, Miss Julie*, among others. The same girl, *the theater, the dancing, the music*, the same name, Ulla Bäckström, on all of them.

But here, still, you might think that at least something would stir something to life inside Susette, a connection, shake her, to something else. *The American girl*. That old story. Which was Maj-Gun Maalamaa's story. The one about *the Boy in the woods*, which she went on about.

Maj-Gun at the newsstand, *kiss kiss kiss*, red sticky lips, glitter. But nah, does not stir anything. Maj-Gun does not exist. "We are two Angels of Death." Which she said once. But nah. *We*. Are nothing. Maj-Gun had stopped existing. They have seen each other today, earlier in the day. The Red One. Another. No connection. Rather Majjunn Majjunn, but for Susette it is something else, has always been: a sound in her head.

I am, in other words, alone here on the Glitter Scene.

So: stirs nothing. Nothing nothing, which might also depend on the multitude, EVERYTHING here. So much, too much, incentive and things, messages, impressions. Takes herself out. Becomes: mute.

Susette does not see them. She *is* inside the old emptiness but here there is no connection between now and then, the one and the other.

"ULLLAAAAA!"

She hears that. That scream. Is standing in the middle of the room and wishes the father downstairs would stop yelling.

"YEEEEEEEEEEEEEEES!" The girl at the open glass door in the panorama window suddenly turns around and yells in toward the room, with everything she can muster too. That enormous voice which sounds even more grand and more special up here. *Not surprising that she likes screaming up here.*

Right in her face. That is how the girl becomes aware of Susette. Has turned around in the middle of everything and, as it turns out, she screams at Susette! About fifteen feet away from her right in her face.

Which is of course comical; the girl, a bit surprised at first, but not so much, starts laughing. "Hi. Who are you? Our guests?" Susette nods and introduces herself and the girl says that she is Ulla Bäckström and runs past Susette to the door at the other end and yells down the stairs one more time: "I just saaaid I waaas coommmiiing!"

Then she closes the door. Takes the wedge out and the two of them are alone up there.

"Ah and then we were rid of him. Dad, he's great, but he can be so naggy.

"It's like this some evenings," the girl continues. "You need to be alone and . . . think. In a strange mood. Can you keep a secret?"

Ulla Bäckström puts a finger over her lips and peers mischievously at Susette. "You'll understand. I'm not allowed to have this door open"—the glass door. "Papa confiscated the key when he found out but I confiscated it back, he has no idea. But, it isn't *always* like this. Just sometimes. Certain nights. Standing there, in the wind, above everything, thinking. I usually think. About everything that is going on. About everything that is going to end. Mortality. In the midst of everything beautiful. On the edge. Do you understand?"

Susette nods, of course, even though she really is not listening, cannot manage to focus. But the girl in the middle of the room in front of her, still, silencing. Those white clothes, the skirt, the ankle boots with a heel, and in her hair, which is swelling around her face, small metal insects: they are butterflies, in different colors, glittering in the sharp light from the ceiling that falls over her like a spotlight. *The Glitter Scene.* That is how it is. Of course. And the girl who on the one hand is like from outer space but on the other is fully conscious of the effect she has on people.

Still: a child. Like her own children. But Susette is not thinking like that. All of that is gone now, she is tabula rasa, she would not be able to be here otherwise.

The emptiness here, *her* emptiness, and the girl, shining, shimmering, in the middle of it. It is confusing.

"Isn't it great up here?" The girl looks around her own room. "I have everything here! And look. What I got today. In the Winter Garden."

It is a mask she is putting on. It is *that* mask.

That stirs a feeling of recognition. The girl, with the mask on, suddenly hisses, almost humorously, theatrically: "I am the Angel of Death. Liz Maalamaa."

That *is* the connection.

Still, Susette is not surprised. Strange, absurd, but like a dream is strange, absurd. And Ulla Bäckström says, "Come," and pulls Susette with her toward the open glass door. They stand there and look out over the darkness, far away there is an island of bright light, before the sea. "The Winter Garden there. How it is shining. Do you know the Winter Garden?"

Susette does not answer, maybe she knows, she does not remember. Everything is familiar and foreign.

"I am the Angel of Death Liz Maalamaa!" The girl is suddenly standing there screaming out into the open, into the darkness. To the wind, out into everywhere that cannot be seen. Toward that Winter Garden by the sea, even farther out, there, solitary dots of light, a ship, a lighthouse.

Susette Maalamaa does not like the scream, she jumps back, steps back into the room.

"What is it? Do you want to try on the mask?" The girl comes toward her laughing and Susette puts the mask on, it is just a game after all, just a game, *kiss kiss kiss*, merry, tippytoe, tabula rasa, clings to it. And: *nothing else happened, she never became older than twenty-nine.* Be nothing, new, that possibility, spinning around around in the avenues, small playful kitty cat.

She is standing in the middle of the room, wearing the mask, the girl is dancing around her.

"The Angel of Death Liz Maalamaa!" the girl calls to Susette. "Here, come and take me! Grab on . . ."

But do not scream. Quiet now. But the girl has gotten started, does not grow quiet. And the girl walks toward the window, come come come. And calls, *but QUIET now.*

The folk song has many verses, the same thing happens in every one. Over and over again.

And Susette cannot hear that, she walks straight toward the girl in the opening now against the wind QUIET now, and pushes the girl—

The girl falls. A quiet fall, *it* is quiet. Maybe it is the surprise. And in the distance: flames jump up from the Winter Garden.

"Look! The Winter Garden is on fire!" Both of them saw that. The girl who turned around at the last moment— but then she just fell, quietly.

And yes. The Winter Garden is burning. What a scene. Susette in the opening. Something she has forgotten.

That impossibility. All impossibility.

Flames in front of her eyes. Rug rags.

"Mama, where is the loom? The rug weaver?"

Susette on the rocks. *Lambada,* among rags, like once, at a disco.

•

She has closed the door and turned around. Walked back across the floor, left the room. Puts on her silver shoes again, they are standing where she left them just inside the door where she, just a minute or so ago, walked over the wooden floor to where the girl was at the other end, in white skirts. But the girl, where is the girl now?

Torn a small hole in the heel of her bone-colored panty hose. A small splinter in her skin, it is bleeding just a little. But she is used to blood, it is not dangerous, she has Band-Aids in her purse, Band-Aids, bandages, you have to be well prepared when you have children.

Leaves the room, goes downstairs again, to the laughter, the socializing. On the stairs she realizes that she has the mask on, takes it off.

"Where were you?" Tom Maalamaa asks when she sits down next to him on the sofa in the bright living room.

"Up there."

But now she is neither here, there, swinging a bit. Flames in front of her eyes.

"Did you see Ulla? She loves oysters. They will be served shortly."

The father who is asking and making an attempt at starting to call for the girl again, with that terrible voice.

"I think she's sleeping," Susette says quickly in order to avoid hearing the scream.

"Sleeping?"

"Looked that way."

"She was just awake. Ulla usually never sleeps. She's hyperactive."

Peter Bäckström laughs, as if calmed by his own explanation because for just a moment he became a bit strange because of Susette Maalamaa. Oysters, Ulla comes to the oysters: he goes to get more wine from the kitchen.

Tom Maalamaa touches her hand.

"You're so cold. Have you been outside? What do you have in your hand?"

Everyone looks at what she has in her hand.

"One of Ulla's thousand toys. It's like the attic of a theater up there. You were there? Ulla loves the theater. A mask. Let's have a look." Nellevi takes the mask Susette hands to her, laughs.

Tom Maalamaa does not laugh.

Nellevi puts the mask on. Buhuu.

Peter Bäckström calls from the kitchen that the Winter Garden is on fire.

Everyone rushes up, around. The Winter Garden is burning, can be seen from the kitchen. But Nellevi does not run there but up the stairs to her daughter's room. "Ulla!" Maybe it is an instinct during times of danger. Susette knows that instinct well, she is a mother too after all.

She has three children, and in the empty living room where she has been left alone because Tom Maalamaa also ran out to the kitchen, she should start thinking about these children—their ages, abilities, characteristics. If someone were left, but no one is left, nor she.

The mother's *screeeaaamm* from the Glitter Scene, throughout the entire house.

Then Susette is no longer in the house anymore. She has taken her coat in the hall and is walking down the avenues where she once walked and where she is walking now, twenty-nine years old, never became any older. It is dark, the silver shoes, the gates are closed. But you can get out from the inside, but not in from the outside, as if she did not know this. *This is the future.* Solveig on the avenues. *You don't need to see with the Eyes of the Old.*

No. But the impossibility. Susette hurries on.

Because she has forgotten something. And how long, almost an entire life.

"Mama, where is the loom?"

LOOM, AGAINST A BACKGROUND OF FLAMES
(Susette at the house in the darker part,
the Boundary Woods, 2006)

HERE IT IS. Susette in the Boundary Woods, she has
run there and onto some path and ended up at a strange,
empty, dark, decomposing house; it is the house in the
darker part. A basement window, flames in front of her
eyes, lighting up the guts, she peers in. Flames and there
it is rising up, taking up the entire basement. *Loom,*
against a background of flames.

And fabric hanging over it and around it like scraps.
All sorts of fabric, silk fabric, ordinary fabric, rag scrap,
velvet, linen—entire large layers and strips, loom lengths.

Sees the loom. She does not get there.

Sirens, ambulances, fire trucks, Spanish wolfhounds.

But at father's deathbed it was like this. He was on his
way away and needed to go and find peace, you could see
that. "Sleep now, dear father. You will get to rest soon."
But her mother who was crying and shouting, "Don't go!
Come back!" "But, Mama—" If you're going to leave then
you're going to leave, it's unavoidable. Then you have to
be allowed to do it peacefully and with love, surrounded
by your loved ones, not filled with anxiety about having
to leave. And there at the hospital, the final minutes, they
had already taken all the tubes out of him so that it had
not been Susette or he who had personally decided he
was going to pass away right then.

It had been at home in the house after the funeral that

378

Susette tried to explain that to her mother. Because suddenly, when they were alone again, the brothers with their families gone home, her mother in the kitchen furious at her, Susette. Because she had not stood next to her father's deathbed where it had just been the two of them and called her father back. Not called together with her mother that he should not leave—

"You let him go. You let him go away." Her mother had said that, of course not: "it was your fault Susette," it would have been too much. Her mother understood that too, of course, because somewhere, at that time, she still had a certain mind for the possible and impossible. She was still also active in her position at the bank, even if she had been forced to go down to part-time due to her husband's illness and also not had time for her position as secretary of the Bankers' Employee Club. But in any case: if you deal with money, particularly other people's money, you have to stay levelheaded, rational in your mind, she said that to herself many times, also earlier in life when she had still been normal.

But half a year later she was put on one hundred percent sick leave. Not a particularly large pension, but that, plus the widow's pension and what Susette earned at the nursing home when she started working there after high school, had been enough so they could afford to stay in the large house.

And then everything had gotten out of control. As if there suddenly were two realities for Susette: one at home, one on the outside. But gradually it was the first reality that gained ground even though she did not want it to. The normal teenage life in the District, which she in and of herself never really was a part of, but it had existed like a background, but that background paled, disintegrated just like the fact that she had once had a real boyfriend too. Despite the fact that it had mostly been a youthful infatuation, Gustav Mahler's music, Sunday dinners at the rectory. Was made unreal. Instead, the nursing home, the empty corridors, the old, the dying in their beds, and two very disobliging hospital cats who saw red at the sight of her.

"I didn't let him go! You're wrong, Mama!" In the beginning then, Susette had roared like a stuck pig when her mother suddenly accused her of having let her father go. And later, calmer, tried to explain the dignity and the importance of the dying one needing to find peace.

Her mother had started crying. Her wailing. But they had hugged, hugged and never fought again. Her mother had said, "There is a lot to cut up. Rags, fabric. Can you sharpen the scissors for me, Susette? My eyes are getting so bad." And Susette sharpened her mother's scissors and took her own scissors (she had her own pair, which she threw away later when she moved out, but her mother's she took with her to the apartment on the hills above the town center) and they had sat down at the rag bucket, each on her own stool. Behind closed blinds, in a once cozy kitchen. And crehp crehp, *let the scissors travel through the fabric, rags, scraps, long strips, loom lengths, which whirled down into the bucket between them.*

"But the loom, Mama. Where is it?" Susette had asked at one point, weeks later, maybe months, when they just continued cutting fabric, rags, and been and collected more, more: transported rags in plastic bags in the wheelbarrow from the nearby houses, and all of the other

*houses in the lush neighborhood below the town center, gone from door to door and rung the bell and knocked. Susette had **not** said to her mother what they both knew: that the rug weaver herself, her in the Outer Marsh, had been dead for a long time already. It was impossible to say. The word "death." Susette had not dared take that word in her mouth even in the house with her mother because it would have been like giving her mother a signal to let everything inside her well forth. Also that terrible thing she had screamed at Susette after the funeral. "The Angel of Death." No, she had not said that exactly, but that was what it had felt like.*

Her mother had not answered Susette's question about the loom, she never answered it. It was probably so, that she did not know. She lost the loom, it had become mislaid in some way, but continued, still, maybe just because, due to her forgetfulness, cutting cutting anyway.

"It is never easy coming to a house of sorrow, Susette." She had said, for example, admonishingly, at the rag-cutting bucket.

And then the funerals, the cemetery again. The flowers to the graves. To her father's grave in the new cemetery where the meadow had once been where they, she and her mother, back when everything had still been normal, picked flowers and brought them to the cemetery. And now her mother was sad about that too: that the meadow was no longer there and her father "was resting" on the new side that she thought was so bare and deserted and she became even more sorrowful because of it, that poor him had to "rest" there, could you even "rest" there, come to peace, which you should be allowed to do after you die?

*Flowers on the graves of others as well. Still, like al-
ways. But the jars they had with them to place the flowers
in were rarely washed and boiled, transparent and clean
like before, rather nasty, sometimes just yogurt jars, helpfully washed, made of plastic—*

*And the funerals, her mother and the funerals. Sit-
ting in the church, listening to the blessings, sorting addresses into neat fans on the tables in the fellowship hall
afterward.*

"The grieving have other things to think about."

*All death, Susette had sometimes thought in secret, in
my hands.*

*But cutting rags with her mother, it had become like
a language. Her and her mother's only way of being together, of communicating. "So ugly," the brothers said
when they, together with their young families, had at
some point in the beginning still come to visit their former childhood home. And father's house of balsa wood
that needed to be collected because one of the kids in the
family was so "interested in construction" but of course
it could not be found anywhere—when it later surfaced
it was broken. Balsa is fragile, thin wood: as if someone stepped right on the veneer sheet on which it was
constructed. Not Susette, maybe her mother, or otherwise
it had ended up under the piles of fabric or other junk,
trash, and been crushed under the weight.*

*"Susette, maybe you should . . ." the brothers insinu-
ated, meant clean, keep things in order. "We can see
mother isn't well, that she can't do things on her own
right now." And snap it had been so that the brothers with
their proper wives and proper small children, self-fulfilled
in their own lives and business like everyone in the whole*

*world, would have such an understanding for "the dif-ficult daily life of a young family," stopped coming to the parental home altogether. Mother had gone and vis-ited them sometimes instead. In office clothes, which she still had. Susette had her job of course and could not get away. On the other hand, she had not actually wanted to go along. Nice to be alone, at least for a few days, now and then. Catch her breath, **not** cut rags. And when her mother came home again she was usually quite energetic and normal, but after a day or two everything was just like before.*

So yes, it had been clear. She, Susette, had not been able to do anything about it. Powerless. And of course in the long run she had not been able to live there either.

So she had left, gone to the strawberry fields in the central part of the country and ended up in a wood and it was not until three years later that she came back, but then, as mentioned, her mother was already dead.

But with the lady, old Elizabeth Maalamaa in Portu-gal, she had been able to get it back. Well, a kind of rec-onciliation. The word "reconciliation" was not Susette's own, she had gotten it from the therapist, therapists, she had regularly seen during her seventeen-year marriage to Tom Maalamaa. "Reconciliation": but a good word, when she, sitting there at the office, had spoken a bit about her mother and Liz Maalamaa.

For example, the following: about what it had been like, in Portugal, December 1989, like coming home. Or another possible image, also fitting: from a road in whirling snow in the District to Tom to Portugal—so self-evident. To Liz Maalamaa, who had become bedridden rather soon after Susette and her fiancé Tom arrived then, *in December 1989, and Susette sat at her bedside for hours when Liz Maalamaa was not sleeping, and sometimes then as well, watching over her, as it were. How she liked Liz Maalamaa. And how Liz Maalamaa liked her. "I want to protect you from everything evil," Liz Maalamaa had even said. "I like you so much, **my** Susette."*

*As if Susette had been her girl and Liz Maalamaa her mother. It had also almost been said: not like a game exactly, but like a silent, mutual agreement. Liz Maalamaa never had a child of her own, and how she longed for a child of her own, she talked about that too. "Susette, my own girl." And Susette had her mother again, but then what had gone wrong with her mother, for real, everything, everything, in the house, that she personally had left and not been there at the end, not even at the funeral . . . could in some way be repaired, now. Liz Maalamaa had also told Susette about her careful preparations for her own funeral, neatly written down in pencil in a notebook that she kept in the drawer of her nightstand next to her bed: "Yes. I haven't thought about dying yet, especially not now when you're here, Susette, my girl, but you never know of course." And then when she shortly thereafter had been dead, Susette made sure to follow all of Liz Maalamaa's funeral instructions to a T, to the point that it was exactly that very expensive porcelain, **a fine china** that her husband's family had so cared for, which should be set out and used at the family's table during the reception in the fellowship hall after the burial.*

"I so like it when you take care of me, Susette. I take my medicine so gladly. It's almost as if I want to be sick all the time when you're here. Now I'm finally getting

some peace and rest, it's been quite lonely, especially after the death of my dog. But now, Susette, here with you."

And Liz Maalamaa had swallowed her medicine: all obligatory portions according to the doctor's prescription and more, gradually, which Susette portioned out for her in transparent, colored medicine cups. She, Susette, was used to it, how medicine should be portioned out, had of course worked so much with the old and the sick during her lifetime.

And she had found more tablets too, consequently, other medicine, hidden away in the medicine cabinet in a special container: bottles, bottles with sleeping pills, calming pills, with a few years under their belt, but medicine as medicine, Liz Maalamaa needed her medicine. "I need my medicine, Susette," she said as well. And Susette had started placing more pills in the medicine cups, and increasing the dosage and even mashing, discreetly, pills into Liz Maalamaa's food too.

"Reconciliation." Though that, about the medication, she had not been able to say anything to the therapist, therapists, or to Tom Maalamaa or anyone else.

But the following, as a backdrop to what it had been like to come home to Liz Maalamaa in Portugal, she had certainly mentioned at one therapist office or another:

"I needed protection. Up until then. I went around carrying a pistol without really knowing why."

The therapist had listened, not moved a muscle. "Yes, it can be like that. We need protection. All of us have a buffer zone that is invisible but cannot withstand being trespassed. And if it has been trespassed upon, it can be the case that you have not been aware of it—especially if it happened during childhood. But it provokes a disturbance, and often such a disturbance, if it originates in the childhood infantile, can take on an absurd expression in adulthood."

That therapist used some of her other patients as examples, granted without naming any names. Some director of a large business corporation who walked around with a teddy bear: a large, large teddy bear who had to have his own seat in business class. A day-care manager with a toy gun in her apron. A movie where someone had lost a sled, Rosebud, which was the key to the mystery his entire life had developed into.

Completely illogical but all of us are irrational beings, especially when we struggle to be the most rational, the therapist had said—but added: "There is understanding. We must try and understand each other. What things say, what language everything we surround ourselves with is speaking . . . We must listen, be observant, speak, speak."

The therapist at the office had spoken, one of those therapists who, in addition to listening, liked talking. Because there were therapists like that too, had been, all kinds of therapists, all manner of schools, Susette had, during all the years in therapy, learned. But the therapist who liked hearing her own voice about the movie and the literature and all the patients who visited her who flew business class had been good, in any case. Aside from the fact that Susette of course understood that the therapist took for granted that it had not been a real pistol, which had been loaded to boot and had ended up in her Fjällräven backpack that she had sometimes carried with her in the middle of the day, rather one of those daycaremanagerpistols, toy, certainly plastic, like the yogurt containers at the cemetery.

On the other hand, the pistol. If she had started thinking about it too much at the office, the offices, then it
would have become too absurd and completely impossible. "We're here to help you build a story for yourself
that has some sort of coherence, context. A story with not
necessarily a happy ending, but a story that you can live
with. There is understanding. It is always easier to look
things right in the eye. Give them words. Then you can
go on living. And you deserve to live, Susette. Your life,
Susette," the therapist had said. "You haven't had it easy,
Susette. But now you have so much that is valuable. It's
your turn now. It's about time you start thinking about
the fact that you have a right to be thinking this way."

So she had forgotten about the pistol. With this therapist and all therapists later. And otherwise. There was a
forgetfulness in her, that was also true. She had forgotten
so much so much and when she remembered what she
had forgotten then it did not come in the form of any coherent stories, it came like breezes, drafts of wind through
her head, images pulled loose, sentences.

But she had cried a lot. There, in Portugal, the crying had
started there, already while Liz Maalamaa was still alive.
She cried at night, during the afternoon when Liz Maalamaa was sleeping and Tom Maalamaa was sunbathing
on the patio. Stood at the window and watched him where
he was lying, wearing sunglasses and reading Gandhi's
memoirs in a deck chair in front of a marvelous sea and
cried. Out of love, and out of sorrow. Something comfort-
less in that crying, everything she was—at the same time,
when she saw Tom, who calmly accepted and would, during their entire lives together, accept the crying as a part of
who she was, a crying filled with leniency, even hope.

Letting the crying out.

"The sorrow doesn't disappear just because of it," the therapist also said, given the crying, the weight, that word: the Sorrow. It was beautiful, fitting. More beautiful than "a life-long depression," which became the diagnosis.

"You can live with depression, as long as you get help . . . And then there is medication—"

So yes, after Portugal, she no longer needed any protection. But the crying had continued. And there had been the thing she had said to the therapists that had not really come out the right way, not exactly how it had been, not due to the information provided, but otherwise just, because it was unexplainable.

Maj-Gun Maalamaa. It was that day in November, the last in the District, when everything culminated: Susette had been on her way to the sea, which she hated, but there, for some reason, going out there, a logic, because she could not live. Suddenly Maj-Gun Maalamaa in the boathouse there at the Second Cape where Susette as a child had been saved in the swimming school—so now when she was going to swim it was logical that it was going to happen, without being saved, exactly right here. Maj-Gun, who had been furious and started hitting. And beating and beating and beating Susette black and blue so that she blacked out awhile in the boathouse and when she woke up again it was dark and Maj-Gun was gone. Maj-Gun who had such power in her blows, and she who had not defended herself, just accepted them. But how strange, that she had also wanted to say to Maj-Gun, afterward, if there had not been so many other things, "Thanks to you I found my way back to life." Maj-Gun saved her life, that had been true. When she had woken up in the boathouse she knew one thing. Away from the sea, not staying here, away from here.

She had told the therapist about that "fight" with her friend, as said. But there it has, as it were, been "diminished," in some way. Become, which maybe it also actually was, of course (there was a lot of jealousy and other frustrations there too), a violent encounter between two friends who were tired of each other and needed to free themselves. "Friendships between women are often like that. You become the other person. A lot of mirroring. And becoming an adult is to free yourself from these reflections. Dare to stand on your own, on your own two feet."

And it was true, of course. Sounded plausible. But still: all she needed to do was remember the frenzy inside Maj-Gun, Maj-Gun's blows, yes, she was going to kill, and her own complete lack of will, her total passivity in the situation, in order to become completely perplexed. Going out into the sea was a gentle way of dying; being beaten to death hurt, damn it.

On the other hand, Maj-Gun, of course you could not tell anybody about her in a way that it would be right. Better said: you did not want to. Maj-Gun at the newsstand, what she had been like there. "We are two Angels of Death, Susette, an eternity." That she had said that, and all those stories she told, which were about all sorts of things, but inside a message about something else the entire time.

Maj-Gun at the rag-cutting bucket. Rug rags. Her dearest, most devout connection. "The loom, Mama, where is it?" A completely unintelligible question in reality, because there was no answer—but Maj-Gun, if you had said that, would have understood it, intuitively.

On the other hand. That Maj-Gun. Did not exist. Anywhere. A figure in your head only, Majjunn Majjunn, a sound from your childhood, in your mouth.

Had been clear the entire time afterward. At the cemetery after Liz Maalamaa's funeral. Maj-Gun had been so different, so stiff, so ordinary. And today, earlier this day, when everything happened, she had been on the Glitter Scene, a girl lying dead in the woods, they found her now, the entire family, but Susette does not know about that because she is at the house in the darker part of the woods now, she has forgotten everything else.

Thinks, at the loom that is rising up inside the basement before her eyes, only her eyes, no one else's eyes: Maj-Gun during the day, that same day. How she should have said something, about something, which Susette had forgotten. But she had stood there and been ordinary, red, slender, and like all of the other people in the world. Had not spoken **kiss kiss kiss** *as she once had at the newsstand, about the silver shoes for example.*

We *are the Angels of Death, Maj-Gun.* **I** *am alone.* **We** *are nothing.*

Helpless in the presence of her story. "A life-long depression. You can live with depression. And then there is medication—"

Liz Maalamaa, the stories, the medication. Liz Maalamaa had already been ill when they came to Portugal, she and Tom, in December 1989. Had been going on for some time, heart failure, dizziness. She had been walking about then, but already the next day she had not gotten out of bed. And then Susette immediately started spending time with her in the bedroom while Tom enjoyed the sunshine on the patio. But he did not dislike it, just the

*opposite, said that it was so nice that she wanted to de-
vote herself to the aunt.*

*And Liz Maalamaa, while she still had the energy to
speak, told Susette about her life. No anecdotes that made
you sleepy listening to them, those people who have it on
their minds to talk and talk about themselves, about their
business, who assume that only they can explain vividly
enough, so that you will sit there in silence and be transformed* **with joy** *too, all ears because it is so wonderful to
just listen. But—if you did not want to, did not have the
energy, to listen? In what way does this affect me? If you
thought like that. And did not come up with a single connection; then that person who was just babbling and babbling was transformed into just babble. But* **quiet now.
Stop screaming**.

*Maj-Gun, at the time she was Maj-Gun at the news-
stand, had caught sight of it. Because everything that
Maj-Gun had told her had, as it were, been something
else, at the same time. Another message, so to speak. A
signal. The rug rags. A bucket. Mama. "Don't be afraid."
"***She didn't give way, your mama.***" At the same time
both of them had been unaware if it too, what it was that
pulled them together.*

*Young and insecure and fragile. There was that some-
thing in each other they wanted to reach, rug rags, but
could not figure out how. So it had turned out wrong, that
too. "The loom, where is it?"*

. *"It's so nice that you're together with Tom," Liz Maalamaa had said in the bedroom.*

"I know Maj-Gun too. We've been good friends."

*"Do you? That makes me so happy. Maj-Gun is a spe-
cial girl."*

And Liz Maalamaa had brightened up considerably and despite the fact that they had not spoken about Maj-Gun or Tom, Susette's fiancé, anymore, whom Susette would live happily ever after with, the fact that Maj-Gun had been mentioned, both of them felt, brought them closer together.

*But otherwise, in the bedroom, which was transformed into a sickroom and to a death room, but soft, normal, when Liz Maalamaa had spoken about her life it, had, in other words, been brief. In occasional images, scenes, some episode from here or from there. The transience, like from an album, **come and see my gallery**, so beautiful.*

*A dog, Handsome. Two swans, Dick and Duck. **Young man against a backdrop of flames**; an image on a wall in a hotel which, for a few terrible moments, looked that way but which later, afterward, had still been something else, just an armful of roses, in a bowl. "You know, Susette, hotel room art, it can be very anonymous." And the silver shoes, which she liked dancing in and her husband too. "Life with him wasn't easy, never easy, but I miss the dancing." And the movie stars she had loved in her youth, Ingrid Bergman, and China where she had never been but traveled to so much in her fantasies that it had almost become real, "that wall, it is LONG, you know, long walk, I think that sometimes, and God and me and reality . . . There is a kind of loneliness too, in God, that loneliness is intangible."*

"I'm staying here. I'm not leaving," Susette had repeated several times and gotten medicine, food, made the bed with clean, fresh sheets.

Toward the end, when Liz Maalamaa no longer had the energy to speak, Susette just sat there and held her hand.

And the very end, the final days, mama Liz mama, **I'm not leaving you, never again alone***, she had crawled up into the bed next to Liz Maalamaa and laid down next to her. "My girl." Liz's arms around her, pulling her closer.*

And there, in the bed, two bodies pressed against each other, something that could have been called Susette's story could have been told, that which was not her mother, but the other, which had also happened. Though without words, words are unnecessary, a story that had pulsated between them like blood in their bodies. And from her to the older woman. From Susette Packlén to Liz Maalamaa.

A story in rags, fragments. Also about what had fallen and would fall outside the actual story, with context, coherence that had to do with coming out of a wood to Tom to here, Liz Maalamaa, Portugal—and farther on in life.

About being in a forest: "Once I was in a wood . . ."

Or, "all walls collapse." About leaving work in the middle of the day, one day in November, just a few weeks earlier at that point in Portugal, but there in the bed with Liz Maalamaa, already an eternity since then. That morning, a project in the city by the sea that she had come to, an independent one that she did not work on together with Solveig but alone and that was that, an apartment in a high-rise in a suburb of the city by the sea, where Solveig had dropped her off that morning.

An old woman there as well, in the apartment, who was playing a film and had the radio on at the same time. "All walls crashing down." A historical moment, in Germany. The wall that had come down in Berlin and now people were moving in hordes, happy, singing, from one side to the other. The woman had recorded newsreels from the day before and was sitting, while the radio was on, playing morning pop songs, watching those clips over and over again, tears running down her cheeks, and said, "a historical moment, all walls are coming down."

Under normal circumstances Susette would have asked about it of course. If the older woman knew anyone in Germany, or if she was just happy about the step forward in history.

But it had not been an ordinary day. She had met Maj-Gun on the walking path in the town center that morning, and Maj-Gun had been angry, an omen that too.

About the impossibility, of everything. And she had taken the rugs out onto the courtyard, hung them over the rug rack, and there, "all walls coming down" ringing in her ears, she understood what it was. What she had forgotten, kiss kiss kiss, as if Maj-Gun had said it too, had she said it? If not, then she should have.

And suddenly she heard the folk song. "The folk song has many verses, the same thing happens in every one. Over and over again—"

The girl at the cemetery who was singing, a song from the company car in the morning. And then Susette had understood: there is no way out of this.

Susette left the rugs on the rack, and left. Took the bus back to the District and came back home and took the backpack and then the bus again, to the capes, the sea, she was headed there.

The Winter Garden. Some scribble, pictures on the wall in her apartment, a lot of words there too. Kapu kai. He had been in the cousin's house, of course, he was there when he was not hanging out in her apartment. She was going to drop off the pistol, she did not need it any longer, she was headed to the sea after all.

But he was in the way. The Boy in the woods, the boy from the woods. But she did not know him. Another story, had always been. All walls coming down. The cat in his eyes as well.

And there had, certainly, been blood, blood, there too. She did not remember. It was difficult to remember. Some things just cannot—

In any case she had not had the pistol or the backpack when she came down to the Second Cape, the cliffs, the sea.

But wait, Liz, about this blood. The Boy in the woods, the following must be said. Bengt, who he was—and was not.

"That once, Liz, I was in a wood." Another wood. In the middle region of the country. Janos, the strawberry-picking fields. Fifteen years old, or sixteen. And she and Janos her second love, "the Pole but actually he was from Lithuania," had gotten lost in this wood after they had run away from the strawberry fields. His idea, but good ideas and most of all, who had been the originator of them is easily forgotten after a day's wandering about in the woods and they had started fighting violently, wordlessly, and suddenly in the woods even Susette had become furious.

He had hit her, she had hit back. That damned unintelligible language, and they had nothing to say to each other anyway. He teased her because she did not know the way out, this was her damned wood, her country. They had not eaten for days, water could be found in the wood, of course, in any case.

He accused her of all sorts of other things too. A scuffle, naturally Janos had been stronger than her. But she had been angrier: might one have been able to tell, in general, have been able to tell a therapist about such a rage? Which just grew inside you, as a result of all the powerlessness in the world, CRASH, someone who stepped on a house of balsa wood, and it went to pieces, The Angel of Death the Angel of Death, someone who was standing and yelling at you. One's own mother. And the cats at the hospital who were hissing, and the manager, Little Susette, Sweet Little Susette, the old dying ones will become so sad if you leave now.

On the other hand. Maybe in hindsight it was a fabrication. Because she had forgotten that moment, would forget, more and more, just here in the bed, with Liz, wordless, let it come out.

Maybe she took the rock just because it happened to end up under her hand there in the middle of the seventymilewoods in the middle region of the country where east was west and north was south, she had no idea, just that it was twelve o'clock somewhere certainly, because the sun was shining that way, as if it were the middle of the day. And Janos had pushed her down on the ground. She took the rock and threw it and it hit him and he sank down to the ground, it was like in a movie, remained lying there.

Moss, mosquitoes, and hunger thirst in her stomach. And a strong sun, as mentioned, and a damned silence, loneliness.

She had continued walking.

"Once I was in a wood . . ." And though she might have regretted it then already that she had left him behind, it really did not matter, the woods were the same the same

everywhere, she still would not be able to find her way back to that place.

And suddenly she had been out of the wood. Almost laughable, maybe just a few hours later after a day of being lost with her second love: found a road where there were cars. And she had just sat down on a rock, taken a breather, out of relief. And fallen asleep. And when she woke up there had been someone who was shaking her and it was a boy, not Bengt, but Magnus, a friend of Bengt's who was in the car. She did not recognize him, or them: she realized first several years later when she met Bengt in the woods anew who he actually was.

Just two guys, maybe in their twenties, who were on their way from somewhere to somewhere like youths are, in a car, loving that vagueness too: "from somewhere to somewhere."

She got a ride with them, and they gave her food, she had been so hungry after all. Fallen asleep in the backseat and when she had woken up again she was in the city by the sea. "Our mascot. We can't leave her here." And she stayed with them for a few days in an apartment in the city by the sea. There was a lot of partying and a lot of beer and a lot of people coming and going, sometimes the guys went to the docks in order to earn money, you could do that sort of thing back then.

"Our mascot." They had been so kind, she had not been Susette but mascot, no one had been allowed to touch her. And as said: no talk of the District, no thought about the District either, just a few youths, she like a little sister-mascot, and the two boys, in an apartment, the city by the sea. And the last thing she wanted to do was tell them

*who she was, where she came from. Because it had been
so obvious: back to her mother, she could not. She had
known that already before Janos, before she left for the
strawberry fields.*

*It had lasted a week maybe, then she left on her own,
gone on her way. Of course she could not have stayed
there with the guys, had to get organized, earn her own
money, a life.*

*And of course she had to do something about Janos too.
That was obvious. It was not that she thought about it all
the time—just the opposite, it almost surprised her at first
how easy it was not to think about it. In the apartment
with the boys, the parties, the beer, Bengt and Magnus.
In the city by the sea, all the people and places, the cars,
buses, all the sounds. Different kinds of weather, sunshine,
rain and thunder. It evaporated; sometimes she had to,
when she was feeling lonely, take Janos's passport out of
her bag (she had not taken it from him, she was the one
who was carrying everything in the woods) and look at it
in order to understand that it was real, it had happened,
something had happened. The rock in her hand, her on
her knees with the rock: an image that remained exactly
that, an image, like in the beginning with Liz Maalamaa,
in Portugal, forced its way out. There, before the crying,
in order to later vaporize again.*

*His name and date of birth and place of birth and simi-
lar facts that are usually listed in passports were listed in
his. The only thing that was not new information was the
first name, Janos. Otherwise she gradually remembered
only someone who had clowned about with her in that
nothing-language, eventually kissing her right in front
of all of the other youths there on the strawberry fields,*

in the middle of Finland, dry hot days, crawling around on their knees in earthy rows, of course gradually hating strawberries too.

But she had nightmares of course. In the beginning, in the apartment, with the boys. But on the other hand there had always been people there, "the mascot," she had liked it, "our princess, so sweet," the one no one was allowed to touch, and as soon as she opened her eyes from sleeping she had been in a story like that.

She had told Bengt and Magnus that she had lost her friend by the side of the road where they found her on the way from somewhere and picked her up in their car. They had not asked any questions, of course, Bengt and Magnus, only tried to say "forget about him," they probably thought that Janos had run off on his own, gotten a ride in some other car and not woken her while she was sleeping on the rock by the side of the road.

But then when she left the boys in the apartment she had said that she needed to find him. And maybe they thought that it was a bit beautiful too, the sweet girl who had not forgotten her friend—had to find him. Bengt, the Boy in the woods whom she met in the woods anew in October 1989, had said that anyway. Something along those lines, at least. Made it clear that he had liked her.

Had to find Janos. She called around a little bit, went to the police station in the city by the sea of course and asked about him, but no one knew anything, nothing happened.

She had not shown them the passport, not to anyone, but she had his full name from there that she could give to the police. But as said, nothing more about that, nothing had happened, no informations, and then she had just about immediately gotten a job in home care and gotten an apartment and at the same time thrown that passport away. Tabula rasa.

Time passed and quickly, gradually, all of that had become unreal. Like the time she had gotten a ride in the car from the boys, in the apartment, like being in a wood, that to.

And she did not want to be in a wood, she was not like that. Not at all. She wanted to live normally, ordinary. And in time, the nightmares disappeared, and Janos, everything with Janos, the reality, the small reality that had existed for her, was pushed away completely, while at the same time Janos, "Poland," became a story to turn to. With her mother, for example, whom she of course got in touch with and called, not regularly but every now and then. "Greetings from Poland," for many years, in different ways, from the city by the sea, and from other places where she lived.

*And with Maj-Gun later, when she returned to the District when her mother was suddenly just dead. Though Maj-Gun had seen through her. "You weren't in Poland, were you." And when she lied about being pregnant when she suddenly, in her childhood home with all of the rug rags everywhere, had gotten such a terrible pain in her stomach, **there must be life** it had also hurt inside her wordlessly, then Maj-Gun unraveled that lie as well. As if Maj-Gun, the only one, who had been able to see the rug rags, the only one who would have been able to understand the question: "Where is the loom?"*

That Maj-Gun, who no longer existed. Or maybe she never existed. Majjunn Majjunn, like a sound only, from childhood, left in your mouth.

As if they had been in the same room. But they were not. Not in the same room.

"Hell, Susette, what are you doing with a revolver in your sauna bag?" *Maj-Gun who should have seen that "need for protection."*

But Maj-Gun had been preoccupied, her talk. Talked, talked about Love. Told her stories, you were pulled along.

No. Impossible. With Liz Maalamaa, in the bed, that story did not exist there, that rag, that fragment, forever, nowhere.

"But don't you understand, Susette? Love like a transformation. Like when the princess kisses the frog, the spell is broken. Or the white cat in the folk song that says to the prince, 'Cut my throat and I will become a princess,' and the prince does and she becomes one."

Bengt. The Boy in the woods one morning in October. Where he had suddenly been and taken her hand as they left the woods. He had not seen through her, he had not seen anything really. And still: "The whole time I thought you were familiar in some way," *he had said, but meant, then a long time ago, in the apartment, when she was the mascot for a while.* "That we would meet again." *He had not forgotten anything. And still you could see it in him: he had forgotten everything.* "Completely washed up," *as Solveig had said, and strange too, there in the woods where she had initially recognized him as something all his own, separate: as the one who had been there, one of them, when she had once come from a wood, and given her a ride, "from somewhere to somewhere"—when she had realized that it was Bengt, Solveig's brother, then she had not been surprised at all. But he looked exactly the way Solveig had described,* "completely washed up," *no entrance there to anything at all. If anything, then a reminder: "Once I was in a wood." When she had met him in the woods again it had been in a terrible moment, just enough to understand that she had to get out of the woods, had been close to ending up there again, but out out of here and now.*

So there on the path she had pulled her hand out of his. They did not know each other at all, had never known. Not she him, not he her. He had shown up, of course, at her apartment, it had not even been a surprise, and she was forced to let him in of course. One time he and his friend helped her, she could not deny him that. But there had not been any "story." He had his drawings on the wall, the Winter Garden, an exhibition, scribbly sketches, screaming meanings, like Screaming Toys, shut her ears to them when she looked at them so she avoided seeing them. And she wished he would leave even if she could not throw him out. But that story he spoke about, a co-incidence that was like a stroke of luck, like winning the lottery, so to speak, "everything has gone to hell but I'm lucky at games," he had said as well, also all sorts of idi-otic things he spoke about while drunk and he was often drunk, almost all of the time. The Winter Garden. His sketches on the walls. A language. He liked speaking it. Kapu kai. Cuckoo.

But she thought it would pass, and she was not there all the time, with him in the apartment. Had her job with Solveig, which she of course naturally had not said any-thing about her brother hanging out in her apartment. She could however remember something that Solveig said about her brother: "a dreamer who goes out of control." And agree. Her personally, Susette, like Solveig, they were parallel, as it were, neither of them in a dream, " a wood."

And Tom Maalamaa, an old love, had started calling too. Life was moving slowly, somewhere. On the avenues. Being nothing, and new.

So, the Boy in the woods. It had been like that. And blood. She could not remember for the life of her what it was like, would never be able to, that was true. The cousin's house, blood. The fragments. "His eyes." "Once I was in a wood."

•

All of what she was not in his eyes, all of what she was not, which she could not be. Someone who came like an old promise that suddenly had to be fulfilled, "We can build here, it is mine, settle down." Good Lord. That in him—but later too, the great sorrowfulness, unavoidable. "Are you thinking about leaving?" Maybe the question had not even been asked, but it was so obvious, so hurtful. In his eyes, are you leaving me or the cat? But she was not something lost, or found, for him a thread to sort out. The mascot. It was he who she had been. Otherwise: a rag. Like one of them, an old layer of fabric hanging over a loom, which she sees one last time, flaming inside her eyes now, 2006, here in the woods at the house in the darker part.

"Sinking sinking like a Venice." Remember this now too, about the house in the darker part. Bengt who had said it, about the house, once. Fluttering through her head. How true.

The blood, the sea, the cliffs, the terrace of the boathouse. "All walls coming down." The morning in her head, the impossibility. Maj-Gun in the boathouse. Maj-Gun Maalamaa!

Who had beaten her to life. And when she had woken she had been alive, to life, and away from here! The sea, the cliffs, nevermore there. She had left, dragged herself over the cliffs, through the pine grove in the snow, back to the cousin's house, into the room where he was lying on the floor in his own blood in pools but only to the hallway where the telephone was, she had phoned from there. First Solveig, that was true. But Solveig in Torpesonia had not been home, it had been some Allison on the phone. She would be in touch with Solveig first the following morning, but then from somewhere else. About the cousin's house. "I think something terrible has happened."

But then she, Susette, had personally already been in another place. Saved to life—because after she tried to get hold of Solveig in the cousin's house she reflected and started crying and called the only person she knew who would be able to save her, that was Tom Maalamaa. And asked him to come even though she could not explain where she was. But she had walked on that road later, forward forward in the snow, and he eventually found his way to it.

That was how it had been, these shreds of something else—"Liz. Mama. I like you so much." This, pulsating, quiet, and everything else, all rags, like blood in their bodies, in the bed, Portugal, between them.

Rug rags. Could not be made clearer. Because clearer than this it does not get.

And immediately in the next moment: true? Was all of this true? "Liz, is it true?" But Liz Maalamaa had caressed her head.

"Little child, little child. Only I would be able to protect."

And the tears had come, started for real there.

But also: a cry of jubilation. Because then, there, with Liz Maalamaa, always there: she had not needed to think, ask about the loom, the rug rags. Nothing, at all.

"If you later come to wander in the valley of the shadow of death no harm will befall you, my little Susette. I want to give you the silver shoes, the finest I have."

And that night she had passed away, Liz Maalamaa. It had been a calm and dignified end. And the funeral— everything. Calm, dignified, an end.

A heart attack in her sleep, Liz Maalamaa's doctor, who came and determined the cause of death, had said. The doctor filled out the death certificate, no autopsy was needed.

So it is clear that life had not bounded away in happiness. The Sorrow, "a life-long depression," it was still there. "But you can live with this."

But no one would need to be left behind anymore, be alone.

· · · · · ·

Loom, against a background of flames, 2006. At the house in the darker part, the Boundary Woods, the basement, a window, but the flames in her eyes have gone out now. She has seen the loom. She cannot get there. She is so small, frozen in the woods. Sirens, ambulances, fire trucks, alarms, Spanish wolfhounds howling in the background.

And the loom, magnificent, covered in old silk fabric, rags, scraps that had never been cut but remained lying there. In an old swimming pool, a house that was decomposing, *sinking sinking* like a Venice regardless of how she, little Susette, standing in other parts of the world, all parts of the world, on heavy floors, admiring views, views everywhere.

The loom. Disappeared. The darkness. She no longer sees it.

Kiss kiss kiss.

Because it was something else, the whole time, *kiss kiss kiss, something white and soft.*

And now she remembers everything. "Kiss kiss kiss," something Maj-Gun should have said. Earlier in the day. Because she was the only one who could have seen. But Maj-Gun, that Maj-Gun, no longer existed. *After the Scarsdale Diet, anything is possible.* Had become one of those, like all the rest.

"Janos isn't dead, Susette. I've met him—"

But information, what the hell was she doing, Susette now, with all the information? And Maj-Gun had also stopped, stood there with the silver shoes in the middle of everything.

Been cut off. The conversation. All connections.

Rug rags. They did not exist, do not exist anymore.

But Maj-Gun, it was not Maj-Gun's fault. Like at a disco a long time ago. Lambada, in the middle of the dance floor, smoke, among rags. Alone.

And always, alone. She sees that now, and everything, all forgetfulness, everything everything. Standing on the Glitter Scene, a girl who is chasing her, running around her, "the Angel of Death the Angel of Death." Could not put up with listening to it, silence her. But it was true of course. It is true, what she is and was.

The Glitter Scene, the girl who fell, the mask, Bengt and blood, the girl who fell and Portugal and her mother, Liz Maalamaa, "never again alone," medication.

The absurdity. But undivided. Maj-Gun, Majjunn Maj-junn, was not there. Where she was, had always been, is alone.

Because there was something else, something white and soft.

And it was not here. Not here. But there.

"Once I was in a wood." Always in a wood, the same wood.

If you later come to wander in the valley of the shadow of death.

It is not possible.

•

And then here, it is possible, for Susette Maalamaa born Packlén in the end. That she leaves the house in the darker part and goes back to the path. Completely dark now, but her eyes see well in the darkness, here in the Boundary Woods. She has been here before, knows where to go.

A bit in on the path, there it is, down to the right. Toward the marsh, the place, what she had forgotten. Off to the side of the path, soft moss, mortality.

And she sees it, confirmed, she goes down to the water.

It is like this, was: that *stardust stardust* from one place to another place the home the scissors the sofa where she once sat and cut again, alone.

And that image when it rushes toward her here, at the marsh.

GOD LIKES, said her mother, THE SMALL-TIMID BLESSED

IT WAS QUIET IN THE NIGHT

SHE TOOK THE CAT AND STRANGLED IT AND THE LIFE RAN OUT OF THE STILL ONE. IT WAS

TERRIBLE AND SHE STRUCK WITH THE SCIS-
SORS AND THEN SHE STARTED CRYING.

The Winter Garden is burning, sirens, Spanish wolfhounds howling loudly in the night.

Flames in the sky, reflecting in the still water in a special way.

Susette is not afraid, never afraid, does not falter.

Bule Marsh, the darkness, the flames. November 2006.

Takes off the silver shoes.

Steps out into the water.

Kitty mine, oh please come back.

DEATH IN PORTUGAL
(*Child in a field, 2006*)

MAJ-GUN IN THE WINTER GARDEN. Who is she? The Red One. Lawyer: after graduating from the university she worked as a lawyer, in family law, for a few years, in the private sector. Quit her job and for the last eight years she worked as the manager of the Municipal Legal Assistance Bureau in the northern region of the country, in a small city where she lives in a big, beautiful house on the outskirts of town.

Has, for a long time now, been able to sand down the "offensive" in herself that she received criticism for during her studies.

"After the Scarsdale Diet, anything is possible." That is also true. She is slender and red, solvent, controlled, "well preserved" for her age, and so on. "The Book of Quick-Witted Sayings." Yes. She still has it. A relic, a memory only, of something, past, old, different now.

The newsstand. But here now, 2006, in the Winter Garden, the Red One, cutting rags. Red rags, long strips. Just an occupation, a loneliness. Evening now, in the Winter Garden.

But who is she? It is difficult to get a grip on it herself. She does not look at herself in the window of the newsstand, where she once was; the window provides no reflection. Nah. Nothing. So: the square. Sees the square, cuts rags, she sees it one more time.

409

Cars drove up onto it sometimes, Hayseeds, from "the pistol awakening," "the revolver revival." Drove around and around—disappeared.

And if someone was on the square, she was then enclosed in the ring. Some girl, of course, to the hayseeds, girls, they were, are, more amusing that way.

Some girl from the junior high, the high school, chin raised, from here in her gaze, Madonna-like.

Or someone else, with big eyes. Older, almost thirty, but still so small. Big eyed, stationary. Susette Packlén. "Djeessuss, Susette," how it whistled out of Maj-Gun's mouth. "The way you look. Don't you get what kind of signals you're sending out? A small poor child I am. In cowboy boots, *boots*."

And Maj-Gun who reeled her in. "I stood here and reeled in the fear," or whatever she had said, does not remember that clearly. That is the truth. She had said so much. The fear? The truth was also that she had become happy. And Susette had become happy. Which she also said, earlier today, 2006, November, during the day. "I liked you more in the newsstand. There was so much life inside you."

But at the same time, with Susette, on the square, in the newsstand as well. Rug rags. Remarkable connections, as if they wanted something from each other, were drawn to each other because of that. Had cut rags together for a while in a kitchen in a house that was Susette's childhood home, after her mother's death. And Maj-Gun, already then, had told her stories.

The Angels of Death, in a timelessness. But all of that is gone now. No longer exists.

Still—not everything can be kept hidden away. The silver shoes. "Death in Portugal." No. It is not possible. Cannot be like that.

And yet: first hours later, she started calling her brother. Not been able to get hold of him, he has not had his telephone on. All of those things she should have said to him. On the other hand, it is so big, so difficult. That she possibly still would not have been able to say it over the phone. "We need to meet. Soon. It's important."

About Susette, his wife. And death. "The Angel of Death." Susette with the big eyes, and all the death, everything strange around her. "They called her the Angel of Death at the nursing home."

A white cat that was suddenly gone. "It got run over." Susette in an apartment, a long time ago, shifting gaze.

And Janos, a Lithuanian, and someone who was called the Boy in the woods—Bengt.

"What the hell, are you playing private detective? I don't know you anymore. You're so different now, Maj-Gun. After the Scarsdale Diet, anything is possible.

"I liked you much more in the newsstand. Why don't you say those other things, like in the newsstand? Kiss kiss kiss—?"

•

Who is Maj-Gun? In the Winter Garden, 2006? She does not know. Cutting rags again. Just a preoccupation. Maybe, for her, it was never anything more than that. Susette at the window.

This day, in the middle of the day, it is evening now, dark—

"This reminds me of Portugal. Death in my hands—"

And it had been then, when Susette started talking like that, that Maj-Gun slowly realized everything. Which she in some way had known earlier, had come like breezes earlier in life, many times, but kept it hidden, because of all of the other things with Susette. She who had almost beaten Susette to death once, blood on her hands. And all the rest. The big eyes. The jealousy. A bad conscience. Own guilt.

Susette at the window, that day, earlier, in the middle of the day. High above everything, beautiful house. There are neighborhoods in the world, they all look the same. Tom Maalamaa lives with his family in neighborhoods like that: wife, three children, aupair-girl Gertrude.

But this has been the homeland, "home now." The mess in the house, things everywhere, paper boxes and bags, clothes, and so on.

And Susette who had been standing there with her back toward her and suddenly starting speaking strangely, about Death in Portugal, her therapy, her life.

"I was terribly depressed. Sometimes I still am. Because of Mama, everything. And I've been afraid of becoming crazy, like her.

"And what happened between us, Maj-Gun, in the end, was the culmination of an acute depression. In a way. No matter how strange it sounds. In the boathouse. I don't think about it often, but sometimes. It shook me. You helped me live. Beat me back to life. And then suddenly, I came here.

"Maybe it was like that. I don't always remember—forget quite a lot. What was it we were fighting about?"

And she has remembered too.

"The Boy in the woods, you called him that. Do you know what it was like with Bengt? Like being in a wood. I didn't understand what he was saying. Like with Janos, 'the Pole,' or the Lithuanian, which he actually was. From the strawberry-picking fields. Just talked and talked and I didn't understand anything. That's how that story goes—"

"But Bengt is dead, Susette!" Maj-Gun suddenly stands up and yells.

"Janos is dead too," Susette says then, laconically, calmly.

"Janos? Dead? No! I've met him—" Maj-Gun started automatically, as it were, but at the same time completely bewildered, not come any farther. Because suddenly, she was standing in the middle of the room with a silver shoe in her hand.

Liz Maalamaa's silver shoe, one of them: both neatly placed in a paper box with glass. Those wonderful shoes, which Liz Maalamaa loved. "Come and see my gallery." The aunt who had sent pictures of this "gallery" in her winter home in Portugal, photographs on the wall, of Maj-Gun also, and other things, "everything I hold dear." And the silver shoes, on a shelf. These shoes that the aunt would become so angry about if you snuck into the guest room and borrowed them from her in secret when you were a child and she came to visit at the rectory—she rarely wore them but always had them in her luggage. Elegant and shimmering. And otherwise she almost never got angry at her goddaughter Maj-Gun Maalamaa.

"Damn it, Susette, do you have to have the silver shoes too?"

Maj-Gun wanted to say, roar loudly, because suddenly with the silver shoe in her hand, Susette turned around and stood there, staring at her, and Maj-Gun understood how everything was. Solveig's little girl Irene who in Portugal, a long time ago when the child had been born in Portugal, had run around like a passerine in the aunt's house, curious, pulling out drawers, opening all the cabinets, which children do. "Look!" Had come running in the midst of everything with her arms full of medicine bottles. Empty, half full, a desert, and there had been more in a certain place in the refrigerator. "SO sick, SUCH a shame about her." Irene's voice full of sympathy. And her mother Solveig who had laughed: "That girl will probably become a nurse when she grows up."

Sedatives, sleeping pills, the like. And Maj-Gun had known at least one thing for sure: that her aunt, after her marriage where she had been drugged with sedatives by the family doctor, instead of being someone in the family, everyone was aware of the abuse that had occurred in the home, who decided to do something about it . . . that after that, she had sworn she would never take a pill like that in her mouth again. "I would rather walk on hot coals, be awake twenty-six hours a day. Clear mornings, Majjunn, are so wonderful."

The aunt who passed away so peacefully in her sleep. "They called her the Angel of Death at the nursing home." That medication, not forgotten directly, just put away. Which suddenly reminded Maj-Gun of something else. Rag-cutting scissors, white hairs, dried darkness, blood? In a kitchen cabinet in that apartment where she had once been and was, and had waited for sirens, justice—certainly put away, but not thrown out, still there.

And stood so exposed in front of Susette, now, without all the words. Susette who paid attention to the bit about Janos, turned around and hissed so strangely about some kind of private detective, and . . . "Shouldn't you say kiss kiss kiss?"

Kiss kiss kiss. Yes. She understood.

A strange moment. When there had been nothing to say. Nothing at all.

And rug rags. All of the strange connections between them. Gone. No bonds.

Susette a stranger. The Angel of Death. Maj-Gun did not know, has never known, anything about her.

And at the same time, such a sorrow in that moment. Such an abandonment, and such abandoning.

And Maj-Gun did not want it to be like that. She suddenly wanted to tell another story, about that Janos, for example, "Black Rudolf," in the corridors of the city hall in the northern region of the country. Been salivating at the mouth, so real and it is as if it has come out of her anyway, one last amusing story, a real newsstandanecdote besides, but Susette is listening now, it was not that bad, listen!

And Janos, the Lithuanian, from the same city in the north where she lives, lives there with his family in peace and quiet. "An engineer now . . . works at the Office for Land Surveying, which is housed in the same building as the Municipal Legal Assistance Bureau, my workplace these days. And one of those conversations over lunch once, you know, in the presence of many colleagues, and there is talk of this and that." And once when a conversation which, as it were in general, was about one's choice of profession, or "life choice" as it is called in those magazines, just as if it is something you can steer rationally. How you become who you become, end up where you end up. How much it's still a matter of chance, really.

And Janos then, a tall jovial man of the sort who normally would not leave anything to "chance" or dreams, who had suddenly started explaining that he knew exactly why he had become a land surveyor and why he devotes himself to orienteering in his spare time. And not only him, but his entire family, all of them are orienteerers, Susette: mom dad all the kids, they run around like wolves, tongues hanging out, with a map and a compass and they try to navigate correctly in the woods. They're smart, one son has even competed in the national championships.

But once when Janos was young, he had really gotten lost in the woods. In the middle of the country, after having run away from a strawberry-picking field where he had not been making any money, while at the same time being expected to be grateful over having been allowed to get out "and breathe the fresh air of the free world" as a link in the international friendship exchange under the sign of solidarity. Because at that time, Susette, there was the Iron Curtain in Europe and Janos was, in other words, from the other side even if he wasn't from Poland not "the Pole," which everyone at the strawberry fields was determined to call him no matter how much he protested. And despite the fact that he would rather have been in any other place on earth at that point in time, for example Paris—he was a first-year student of French—he, without grumbling, had to take the only opportunity that was offered to him to spend a few days "in

the free world" somewhere. "The free world, the strawberry field, the same berries berries as at home on the
collective farms, ha, ha, ha, ha." So in other words, that
summer: plants plants is what he had in front of him
and he quickly understood that in addition to plants, it
also wasn't the idea that he was going to see much more
before, *pjutt*, a few coins in his pocket, and back to the
homeland behind the Iron Curtain again.

But as luck would have it there had been girls there
then. There were always girls, "cute girls." And one of
them—with such amazing hair and these blue eyes—he
had especially spent time with, so that shortly thereafter
he and this girl had just run away, in the middle of the
night.

And ended up in a wood. Walked and walked for days,
just hills bushes moss around them. There had been water
to drink, brooks, small forest lakes, pools, the like—and
raw mushrooms and berries to eat, but the hunger was
not quieted by them, and the more time went on, and the
less they got anywhere, both young lovers were transformed into two small animals. Became *"les petits animaux sauvages"* with each other. All of the sweetness in
the girl washed away, just silly and idiotic weakly unfo-
cused staring big-eyedness left over. And of course they
couldn't say a word to each either; her English had been
just as bad as his, and it was her only foreign language.
And like a frustrated speedball he had made trouble with
her. The strength that was running out, the exhaustion;
a great fight had broken out. He had pushed her, *splat*,
she landed face-first on the moss and he had done that
to her over and over again. But suddenly, she caught on
fire, and one time when she crawled up on her knees, she

had gone after him like a vixen. With unforeseen powers, besides: hit him with a rock. And he had passed out for a few minutes, but when he came to again he had been alone in the woods and the girl had been gone forever.

So it wasn't that bad, Susette. You didn't kill him. And pretty soon after that he had gotten out of the woods and come to some farm where there had been kind people who took care of him. And then, in other words, after that, Susette, Janos decided there wouldn't be any more French, *les petits animaux sauvages*. To the School for Land Surveying, to learn to always have a map and a compass with him.

And how did I know that girl was you, Susette? Because something in that story sounded familiar and so afterward I quite simply went up to him and asked what the name of the girl in the woods was, did he remember? And ho-ho, Susette, poke and blink and pinch in the corridors of city hall, of course he remembered. A beautiful name, like a chocolate waffle, he said, she had also been a bit like that . . . and a little more poking and pinching, "see Black Rudolf he is dancing, all of us have been young once . . ." But Susette, he liked telling stories too, just like me. So he didn't ask me why I had decided to ask him something like that, but carried on with his youthful reminiscence, the strawberry-picking fields, all of that. And the song "Black Rudolf," which had been the first song he learned in "the free world": at a social gathering in the fire station for the area's residents, it was a religious area, so Susette, no dancing. Just this community sing-along that had resounded, drawling like a hymn from the mouths of the area's gathered residents and from other parishes, berry pickers including "the international brigade," which had been transported there in their own bus for what looked like was going to be the only evening entertainment for the *month*. "Iltamat," a dance with songs to which the text had been handed out to everyone so you only needed to sing along as a warm-up before the evening highlight, which was going to be some minister on summer work who was going to give a "speech to the countryside" while his wife was buying local weavings to hang on the wall in the cottage.

"In the middle of the song I thought," Janos said, "that I'm never getting to Paris, I will die in exactly this spot. But then, Maj-Gun, in the next moment I thought that *if* I die I will die with the words to 'Black Rudolf' as black as a tropic night on my lips and then it suddenly became funny, I started laughing, at everything. And in the middle of the laughter I looked around and my eyes met her eyes . . . the chocolate waffle's." And poke again, Susette, and blink blink blink. "And the chocolate waffle was squirming just as impatiently as I was and she smiled at me, and Jesus Christ, those eyes . . . Maybe, Miss Leading Legal Aid Assistant, a little bit of romance anyway, *hein?*"

Hein? Susette. But sure enough, a story too long to tell in just a few seconds, seconds during which you understand everything. A silver shoe in your hand, but you don't want to understand anything.

One final story for you, Susette, but in silence only.

Because for real, there in that house, Susette in front of her, she has not said anything at all.

Susette a stranger. The abandonment, the brokenness.

And maybe the same sorrow in Susette too, one moment. Because she has suddenly recovered, said: "Sorry, Maj-Gun. It spills over sometimes. It's so messy, rags

everywhere. You get irritated. Yes, the shoes. Liz Maalamaa gave them to me before she died. She liked me, she
said. And wanted me to have them.

"And Tom likes them. We go out dancing sometimes,
just the two of us together. And tonight we're going out.
If the shoe fits. Liz and I, we had the same size."

•

And Maj-Gun has of course understood that she is powerless. With Susette. Nothing she can do here.

"And don't misunderstand me, Maj-Gun. I'm not unhappy. I'm doing all right. A life I never thought I would
have . . . Maybe it's strange but I have missed . . . you.
Sometimes. My mother. I have a bad conscience. I was,
to put it simply, depressed."

There are no collected conversations. Is left unfinished, Susette at the window. Maj-Gun left the room, the
alienation.

•

In reality it is not even Susette she has come to see, but
her brother. For a different reason, suddenly just wanted
to see Tom, such a confusion about everything.

•

"How did you know Susette anyway?" Maj-Gun had
asked Solveig earlier in the day.

"She worked for me at the cleaning business and came
from here, of course. She worked for Jeanette Lindström
too, and for a while when she was terribly young she
was employed at the private nursing home for the elderly
and demented. At the nursing home they called her the
Angel of Death. Jeanette Lindström told me that.

"How adults can be so brutal. It was probably that
paleness, the big eyes. Her mother wasn't really right

those final years. Dragged Susette with her to all sorts of strangers' funerals—"

"She had a pistol in the bathroom," Maj-Gun put in. "I saw it with my own eyes."

Solveig and Maj-Gun: they met at the café up in the town center earlier in the morning. And they had spoken about the past, despite the fact that it was Maj-Gun who had called Solveig and wanted to meet her even though she had come on entirely different business, which she still had not managed to get out later.

"Solveig," she started instead, "sometimes I think about everything with—Bengt. What really happened?

"I saw him lying in the house, dead," she added.

"You've said that."

"Have I?"

Solveig did not answer, did not comment on the bit about Susette and the pistol in the backpack in the bathroom at Susette's apartment: passed over, as if she had not even heard it.

But suddenly said instead, "Is that why you're here? Is that why you've come now, Maj-Gun?" And focuses her eyes on Maj-Gun there at the cozy local café, Frasse's Pastries and Coffee, authentic through and through, "provincial," of course, really looks the way it is supposed to. But still in some way sterile, fabricated like an exhibition, "the coziness." Solveig who had asked, in the middle of all that familiarity in her eyes even if it was a long time ago, "a wild pain."

No fear, no avoidance, just that pain.

Well, no. Maj-Gun was not able to answer that properly either. It had not been because of that, shrug of the shoulders . . . "I don't know."

And then suddenly Solveig said she was the one who burned down the cousin's house. Set fire to it, she did not care about the consequences, had gotten the insurance money. But speaking of Susette, she was the one who called Solveig and told her about Bengt in the cousin's house: "I think something terrible has happened at the cousin's house." She had said, almost whined, early the next morning, when she had, in other words, phoned from where she was, with her fiancé, in the city by the sea.

And it was she, in other words, who had alerted Solveig to the fact that she had found Bengt dead in the house, he had probably shot himself. She had not said that, of course, but sounded truly shaken and worn out and Solveig had seen it later with her own eyes.

And besides, Solveig continued after a brief pause in the café, spoken softly but calmly as always—that yes, if there was something strange about it all, something else, in other words . . . then it might as well have been in another way. Maj-Gun herself, for example. Whom Solveig had spoken to on the phone before she got the chance to speak with Susette, already the evening before. Solveig had come home late to Torpesonia where she was living at that time and some Allison told her that Susette had called. And Solveig had, despite the late hour, dialed Susette's number because she had been a bit angry but certainly worried too about what happened with Susette who had just up and left an independent project in the middle of the day. Just left without saying a word, which was, despite the fact that Susette could undeniably be a bit scatterbrained, rather unlike her. And then it has, in other words, been Maj-Gun in Susette's apartment who lied on the phone about Susette being there but that she could not come to the phone because she had a bad case of angina.

And speaking of the cousin's house, what it had been like when Solveig had gotten there and found her brother the next morning, "those cigarette butts, in all of the ash-trays." No lipstick on the filters, but cigarettes of such a brand that certainly no one else in the whole District smoked except one, whom Solveig personally happened to see with her own eyes somewhat later, one day in January, when she and Maj-Gun had run into each other on the square and Maj-Gun had been weighed down with things from her old place of employment. All of those things Maj-Gun lost hold of in the midst of everything and the splendor spilled over the square, including those unusual cigarettes. As obvious as she could be, Solveig remembers, she personally helped pick up Maj-Gun's belongings.

You still seem convinced that it is a question of some sort of Immaculate Conception Virgin birth, the storks in Portugal?

Maj-Gun had the desire to point out in a loud, old newsstand voice in the middle of the picturesque café silence among the pastries and the homemade textiles. *Djeessus*, Solveig. I'm just saying. *Djeessuss*.

But not gotten anything out at all, instead she just sat there with her mouth open and in the midst of it all understood that it would not matter for Solveig if she were to mention the Fjällräven backpack that she had also seen when she looked in through the window and seen what she had seen, the terrible. Susette had personally called—from where? Certainly from the house. And then she had gone on her way and taken the backpack too.

But suddenly, at the café, Solveig stopped herself and almost started laughing.

"But take it easy, Maj-Gun. For Christ's sake. Let it go. What do you think of me anyway? I've never thought it was you. I know. Tobias told me—about Susette's apartment. How he found you there and that you were pretty miserable and feverish and made sure you got to the rectory and were able to rest."

"Tobias?"

And Solveig later said, that yes, she and Tobias had been good friends, and now that he was gone, how she missed him sometimes, so much that she could be completely upside down in the middle of the day. "Sometimes you realize how much you care about someone and how much you value him first when it's too late. That you should have shown your gratefulness. Not much would have become of me if it hadn't been for Tobias. He was always there, always, for everything—"

This and more, Solveig has talked for a while so that without being mentioned directly Tobias also knew that the house had been set fire to and maybe he had possibly had, via some brother at the Lions Club, connections at the insurance company too.

"But I guess that's the way it is, Maj-Gun," Solveig said at last, in general, as it were. "Been there done that.

"But one more thing, Maj-Gun, which I still want to say. That regardless of Tobias or anything else, I would never seriously have been able to think poorly of you. Because this is how it is with me, Maj-Gun. That either I like someone or I don't . . . and I liked you from the very beginning. That's how I am—"

And Solveig suddenly started telling a story from her childhood, a Christmas bazaar in the fellowship hall, some fruit basket her brother Bengt had won in the lottery and he had immediately given it, the entire basket, to their new "cousin" Doris Flinkenberg who had recently come to live at the cousin's house. Just because Doris wanted it and she was so little after all, and besides, she had had such a terrible time with her real parents there somewhere in the Outer Marsh and now that she had finally gotten a real foster home she deserved all the joy and love and all the presents she could get in this world.

But then the Pastor's daughter Maj-Gun had been there wearing a terrible mask over her face and stolen the largest green apple from the basket. *Scratsch,* just stuck her hand right through the cellophane, not paid attention to Doris, just taken it for herself.

"That was funny," Solveig determines in the presence of Maj-Gun who of course has no memory of it. Who remembers things like that? "Though I didn't dare laugh then. It was such a shame about Doris. You couldn't say anything bad about her. And yes—well. Despite everything that happened later, you know she killed herself, of course; I just didn't like her.

"I guess that's my secret, Maj-Gun. Because Doris just came and took everything away from you."

"You remember all the cuckoo stuff later." Maj-Gun could not help but smile.

"But that's how it is for me, Maj-Gun, as I said. With Susette too. She is who she is. Did you know that I saved her life once when we were little? She was close to drowning, in the swimming school. I was wearing a blue bathing suit, was Tobias's teacher's assistant, I was Sister Blue.

"And she, Susette, had helped the cousin's papa for several years and God knows that there was a revolver lying around in that house and she didn't do anything with it—"

Solveig grows quiet for a few seconds, but then she says again, in conclusion, as it were: "Been there done that, Maj-Gun. That's how it is, has been for me, with Susette too. Like with you. You either like someone or you don't—"

So: no more about that. They had gone their separate ways at the square in the town center, Solveig, Maj-Gun Maalamaa. Solveig asked again, as if in passing, "And how long are you thinking about staying?" Hesitation, and for a few seconds that wildness in Solveig's eyes.

The girl is there of course, the child, an old agreement. "Not very long. I'm going to see my brother, then I'm leaving." The child, one had to carefully deal with everything important, for her sake, Johanna's.

Been there done that. Maybe it is like that. In the middle of the square in the town center, which had been transformed into some sort of parking lot; both of them had their cars parked there, so not because of that. No newsstand at the square either, incidentally. Though Maj-Gun there next to her Volvo did not ask Solveig who got into her Toyota with the name of the real estate agency on the side about the newsstand. Not even in passing, as if it had been raining: "And where is the newsstand these days?"

It has not been raining, but snowing a little, hesitant flakes, sparse, descending. A horde of youths who have come wandering across the square, filling it with their own business for a few minutes. Laughter and jokes and shouts: no ordinary country bumpkins, no sir. There has been something precious about them, exclusive, talent . . . the theater, the dance, the music. And in the middle of the group someone in particular catches your eye: a girl with big, teased hair that falls around her, over her back, shoulders, small small butterfly clips in her hair, many, many, shimmering. The most merry, the obvious center point: suddenly she stays behind the rest and runs out among the cars to the very center of the square and stands there laughing and looking around, everyone looks at her as if she is on a stage, and catches snowflakes, slowly falling around her in the chilly November day, with her tongue.

A bewitching girl, who looked at everyone, looked at no one, laughing, snowflakes on her tongue.

"Come on now, Ulla, we're going to be late!" one of the youths who is waiting for her in the group on the other side of the square calls out.

"I'm COMMMMIIIING!" How she shouts, what a voice. Unforeseen vocals, sounds like it is coming from the abyss—looks around, again. As if: did you hear? Yes. Yes, we certainly did.

•

But, one moment there, then gone and neither Maj-Gun nor Solveig remained on the square to express her admiration for the small spectacle of the unusually dramatically talented girl in more detail. Solveig drives off and Maj-Gun starts the Volvo's engine, heads away, at full speed to the other side of the city by the sea, an hour's drive to the address her brother had stated that he and his family would be living at for the coming years. "See my brother," which she had said to Solveig, not that it was planned, but as soon as she is alone and sitting in the car she knows that is where she is heading. To her brother, to see him, no one else.

Her brother Tom: they had gotten back in touch with each other over the last few years, not very intensely but they had spoken on the phone now and then. Not about great important things but about work, the like. Things in general, so to speak. About how the doldrums can grab hold of you during the day. "You want to make a difference, Tom, do something for someone, not sit in a dusty law firm and for the clients tally and distribute their money in the most beneficial way between rich people."

Still, there could be the same crap at the legal assistance bureau as well. Not in the same way, not as much money, for example, but in some way still the same. "These people without legal rights," which she, like her brother Tom Maalamaa at some point, had spoken about grandly, not held lectures like him, but certainly spoken that way with him, privately. All of those who come to her, without money. But money no money, the same hunger. People are prepared to do almost anything for nothing.

For example: a crime that had attracted a lot of attention not only up there, in the north. A woman had shot her husband and her child and then run away and chased her departed lover who, when he refused her, got shot as well. And then sat there on various chairs and got in the papers too and stammered about "ménage à trois" just as if she knew French. Because that woman had really been in love then, had too much beer to drink too, had sex had sex and et cetera. "All of this climbing toward a story that gives life meaning—" Become someone who at least can stammer her way to some unusual drama and be the center point of it.

And when she had told her brother about it on the phone she added that sometimes she can hear papa Pastor, as it were, laughing rascallike at the Sunday dinner table in the rectory at certain ministers of the new school who wanted "the language of our time" and everyday trite similes in order to dramatize all of the big mysteries found in the church about life, death and make them understandable. Red light. Green light. "Tom, sometimes I've started thinking, imagine if people would first learn to stop at a red light, drive on green, and stop for all of the pedestrians in the crosswalk."

"Ha ha ha." Her brother Tom Maalamaa had laughed. He has been the only one with whom she has ever been able to carry on such conversations, despite the fact that he had then said what she really wanted to hear, which granted she understood first when she heard him say it. "Hey, Sis, what's wrong? Got up on the wrong side of the bed?" Or . . . "Come on, the metaphysical doesn't suit you. Me neither, for that matter. You must remember that from our childhood, which in certain respects was boring. We were rather alike. But I don't remember anything about myself that was particularly funny, but certainly a lot that was funny about you. The Girl from Borneo. Get real, you were more fun as the Girl from Borneo, you know.

"Hey, Sis, what's wrong? Isn't it something else? Have you heard this one? 'You become moral as soon as you become unhappy.' I came across it on a blog once. Joking aside, Maj-Gun, you know that you can always come to me, I'm you're brother, you can tell me anything—"

So yes, Tom. Now, that morning, she wanted to tell him . . . that, Tom, in the middle of everything, such a confusion about everything. *Had in addition to the story such a burning low-voiced interest for*—yes, what had it said in the obituary? Nature, roses? Music? She did not remember or, of course, she did, of course, but it was the formulation, "an interest, discreet, burning," that has been eating away at her. So Tobias, so to a T, him. That text she had consequently found in her home, an old issue of the local paper, almost a year old, from the District, that she had at some point started subscribing to but never had time to read. Old issues strewn around her rooms. Happened to open a paper lying on a shelf even though she had actually been looking for something else.

That was of course what she had wanted and had thought about asking Solveig, that was why she had come—suddenly been in the District without letting anyone know ahead of time, which had been outside their agreement regarding the child, Johanna. That Tobias had died, why had no one told her?

But she, Maj-Gun, had not gotten it out, of course. Maybe because as soon as she was sitting in that café with Solveig, she understood that there possibly was no logical answer to that question. Solveig, Tobias. At the same time: there had never been any "pact" there—Solveig who had calmly said when she told Maj-Gun that Tobias had told her about Maj-Gun in Susette's apartment, that Tobias had taken care of Maj-Gun then and made sure that she got to rest at the rectory. *Flaming Carmen.* Oh, no. Regardless of what Solveig had known she had not known that. No one had known.

But that confusion toward her brother. But her brother had not been home; at work, of course. Susette alone in the home, among the moving boxes, unmoving, at a window later, the children at school, the aupairgirl at the store.

And what were you supposed to do with Susette? In that frame of mind? Say to her: "Everything in my life has happened in the wrong order," as you would have liked to have said to Tom, your brother, so that he would then say, after having comforted you, "Hey, Sis, it's not that bad." And that if you started thinking like that, "your life," then you would lose your sense of reality, it became pretentious, metaphysical, too big. "And yes, Sister, I still think we're doers, not talkers."

But *my life*. Which despite the fact that it had not been said to Susette it still hung in the air between them, *my life*, like in the newsstand once. "Everything in my life . . ." Like something to write down in "The Book of Quick-Witted Sayings," yes, she still has it, like a memory only, a relic.

Still as if just that saying existed between them because that is when Susette walked up to the window and started speaking strangely about *her* life.

The Boy in the woods, Janos, . . . and Maj-Gun caught sight of the silver shoes.

And Maj-Gun, it stands to be repeated, understood, during the span of a split second, everything. In addition to the alienation, the shock, the surprise—understood that Susette was unreachable, she could no longer do anything for Susette.

Like a towel over her face, an anesthesia that had lasted a long time afterward.

Ringing in her ears, Susette's: "You are so different now, Maj-Gun. After the Scarsdale Diet, anything is possible. I liked you much more in the newsstand. There was so much life inside you."

And: "Don't misunderstand me. I'm not unhappy. I'm doing okay. More than okay. I have a life I never thought I would have. I still want to thank you for making it possible."

An anesthesia that has lifted only hours later, in the Winter Garden.

And only then has she started calling Tom; you just can't push it away. The silver shoes. Aunt Liz. The medication. "At the nursing home they called her the Angel of Death."

•

So in the Winter Garden, she is there again, Maj-Gun, afterward. Cutting, cutting red, whirling strips. But: it is only a preoccupation, almost an image. A preoccupation among other occupations, an image among many.

There is a girl, it is the one from the square, the Troll Girl, with the voice, butterflies in her hair, shimmering, who is suddenly there, outside, wandering in the corridors. "I'm searching, searching, for rooms under the earth, the truth about everything, I come here sometimes."

An old story. The American girl. "Do you remember?"

Stories, informations. The girl in her room. The Winter Garden. And red whirling, scissors cutting, rug rags. Everything you can think about and share if you want to. "Do we know each other?"

Yes. They do. In some way. But a while ago. The American girl. The Boy in the woods, in a different way. He is a love story. The American girl, in that way. A story that in different ways parallels Maj-Gun's life, *my life*, and now she is suddenly sitting there laughing about it too. A story that has not belonged to her, not to the girl either, in the way they are, have been, alike. At some point they have e-mailed, chatted a bit. "Hey, Theater Girl." The girl who talked about a play she was working on and Maj-Gun who had gotten in touch with her on a site for unsolved crimes where the girl had posted a question about wanting to get in touch with someone who knew something about it.

Maj-Gun had replied, then, with about the same thought she had when she started subscribing to the local paper even though she did not have the energy to read it: no sensible thought. Or: you can't step into the same river twice, still you have to go there with your foot, dip dip, over and over again, move it around. Or maybe not. Maybe she wrote to the girl only because she felt some sort of protective instinct because the girl probably was not fully aware of what she was doing, what signals she was sending out, by posting a bunch of pictures of herself as the American girl on a cliff, in the moment when she falls and dies. "Here I am singing a song from my upcoming play that is called 'Don't Push Your Love Too Far, Eddie,' the song about the American girl, the final song about her." Suggestive black-and-white photographs.

And now, in the Winter Garden, Maj-Gun sees that it is her, despite the fact that the girl is older, looks a bit different, has become more woman, so to speak, has different clothes—ordinary clothes, jeans and a shirt. The same girl who was catching snowflakes with her tongue on the square. That morning, and even though it is only afternoon now, after the visit with Susette: eons ago.

Ulla Bäckström from the Glitter Scene, Rosengården 2. "My room, EVERYTHING is there . . .

". . . and my band, Screaming Toys."

Informations. Everything that Maj-Gun has also known, knows, regarding for example the American girl. Countryman Loman who covered things up. She has known that since her college days: some female classmate who had devoted her time to things like women and crime. Old cases, maybe not unsolved but with something strange about them.

And other strange things. Some of it said, some of it heard, sometimes one plus one becomes two aching in your head, not conscious of it. "Three siblings, a secret that drove them apart. The three cursed ones."

Also: an eternal memory, impossible to really share with anyone. Except for one who had communicated it, Susette, but in connection with another story, somewhere else.

A girl is standing at the cemetery. She is afraid. Her name is Doris Flinkenberg.

The folk song inside her. "The folk song has many verses, the same thing happens in every one. Over and over again."

Calling forth the fear. Maj-Gun with the mask, a teenager. Angry. Doris who is afraid, but not of the mask, it is something else. But Maj-Gun never finds out what, more than a few random words, sentences, because Maj-Gun putting the mask on only irritates Doris—she leaves, runs away.

Like the girl here now in the Winter Garden, Ulla Bäckström, is going to leave, run away in just a second. Meet Johanna in the house in the darker part, scare her or call forth an earthquake—and then home home to her fate, the Glitter Scene, the open glass door . . . Susette in the silver shoes, all of that you do not know about yet that is going to happen in a few hours.

Then it is all too late.

And Maj-Gun sits there with the girl, even though it does not matter. And then she says anyway: "I'm going to tell you another story. Which might make all of the incomprehensible comprehensible. Not the truth about everything, the rooms under the earth. But about two people in a newsstand once."

The girl yawns. Looks around, says uncertainly, "You have to let go of your childhood. I don't think . . . that is interesting for me anymore."

And adds: "The American girl in a snow globe. I think I gave it to Johanna."

Discovers the mask, a relic that Maj-Gun sometimes has with her—like "The Book of Quick-Witted Sayings," *there is so much life inside you.*

"Buhuu those girls," Ulla Bäckström shouts at Maj-Gun Maalamaa in the Winter Garden with the mask on, "and lady, here's another thing." Laughs suddenly, almost cheekily. "Why are you always asking about Johanna?"

And with these words the girl with the jungle voice is "like from the abyss," shimmering, with all of the theater the dance the music inside her, gone.

Here for a while, then gone.

And has, of course, swiped the mask too. Ha-ha-ha, Troll Girl. It definitely is no surprise.

•

But—

The Angel of Death Liz Maalamaa. You cannot always be getting rid of everything, pushing it away.

And when the girl has left: no, Maj-Gun is no longer cutting, she understands, she has to speak with Tom Maalamaa. And only then has she started calling, late afternoon, early evening, and Tom Maalamaa has turned off his phone.

•

Thrown away rags, put on her clothes. Maj-Gun heads out into the night, the darkness, runs out. Yes: so this, on the one hand. Blueblueblue images in her head now too. The Winter Garden. A blue child who is screaming on a cliff. An old story in images told again. Existed on a wall once, in a room, another room, an apartment where she was for no time. Words on the walls, a language, *Kapu kai*, the forbidden seas. They had a game. The Winter Garden.

"Three siblings who shared a secret that united them but turned them against each other."

The Winter Garden, like a place. Rooms under the earth, the truth about everything, the Rita Strange Corporation.

Bengt lying dead in the cousin's house.

And Solveig, Sister Blue. Who said that morning, "I saved her life once in the swimming school. I was Sister Blue."

Ulla Bäckström's words: "The American girl in a snow globe. I think I gave it to Johanna.

"And another thing, lady. Why are you always asking about Johanna?"

Johanna. *My child.*

•

Throws away the rags, puts on her clothes, runs out. On the other hand, honestly: that is not why she is running, Maj-Gun Maalamaa. Out of the Winter Garden, leaving it behind her. Stories, tales. What it was like what it was not like, tear to bits: there is also goodness, regardless, and beauty, flowers, blue skies.

Stories, tales are not the body, the blood, the longing, here.

What exists is here.

The Red One on a field. She is there.

Outside the house and inside the house another one with stories, projects. Project Earth, tear to bits, has been torn, old, finished playing its part. A girl pounding with loneliness, with another story, about rhythm and secrets—

Whirls of fear in the girl's head, until nothing is left. One book, one image in it. Blueblue, that one too.

But tear to bits.

Johanna sees the Red One. Never more afraid, never more certain. Johanna goes out, to the Red One.

The Child, fluorescent. Explosion, transcendence?

Images to take to the Winter Garden: mother, child on a field. Or?

No. Maj-Gun holds her daughter, Johanna, tightly, Johanna holds her mother tightly back.

Explosions? Oh, bother.

Because then, exactly then, flames rise up behind them.

During the embrace, Johanna looks around the field.

"Look, Mom! The Winter Garden is burning!"

EPILOGUE

SOLVEIG, SISTER BLUE
(and what it was like with the American girl, 1969)

I LIKE THE PARLOR in the cousin's house. That's my secret. I have a habit of going there and spending time there, even though it isn't allowed. Not even Rita, my twin, my sister, knows; we live together in our own cottage on the field across from the cousin's house. The cousin's mama, the parlor, it is her creation. There's a round table there with a white, embroidered tablecloth and a glass cabinet with china. The cousin's mama has arranged it, it wasn't there before her time. The parlor is used only when there is a party. Then the door is opened wide, the table is laid with coffee cups, napkins, plates. You spend a few hours there, then you leave. The door is closed, and until the next grand occasion no one is allowed to go in there again.

I still sneak in there sometimes. There is a closet in the parlor. That's where I stay, on the floor among the shoes, I can fit without a problem, I am so small. I sit and listen to everything around me, inside the house, outside. The walls in the house are thin, sounds are easily heard. Off to the side, but still a part of things. In peace, but not alone. The calm and the quiet in the parlor, while the normal time that has come to the cousin's house together with the cousin's mama and Björn continues outside.

Someone shouts, "Where's Solveig?" The cousin's mama, I wouldn't have anything against that. Usually just my twin sister, Rita. We're always together, Rita and I.

I don't go out when Rita calls. By chance my hands grope around in the darkness in the closet. That's how I discover the cloth bag with the cousin's papa's money. Stuck inside a boot with a high ankle, dried dung on the leather. A lot of money, bills. I don't think I'm going to take them and go out into the world and build the Winter Garden when I grow up. Just "aha, it's there." The cousin's papa's stupid secret. The cousin's papa is one of those old men who prefer to save their money in an old shoe instead of taking it to the bank.

I'm not like my siblings Bengt and Rita. I don't have any visions, fantasies. I'm just there inside the closet, for a while, in ordinary time.

When I have been in the parlor I sneak out again.

•

Astrid Loman. That's the cousin's mama. She has a son with her when she comes to the cousin's house. His name is Björn and he is fifteen years old, a few years older than Bengt, my older brother. Astrid Loman is the kind of person who draws children to her. All children, especially the small and mistreated.

Astrid and Björn are from the next county over, where Astrid, who is countryman Loman's daughter, was born and raised. Countryman Loman works periodically as the substitute police commissioner in the District.

Astrid. What a beautiful name. Still, it isn't used particularly often in the cousin's house because the cousin's papa has, from the very beginning, had a very special way of saying it. He stresses the last syllable: sounds like ASTRIID, which is the cousin's papa's intention: as if it were impossible to have a name like that.

The cousin's papa three sheets to the wind, in his room next to the kitchen where he almost always is, the door flung wide open. Three sheets to the wind means drunk in Districtish.

For the most part all of us say cousin's mama after that.

•

But the cousin's mama doesn't care about that. Hums a song in the kitchen. *I walk up the mountain with my lonely heart.* She's allowed to hum rather loudly and persistently. In the very beginning, at first, there is no transistor radio or cassette tape player that you could turn the volume up on.

Astrid, the cousin's papa. It takes time to get used to it. Astrid hums, grows accustomed.

Otherwise, who is she? Someone who likes crosswords, pop music, and magazines. Family magazines, and a popular magazine called *True Crimes*, has a bundle of old issues with her when she moves to the cousin's house. Maybe they belonged to countryman Loman. Then the daily paper of course, where Astrid carefully follows what is happening around the country.

The first swallow has come, a cat has run away. Three small siblings who have become orphans as the result of a car accident.

•

"Children's mama." That is what some people in the District say about the cousin's mama. When I get older I understand of course that it doesn't just mean she has all of these children, which aren't in fact hers. Björn has no father; actually, there are a lot of children like that everywhere—in the wake of the war, for example—who get to come home to her and whom she takes care of. The children in the cousin's house whom she never abandons, that's true too. Left there after Björn, the cousins and Doris Flinkenberg.

When Astrid comes to the cousin's house her contact with her parental home ends, I don't know why. But maybe you can see it like this: that countryman Loman was a bit relieved to have his child-loving daughter placed somewhere. Maybe having all of the children come to Astrid Loman wasn't an easy thing for the police commissioner and his wife to deal with, people who were approaching retirement age and the love between a man and a woman was something Astrid Loman liked learning the words to when she heard them in the songs played on the radio.

•

Because the cousin's mama likes children most of all. All children everywhere, but particularly children you feel sorry for, who have ended up alone in life. That's why she settles down at the cousin's property where Rita and Bengt and I have been living alone with the cousin's papa since our parents' fatal accident. It happened when we were much younger. They say these parents were professional dancers, I don't remember.

Sitting at the stone foundation of the house on the hill on the First Cape, me and my siblings, Bengt and Rita. Sitting at the stone foundation of the house after the car accident, before the cousin's mama comes, me and my siblings Bengt and Rita. Three of us in the high grass. Pressing ourselves against the stone foundation, cold in the shadows. Hearing rumba tones through the cold stone. A pounding rhythm in the stone, through stone, into our bodies.

Sucking, temperamental and dancing. To someone who understands dance, that is. For the one who wants to dance, or can.

We three siblings don't want to. Can't.

We build the Winter Garden instead. A world. Everything exists there. Whatever you want. Dreams, fantasies, reality, whatever you want. Bengt sketches, draws maps. The Winter Garden has its own language. We speak the language. Make up our own words, names, expressions. Bengt and Rita make them up. That's how it is for the most part. I don't have as much imagination. After the cousin's mama comes I would rather be with her below the hill. I like the cousin's mama.

But it's hard to leave Bengt and Rita, especially for me, leaving Rita. I wait until they're finished. We remove ourselves from the spot. Go down.

Bengt goes to the cousin's house where he slept by himself in a room on the second floor before Björn came. Had a ladder on the outer wall of the house so that he could use the real entrance as little as possible. It isn't necessary anymore now that he and Björn are sharing the same room upstairs. As I said, Rita and I live in a separate cottage on the other side of the field. It's an old baker's cottage, says the cousin's mama. Where you used to bake bread, and have children. I like it when the cousin's mama talks about things like that. I listen carefully.

Before the cousin's mama it's like this: another landscape.

•

But so, when the cousin's mama and Björn come everything changes. It becomes another time: the time that most other people live in. Daily paper in the mailbox, pop songs of the day, pop music that Björn listens to on his transistor radio, which hangs on a hook hammered into the side of the barn, while he tinkers with his moped in the yard. Carefully lifting the transistor from its hook when it's time for supper, all of the cousin's children, in the kitchen. Sets the transistor on the fridge, plugs it into the wall if the batteries are dead—so that after supper, tea and cheese sandwiches, evening pop music floods over the entire kitchen. Astrid sings along, closes her eyes. Björn laughs, ruffles her hair. Bengt, Rita, Solveig: we watch. The lyrics aren't familiar, we can't sing, but it's fascinating to watch. Björn and the cousin's mama: they *are* from another landscape. It's so obvious in that moment. The cousin's papa is sleeping in his room. He is rarely awake on peaceful supper evenings.

•

Björn bought the transistor radio with his own money. He works as a mechanic's apprentice at the service station in the town center. It's the same radio he lifts down from the nail in the barn wall a few years later when he's going to walk back and forth along the road with his first girlfriend, the American girl Eddie de Wire.

The radio in one hand, the first girlfriend in the other: being teenagers together. "Eating" music. Even though rather often, when it's time for these walks, the radio isn't playing anything other than the weather report. The sound on the machine can conveniently be turned up anyway and the antenna pulled out to its maximum length and when pointed a bit to the side you don't hear too much static.

Don't hear much of anything else either. For example, talking.

And that's okay.

Because talking with other people is something that Björn has a hard time with, especially together with his first girlfriend, the American girl Eddie de Wire.

When Björn is together with the American girl he's a little bit like my brother Bengt is in general. Not sullen, but quiet.

·

But for Bengt, exactly that changes with the American girl Eddie de Wire. Björn's first girlfriend: and Bengt, in the company of Björn and Eddie de Wire, finds his tongue in the midst of everything. Really energetically too, when after his initial shyness he wholeheartedly affiliates himself with the couple. They hang out in the opening of the barn in the evenings. You can hear the voice from a distance, Bengt's voice. With the older teenagers', Bengt's, who is three–four years younger, his mouth moving.

·

Otherwise Björn and Bengt are best friends, and together with Björn, Bengt becomes different, so to speak, softens, relaxes. That prickliness that in and of itself is always going to be a part of him is evened out. Bengt is peculiar after all, has always been too: "his own kind." Which doesn't mean what the cousin's papa says: crazy. The cousin's papa and Bengt don't get along. According to the cousin's papa, Bengt isn't good for anything, walks around and mucks about. A dreamer, Astrid Loman tries to say, but then the cousin's papa says deranged and he hits. Bengt isn't someone who lets himself be beaten, he hits back. He has always hit: arms flailing in the empty air when the cousin's papa held him when he was younger. The cousin's papa laughing. Wiggle fish. But as is often the case with these kinds of stories there comes a time when the smaller one grows and acquires some force behind his punches—and hits right in the face. The cousin's papa isn't particularly strong either. And we three siblings, Bengt and me and Rita, are all rather tall. We have that in common: the height, the stature.

So already before what happens with the American girl and with Björn, after which Bengt moves out to the barn on the cousin's property, the real fights between Bengt and the cousin's papa have stopped altogether.

Crazy. The cousin's papa continues saying it when he's in that kind of a mood. From his chair, panting. Bengt imitates him sometimes. At a distance. Then he goes out.

•

Of all the children, the cousin's papa immediately prefers Björn. Because Björn comes from a different landscape? Probably not. What does the cousin's papa know about that, inside his room, three sheets to the wind? He drags himself out into the yard only when it's cleaning day. Sitting in an old blanket with holes in it, which the cousin's mama throws over him so that he won't get cold, like a mean old Indian chief. Sits in a recliner in the yard, fifteen feet from the barn wall where he's throwing darts. Then back inside.

And in that "landscape," if he then one evening on his own accord happens to wander out into the yard, "propperty": waters the flagpole with the spray bottle. His woods, which he stands and asserts with determination to no one in particular. It is of course unclear whether or not he knows that the flagpole isn't one of the trees in the woods that he owns or just an old rotten flagpole that will eventually break in a storm. But that's how it's supposed to be: this ambiguity. Uncertainty. That's what it is and has always been like being in his landscape.

But what the cousin's papa appreciates most about Björn is "his skill." Björn does carpentry, hammers on old boards in houses and barns and it results in something. And when Björn saves money for a moped and becomes impatient because it is taking too long, the cousin's papa gives him the outstanding amount. "There's always more money."

•

Björn is also the only one who can actually stand to listen to all of the ideas Bengt has in his head. The houses on the Second Cape, which he had on his mind when they are being built, knows everything about them. In and of itself, he has them on his mind just as much later, when the summer residents who have bought the houses arrive, he runs around there. It's pathetic, sometimes you're ashamed of him. If someone asks, "Is that your brother?" you don't want to answer. Then it's nice being together with Rita. She answers back, fiercely. Certainly not because she doesn't think that Bengt is making a fool of himself, but because she *is* someone who always answers back. There are those who are a bit afraid of her even when she's still young. But there is one good thing about Bengt's preoccupation with the houses on the Second Cape: not a lot of talk of the Winter Garden anymore. When we walk up to the house on the First Cape, Rita and I, it's usually just the two of us. And then we don't do anything in particular. Stroll around in the old abandoned garden. The beginning of an English Garden, says the baroness whom we call Miss Andrews, whom we swim with in the mornings at Bule Marsh. I look at my reflection in the crystal ball sitting in the middle of the tall grass surrounding the houses. My face looks funny. We laugh.

Björn listens to Bengt, as I said. Björn in the yard with his moped, Bengt is sitting in the opening to the barn wearing a cap and is explaining things to him. When he notices that Björn is listening, the words just pour out of him, like they will flow later as well, all the time, with the American girl. Bengt so excited he's almost stammering. Björn who's listening and asking normal questions that you wouldn't dare ask yourself, not me in any case, because then Bengt becomes furious.

"How is it possible?" and that question, from Björn, Bengt loves answering. Though I'm certainly not listening to what he's saying. "Why didn't you say that right away?" Björn says. "NOW I understand." And only then does Bengt become happy. Even if it can be the case of course that Björn says that only to make Bengt happy.

But it isn't bad. Because I've actually started thinking that it's still a bit beautiful in a way. Bengt a dreamer, head filled with dreams. Which the cousin's mama tried to tell the cousin's papa, who got angry at her.

And besides: you can't get away from the fact that Bengt draws really well.

"A budding artist," Miss Andrews says, at Bule Marsh.

•

Bengt and Björn: in other words they're the ones who have both fallen head over heels for the same girl. Björn's first girlfriend, the American girl Eddie de Wire. Then on the other hand, the difference between them

will become that much more obvious. Not "the skill," as
the cousin's papa goes on about, that sort of thing barely
makes a difference now. But otherwise.

Maybe it's the case in general that what is different
about two people who seem to be on the same wave-
length on the outside stands out the most, sees the
chance to stick its head out, in relationship to a third.
Like with me and Rita and Miss Andrews at Bule Marsh,
for example. Miss Andrews, the baroness from the Second Cape: the name she makes up in order to tease us,
I know that. Rita takes it much more seriously, takes an
exception to Miss Andrews, and Miss Andrews exactly as
Miss Andrews, not the baroness, more than I do.

At Bule Marsh in the mornings we teach Miss Andrews to swim and she teaches us English. It's a business
exchange, but also, mostly, a game. And actually I would
rather practice swimming. I don't mean all the time. But
when we're there. Sometimes I also suspect that Miss
Andrews isn't as bad a swimmer as she says she is. She
seems to float pretty well, in the water I mean. In and of
itself, I think she comes to the marsh because she wants
to put on a show for Tobias who also shows up there
quite often. Tobias is our "almost" godfather, mine and
Rita's.

Rita and I have decided that we're going to become
swimmers. I'm a better swimmer than Rita. I'm a little
faster. I'm not afraid to jump from Lore Cliff. Headfirst.
High up for the ladies: a vault in the air. When my body
breaks the surface of the water I quickly swim away. Away
from the current, it is strong. You have to have strength
for this, and precision. Rita doesn't. Maybe she's afraid.
Doesn't dare: that is an amazing idea, new. Sitting on the

beach, making froglike movements in the air, showing Miss Andrews a swim stroke. Talking about the Bermuda Triangle with each other, in English.

I come out of the water after this jump. "Did you see?" Yes, it was nice, Miss Andrews says absentmindedly. Rita too. Saw but didn't see. Then I get angry. A little. When I get angry I don't let anyone see. Except for Rita. I mean, we're twins, she knows.

There comes Tobias from the woods. Then we can talk about swimming practice again. Rita is standing in the sand, concentrating now, digging her heels deep into the sand. "Come, Solveig."

Then we swim. And we swim.

We are swimmers, we are going to amaze the world.

We aren't the type to stand on the beach and crow about it, pounding our chests, so to speak. This is serious.

Later when Rita has left I will think about Rita on the beach like that. Switching from the one to the other. Suddenly in one world, then in the other. It will be an extenuating circumstance. It is admirable. But it also gives a false image of what you're actually able to do and what you can handle.

And Rita has a violent temper. It isn't a temperament, it's a mood. Temperament can be seen on the outside, it exists inside someone who always has her own show going on, like Doris Flinkenberg. And now I don't mean to say that Doris was false. No. As clear as water. But she had show.

No, besides. I don't want to tell it this way. About my reflections about Rita and myself in that way. Or bring the future in now. We don't know anything about the future in the present. Maybe it's best to say it like it is.

I'm a better swimmer than Rita. A little better. Rita lacks stamina and precision: not completely, of course, and in everyone's eyes it can't be seen, but she doesn't have as much of it as I do.

I was the one who was Sister Blue in the swimming school that existed on the Second Cape before the public beach was moved to Bule Marsh. I was the one who saved Susette Packlén from drowning and got the Lifeguard's Medal, which I still have. Rita saw but didn't see. Not because she didn't want to but she didn't take control. Rita is preoccupied with Miss Andrews. Miss Andrews is the baroness on the Second Cape, an acquaintance. And I say the baroness, Rita says Miss Andrews. But just as much, or even more, I want to be with the cousin's mama in the cousin's house, the District. I don't like being on the hill on the First Cape that much, being at the stone foundation and playing the Winter Garden. I would rather be with the cousin's mama in the cousin's kitchen, a helper with all of her chores.

•

So if the difference that exists between me and Rita, despite the fact that we are twins, comes out in relation to Miss Andrews then you could say that the difference between Bengt and Björn is most obvious in relation to the American girl Eddie de Wire, who gradually becomes Björn's first girlfriend. There, suddenly, Bengt and Björn are like night and day.

Björn and the American girl Eddie de Wire: in the future Björn is going to marry her and have a family. Here in the District, or close by. It also isn't something that needs to be stated in words. And if not with his first girlfriend Eddie de Wire, then with some other girl.

Eddie de Wire is actually the first girl who happens to come by. Literally, slowly wandering down the road from the Second Cape where she's living in the baroness's boathouse that summer, it is the year 1969, she is in the District. One evening, two evenings, back and forth on the road she walks, in the sand, on the side of the road, sauntering. Restless teenager in light-colored clothes, walks past the yard where Björn is with his moped. Tinkering for all he's worth. A teenager's intuition tells him that he should do something about this. Ears burning, damned shyness.

Up until that evening when she finally calls to him from the road: "Do you have a cigarette?"

After which, since Björn had answered in the affirmative, she comes to him across the yard.

Transistor music, cigarettes glowing in the summer twilight.

•

On the other hand, not much later Bengt will be hanging around with the American girl during the day when Björn is at work. And as if transformed. Is GOING TO do a lot of other things too, and precisely with her, everything. Run away. The world. The Winter Garden. Everything. Babbling on the terrace of the boathouse. Eddie with her guitar. Yes, she's talking too, looks happy.

•

I don't know the American girl Eddie de Wire. I don't know anything about her. I have no idea how she relates to everything, or which boy she prefers. But you can also think like this: that if you're Eddie de Wire, both alternatives are pretty attractive. Bengt and Björn.

Two who are head over heels for her.

Eddie Young: inside each of us there is that eternal YOUNG that wants to glitter, be loved, *BE LOVED* mercilessly.

.

And: not a bad way of spending your summer.
It's so boring at the baroness's.
You can see it that way too maybe.

.

But this I know: that I prefer it when Eddie and Björn are together.
Moped, transistor radio, cigarette, going out for a walk.
And cigarettes: spots of light in the opening of the barn, a calm, green summer evening in eternity.

.

Though it must immediately be said anyway: regardless of what it's like with Björn and Bengt and the American girl, Björn and Bengt never fight with each other because of her. In Björn's eyes, Bengt is always a cousin, a brother, they are friends. She is the one who betrays and it's obvious that you would become furious if you're Björn when you find out about it. But it isn't something you kill over. Not her, or yourself. That isn't why he hanged himself in the outbuilding.

When Björn realizes that Eddie de Wire can't quite be trusted he does what guys do when they have been left by some girl. Ride off on their moped, come back with a lot of beer, and go out to the barn. He gets drunk, of course.

That evening which is the last evening, night, I will be in the closet. Incidentally there's also a pistol there. In a shoe box: it is our pistol. Mine, Rita's, Bengt's. Our inheritance, which the cousin's papa has taken away from us. We're too young to be playing with pistols. I have it under the palm of my hand, I feel it.

•

We're in the garden on the hill on the First Cape, me and Rita, we are looking at our reflections in the crystal ball, looking around. You can see a long way from the hill, down to the Second Cape, and also a glimpse of the Glass House.

"Look, Miss Andrews!" Rita says suddenly. We see the baroness from a distance. On the cliffs, by the sea. And the house, with the large veranda with the windows that can swing open toward the sea when it's really warm. Her Winter Garden, which she had talked about once. Welcome girls to my lovely garden. That's just something you say, it never happens. The swimming and the English at Bule Marsh are, so to speak, for the baroness, games, another place. I know that better than my sister Rita.

"What now?" I ask because I don't want Rita to become disappointed.

Rita doesn't say anything. But she gets angry at me, you can see that.

But otherwise it's nice up there, you can see in many directions. The coast, the sea, the houses, the woods. Everything is there. Being here.

On that July evening with my twin sister, Rita, it's not the stone foundation, here we belong together. And of course, naturally in some way waiting for the cousin's mama to come out on the steps of the cousin's house below the hill and call us home for supper.

"Come, all my boys!" she calls, but all of the girls are included too, of course. Me and Rita, Rita, me.

And all of the boys come. Björn and Bengt from their

directions, often together. From the barn, for example, where they have been lurking with the American girl, the three of them. Carrying out lengthy, quite normal teenage conversations that don't say much of anything. Because normal teenagers in full possession of their senses don't stand there and hold speeches for each other.

In other words Bengt, then, as said, the one who has been keeping the group alive.

"Πολιτική."

Says something in ancient Greek.

In order to impress the American girl. *Teach Yourself Ancient Greek.* Since she has a book like that and has lent it to him.

But the cousin's mama who calls and the boys, separate from the girls, to the supper table, all four kids together.

•

"Wait for meee!"

But then one evening, another hungry, thirsty one shows up on the road. Doris Flinkenberg, the knocked-about kid, who becomes, for a while, "the fifth duckling at the table." That's how Doris expresses it herself, when the cousin's mama quickly sets out a teacup and a plate for her too.

The strange, wonderful, but poor little Doris Flinkenberg.

That it's a shame about Doris, everyone knows that. Doris, from the Outer Marsh, who wanders around in different places because she has a hard time at home, seeks out calmer places to be. Places where she can rest. So tired. How Doris slumps together after tea and sandwiches, falls asleep in her chair.

But in the middle of her deep sleep, watchful. On the alert at the slightest foreign sound, movement. Her eyes open, wide-open.

Looks around: the danger, the threat, where?

And then it's just something ordinary. For example the cousin's mama who turned on the transistor radio, which Björn had brought with him, when everyone had finished eating.

The pop music floods through the kitchen.

Doris immediately relaxes and starts singing along with the song, even though she doesn't master either the lyrics or the melody. The cousin's mama who, in contrast to everyone else in the kitchen, knows the song, joins in: Doris raises a cry, the cousin's mama raises a cry—and in the middle of the song, how Doris looks at the cousin's mama with teacup saucer eyes as if at a creature from an unknown planet. *Like mother, like song.* Is it possible?

Delightful new acquaintance.

And Doris, still in the song, slides off the chair and steps out on the floor and onto her toes and starts dancing. Silly, in and of itself, Doris can't dance after all. But she dances anyway, bumpily, because she is also rather small and plump too. And how the cousin's mama, while the song is playing, sings, Doris dances, looks at Doris so, tears in her eyes but so happy. Doris-light!

And Doris: you can see how a wonderful view unfolds in those eyes. In the middle of the Doris-song, Doris-dance, rosy cheeked, loud voice, and—marsh cunning-ness. A small glitter; but you can't say it in Doriscontexts, it sounds so awful.

Afterward, Doris comes to the cousin's house more

and more often. Almost every day. Is drawn to the cousin's mama, the cousin's house like a magnet.

Starts staying the night as well. Not in the cousin's house; it isn't possible because of the cousin's papa. But, for example, with me and Rita in the middle of the room between our sleeping bags, you have to, says the cousin's mama of course, "have pity." Lets herself be found in different places nearby. Out in the barn, up in the house on the First Cape where she, despite the fact that all the doors are locked, easily makes her way in.

But at the same time: it's a terrible shame about Doris.

But always, if she doesn't go herself, she is taken away anyway. The cousin's papa is angry, eventually he even calls the police and says that they should come and take the child away. The cousin's mama is crying. Doris is crying. Even tries, when she sees how sad the cousin's mama is, not to show her own sadness. Brave girl, brave Doris!

Doris who is taken away, Doris who comes back. The cousin's mama who snaps—

The cousin's mama who goes to the cousin's papa.

•

He likes that, the cousin's mama doesn't know that, she doesn't know him. That the more she asks and asks, the worse it becomes. She is countryman Loman's daughter and knows this sort of thing can be arranged, the child must be looked after, and it has always been the case that all children should come to her! Astrid Loman, "children's mama."

But it is so that the cousin's mama is no daughter anymore and this is not the neighboring municipality, which he, in various ways, explains to her. Loves explaining to her, the more persistent she is with him. It's terrible to see because it's quite likely, or I'm sure of it, that the cousin's papa would, if Doris just came to the house and stayed in the house without there being a big fuss about it in that way, even like it. Wouldn't have anything against Doris, actually, but now, here, with Astrid Loman, the countryman's daughter, he sees the opportunity to play a game. He likes games like these, give with one hand, take with the other, have an opponent whom he always makes sure is at a slight disadvantage, floating around in uncertainty. Uncertainty, obscure promises that he takes back, only to make the same promises again the next moment, or even just fulfill the promise suddenly when you've just stopped hoping.

Negotiate the matter, it costs money. Which means that the cousin's papa, for fun, names a sum of money that he claims he has seriously calculated it would cost to take care of a girl like Doris until she becomes an adult, including the money to pay off the people in the Outer Marsh and so on. If she gives him that sum of money, to be delivered by hand, he might possibly take the matter seriously under consideration. Not even rotten eggs are free, the cousin's papa repeats. Rotten egg is the cousin's papa's nickname for Doris Flinkenberg. Comes from Doris herself, actually: how Doris has a habit of imitating the cousin's papa's way of saying the word, which he often says anyway, in general so to speak, in relation to everything and everyone, but the cousin's papa imitates Doris only when she isn't around.

Something in Doris makes it so that when Doris is in the cousin's house the cousin's papa stays out of sight. But Doris is also good at noticing things; all of her senses on alert, observant.

The cousin's papa names this sum and the cousin's mama believes him. Aastriid. A ray of hope lights up in Astrid's eyes. At closer reflection: is extinguished again. Cannot give in. Is lit.

I go up to the mountains with my lonely heart. It is rather terrible to see.

"Children's mama." For a moment I forget that all of it is a game.

•

I'm with the cousin's mama in the washroom with the big washing machine and the mangle set up in a basement up in the town center. We have taken the bus there. With dirty laundry, bedclothes, and light-colored clothes, from some summerhouse on the Second Cape.

We stuff the dirty laundry in the machine. I fumble a little, and the cousin's mama, who never loses her patience, suddenly becomes angry and yells at me. I start crying. Then everything falls apart for her as well and she takes me in her arms and talks about that child, Doris, whom she's thinking about all the time, it's so terrible to see.

"Solveig. If only one could come up with a solution." And that she has money, but it's not enough.

The cousin's mama has been saving and she counted all the money she has, but it really isn't that much, coins and some bills in a glass jar and now she takes all of the cleaning and washing jobs from the Second Cape that she can get, but it isn't enough. The cousin's papa says so too, all the time: "So much more is needed."

And thinking about Doris, how time is passing.

I nod.

Not enough. Both of us know that, the cousin's mama and I. But I know, as said, something else that I will know the whole time. None of the cousin's mama's money will ever be enough. Because for the cousin's papa, it isn't a matter of money. This is a game to him, a game, something to pass the time with.

The cousin's mama doesn't understand, still. Can't take it in. "Children's mama." Yes, maybe. But also: she comes from a different landscape. And that's why I can't say anything to her; I am ashamed of the other landscape, about the fact that I suddenly know it inside and out, as if I were there. I'm not there. I'm not there.

I'm here, cousin's mama, another landscape and it truly is—and look, cousin's mama, sun cats!

And that is what overwhelms me in the midst of everything. The sun that has now started shining anyway, after it having been so cloudy all morning.

"I like your name." Which the cousin's mama said to me many years ago when she came to the cousin's house. "Solveig. There is so much sun in it."

"Look, cousin's mama! Sun cats!"

Then, in the basement washroom, I do the following: I start dancing. Like the sun cats are dancing. Call to the cousin's mama again, look at the cats! How they are forcing their way into the washroom under the ground through a window that is almost in the ceiling. But still, in any case, dancing over the heavy mangle that is turning, creaking over the wrinkled, slightly damp sheets.

How I am dancing! Carefully going up on my toes, before throwing myself head-first pretty much, like the high jump for women from Lore Cliff, Bule Marsh, in the dance.

Carrying out my own sun cat's dance to sun cat accompaniment, on my tiptoes!

Doris-light.

This occupies me completely, precision: because I don't know the dance, rising up in the dance is difficult, because it is also the idea after all that my dance should be reminiscent of how Doris Flinkenberg dances in the cousin's kitchen in the evenings.

And: dancing in order to make someone happy. The cousin's mama, who has become so inconsolable.

And of course, which I know at that moment but prefer not to think about. So to speak influence myself into the right mood by suggestion. To another landscape. Where I should be quite naturally, not in this knowledge: that shit of hopelessness.

Regardless of how I stretch. Tiptapandontiptoe.

I have gone up on my toes. Become tall, tall, so large. And it is impressive, of course, so tall for my age.

But from that skyscraper height I suddenly don't see stupid little Solveig without fantasy, who *has to* think in order to go up in the dance. But something else. The opposite. The influence of suggestions inside a square. Applause. What a performance.

"You did that well, Solveig."

"Look look, Astrid! Sun cats!"

"Don't be silly now, Solveig." The cousin's mama smiles a bit tiredly. "We have a lot of sheets left."

I go back to work. But hopeless. What happened, what was thought in the dance, does not leave my head. A plan that unfolds, a secret to everyone. "You did that well, Solveig."

In vain, from the beginning. But the other, it is so much stronger.

•

The cousin's papa's money. The parlor, the cousin's house, the closet. The cousin's papa who is an old-fashioned idiot who can't imagine keeping his money in the bank. He brags about it too, in general, in vague terms, about all the money he has. Sometimes you've seen some of it, in the open. Like when Björn was going to buy the moped, for example.

"There's always more money."

If you sell the Second Cape you get a lot of money.

Is kept in an old, dungy boot, in a closet. I'm the only one who knows that secret. In addition to the cousin's papa, of course, but he doesn't know that I know.

I haven't told anyone about the money, not even my sister Rita. Because from the beginning Rita was more impatient than me, despite the fact that we look so alike. Just as tall, dark. So different, essentially different, compared to Doris Flinkenberg, for example, small and plump, flaxen hair, light. In general, light.

A bag with money somewhere would for Rita be something you needed to do something about; not necessarily take it and go, but still, attend to in some way.

And now. Maybe lacking that necessary caution, that mood, for example, which would cause everything to go out of control. It can't get out of control. It's a matter of Doris Flinkenberg, a child.

And now in other words it isn't so that Rita would have been badly affected by little Doris's fate, that she would, for example, have anything against Doris Flinkenberg becoming the fifth wheel at the supper table for good. After all, Doris has spent many nights in our cottage.

Rita detests the cousin's papa and feels sorry for the cousin's mama, just like I do.

So in that way it would be much easier, with Rita, together, having a plan. But as I've said, that thing about
the mood, caution . . .

And another thing. Up on your toes, in the sun. I want
it to be me. Only me.

"You did that well." The cousin's mama will be happy
afterward and applaud me and no one else.

•

So one day I sneak into the parlor and take the money
out of the cousin's papa's hiding place in the boot in the
closet. I don't count how much, a wad of bills, I think it's
enough, and I put the money in my underpants which
have a strong elastic band, it's held in place, I tested it
ahead of time with ordinary paper.

In the middle of the day, no one else is in the house.
I will also remember that day, maybe more than what I
do, that entire business. We had been cleaning the entire
morning, I helped the cousin's mama inside the house
and now she's busy with the rugs outside. It's almost late
summer, the saturation of summer, me in the parlor, that
feeling I like. Everyone else somewhere else, me off to
the side, yet not alone.

The others are in the yard, I hear sounds from out
there, I stand for a moment and sneak a peek, hidden
behind the curtain, of everything that is going on in the
yard, like a play. Carefully, so no one sees. The cousin's
papa is throwing darts, the cousin's mama is beating rugs
that she hung over the rug rack that Björn has made for
her out of some boards. Rita and Bengt and the cousin's
papa are throwing darts: some sort of mediocre competition seems to be going on. The cousin's papa has actually

gotten out of his chair, which always needs to be dragged out for him so that he has somewhere to sit when it is cleaning day at the cousin's house. Now he's dragging himself around in the yard, in the same blanket with holes, like a chieftain.

In the silence of the parlor this afternoon: the sound of darts hitting the dartboard on the wall of the barn. *Plonk, plonk*. Rugs being beaten: *damp, damp*. The voices in the yard. I can't make out what they're saying, but ordinary voices, no particular energy or excitement in them, but not anything else either.

All of this which is going to disappear. I don't know that yet. But still, I know it, right in this moment. The saturation of summer, the completion. Me in the parlor, off to the side. Sweaty bills in my underpants, but suddenly in my head, me, so exactly in the middle. Everyone who is suddenly looking at me, clapping their hands loudly. The cousin's papa too, he isn't impossible either really, Rita and Bengt and the cousin's papa, in the yard. They're even laughing at something together, a dart that lands in a funny way with the feathered side first on the dart board. *Bonk*. Ends up on the ground.

At the same time. Exactly because of that. The moment that will follow, unavoidable. The summer that throws you away. The ordinary time that disappears. And that is now.

The cousin's papa has turned around and thrown a hasty glance at the cousin's house. Looks in my direction. Doesn't see me, it is impossible anyway. Turns toward the dartboard again, throws the dart toward the barn, it strikes the ring, right in the bull's-eye.

An omen that nothing can become like it is now.

•

I'm back out in the yard again. Same day, in the afternoon. Money in my pants. What now?

Alone at the cousin's property. I shilly-shally up toward the mailbox where there are rarely any letters addressed to me, except when I got the Lifeguard's Medal from the Lifeguards' Club a few years ago, in the winter after the summer I rescued Susette Packlén from drowning at the public beach on the Second Cape—a registered letter that required the signature of the addressee, so the postal worker drove onto the property and came up and knocked on the door to the cousin's house and I got to sign myself and confirm the delivery. I who had been Solveig in the blue swimsuit, Sister Blue, during the summer.

•

Everyone has gone inside except Rita and Bengt who have disappeared off somewhere else. Bengt to the Second Cape probably, where he is spending more and more time together with the American girl Eddie de Wire, especially on the days that Björn is at work. Rita to our cottage, maybe to look for me. "Where's Solveig?" she had shouted out in the yard while I was still inside the parlor. To the cottage; she thought I was there.

I stand in the yard and think about my plan. Brilliant. And if you have a brilliant plan then you shouldn't shout it from the rooftops, everywhere.

The problem is simply this: money in my pants, I realize right here in the yard, that I don't have a plan.

So now what?

Go straight to the cousin's mama? No, not that. There would just be trouble. The cousin's mama is the police

commissioner's daughter and understands the difference
between right and wrong—all of these old magazines,
True Crimes.

"HAVE YOU, Solveig?" The cousin's mama would ask
and all the sun cats would disappear, smack, because
when the cousin's mama looks at you in a certain way
then you can't lie.

"Now you go and return that money to the cousin's
papa and then you say you're sorry."

The cousin's mama would say that too. Regardless of
whether or not all hell would break loose because of it,
regardless of the intention and the goal.

•

"Cat got your tongue?"

But there comes someone driving home on his moped.

It's Björn, who is shouting.

No not that!

Suddenly this power inside me, deliverance, how I become happy! Björn and me: the two of us, we're the ones
who will. There it comes, like a letter in the mail, in just
that moment it feels like I've known it the whole time.
Björn and me. And everything falls into place inside my
head.

"I have something . . ." I mumble, pulling Björn after
me inside the barn where I initiate him in a plan I don't
really have. Afterward it's uncertain what is said and
actually what is agreed upon, if anything at all. I don't
think about that then, I'm just so relieved.

Not many words are exchanged: Björn is not someone
with whom you sit and discuss, so to speak. And I am too
shy: suddenly there in the barn with all of that happiness
I get the idea that I have a crush on him. That love comes

up right then and exactly in that second: maybe *we* will get married when we grow up. Despite the fact that we're cousins, we aren't blood relations and it's rarely the case that your first love lasts a lifetime. If you lose one you get another thousand! And suddenly I'm one of these thousand, maybe downright already the second one, or the third one, and besides I also have a pretty hard time in a discreet way, back turned toward Björn in the darkness of the barn, getting those damp-with-sweat-bills out of my clothes.

But something is decided, with the plan, that is to say. For example, Björn's surprise when he sees the money and when I tell him where it came from and how I found it. And about the cousin's papa, the cousin's mama. Doris Flinkenberg. I'm just about to tell him about the parlor too, in a general kind of way, about my own special place that is just mine and no one else's. Initiate him in the secret too, like when the words can start pouring out of someone who is otherwise taciturn like Bengt with the American girl because you've fallen in love.

But then suddenly before I've even gotten started, Björn's instant surprise about the money and the entire story about the cousin's mama and the cousin's papa and Doris Flinkenberg is gone and it turns into pure and simple rage and shortly thereafter the American girl arrives.

"That idiot," Björn has time to utter, so furious in the midst of everything, like I have never heard him before. Under ordinary circumstances when Björn gets angry he goes off on his own and comes back after a while and then everything is normal again. "That idiot," he spits out again and that it can't go on like this and that's saying a lot coming from Björn but then both of us see the

American girl Eddie de Wire come strolling across the yard in the direction of the barn and there is no opportunity to say anything more at all but he has time to take the money and say, I think, we are going to take care of the matter and that this will stay between the two of us and that neither of us is going to say anything to anyone—and we shake on it.

Then Eddie de Wire comes.

•

"Hey, girl!" she says to me as I'm leaving all excited and almost rush right into her arms. "Don't run away."

Lights a cigarette. Björn also gets out his pack and lighter.

I don't run away. So then I'm there for a while, in the opening of the barn, at the cousin's property, Solveig, with two teenagers, the three of us together.

•

The time it takes for a teenager to smoke a cigarette: that is what I experience of the American girl Eddie de Wire while she is still alive. Eddie, in white pants, white blouse, and a light blue sweater. All three of us sitting in the opening of the barn, silent. Björn and Eddie next to each other, me a little bit farther down on the steps. Eddie is humming a song. Not the song like the messed-up song that Doris and Sandra start singing much later. Just an ordinary one. Ordinary pop music, the kind that's popular back then. Björn puts his arm around her. They giggle. Not meanly toward me or anyone else, because they aren't talking about anything in particular, just giggling. The way two teenagers do, quite simply, together; two who like each other in a normal way too. Naturally I understand exactly during those minutes that I'm not going to marry Björn later either, he's just way too old for me, so I giggle a little bit too.

Then Eddie says something about the baroness, in a low voice, that the baroness is a real shit, says it in a teenager kind of way, who doesn't leave Eddie alone and let Eddie do what she wants to do. The baroness said that Eddie will have to leave if she doesn't change.

Imitates the baroness: "chaange." Jumps on the word, sounds a bit funny too, I start thinking about the fact that the baroness at Bule Marsh probably does talk a bit in such a way that you become impatient, we're going to swim, not talk about art and life and Uffizi galleries and then the American girl has that American accent in her Swedish as well, which is due to the fact that she's actually from America.

But nothing more about that either. Otherwise, I mean with the baroness. Of course I understand that that's the way youths can talk when they aren't in agreement with the adult generation, which is a different generation and doesn't understand the younger generation's striving for freedom.

And most of all I'm not sitting there on high alert putting two and two together, the baroness, Miss Andrews, who has been pretty nervous lately and scatterbrained in a different way than normal in the mornings at Bule Marsh.

To me the baroness, who is Miss Andrews at Bule Marsh, is mostly a game, at Bule Marsh, sometimes Tobias is there as well. They like each other, he and the baroness, it sometimes is, rather often too, a very pleasant atmosphere.

And it has nothing to do with the baroness and her boarder Eddie de Wire in the boathouse.

Eddie's striving for freedom. I don't really know anything about that either, I mean, I never will, even after she's dead. What I know is that the baroness is going to try and send her away a few days later and that things are going to end in a tragic way for the American girl Eddie de Wire, due to all the unexpected circumstances.

Which have to do with my story, but not cause-effect, in that way, in such a crystal clear way. Circumstances, coincidences—that's how it is, and remains.

But now nothing has happened yet, Solveig, a moment in the teenagers' world. An entirely different world too from Miss Andrews and Rita who speak English with each other at Bule Marsh. Not in the water, where I am, but on the beach. Tobias comes and then at least Rita and I can focus on the essentials again. Swimming, that we're going to become swimmers, Rita and I.

The teenagers' world: it's peculiar in and of itself and for a moment entirely enough.

Eddie suddenly asks, "Are you Solveig or Rita?" and adds, as if she's already lost interest in the answer while she's asking, which you do when you're young and your head is full of more important things: "It's quite difficult to tell you guys apart."

But I answer the question politely. "Just Solveig."

And that's the first and only thing I ever say to the American girl, answer a question politely. Because I don't say anything about the next thing she says, though, in and of itself, she mainly just tosses it up into the air, a bit ironically too.

"I'm sure it's fun swimming with the baroness. Splashing around with her in Bule Marsh. She and her boyfriend. What's his name? Tobias?"

I don't answer, as I said. First: I have never thought about it in that way. And if it really is like that, that Tobias is the baroness's "boyfriend," what's so special about that then?

Personally she, Eddie de Wire, had TWO boyfriends. But you can't exactly say that out loud since Björn is here and you just can't gossip about certain things, some things a man has to find out on his own, and besides, Bengt is my brother and Björn and Bengt are friends and I don't like it when there's arguing and fighting, who would do that? And then I'm too young to be going around putting two and two together about people in that way.

And then to start bickering with Eddie de Wire, Björn's first girlfriend, right here and now.

And sure enough, it passes. Just something that swished through the teenager's mind in order to disappear in the next second. Darkness falls, Björn switches on the transistor radio, the cigarettes have been finished. "Hm. It's cold," Eddie says in the opening to the barn, pulls her sweater more tightly around herself.

Björn pulls her toward him, holds her more firmly.

I get up and leave.

"Bye," Eddie de Wire calls after me. Björn too: "Bye, Solveig."

When I'm on my way, across the yard in the direction of Rita's and my cottage on the other side of the field, Bengt is coming, at a high speed. He barely sees me, straight ahead, toward the opening of the barn! Eddie and Björn are there, of course, and as soon as he catches sight of them he starts talking about something learned and silly even before he has made it to where they're sitting.

Something from "shopping mall theory," in order to impress the American girl. She also has a book like that which she lent him but barely read herself, some old birthday present, but *he* has read it, really studied it now! Bengt, ears aflame, as if it were important.

Bengt and the American girl Eddie de Wire, maybe we can talk about that here, say something about that as well, a few words, what I know.

I see it, like a scene: Bengt and Eddie on the veranda on the Second Cape, Eddie with the guitar, Bengt who's drawing, talking. Eddie who's trying to sing, nah, she doesn't have a singing voice, doesn't remember the song, starts laughing. Bengt who's laughing. The sea in front of them, blue and foamy, and waves that are crashing, wind, you can't hear what they're saying, what Bengt is saying, the American girl, but she's talking too, they're talking at the same time. Can see them that way, from some house on the Second Cape where I'm cleaning with the cousin's mama, lock my gaze on them in the middle of cleaning, see. I don't know what I'm seeing, as I said, Bengt and the American girl, but I can imagine, Bengt and Eddie, that is also true, it is also, was also, as it should have been. So true. So right.

•

"What did the girl want?" Eddie asked Björn there in the yard by the barn when I got up and was almost out of earshot, just before Bengt here, now, is tumbling head over heels with his stupid theories.

"What did the girl want?" I don't hear Björn's answer, almost nothing at all. He's already in another world, he and Eddie, in their own teenage world. New music on the transistor, trallallaa, new pop song, that's the way it is.

Even if the summer will soon throw them away, though they don't know that, I don't know that either, yet. My plan: that is something I've also completely forgotten for the time being.

Walk calmly to Rita's and my cottage, let myself be filled with Eddie, Björn, cigarette smoke, the steps. I'll tell Rita about it. I'm burning with desire and excitement, hurry up the stairs, run the last bit.

•

Three evenings later, or it's almost night then, Björn throws all the bills I gave him in the barn right in the cousin's papa's face in the kitchen of the cousin's house. You can imagine: all of the money flying about, raining down over the kitchen where the cousin's papa is sitting in a straight-back wooden chair, with his cane. This evening he has crawled out into the kitchen from his room, the cousin's mama crying, or it's more than crying. Loud shrieks, sobs, and scream scream, terrible. Björn who hasn't known what to say but who does that. And rather drunk, so that too. Has been sitting in the shed with beer bottles the whole evening up until now. Björn who doesn't say things like that, who doesn't know what he's going to say, who never knows, he isn't someone who talks, but the cousin's papa is someone who talks, can destroy with his talking.

Doesn't Björn understand? And me, about Björn— don't I understand?

Björn from another landscape. And the cousin's mama, Astrid. "Children's mama." Only the two of them in the kitchen with the cousin's papa. In that landscape. Exposed.

Everyone else somewhere else. Rita and Doris Flinkenberg in our cottage, where I should also be. Bengt and the American girl Eddie de Wire where they are now: in Eddie's boathouse on the Second Cape. Bengt hasn't been around all day.

I'm in position. Though still not. Because I'm sitting in the parlor, in the closet. In my closet. The whole time. Shaking, curled up, listening, but I can only imagine what's going on in the kitchen. In the closet. Like always: no one knows that I am there.

I have snuck into the parlor and the closet at the beginning of the evening and now I can't get out. I know what's going on in the kitchen, I don't need to see it with my own eyes. But at the same time I don't know, I have no idea. That it isn't going according to plan is clear. But as soon as I have the chance to think "plan," then I also think that Solveig, idiot, there has never been any plan. "What did the girl want?" The American girl's question, an unbearable question ringing in my ears, hits home, "You did that well." That was where I was going, the cousin's mama's shining eyes on me, but the road there was murky, gave the money to Björn and that was almost a relief, and then it ended up like this.

When I at long last, it's a long time afterward, maybe a few hours even, when it has been quiet in the kitchen for some time, dare to come out, there is barely anything left of what I heard with my own ears in the closet but only been able to imagine. No money is lying scattered about. They've done the dishes, no pots on the stove, the kitchen table, the counter shiny and clean, even cleaner than the day before. The magazines, newspapers, *True Crimes* and the family magazines with all of the crosswords, which the cousin's mama likes to solve, in a neat pile on top of the refrigerator. Ordinary. The cousin's mama understands that too.

For a moment I think I've imagined it, that nothing has happened. Then I see the transistor radio. On the windowsill, behind the curtain that I lift up. Broken to bits. In a mash. Yes. Unbelievable. But that's what can happen if you throw it on the floor and go after it with a cane. That landscape. I've been there.

Ordinary. But the cousin's mama who understands that, as said. Has done the dishes and cleaned the kitchen again, in the middle of the night. So that it will be just as nice as after yesterday's cleaning, during the day. Even cleaner and nicer. Early morning, it's getting light outside. The counter is shining, piercing the eyes. I was the one who cleaned it and polished it yesterday, during the day.

The cousin's papa is sleeping with his clothes on in his room, the door is ajar, snoring, sawing wood, the house shaking, no exaggeration.

The cousin's mama is also lying in her bed, in the bedroom, unmoving, the covers pulled almost all the way over her head. Maybe she's sleeping, as well. Otherwise maybe she would be paying attention to the sounds that, despite everything, can be heard from me, in the kitchen, in the hall, from the parlor too. I couldn't open the door without it creaking when I finally dared come out, the hinges aren't oiled; the parlor, people rarely ever go there. The sound of a small rat, from a closet. From the parlor, besides. The forbidden room, but rats there as well. But forbidden and forbidden, now, after everything, you wouldn't think it would matter.

But she's lying still, not paying attention.

The cousin's mama's crying, the screams, the shouts. Over. And Björn who has gone out, has been a few hours by now. The cousin's mama who has remained, the cousin's papa who has fallen asleep sometime later, in any case, finally.

The cousin's mama who hasn't gone out after Björn then either. But has gone after the kitchen table, the dishes, the pots and the kitchen counter, polished, rubbed rubbed. It's natural in a way, like it's supposed to be, that too. But still, in the closet, I haven't really been able to imagine exactly that.

Now, when I'm standing in the hall, looking into the bedroom, how much time? An eternity, but the cousin's mama is breathing, lying on her side, not paying attention. I don't dare open my mouth, not after everything. Terror struck, and I have a pistol in my hand. For protection. Otherwise I never would have dared come out of the closet, here, back, out.

It's just that Björn left like he usually does when he's angry. But this, this is more than angry. I know that already, the cousin's mama knows, us in the house, everyone. Or does everyone, know?

Björn has left, and in contrast to other times, ordinary times when he gets angry, this time Björn won't come back but stay away.

But when he left he was alone! Astrid. Didn't she see that?

Oh. That's just the sort of thing you think about, afterward.

Me in the closet, the parlor. I was also scared. And only when it had been completely quiet, for a long long

time, did I dare come out. The pistol, the inheritance
from the shoe box, in my hand. For protection. I have it
with me now too, when I, in the silence of the morning-
night sneak out just as quietly as I have moved around
inside the sleeping house.

·

Björn was in a bad mood the night before. That's how
it starts. In and of itself, maybe it already started earlier. During the day, even if nothing had been noticed
yet. Björn had been at work as usual but came driving
home on his moped at a high speed somewhat earlier
than usual. Left the moped in the yard and gone straight
to the Second Cape where Bengt is intensely hanging out
with the American girl Eddie de Wire, mainly during the
day, which most everyone except Björn has been aware
of for quite some time, at least a week. And a while later
Björn came back, and got on his moped and drove off
and got some beer. Came back, to the barn, and started
gulping it down.

Up until then the day had been deceitfully good,
which if you think about it is of course normal right
before catastrophes. Sunny weather, insidious of course
too, because in reality, summer has already thrown you
away.

When it comes to the plan, it has been going back and
forth in my head. Sometimes as if it hasn't been there
at all. But, confidence. Björn has been initiated, it will
happen soon. It? That Björn will go to the cousin's papa
and talk some sense into him? Give all that money to the
cousin's papa and say: Well, Doris? Now we have, the
cousin's mama and Björn (and me, but that comes out
later when everything is okay and we have, what, a party

mood and the table has been laid in the parlor?), carried out our end of the agreement.

The cousin's mama. Maybe Björn has spoken to her? And they have their own little secondary strategy, because they're older and can think about the practical details better.

Björn and the cousin's mama: I haven't asked Björn about it directly, but the cousin's mama and Björn talked to each other in the barn for a long time the previous evening.

On the morning of that day, after breakfast I tried winking in Björn's direction, but he hadn't had the chance to notice it. Rita was there of course. Always together otherwise, me and Rita. "Got something in your eye?" and sang happily, but thank goodness so softly that neither Björn nor anyone else heard: "Aha, I understand. *Daj daj daa.*" It didn't exactly make things better because then I had even less of a chance to look in Björn's direction in order to send signals about our agreement.

The fact that the cousin's papa might occasionally count his hidden boot money has also flickered through my mind. From the beginning. Yet another factor that is taken away when considering if you should have a plan like this at all.

But I'm so little, of course. You can't expect me to be able to think about everything. On the one hand that. On the other hand, a logical false conclusion that you can make exactly if you haven't grown up yet, and I haven't grown up yet; this, exactly this day, is actually the last day I am ever a child even though I don't know that yet. A small thought here, or along these lines: "There's always more money." Which the cousin's papa has a habit of saying pretty often, contentedly, as it were. On the one hand he meant, insinuated, his own money. All the money he has and that Rita is going to steal from him when she runs away as a teenager, which he has hidden somewhere. On the other hand there has also, in his tone, been something that can, by a sharp person, be understood as happy expectation. All the money that isn't yours yet but that can be attained, get and have. That attitude, that money in general, makes you happy. And then of course you really become pleasantly surprised if you get even more money, in general so to speak. Especially if the amount you're offered is in exchange for peanuts—my God, the house is big, there are several houses on the property, Doris, there's probably room for everyone here—maybe doesn't just match but rises above the amount you had asked for in the beginning. In addition to the fact that the "sum" I stole out of the boot, which I didn't count, has taken on mystical proportions in my head and what the cousin's papa wants to have for Doris is something I haven't even paid attention to in the beginning, just a lot, granted—but in addition to that I have, in other words, seriously recently, while nothing is happening except that I am waiting a bit nervously, seriously started imagining that the cousin's papa will be happy too. The cousin's papa's joy and the cousin's mama's joy and Doris's joy and everyone's joy—for eternity afterward, in the cousin's house.

"Go and hang yourself, fathead."

"*Daj daj daa,*" Rita has been singing in the yard, in other words, meaningfully, in the morning, after breakfast, Björn has gotten on the moped and gone to work.

"Come now, Solveig. Morning session. Training."

And actually that has been the best thing of all.

He who likes Björn so much too, especially Björn out of all the children. Had given some money for the moped, and for the transistor radio, in the beginning. The boy's practical skill. In contrast to the shitkids, really. Björn will certainly in some way find a way to put the plan into action. Solveig's plan. I am in other words convinced of it by just looking at him, which I still don't get a chance to do very often because of Rita.

"*Daj daj daa,*" Rita sings as it were, meaningfully.

"Come on now, let's go and train a bit more."

And in reality that has been the most fun. Not standing there pondering. Taking my blue swimsuit, my blue towel, Rita her red swimsuit, her red towel, and running on the path through the woods to Bule Marsh, jumping in. In peace and quiet, of course. Miss Andrews, the baroness, usually comes only to the very early morning session.

•

In the afternoon there has been big cleaning and scrubbing of floors and on days like this the cousin's mama is always in a wonderful mood, she likes cleaning. She's been singing unusually a lot this day. The cousin's papa has been throwing darts from his chair in the yard. *Plonk plonk.* The darts on the board. He has better luck when he isn't three sheets to the wind. Still, not in the center, not today. Not even the eight or the nine. Just like Rita who has been there, Rita is terrible at darts; the fact that she lacks precision is truly obvious when it comes to throwing darts. And Doris Flinkenberg has shown up as well. Wanted to join in. Been allowed to. Thrown darts around her in general. But she's so little that it doesn't matter how she throws.

And *so* little too that she can't help Solveig and the cousin's mama with the cleaning. Doris isn't particularly good at cleaning either, though she's careful not to say it out loud. Later, when she's living in the cousin's house and becomes older, it is still the cousin's mama and I who continue having most of the responsibility for cleaning in the home.

The cousin's papa has even been in an excellent mood out there in the yard, felt like some sober joking in the middle of the dart throwing. With Rita: about what bad dart throwers they are. "Have you tried poker, Rita?" Maybe it would go a bit better for Rita there, the cousin's papa joked meaningfully, because in poker it isn't really about the skill as much as the luck and the art of reading your opponent, which is decisive. You have to have a certain amount of patience. A real game of poker can take a long time. But you can learn patience, determination. The cousin's papa knows to say, does Rita know that?

The cousin's papa laughs and Rita has to get her act together to laugh too. I can see it. Rita can't stand it when anyone tells her that she's bad at something. But not even she talks back to the cousin's papa when she doesn't really need to. Saves her energy. Rita can do that, she will get better at it in time. A certain feeling for the right timing. Like when she has left and taken all the money out of the cousin's papa's new hiding place, which I don't know about because it's farther up in the future and after that day, the last day of childhood, I won't be interested in things like secret stashes of money or anything that has anything to do with the cousin's papa anymore, not—when it happens, and the cousin's

papa notices it, afterward. Then he'll be completely perplexed, genuinely surprised.

And in some way also give in to her. Afterward. When
Rita is no longer there, because she never sets foot in the
cousin's house or on the cousin's property again after
leaving the District when she goes to the Backmanssons'
after Doris's death and she's seventeen years old.

Which means that he isn't going to try to find out
where she is, persecute her, take measures. No. He'll sit
here. In the cousin's house, on the cousin's property, for
eternal time. Sit, sit. Become even more sheets to the
wind than he already was.

He'll admit to being defeated by her. Rita's victory. But
what? Because then he will in turn have defeated everyone else, except me, of course. The cousin's mama who
doesn't have the strength to remain, almost doesn't have
the strength to be at all, even though she has already put
up with most things with the cousin's papa on the cousin's property here in the house, after Doris's death. Then
she collapses and has to be taken to the District Hospital
in an ambulance: I call the ambulance. And she never
comes back. Astrid Loman moves back to the neighboring municipality where she came from. In order to take
care of all of the children, "children's mama," in the best
way. But I won't blame her, ever, at all.

I'll keep visiting her, bring chocolate and crosswords
and flowers. I will be kind. Maybe she didn't do what she
should have done, maybe she—something terrible. But
I, and no one else or anybody else knows it, will ever tell
anyone, ever, because she was here, she stayed with us.

I'll be here then, afterward. And no longer, with the
cousin's papa, be "nice."

I'll just leave him, but still be gripped by a guilty conscience and I'll have the cleaning company then because
I'll be grown up, have my own life, my own child, which
I'll have to wait a long time for, many miscarriages, but I'll
have that, Irene. So I'll ask Susette Packlén to go and
check on him sometimes.

The pistol will be lying out, on the refrigerator, but no
one, there in the house, with the cousin's papa, while
he's alive, will shoot anything, anyone with it.

Well. Not now. Going through events in advance.
Being here.

•

Doris Flinkenberg in the yard outside the cousin's house
during the dart throwing, which she takes part in in her
childish way laughs when the cousin's papa explains
the finer points of playing poker to Rita. In her special
Dorisway, which undeniably pulls you along, and then
she tells her own childish contextless Doris-story that
becomes funny mostly because of the way she tells it.

And the cousin's papa laughs suddenly, a friendly
laugh about the story too—or just laughs, friendly, at
small smart Doris Flinkenberg, in general. It isn't that
he doesn't like her. Doesn't really think anything about
Doris Flinkenberg. Just "knocked-about kid," another
clan. And in turn that means that he doesn't have anything to do with Doris's terrible circumstances in the
Outer Marsh, in general so to speak.

The cousin's papa laughs along with Doris Flinkenberg. You can of course if you're from someplace else
allow yourself to be duped by that laugh, take it for
something other than what it is: a temporary happy flaming laugh after you have gotten to explain to Rita about

playing poker. But the cousin's mama doesn't understand the finer points of card playing, she just sees that the cousin's papa is, if not "kind," then leaning in that direction, and in a sober state of mind for once, and yes, well, happy. Is that why the cousin's mama has been singing more than usual today?

I have as I said not been there, throwing darts, but scrubbing the kitchen floor and washing the windows in the parlor and been able to cast a glance out in the yard now and then and hear a bit of what is being said.

And Doris, about her then: this is what I remember most about Doris from that day, the last day we were at least wholeheartedly able to imagine that everything was normal: Doris who was joking with the cousin's papa without me knowing what they were joking about, the cousin's papa who was laughing. Just Doris's way of being, with the cousin's papa. On her guard but at the same time open, fearless. But the whole time with that kind of a nonchalance lying underneath: "I don't care about you, old man."

And just as fearless then and yelled, "Hey, cousin's mama!" to the cousin's mama who has been busy with her rugs, *pisk-pisk* on the rack, sung and waved and sung even more loudly just from having seen Doris.

Doris not from a landscape, or another one. Doris from all landscapes at once. Something invincible about it. Doris, a bit like the joker in poker, in other words.

I hate Doris. But it doesn't mean anything. I'm not going to do anything about my hate. I'm going to be sad when she shoots herself and think that it's unnecessary. There were reasons. Her friend Sandra from the house in the darker part whom she started hanging out with a lot not long after coming to the cousin's house—who didn't want to be friends with her any longer, they were in love. She was at a loss, confused, suddenly not a child any longer and didn't know which foot to stand on, who she was. And all of those experiences in her from the Outer Marsh, they hadn't left her, they were still there.

But first much later, I will be able to understand why Doris really took her own life. Why Rita in some way understood, she heard the shot, and ran, ran out into the woods, but it was too late. Blood on Lore Cliff, blood everywhere on Rita. Then in that moment, right afterward, I thought it was over for Rita.

But it wasn't. It's never, ever over for Rita. I know who Rita is, I'm like her, we're twins, I am, could be Rita. So alike.

Rita doesn't tell me that Doris has asked about something that causes Doris to realize something else. Which she had certainly known the entire time, in some way, but due to all sorts of things, also her light, her love, for everyone, mama, the new world, the cousin's house, everything everything, wanted to keep hidden.

And Rita never planned on telling her the truth. But she, Doris, that last fall asks her. And Rita replies, in some way, which makes it so that Doris understands anyway.

And then things fall apart for Doris Flinkenberg for real.

When I find out about this, I am already deep into my own life, have had a child, am living in Torpesonia at Bule Marsh, everything has already happened. I'm in the cousin's house, the cousin's papa is in the yard, I'm organizing things. "Good" girl, but with him it's just a façade. A pile of old newspapers, in an old cabinet, otherwise just filled with disgusting things. A lot of old crosswords there. Doris and the cousin's mama liked doing crosswords together, of course, in the cousin's kitchen, during the time when Björn was no longer there and Doris had moved into the room upstairs. But Doris never really had the patience for solving crossword puzzles properly, she got bored and started filling in her own silly words inside the squares. Too long, too many letters in each square, several squares where there was only supposed to be one. The cousin's mama didn't get angry at her about that either, just the opposite, it was just a Dorisoddity.

Well, I'm going to see one of those old magazines, one of those old crosswords with Doris's own letters in it: a newspaper dated from exactly that fall, about a week before Doris died.

It will be listed there clearly in the squares. Helter skelter, too many letters, but still.

And when I have seen that I will never be able to return to the cousin's house again. I mean, when the cousin's papa is there.

Wait, I'll explain more later, about the newspaper and what is listed in the crossword puzzle.

I just want to say two things, now. First, Doris. I hate Doris but Doris is a joker and Doris will, in her own way, save life at the cousin's house. Will make it possible to go on afterward. Move on. Live on. Doris-light. And when Doris moves to the cousin's house the cousin's papa calms down too. Doris and the cousin's papa will never fight with each other. Nor will they be "close" either. When Björn is gone and Bengt has moved out to the barn and Doris is the only one of the cousins left in the house, the cousin's papa will shut the door to his room next to the kitchen. Coexistence.

And second: those of us who know what happened that night, with the American girl, and I who know about Björn, about everything—will never say anything to Doris about it.

Maybe we don't do it for Doris, I don't, in any case. But for the cousin's mama. But that is no plan either. Nothing uttered. We just know, we three siblings, and what we know we keep quiet about, forever. Others know too. They're keeping their mouths shut as well. The baroness, countryman Loman, maybe someone else.

•

But now back to the sunshine day, Doris who's yelling "Rottenegger" at the cousin's papa this day in the garden, imitating the cousin's papa right in front of him when he has sat down in his chair again now and Doris is dancing around it.

He doesn't get angry, just mutters; when Doris is in a dancing kind of mood it's impossible for anyone to be angry at her.

The cousin's mama is running in and out with the rugs. In the midst of all this she comes to me where I'm busy in the kitchen, the counter that needs to shine, whispers in my ear, "It will all work out!"

And winks, and without hesitating even though I don't know the reason, I wink back. Will work out, in general, so happy.

•

Then evening falls. Björn who has gone to the Second Cape comes back, is drinking beer in the barn. Bengt whom there has been no sign of, no sign of, is with Eddie de Wire, for sure, in the boathouse on the Second Cape.

The cousin's mama is not aware of these love affairs. She has never been interested in the story between Björn and Bengt and Eddie de Wire: in her eyes Bengt and Björn are her children, are still in some way just children.

And she's thinking about other things now. Because just about then the cousin's mama, who still has the summer day inside her, has—and Doris and the cousin's papa who were joking with each other in the yard!— gone to the cousin's papa in his room.

Set out for the cousin's papa: money. Everything she saved in the glass jar, a bit more than she had a while ago, which wasn't enough, in the laundry room up in the town center, and a little that she has borrowed from Björn too, he had some left over from his paycheck.

"Enough!" she said, triumphant. Then the cousin's papa smiled his most sneering smile. He has been waiting for this, you see. I who have been in the kitchen and heard everything have suddenly understood this, like a bolt of lightning in my head, now, though one plus one, it should have been sorted a long time ago, already with the dart throwing in the yard. How the cousin's papa was talking with Rita about the art of playing poker: you have to learn to read your opponent.

And this was in other words the moment the entire day was supposed to lead up to, he has decided, ahead of time. That is why he has been, and is, relatively sober too.

Some rat has been gnawing on his purse strings. Suddenly he had this "bag" in his hand too, held it up in front of Astrid. Has Astrid taken him for a fool? The cousin's mama stood there for a few long seconds, lost her power of speech, not understood a thing.

The cousin's papa did not care a bit about what the cousin's mama has or hasn't understood: he had a damned rat in his trap, damned Astriid, that is the main thing. Followed after Astrid who backed up, terror-stricken into the kitchen and hit the transistor radio that has been in the house during the cleaning that day and that Björn, this evening, because he has been drinking beer in the barn has not come to get, on the wall.

And thereafter, he went after the cousin's mama. Rita and Doris disappeared from the yard where they had been waiting for supper, Rita quickly pulled Doris with her into the twins' cottage—"Come, Doris, we can play cards." And Doris who has an intuitive timidity for similar situations followed along. I was not able to go with them, I had to stay, I had understood that much inside, stay. It isn't Astrid's fault after all.

I ran out to the barn and got Björn.

Björn came to the cousin's house.

I snuck into the parlor, to the closet.

•

There isn't so much more to say about that night. The cousin's papa who went after Astrid, Björn who got in the middle and put a stop to it.

And then he confessed, about the money. He had taken all the money, him and no one else. Grown out of the moped, wants to buy a motorcycle.

No one else's name was mentioned. As said. I'm in the closet, the parlor, even if you can't see, you can hear.

The cousin's papa didn't believe Björn. Björn went to the barn, got this money. What is left, after what he gave to the cousin's mama, and what hasn't been spent on the beer.

I don't even think he threw it at the cousin's papa, over the kitchen. Said, simply nothing. Just stood there, it seems, accepted it. An eternity. While the cousin's papa was really crazy, no game anymore, told Björn who Björn really is. The genes. Bad blood. Björn was someone on whose birth certificate it read "father unknown." The cousin's mama's sobs, crying.

Björn grew still, remained silent, accepted it.

All of the time that had run away from him, all of the unused teenage years. I guess. I don't know.

•

Björn leaves, stays away.

No one, not even the cousin's mama, follows him.

I'm in the closet and I'm afraid. Just afraid. I have the pistol. If someone comes I'll shoot.

That fear is over when I sneak through the house out into the yard a few hours later. I have the pistol with me. I no longer know why I'm holding it in my hand.

•

Movements in the morning-night, many people are in motion. I don't know that. Nothing about Bule Marsh, the American girl. At least not for the time being. I don't go there.

A moment, when I have come out. Then it's like this. If not like another landscape, then another place. Outer space. The surface of the moon. Where I am an astronaut, heavy movements in a space suit, reflective glass over my eyes, and a helmet on my head.

Then it passes. The day, the morning comes to me. Not normal, but real, in any case. Rita, I need to see Rita. How

I had forgotten about Rita, not just this night, but for a long time already. How I almost wanted to get away from her.

Early morning, the sun rising, the glitter of sunshine between the trees—so wonderful, and me here. Dew on the grass, it is late summer, usually tickles in an especially disgusting way when Rita and I run to Bule Marsh from the twins' cottage. Barefoot, that is also an idea. Hard skin that needs to be toughened, us in our swimsuits, towels wrapped around our bodies, my towel is blue, Rita's red. It must still be a little after that point in time that I draw near the twins' cottage.

Suddenly, a brief moment, astronaut again. Or: alienation. Caution. Hesitation. Or maybe just: intuition. I don't go in right away, peer in through the window on the side facing the field first. That is lucky.

Rita's bed is empty. She has already gone to Bule Marsh. Without me. But in the middle of the room in a sleeping bag like a stuffed sausage, Doris Flinkenberg. She's still sleeping.

Doris. Not Doris now. Turn around, carefully. You don't know with Doris. She's always, even in her sleep, you've seen it in the cousin's kitchen certain supper evenings, on her guard.

What I don't know, am not going to see then, is how Doris, maybe awakened by some movement outside the twins' cottage, wakes up, sees Rita's bed, and is in a hurry. Rita who promised to wake her and take her with her to the marsh, she was going to get to participate in the training. Doris with hasty steps takes the blue swimsuit and the blue towel that are hanging to dry on the damper of the kitchen stove, *my* swimming things. And runs out. Doesn't look around, is thinking only about Bule Marsh, a new experience, swimming practice, Rita—maybe she'll become a real swimmer, too?

•

A little while later at the twins' cottage I turn around and start walking. Hesitation again.

But the summer day, here, it is still coming toward me! Bule Marsh, Rita, Miss Andrews!

That is when I notice that I have a pistol in my hand. I try and put it inside the waistband of my pants, hide it. It doesn't work, it's too heavy. And otherwise too. I can't carry a pistol with me, not anywhere.

I go back toward the cousin's house, I need to take the pistol back.

•

The closer I get to the cousin's house the more terror-stricken I become. Like a stain among everything that is beautiful, despite everything, in my head.

Björn, the barn, I go there. The barn is empty. Beer bottles.

Then I see, from the barn, the cousin's mama. She is coming, walking from an outbuilding that is located at the edge of the woods to the left, a ways away from all of the other buildings. I don't know it then. But she is walking quickly, she is pale, she almost doesn't see me even though I run out and stand in front of her.

She says with a voice that makes me understand something about the outbuilding that of course I don't understand then, but terrible, certainly enough, that I should go away, home and *not* to the outbuilding.

She's angry too. She is panting. Fury. In any case, I give her the pistol. Suddenly I think something strange. The cousin's house. "The idiot."

It's a strange thought. As luck would have it I don't say what I am thinking out loud. It isn't real either. It is a dream.

The pistol. The cousin's mama looks at me. Then, in that moment, I see all of my idiocy. My landscape, where I am and have always been. In her eyes.

She hisses in anger that I should take it back.

To reality. I run into the house, the parlor, with all my might, I leave the pistol in the closet and run out, and away, away from here, up up to the hill on the First Cape, the house, the stone foundation, that is where I end up.

And there I am, back leaning against the foundation, the whole time, while I am waiting for Rita to come back. Or maybe I'm not waiting for Rita. Maybe I'm not waiting for anyone in particular. It's the first time I'm completely alone.

It's terrifying. I haven't slept, I'm confused, what I experienced is atrocious. And it will continue, a long time. But in that loneliness there is also something else, something special. The summer day. Or, the winter day, or the day, the night—I'm here. My place.

And it is not the Winter Garden that we, some siblings, have been sitting here and "playing." A game I don't understand, I don't have any imagination, I want to be here. I can be here, and alone. The summer day, glittering, here, which is spreading itself out, a panorama. The cousin's house, the twins' cottage, the woods, the outbuilding, the barn, the road. I see everything.

Yes. After this we're going to sit here. Bengt, Rita, me. Three siblings, people look at us for a while in the District a bit strangely. It will pass. I am here.

And we'll play the Winter Garden. Maybe even more intensely than before, for a while. Bengt when he has gotten over the shock, gets his speech back. But more hot tempered, so that the game falls apart for him, so to speak, despite dreams, buildings, don't disappear anywhere. And Rita, who will "play" so that there will just be some quotes around it. She's going to do something else. Maybe not that Winter Garden, *Rita Strange*, as it turns out. And not much will come of that either really. When the Winter Garden is there, for real. And I know that, the entire time. That it won't be like that, because I know Rita, I know everything about her. She doesn't really have—well, she lacks a certain perseverance. She grows tired. And besides, I know that too, you can't make, build, for real, regardless of how much money and how many opportunities there are, out of opposition, like a revenge.

So in that way, even though I lack imagination, I know that I would have done it better. In a different way. The Winter Garden, on the Second Cape, I mean.

After this morning, this day, when the American girl dies in the woods at the marsh and Björn is also dead—there is already someone who knows, the cousin's mama, with certainty, I just simply know: something terrible—being up here for a while. Rita and me, Bengt. Playing the Winter Garden.

It may look that way, on the outside. But it's like this: and that loneliness which also gradually becomes a happiness, a confidence, it also starts here, exactly this morning, right here. *I* am not going to be there playing along. Even though it might look that way, I am sitting with them because it is easier. It is after all, me and Rita.

I will sit there but my thoughts will be somewhere else. And later we will be grown up, a life will come later, and I will also have a lot, things that mean much more. And I will be here, continue to be here. But not my siblings. I am going to be able to leave the game, the Winter Garden, the stone foundation and everything. And then of course the most impossible: leave Rita. In my head.

•

Susette Packlén isn't going to do anything to the cousin's papa with the pistol even though it is lying out in the open. She is a colleague, but a friend as well, in some way: we knew each other, for a while. Are parallel so to speak, the same tenacity in both of us. Sun cats. Susette who is dancing on a floor, in one of those beautiful houses in Rosengården 2, in Rosengården, and on the avenues, stupid girl, but playful. She isn't going to do that with the pistol to the cousin's papa, which I regret that I had even thought. The cousin's papa, what is that? That sort of thing passes too.

Bengt who inherits the house. It is a shock, I still thought it would be mine. That the cousin's papa would have thought about me so much. But that passes too, almost right away—that resentment.

I will come back here, to the cousin's house, one morning in November 1989. My brother Bengt will be lying in the parlor. Will have blown his head off. That is how it is. I know—he was washed up.

Then I will set fire to the house. There will have to be enough of tomorrows, consequences. It will have to be here and now. And it will come to me, and Johanna too. And Maj-Gun Maalamaa. I like her. Always have. In reality that feeling started early, I was just a child. It was during the time when Björn was gone and Doris was suddenly in the house and was taking up everything, had to have everything everything—was so happy and fulfilled, and you couldn't deny her anything. At the same time, how you disappeared. And the cousin's mama who disappeared completely. But you were simply, not a child. And yet, everyone saw it, of course, everyone felt it, Doris came with life, light, the future, and everything. As I said, we would have gone under otherwise, without Doris Flinkenberg.

But still. Doris. For example that first fall after everything, before you had really gotten used to everything new, found your place, that state between child that would gradually become a real youth, it would be a relief as well—but then, you got tired and irritated, even though you were supposed to be an adult, restrained, happy despite everything with Doris and for the cousin's mama (which you were, of course!) but still, there was never really space for that happiness inside you. And Bengt who was gripped by the general giddiness of giving a lot of welcome gifts to Doris who, after all the grief and woe, was allowed to come to the cousin's house and become a full member there, and the cousin's papa who also hadn't become "kind" but "bearable," we were at a Christmas bazaar at the fellowship hall, the cousin's mama and all the children, and Bengt won the big fruit basket that was the first prize for the Christmas lottery. And gave, because Doris had become delighted with all of the beautiful fruit, the basket to her immediately. But then there came a girl, the Pastor's daughter, Maj-Gun Maalamaa in a creepy mask, and quite simply *scratsch*, stuck her hand through the cellophane that was covering the contents of the basket and took the largest, most beautiful green apple, right in front of Doris Flinkenberg's nose. Who became angry of course and stamped on the ground and Maj-Gun Maalamaa had to say she was sorry several times, in the kitchen of the fellowship hall, and the Pastor himself furious at her. But we got, all of us children, candy that the Pastor offered us because he was kind, and Maj-Gun accepted the scolding but ha ha ha she finally shouted at last and just ran away, she didn't regret it. Can't be helped, but it felt good. And I've told Maj-Gun about it too, maybe I'll tell it one more time, it will be part of this story. That certain things, scenes, at first glance meaningless get their claws into you from the beginning and make it so that you can never doubt them or hesitate about them, like in your heart, as the cousin's mama would have said.

That is how it was, has always been for me, with Maj-Gun Maalamaa. And maybe I regret it now, that maybe I should still have told Johanna more about her.

•

Well. No more about that now. It exists in a time in the future, which is many years from now. This morning. So terrible, but still exactly, just because of that, so glittering, meaningful. That you have to go through the terrible in order to come out on the other side. But for the most part if you have determination, you will get out. And then everything is that much stronger, more beautiful, also the smallest tiniest good thing has meaning. I believe that.

The time starts now. When I leave the hill in about an hour and walk down. And I have to do it. I don't want to, not right then, but there is no choice.

Up there, at the base of the house. If you don't play the Winter Garden and aren't filled with your own fantasies, then you see clearly. A great panorama that reveals itself right here.

I am sitting here this morning watching what is happening below.

•

The cousin's mama on the cousin's property again. Where I met her when she looked at the pistol and looked at me like a crazy person and an idiot—but her rage! And I landed solidly on the ground with both feet, ran in with the pistol and ran away.

But the cousin's mama can't run away. She has been to the outbuilding, she has seen, what I know later, Björn there, and now she is standing in the yard calling for someone. Bengt! Not for me. Maybe that's better. I still wouldn't have been able to help her. Or anyone. In such a way.

Later I understand that the cousin's mama is standing in the yard due to the fact that she still doesn't dare go inside the cousin's house again. The cousin's papa is there—who's probably still snoring, he was just a little while ago, when I was inside with the pistol, but then I wasn't thinking about waking him anymore—and there was everything that had led up to this.

The cousin's mama is appallingly alone. Doesn't know where she should go. What she should do.

Then someone comes running along the road. From the country road, not from the Second Cape where she actually lives.

It's Eddie de Wire the American girl. She comes running toward the cousin's property in a red coat, on fire, an alarm. Whom is she looking for? Which one of her boyfriends? Bengt? Who is waiting for her somewhere else, he has her bag too. He has packed it because they are running off together. Nonsense. But in the middle of all of those dreams, the American girl has been called to the baroness, she has stolen something there. Now she has to leave. The baroness had enough. She arranged it so that someone with a car will take the girl away.

Locks her inside a room while she is waiting for the person who is going to take the American girl away to arrive, I don't know. What I do know is that Bengt isn't there with her then. He's waiting somewhere else. Somewhere simply. Not in the barn, not in the cousin's house, not on the hill on the First Cape, not at Bule Marsh. In the wrong places, quite simply. Where he usually is.

With her bag that he is going to have with him later and will place under the floor in the barn when he moves out. Keep it like a relic, a souvenir. A real memory, of something unusually beautiful. Some sort of promise about something, somewhere, he never got too, never came.

And that promise may not have BEEN the American girl Eddie de Wire as she was, or is—but she was a figure for it. Or maybe, what do I know? I will also think about Bengt and Eddie on the terrace of the boathouse. Right in front of the sea, the guitar, Bengt with his sketchpad, the music. Laughter, talking, both of them talking just as much. Maybe it was the way it was, the two of them, one plus one and true.

•

But Björn was also the American girl's boyfriend. And she comes running toward the cousin's property now, to the barn, maybe Björn is there, she barely sees the cousin's mama who is standing in the middle of the yard. The cousin's mama walks toward her.

I don't know what they say, but it is soon evident that it is an argument. Almost a fight. "Children's mama." Is that what she's like when she is beside herself? My body is pounding—but I see, I have to see.

But then they disappear too. Eddie runs toward the woods, the path. And the cousin's mama runs after her, it's like a dance. They disappear, the cousin's mama is chasing her, screaming and shouting can also be heard. The cousin's mama who grabbed her as hard as only the cousin's papa usually does in the yard.

She's so angry. Björn, suddenly it's as if everything that the cousin's mama can't control or understand is, or could be, the American girl's fault.

I don't know.

That is where they are running to now anyway, toward the marsh.

The cousin's mama can't know how strong the currents in the water under the cliff are. She's just beside herself. Onto someone. Who is not her "child," who has taken her "child" away from her.

And you achieve nothing by raging against the cousin's papa. You're powerless against him. She knows it in her bones now.

It is quiet, some time passes.

Shouts again.

The cousin's mama comes running from the marsh, she runs into the cousin's house and shuts the door behind her.

Doris a little while later, from the woods, in a blue bathing suit, crying. On the steps of the cousin's house, pounding on the door, but no one opens, she doesn't get in.

She sits down on the steps, Doris crying, Bengt who shows up, has a bag in his hand.

He runs to the marsh, and back. Doris on the steps across from him. But Bengt in the wrong places, everywhere.

First he runs to the marsh. And then to the outbuilding— yes, he runs there too.

And Doris after him, Doris in a blue swimsuit, crying, toward the outbuilding behind Bengt. He goes inside, knocks Doris over, but only so that she won't go in! It isn't Bengt who is screaming in the yard. It is Doris Flinkenberg.

•

But I don't see that, then I'm no longer there.

I have left the hill, gone down, straight through everything, to the twins' cottage.

It has become morning for real—me through the beautiful morning, the sun that is already high in the sky, but everything is still completely still. How everything is glittering again, it is getting windy.

Home. Rita. The twins' cottage. Rita is back.

I come to the cottage. Walk into the cottage. Sun. Pouring in through the windows and with the wind and the trees the sun makes sun cats, which are playing on the floor where I am standing. In the middle of the room in the house, next to Doris's rolled-up sleeping bag.

A glance in the round mirror on our wall. So long, stately, tall. Solveig. She is lying in her bed on her stomach, Rita. In her swimsuit. The red swimsuit, even darker. Dirt on the bottoms of both feet and around her ankles and calves. The towel over her head.

"Rita." She isn't sleeping, she's awake. She is moaning, her body is shaking.

I carefully get closer. "Rita." Then she turns over and I get a red towel thrown in my face.

•

I was the one who was the lifeguard, Sister Blue.

I know that. I know everything about Rita.

Then we are also, from that moment on, together but also apart. But also. Such tenderness.

Which will never disappear later. Even though we don't see each other anymore, despite the fact that Rita doesn't return, you're sad at first, but that's how it goes.

And, understandable—that she doesn't come back.

It was Rita who was forced to lie the most, to Doris Flinkenberg. She and Doris at the beach at Bule Marsh. First Rita alone, then Doris Flinkenberg. No one else, no Miss Andrews. She was still in her house, because of Eddie de Wire.

And Tobias was away during these weeks. Sometimes I have thought that things could have been different if Tobias had been there. With his swimming ability, for example. Or just because.

And among everything that is falling apart, cracks, there is always something else. Something just as meaningful, maybe more meaningful, even if you don't see it right away. With Tobias, for example, when he comes back in a few days and finds out everything. He comes to me and Rita in the cottage, like before. We don't hug each other or anything. It is never like that with Tobias. But he, in some way, without a lot of fuss and big gestures, without words, walks beside us.

For me it is enough. I'm here. Even more.

•

But it was Rita who was there and saw everything and has to tell Doris a little lie. The American girl who ran out onto Lore Cliff, the cousin's mama after her, and the American girl couldn't get any farther.

The cousin's mama on the cliff who remained standing there. Doris up onto the cliff to the cousin's mama, but the cousin's mama had already run away. On the cliff, Doris who was standing and screaming, blue, in my bathing suit, as if she were Sister Blue.

And turned and ran after the cousin's mama.

Rita alone, who came home.

Told Doris Flinkenberg that it was a game, "she came up again later." You can believe that sort of thing if you want to, if you're young and a child.

Even if it still doesn't leave you, it remains there. Is that why Doris needs to drag her new friend Sandra Wärn from the house in the darker part into it a few years later? Into the story? Start over again, "find out."

Possibly. I don't know.

But we lied to Doris, everyone lied to Doris, it was never written down on paper like an agreement.

The cousin's mama, the "children's mama," who really didn't know what she had done. But then there was also Björn.

She stayed with us.

And we, all of us, wanted it that way.

•

But later, when Doris grew up and was unhappy, then she wanted to know how things had been. So. Asked Rita. Rita had to answer.

In any case: in the newspaper much later when I take care of the cousin's papa alone and am cleaning up in the kitchen, find in a cabinet, a newspaper from the fall Doris died, there is a crossword puzzle, half finished. There is a last name in the row where the correct word is supposed to be filled in: "Astrid a pop song for the day." And it is the idea that you're supposed to fill in the surname of the singer who had sung that song some time during the '60s I guess it was. "A song for the day."

I don't remember that song. Doesn't mean anything to me.

But it is the name, Astrid. And after the name, in straggling angry teenage letters there is a long word that doesn't fit in the boxes following it, there are only four of them. Letters on top of each other, a terrible word, I'm not going to say it, but something with *m*.

•

I never showed it to the cousin's mama when I went and visited her, she was living in the neighboring municipality back then. I threw the paper away. I forgot. And have forgotten.

•

"The folk song has many verses, the same thing happens in every one, over and over again, an eternal repetition of time and space. Such a different way of looking at time."

Doris Flinkenberg who is singing folk songs on an old cassette tape, talking about the folk songs between the songs. "And the girl she walks in the dance with red, golden ribbons"; "I went out one evening, out into a grove so green"—those kinds of songs, others like them.

I used to play the old cassette in the company car sometimes. Susette, my colleague who was sleeping next to me, in the morning. I turned up the volume so she would wake up, sometimes just the news and especially the weather forecast; a morning sleepy person who otherwise could sleep almost anywhere, standing, and sitting then, in the company car.

I don't know if I liked those songs Doris sang, in some way it already felt so big, bewitching, exaggerated. But you could of course also see them as Doris's message to all of us who would be left behind and live on after her too. I don't know. I didn't think about that then, at least. Rather mostly that they could still in some way carry me back to certain memories that I had from when it was still so beautiful in some way, but not in the way that you wanted to talk about it anyway.

Or maybe to muffle a bad conscience because I was never able to like Doris Flinkenberg. I don't know.

In any case. After Bengt's death I stopped playing that cassette almost completely. That simple. Just turned it off.

Turned the radio to the morning news and the weather forecast instead. The sea level, all of the lighthouses. *Bulleholm southwest eighteen.* But for a while it only made me sad. I came to think about Susette, my colleague Susette, and missed her. Susette, who in order to show me how awake she still was in the morningcar even though it looked like she was sleeping, would start rattling off those reports in the middle of the workday too. Idiotic. But also charming, a bit.

Started thinking about what became of her. Here for a while, then gone. I've never been angry at her exactly, definitely not, but I thought that it would have been nice to hear from her, that she could have been in touch, sent a card, the like. On the other hand, of course, we were colleagues, had our own separate lives, we didn't know each other.

And then I closed the cleaning business, sold it to Jeanette Lindström, who naturally, when her entire "imperium," which she called it in her prime, fell in connection with the recession at the beginning of the nineties, drove it into bankruptcy. Four Mops and a Dustpan; *but shall I grieve*, as Doris sings, I had already started my real estate business instead at that time. And Irene was there and Johanna—all of us living in the newly built house below the hill on the First Cape. Tobias came by a lot, it was a new life, a different life, a good life. And nothing more about that here, now.

•

But Rita and I, still on this morning. The moment before I get a red towel thrown in my face—but I don't care so much about that, I know Rita, her anger too, her fear too, her still, like my own, smallness.

Sun cats that reflect in the room, like a dance. I stand there where they are dancing over my body, warm beams, here in the room, it is warm.

Rita and I, Bule Marsh in my head, like an image.

The beaches at the marsh: root ends winding around each other. But you see that only when the sand around them has washed away, which will happen in the time to come, gradually. When the sandy beach washes away, it wasn't natural either, transported there. Heavy, thick roots, with large knots, which are hiding underneath, and in the reediness.

That image can't really be explained. But it exists. Has an effect on you, always.

And we won't become swimmers, Rita and I.

•

I drive home. I have been at exhibitions, looked at a few new objects in another part of the District. It is the month of November 2006, in the evening, late, maybe already night. There has been a fire at the Winter Garden, fire trucks pass me on the road. You don't see much of the fire, it has already been put out. The darkness suddenly falls now and it's only when I drive past Tobias's old greenhouse on the side of the road that it hits me that it's due to the fact that the lights from the Winter Garden aren't on, the fire that has been neither large nor destructive seems to have taken out the lighting, goodness knows what it's good for: the Winter Garden, I have never been there.

Light in the window of the house.

I come home. Johanna and Maj-Gun Maalamaa in the kitchen. We drink tea, and eat sandwiches, and then I tell them this.

JOHANNA, THE GLITTER SCENE, 2012
(OTHER SONGS)

PROJECT EARTH. ORPHEUS was going to his Eurydice. What had been lost. There in the underworld. The Winter Garden. Underworldly rooms. Which are burning, disappearing. No one was ever there. And yet: you were there the whole time.

I am Johanna, I'm growing up. The Winter Garden, on the Second Cape. Doesn't exist, but does. For real. Was something else. Becomes something else, "SPA-ponderings," further changes.

The old stories, tales aren't there anymore. For example the story about the American girl, *the American girl in a snow globe*, the souvenir shop, it is fading. The story itself lives on in the District but is also fading. There is so much else after all, a lot of other things that are happening. There are other stories, more brutal ones, more terrible, violence, murder. Like what happened with Ulla Bäckström, for example, in November 2006. How she fell from the Glitter Scene, died.

For a while after, in school, in the entire District, the shock was intense. But later, almost more shocking, it passed. Rather quickly, faster than the American girl was ever forgotten. The Bäckströms moved away. New girls came, and new girls come, all the time, *the theater the dance the music*. But then I was no longer there. Came somewhere else. To the music, the stories. Yes, you could put it that way.

That was in any case when I got out all of the old stuff, my stories, the beginning of my Project Earth. The Winter Garden, what existed for real and in my head, all of my "material." The Marsh Queen too, an eternal first chapter, *where did the music start?* What was left, in other words, still quite a bit, which I never tore up. And then I had so much of it in my head, of course.

And started writing a story about me and my cousin Robin whom I miss sometimes, he moved with Allison as said, I never heard from him. But a story about how we are children and left the house at the foot of the hill on the First Cape, and the Winter Garden reveals itself in front of us, an island in darkness, all the promises, beaming with light. A feeling that can exist only when you are young, a feeling you have never felt before: *to there*. Must go there.

The girl in the story grows up, but the same longing, the Winter Garden. And into the story comes a boy, his name is Glitter (!). He is the Marsh Queen's son and returns in the story about a Project Earth, which you do together because you don't want to do it alone. Because you already know that "lose an innocence, find a treasure," it can truly be frightening, turn everything upside down. *In the middle of the Winter Garden there is* Kapu kai, *the forbidden seas*.

"Underworldly rooms, pictures on the walls, it happened at Bule Marsh, the truth about everything." Ulla Bäckström who whispered all of that, on the field. White Ulla, red roses in a basket, the Flower Girl. Shimmering clips in her hair, in the light from the Winter Garden that became ever stronger in the dusk.

"Ille dille death," she hummed, laughing, training her eyes on me, teasingly, I was so young. "*I am Ylla of death.*"

A memory that comes so strongly right then, forces everything else away, makes it impossible to say anything about the Winter Garden, that loss, that kind of longing, and everything else that belonged there, in general.

But stories, music. There are other stories, other music, the world is filled with stories, music. And I make my story about the Marsh Queen instead, the Marsh Queen and the punk music, the first and the second chapters and so on, to the end. In my way, with my language, but it is a true story of course, because the Marsh Queen, Sandra Wärn, is not a made-up person, she exists, existed. *Death's spell at a young age.* How she sings that song, it is dreamlike, it is hard, it is unforgettable.

And it becomes a good story, and after that story other stories follow, other songs. But about the Winter Garden, Ulla Bäckström, I can't say anything, it is too painful.

Though gradually that story, the one about the Marsh Queen, when it has been told, it fades away. A story among many others. Though everything continued, continued anyway, changes.

Like in reality, with reality, in the District, everywhere.

The Boundary Woods disappeared. A new Rosengård was built, number 6 or 7 in that order, family homes. Around Bule Marsh, which has been drained down to something that looks like a properly bred pool in the middle.

And the house in the darker part of the woods no longer exists either—where the Marsh Queen once lived: a little girl, Sandra Wärn, wrapped in silk fabric from which the Marsh Queen was born, like from a cocoon. The house sank deeper in the mud and was torn down. What remains, a stairway in the woods. A single stairway in the middle of nowhere. Cannot be seen from here because of all of the houses. But imagine it. A great staircase in a wood. Moss that is growing on it, weeds in the cracks, concrete decomposing.

Beautiful? Maybe. As I said I can't see it, not from here. Where I am now, on the Glitter Scene, in what was once Ulla Bäckström's room.

Alone here now, for a while, at the window where there no longer is a door. In this landscape, I don't live here, I live somewhere else, I am in the music, my stories, I have everything, otherwise, another life.

•

But here in the house in Rosengården 2 with Solveig, one last time. I have been visiting Solveig, who still lives in the house at the foot of the hill on the First Cape and she has told me that she is going to sell what once, several years ago, was the Bäckströms' house in Rosengården, for the new owners, and I have asked if I could come along.

The Glitter Scene. An empty room. Nothing up here. And what a space and all my dreams about what it was like here and would be like here. How I wanted to come, also here. Ulla Bäckström, Ulla with butterflies in her hair, Ulla in the corridors of school. And I who stood there and looked at her from off to the side, but she didn't see me. *Dark sad groupie.* And when I occasionally happened to walk behind her in the hall she turned around and said and laughed so that everyone heard, "Don't step on my shadow, Lille, turn around."

Don't step on my shadow, turn around. How I hated her—and loved her. Still, she was mine. Is mine.

An image I carry with me: Ulla on the field, Ulla in the Boundary Woods, *my world*, catching snowflakes on her tongue. Says wonderful things. That was *who* she was. Even if I didn't know her, knew nothing about her.

And she didn't know me, knew nothing about who I was. No connection. Understood nothing about her stories, what she was doing, how important it could be for someone like me. Like the story about the American girl. Just a play to her, new idea, new songs to sing, to hum. Weave herself inside something for a while, then weave herself out. And go on, *the theater the dance the music*, as if nothing would leave a trace.

But still, a connection, and here, now, I am the one who would see it.

Suddenly, here on the Glitter Scene, everything coincides, or can be fixed, in some way. In another image, *my* image, and it was Ulla Bäckström who brought me to it. Before everyone else, before my own mother too. And I see it more clearly than ever now, on the Glitter Scene, Ulla's room, a cloudy day in January 2012.

It is Bengt, my father, and the American girl Eddie de Wire, on the terrace of the boathouse, one day in August 1969, a few days before Eddie disappears forever.

Eddie de Wire and Bengt on the terrace, just the two of them, and their mouths moving.

Feet dangling over the water, the sea opening up in front of them. Eddie with the guitar that she is plucking at, amused, Bengt who is drawing, talking. He who was always so quiet, as if transformed—suddenly something happy about all of it.

On the Second Cape otherwise, the summer life that is continuing on its own path around them and all of the other people in the world somewhere else.

But the unusual characters on the terrace of the boathouse. Brace yourself in them. In this moment, they are the ones ruling over everything.

Northerly wind. The sea dark, foam on the waves.

Eddie and Bengt. Ideas flying around, long, happy, excited.

What is Bengt saying?

The hacienda must be built?

Something else?

You don't know. You won't know. It can't be heard. Travels away with the wind.

·

But, where did the music start? Here. Exactly right here, in any case.

And: it is *not* an image. It is how it is. Bengt, my father, and the American girl Eddie de Wire who in one eternal moment rule over everything.

And at the same time, on the Glitter Scene, this room now. In the sun that suddenly, for a few seconds, peers out and lights up everything, the first rays of sun in January. The great deserted wooden floor is glittering.

With tinytiny butterflies. I turn around. Now I see.

That what remains up here in the empty room is tinytiny butterflies wedged in between floorboards everywhere. Velvet insects, different colors, in silver clips. The ones that fell out of Ulla Bäckström's large, wonderful hair.

·

"JOHANNAA! Come now!" Solveig calls from the floor below. I leave the room, have to go.

Author's Note

"It is a terrifying thing to fall into the hands of the living God," which occurs in several places in Susette's and Maj-Gun's stories, is from Hebrews 10:13. "The roses had the look of flowers that are looked at" (page 215) is from T. S. Eliot's poem "Burnt Norton" in *Four Quartets*. "Ready to be gone," about the Glitter Scene (page 338), is from Jean Cocteau, *The Holy Terrors*, translated by Rosamond Lehmann. The idea about becoming moral as soon as you are unhappy (page 429) is Marcel Proust's (thanks to Malin Kivelä).

I took the characterization of Gustav Mahler's Ninth Symphony and several statements about Mahler and his music from a fantastic article about Mahler and the philosopher Martha Nussbaum: "Närhet och utanförskap" (Proximity and Exclusion) by Lena von Bonsdorff, published in *HBL*, June 2008. This article, which breaks down intellectual defenses, was an important source of inspiration for me.

The people and places in the novel are fictional through and through, but I have taken the liberty of borrowing the names of the captains' homes, Java and Sumatra, from reality; these are the names of two of the most beautiful houses in Hangö. The islands of Java and Sumatra are of course located where they are in the Indian Ocean, next to each other with Borneo just above; it was not really possible to find other nonfictive examples.

Thanks to Silja and Tapani for their indefatigable support and encouragement, and thanks to Hilding, more than words can say.